THE WORLD'S CLASSICS

THE MISFORTUNES OF VIRTUE AND OTHER EARLY TALES

THE MARQUIS DE SADE (1740–1814) was born in a palace and died in a madhouse. He spent twenty-seven of the intervening years behind bars. His real crimes were few and he was not deprived of his liberty for what he had done but for what he represented. His true crime was fathomless and unnameable. Successive regimes recognized him as an affront to civilized values and a threat to the fabric of society. Indeed, the fact that even during his lifetime his books were banned and their author kept under lock and key by monarchical, republican, and imperial powers in turn suggests that there is no government of any political colour which would willingly permit him to walk free. It was not Sade the practising libertine or the atheistic philosopher who was removed from circulation, for his achievements in these fields were modest by contemporary standards, but the unblinking monster who spat on the common decencies and released pure poison from the Pandora's Box of social compromise which must remain forever shut. Sade contemptuously swept away all established social and moral values and simply called for a new start. For this, he has been called the greatest of all subversives. In comparison, Freud merely hovered politely at the door of our personal and collective lives, and Marx did no more than redistribute a few domestic chores. Sade gleefully demolishes the whole private and public edifice and proclaims rubble to be our true, our only, our deserved destiny.

DAVID COWARD is Professor of French at the University of Leeds. For the World's Classics, he has translated Dumas *fils*'s *The Lady of the Camelias* and a selection of Maupassant short stories, and has edited *The Count of Monte Cristo*, *The Three Musketeers*, and *The Man in the Iron Mask* by Alexandre Dumas. His most recent book is a study of Restif de la Bretonne, Sade's contemporary and his wildest critic.

THE WORLD'S CLASSICS

THE MARQUIS DE SADE

The Misfortunes of Virtue and Other Early Tales

Translated and edited by
DAVID COWARD

Oxford New York
OXFORD UNIVERSITY PRESS

Oxford University Press, Great Clarendon Street, Oxford OX2 6DP

Oxford New York

Athens Auckland Bangkok Bogota Bombay
Buenos Aires Calcutta Cape Town Dar es Salaam
Delhi Florence Hong Kong Istanbul Karachi
Kuala Lumpur Madras Madrid Melbourne
Mexico City Nairobi Paris Singapore
Taipei Tokyo Toronto Warsaw

and associated companies in
Berlin Ibadan

Oxford is a trade mark of Oxford University Press

Translation and editorial material © David Coward 1992

First published as a World Classics paperback 1992

British Library Cataloguing in Publication Data
Data available

Library of Congress Cataloging in Publication Data
Sade, marquis de, 1740-1814.
[Selections. English. 1992]
The misfortunes of virtue, and other early tales / Marquis de Sade;
translated and edited by David Coward.
p. cm.—(The World's classics)
Includes bibliographical references.
1. Sade, marquis de, 1740-1814—Translations into English.
2. Erotic stories, French—Translations into English.
I. Coward, David. II. Title. III. Series.
PQ2063.S3A235 1992 843'.6—dc20 91-38940
ISBN 0-19-282863-0

7 9 10 8 6

Printed in Great Britain by
Caledonian International Book Manufacturing Ltd
Glasgow

CONTENTS

CONTENTS

INTRODUCTION

WHO or what is Sade? Not a man, for biographers have always found him an elusive subject. Nor a philosopher: though his ideas have an antiquarian interest they have long since been superseded and no longer bear the weight of the structures he placed upon them. Is Sade a part of literature or the property of science, social psychology, and psychoanalysis? He himself is not a satisfactory case study (there are always certain difficulties in psychoanalysing the dead), though his catalogue of psychopathological impulses is without equal. Nor is Sade a body of work, for, like Freud and Marx, the Great Unreadable is also the Great Unread. Sade is a myth, a convenient vessel from which extremists have always drunk. Anti-conformists instinctively recognize him as an ancestral folk hero, the ultimate apostle of freedom who exposed the hypocrisy in which all societies are rooted: he dared think the unthinkable, imagine the unimaginable, and write what should not be written. To the defenders of established values and social structures, he is the eternal bogeyman, the embodiment of gloating cruelty, the vilest obscenity, and the threat of anarchy. Sade, the would-be liberator of the beast in man, raises in extreme form questions which confront all free societies which strive to balance the rights of individuals with the good of all. Revered by some and reviled by most, Sade makes a fearsome case for the total emancipation of the individual from the bonds which tie citizens to each other and to the state. Unlike most pornographers, who titillate for money, he rooted his uncompromising brand of anarchical liberation in philosophical principles and threw down a coherent challenge which no mature society can afford to ignore. We have still to answer that challenge.

The terms 'sadism' and 'sadistic' have long been psychoanalytical shorthand and a boon to blurb-writers.

But Sade was an aristocratic name once borne by Petrarch's Laura. The family was of old, landed nobility and for six centuries had been prominent in the civil and ecclesiastical life of southern France. Since 1627 the Sades had been lords of the Château de La Coste which, now ruined, still stands on a rocky outcrop on the northern face of the Lubéron mountains due east of Avignon. But Donatien-Alphonse-François was born in Paris in 1740 at the Hôtel de Condé, the residence of one of France's most illustrious families. His father, the Comte de Sade, a soldier-turned-diplomat, was on official business in Cologne at the time, and after the birth his mother, lady-in-waiting to the Princesse de Condé, stayed on at the Condé Palace where Sade's natural arrogance was compounded by the indulgence of servants and the neglect of his parents.

In 1744 he was sent to Avignon where he was fussed over by aunts. When he was 6 his education was taken over by his uncle, the abbé de Sade, sometime friend of Voltaire and a noted antiquary, from whom he acquired a taste for history and the habits of a feudal *grand seigneur*. In 1750 he was enrolled at the Jesuit college of Louis-le-Grand in Paris. There he was taken in hand by the kindly abbé Amblet who gave him a measure of discipline and a sense of intellectual values: Sade always remembered him with affection. In 1754 he transferred to the military college at Versailles, for he was to be a soldier. Promoted Captain in 1759, he saw active service in the Seven Years War and, during spells of leave, in the stews of Paris. Reprimanded by his father who concluded that he was 'furiously combustible', Sade wrote contrite letters and promised to mend his ways.

Sade's military career, jeopardized by his dislike of currying favour and the shortness of his father's purse, was dislocated by the outbreak of peace in 1763. To mend the family fortunes, the sly, mean-minded Comte de Sade decided that he should marry money. Though Sade's affections were, perhaps for the only time in his life, genuinely engaged elsewhere, Renée-Pélagie de

Montreuil became the Marquise de Sade in Paris on 17 May 1763. The Montreuils had been recently ennobled. Her father, a former President of the Paris tax bureau, the Cour des Aides, had retained his title, and her mother, the Présidente de Montreuil, a steely, ambitious woman, was dazzled by the prospect of a brilliant alliance. She knew nothing of her future son-in-law's unsavoury reputation and the Comte de Sade saw no reason to enlighten her. Sade always thought his wife's parents irremediably middle class, though he got the worst of the bargain. The marriage settlement was arranged in the form of a trust and the couple were allowed just enough to support a modest style of life. Sade was never to have the kind of income which he felt was his birthright.

Still neglecting the court at Versailles where advancement was to be had, he immediately resumed his debauches in Paris. In October 1763 a fan-maker named Jeanne Testard, who supplemented her income with casual prostitution, lodged a complaint against a man, described as fair-haired, slight, and about 5 feet 6 inches tall, whom she subsequently identified as Sade. Her complaint, that he had abused her physically and indulged in 'horrible impieties', was investigated and Sade was sent to the prison of Vincennes for debauchery and blasphemy. The family intervened and his prison sentence was commuted to a year's banishment from Paris. But by the following summer he was back in the capital. The police warned brothel-keepers that they were not to supply him with girls but in any case Sade was now launched on a series of ruinous liaisons with actresses, the most notorious of whom he passed off as his wife during a visit to La Coste in 1765. He was living far beyond his means and the death of his spendthrift father in 1767 brought no relief. Though he was now Comte de Sade, he never used the title and continued to be known as Marquis.

On Easter Sunday morning 1768 Sade picked up Rose Keller, an unemployed cotton-spinner, and took her to a house he rented at Arcueil. She claimed that, against her will, he beat her, cut her flesh with a small knife, and poured hot sealing-wax on to the wounds before she managed to climb out of a window and escape. Sade admitted the beating but denied having used a knife, stated that the 'wax' was a soothing lotion, and added that whores were paid for what they did and should not complain. The record of the trial reveals inconsistencies in the plaintiff's evidence and even the Présidente de Montreuil, who had no cause to be lenient towards him, considered that her son-in-law had been unfairly treated: what he had done was, she wrote to the abbé de Sade, 'an act of madness or debauchery which cannot be excused, but it was marked by none of the horrors with which it has since been overloaded'. Rose Keller's dramatic version of events was accepted and though she was given handsome compensation to withdraw the charge, Sade was gaoled. He was released in November on the condition that he returned to La Coste.

In the autumn of 1769 he toured the Netherlands and wrote an account of his impressions. The following year he attempted to resume his military career but his reputation had preceded him and he was not welcomed. In 1771 he was imprisoned briefly for debt. Since his marriage, he had spent 60,000 livres more than his income and had borrowed heavily. He now had three children and considerable expenses to meet, but the bulk of the money had gone on his pleasures. At La Coste, where he lived like a lord, he indulged a passion for amateur theatricals and, possibly with the complicity of his wife, began a liaison with his sister-in-law, Anne-Prospère.

In June 1772, accompanied by his valet Latour, he travelled to Marseilles to cash a letter of credit. Four prostitutes were engaged for a modest entertainment during which Sade handed round 'sweets' which were in fact a preparation of cantharides or 'Spanish fly', widely believed to have aphrodisiac properties. Marguerite Coste, one of the four, subsequently became very ill and the authorities intervened. Sade absconded to Italy, tak-

ing Latour and Anne-Prospère with him. He was tried
in his absence and again the surviving legal proceedings
suggest that the case against him did not wholly reflect
the facts. In particular, the medical report on Marguerite
Coste failed to reveal any trace of the poison which Sade
was accused of administering to her. Sade and Latour
were found guilty of sodomy and attempted poisoning,
both capital offences. The Marquis and his valet were
sentenced to death and were burned in effigy.

From Italy, Sade made his way to safety at Chambéry
in Piedmont, beyond the reach of the French authorities.
However, he could not escape the Présidente who,
anxious to spare the family further disgrace, arranged for
his arrest and detention at nearby Miolans. Sade fumed,
wrote blistering letters of protest, and after five months
of captivity succeeded in escaping. He returned eventually to La Coste and made efforts to persuade the
Parlement of Aix to withdraw the sentence against him
and the Présidente to desist in her persecutions. At the
end of 1774 he presided over an orgy at La Coste which
led to further complaints. Again he fled to Italy where
he began collecting material for a book which was never
written. On returning to France in the summer of 1776,
he was involved in a further scandal at La Coste. The
father of one of the girls whom he had abused was so
incensed that he fired several wild shots at the Marquis.
A month later, in February 1777, Sade and his wife
travelled to Paris perhaps to see his mother who was very
ill and died before their arrival, and partly to clear his
name.

On 13 February 1777 the King granted the Présidente's request for a *lettre de cachet* (see note to page 46)
against her son-in-law who was a disgrace to the family
and possibly a danger to himself. Sade was arrested and
sent to the prison at Vincennes where he believed he was
being held pending the revision of his trial. The
Présidente made her view plain: only by admitting that
he was mad could he hope to overturn the capital sentence against him. Sade refused to plead insanity and in

June 1778 was escorted to Aix-en-Provence to face his
judges who, after considering the facts and taking account of the interests of the family, upheld the verdict
reached in 1772 but commuted the sentence to a repri-
mand, an injunction to mend his ways, and a ban on
visits to Marseilles for three years. Sade's relief was
short-lived, however, for on leaving the court he was
immediately rearrested, since the *lettre de cachet* against
him had not been rescinded. He eluded his escort but
two months later, in September 1778, he was apprehended and returned to Vincennes. He never escaped
again.

He was a difficult prisoner. He grew angry with his
gaolers and wrote letters so violent and so obscene that
his correspondence was on occasion suspended, as were
the visits from his wife whom he suspected of infidelity.
He demanded to know the term of his sufferings and
became obsessed with numbers. In the number of lines
in a letter, the number of times a word or part of a word
reappeared, were clues to the date of his release. By late
1779 he had begun to write plays, for which he had no
talent. But he also read widely and by 1782, when he
wrote the 'Dialogue between a Priest and a Dying Man',
he had established the basis of his philosophy which
stated that since everything is natural, nothing may be
judged by human standards. His philosophy insulated
him against guilt and his literary activities channelled his
intellectual energies. In 1784 he was transferred to the
Bastille where he continued to be given the privileges
accorded to prisoners of rank. He complained of stomach pains and eye troubles and by 1787 was obese. By
that date, always working 'prodigiously' fast, he had
completed what was ever written of *The 120 Days of
Sodom* (1785) and *Aline and Valcour* (1785–7) which he
called his 'philosophical novel'. *The Misfortunes of Virtue*
was written in two weeks in the summer of 1787 and by
the following year he had written the thirty-five tales (of
which a third are lost) which he thought might make him
'the French Boccaccio'. In October 1788 he drew up a

list of his completed works which, he later estimated, would have filled fifteen printed volumes. And all this time Madame de Sade remained faithful and the Présidente implacable.

On 2 July 1789 he improvised a megaphone and, according to the prison register, 'shouted repeatedly from his window that the prisoners inside were being slaughtered and that the people were to break in and free him'. For this, he was transferred on 4 July to the insane asylum at Charenton, four miles south-east of Paris. When the Bastille fell ten days later, his furniture was looted and many of his manuscripts disappeared. He remained at Charenton until April 1790 when he was freed by the amnesty granted by the Constituent Assembly to all prisoners held by *lettre de cachet*. Madame de Sade refused to see him and began separation proceedings. In August he met Marie-Constance Quesnet, a sweet-tempered woman, who was to remain faithful to him for the rest of his life.

The world outside had changed dramatically but Sade was at least in charge of his life once more. He chose to remain in Paris not because he endorsed the Revolution but because he feared the democratic gibbets in his native South. He lamented the abolition of aristocratic rights, the attack on noble property, his King in chains, and 'the thirty thousand brigands' who now ran the country. His political views remained moderate. He came to despise Louis XVI who, by fleeing to Varennes, had broken his kingly oath, but in private he favoured a form of constitutional monarchy and the restoration of the nobility. When La Coste was looted by Revolutionaries in 1792, he spoke harsh words of the 'marauders' and 'robbers' who had destroyed his private property. But he dutifully mounted citizen's guard, wrote occasional political pamphlets in support of the Revolution, and became secretary and eventually president of his district of Paris. He served on a commission which recommended humanitarian reforms in the hospitals of the capital, was horrified by the September massacres of

1792, and in August 1793 used his influence to ensure that the Montreuils did not figure on a list of suspect *émigrés*: 'If I had said a word', he later wrote, 'they were as good as dead. But I kept silence: that was my revenge.' His habit of showing leniency to victims of persecution did not make him popular with extremists and eventually he was arrested for 'intelligence with the enemies of the Republic'. From his prison window, he could see the heads roll. On 26 July 1794 he was sentenced to death but, in the confusion, could not be found when it was his turn to be called. Two days later Robespierre fell and the killing stopped. Sade, who refused his fictional characters the consolation of Providence, was saved providentially.

On leaving Charenton in 1790 he had tried to make a career in the theatre but had met with small success: his best effort, *The Comte d'Oxtiern, or the Effects of Libertinism* (1791), was shouted down and closed at the second performance. In June 1791, for money he said at the time though subsequently he disclaimed all connection with so vile a book, he published *Justine*, an amplification of *The Misfortunes of Virtue*. When he was released in October 1794, he tried again. *Aline and Valcour* finally appeared in 1795 along with *The Philosopher in the Bedroom*. But success eluded him. By 1796 he and Marie-Constance were destitute and La Coste was sold. Though he remained the owner of other properties, he was wrongly listed as an *émigré* and as such disbarred from collecting his revenues. In 1797 he published *The New Justine, or the Misfortunes of Virtue, followed by the History of Juliette, her Sister, or the Prosperities of Vice* which made no money and brought much unwanted notoriety. In 1799 he was working in a theatre at 40 sous a day and played Fabrice in a revival of *Oxtiern*. The first days of the new century found him, 'infirm and penniless', in the public ward of a hospital.

He had not stopped writing, however. He published a collection of tales, *The Crimes of Love*, which was denounced in the press, and a new edition of *Justine*, with obscene illustrations, which was seized by the police. For after a decade of revolutionary upheavals, there was a new puritanism abroad. Sade was arrested and imprisoned in 1801. Two years later, for making advances to newly arrived prisoners, he was returned to Charenton where an official report described him as 'incorrigible' and his condition as 'a permanent state of libertine dementia'. Though many believed that he was not mad, but bad, and attempts were made to transfer him to a secure prison for conventional criminals, Sade remained at Charenton, writing—the manuscript of *The Days of Florbelle* was confiscated in 1807—and helping to stage plays which the hospital's director regarded as a form of therapy. Still obsessed by numbers, still visited by Marie-Constance whom he passed off as his daughter, Sade turned into a morose, shambling relic who was invariably described as a 'monster of depravity' by those who visited or inspected the hospital. In 1813 he began an affair with the 16-year-old daughter of a cleaning-woman. He died suddenly at the end of 1814. His will requested that he should be buried in an unmarked grave which should be allowed to grow wild so that 'all trace of my resting-place should disappear from the surface of the earth as I flatter myself that my memory will disappear from the minds of men'.

But was Sade a monster? His treatment of Jeanne Testard, Rose Keller, and the prostitutes of Marseilles would suggest that he was. Categorical judgements, however, are less easy to sustain when he is set in context. The French eighteenth century may now seem a lost age of wit and elegance, a lavish production (decors by Watteau, music by Rameau) staged for our aesthetic pleasure. But the reality was quite different. In Paris, pimps and bawds bought and sold children. They procured shop-girls and country hopefuls who had little choice but to submit to sexual slavery and, not infrequently, to the perverted tastes of their clients. One in seven women was implicated in the vice trade. According to contemporary estimates, 150 million livres were spent annually on 'the pleasures of Venus', a figure which, if correct, was fifty times the sum spent on the relief of the poor, twice the trade shortfall for 1781, and half the size of the Royal debt in 1789. The lead was given by the King who kept a deer-park at Versailles staffed by barely nubile girls: royal bastards were so numerous, it was said, that there was probably a great deal of literal truth in the political platitude that the King was the father of his subjects. 'Gallantry' was an empty sham—in the jargon it was a euphemism for venereal disease—and the Don Juans of the age simply bought their conquests: of a lady's favours, only the last had any value. In 1774 the Duke de Richelieu was prepared to burn down the house of Mademoiselle de La Popelinière the better to have his way with her. When he died in 1776, the Prince de Conti left a collection of several thousand rings, each a souvenir of the women he had pleasured. Churchmen who patronized the capital's bawdy-houses were arrested in droves—and among these sporting clerics was Sade's uncle, the abbé de Sade, who was apprehended in 1762 and charged with debauchery. Although moralists rightly protested, the abbé de Sade continued to be the absentee Vicar-General of Toulouse he had always been, and the career of Richelieu was in no way impeded by his notorious depravity, even though he, like others, was suspected of adding satanic and sacrilegious practices to his portfolio of depravity.

Nor were the crimes for which Sade was punished in any way exceptional. Masters regularly seduced servants and gentlemen abused, sometimes to the point of maiming, the girls they paid. The vogue for flagellation was widespread—a police report commented in 1765 on the 'prodigious' consumption of brooms in the brothels of Paris—and lesbianism and homosexuality were in fashion. By the 1780s there were reckoned to be 40,000 practising homosexuals in the capital ('from Dukes to their lackeys and the common people'). Sodomy was a capital offence, but the authorities trod warily. Their discretion was generally approved. In 1781 the *Mémoires secrets* commented: 'This crime has become very common and is rife at Court. It calls for a sensitive handling which would not be possible if the laws against it were to be rigidly enforced; it is preferable that a blind eye be turned to those guilty of it than that it should be further propagated by being brought to the attention of the public.' True, a sodomite named Pascal, an ex-priest, was broken alive on the wheel in 1783. But his offence was extreme and his case was regarded as exemplary.

It is clear that Sade too was regarded as an exemplary case. In the Rose Keller affair, he was the victim of a moral backlash which might as easily have fallen on a score of aristocratic rakes. In the matter of the prostitutes of Marseilles, he was a pawn in the wider political battle between the aristocracy, which he represented, and the Parlements, who passed judgement on him. He was a victim too of the *lettre de cachet*, a system of arbitrary justice which many denounced as patently unjust. In 1800 he fell foul of the new moral climate and of a response which has since become a standard method of dealing with political dissidents: he was called mad and locked up in a mental institution. Sade's behaviour, however appalling it may now seem, was not much worse than that of many contemporary libertines, and when it is further set against the horrific tortures and brutal public executions which were a routine part of the legal system, he seems a very unadventurous sadist indeed. In 1781 he wrote to his wife: 'Yes, I am a libertine, I admit it freely. I have dreamed of doing everything that it is possible to dream of in that line. But I most certainly have not done all the things I dreamt of and never shall. Libertine I may be, but I am not a criminal, I am not a murderer.'

But would he have tried to make those dreams come true had he been left at liberty? His judges, his gaolers, and even members of his own family called him 'incorrigible' and 'mad' and clearly thought that he would. But the evidence does not substantiate their misgivings. When he was freed in 1790, he did not run amok. He did not seize the unique opportunities offered by the Revolution to enact the atrocities which he continued to invent for the heroes of his books. The Terror which Robespierre achieved in reality, Sade merely imagined on paper. He settled for domesticity with Madame Quesnet and could not even bring himself to send the Présidente de Montreuil to the guillotine, though it was in his power to do so.

But Sade's behaviour during his decade of freedom is not merely a chronicle of lost opportunities but typical of the contradiction between what he wrote and what he did and believed. Before 1789 he looked forward to the violent overthrow of the social order, but complained bitterly when prevented from behaving like a feudal tyrant. He was a modest supporter of the Revolution when it came, but he rejected the equality and fraternity it stood for and clung fiercely to his entrenched individualism. As a philosopher, he knew that it was a matter of total indifference to Nature whether an individual were alive or dead, free or in prison, yet he never accepted the cosmic arbitrariness of his own fate. He wrote dithyrambically of the domination of the weak by the strong, but it never occurred to him to regard the Présidente as a successful illustration of his doctrine, though she did to him what the bullies of *The Misfortunes of Virtue* do to Justine. In a word, the attitudes and cruelties expressed in Sade's fictions are at variance with almost everything that is known of his conduct. Rather than a 'monster of depravity', it seems far more likely that he was a not untypical *grand seigneur* who, though intellectually enlightened, regarded most people as his inferiors and treated them with patrician contempt.

Sade's inveterate class snobbery clearly worked against him. But so did rumour. Within a week of his arrest in 1768 Madame du Deffand, the first lady of the Paris *salons*, sent Horace Walpole in London a lurid account of the Arcueil episode in which clear echoes of the current scandalmongering may be heard. 'He brandished a pistol which he produced from his pocket . . . flogged her cruelly . . . and with his knife made incisions all over her body'; 'far from denying his crime and hanging his head in shame, he claimed to have done a fine thing and to have rendered the public an important service, viz., the invention of an ointment which heals wounds quickly.' When news of the Marseilles affair broke in 1772, Sade's intimate *partie de plaisir* was reported in private and public as a bacchanalian orgy; it was said that the sweets, which he had deliberately poisoned, had caused the death of 'numerous' people, including Madame de Sade. By 1788, when Restif de la Bretonne retold the tales, Sade had become a vivisectionist. Restif claimed to have questioned a woman who had by good fortune escaped the fate which had befallen Rose Keller. Sade had considered her a suitable subject for his physiological researches and led her into a secret chamber. 'She swears that she saw three bodies there: one which was skeleton only; another which had been cut open and was preserved in a jar; and the freshly killed corpse of a man . . . '. Restif also claimed to have seen the murderous orgy for himself, though in his account it is transposed from Marseilles to Paris. 'De S* laughed as he opened the door. Inside, we found young persons of both sexes lying in heaps, some in pools of their own blood, others reduced to the most appalling condition by the drugs which had been slipped into their wine.'

Such sensational exaggerations of Sade's crimes were all the more believable because they both reflected and fuelled popular fears. The strong hint of the *droit de seigneur* in his actions identified him as a feudal tyrant, while the charge of sacrilege was proof that he believed in nothing at all. Both affairs reeked of a contempt for human decency and kindled thoughts of satanic practices. His intentions were murderous, but worse, the horrors he perpetrated were cold and calculated. The claim that he was testing an ointment on Rose Keller, together with his knowledge of poisons, gave his cruelty the character of a heartless scientific experiment. Sade was more than hated for being the standard noble auto-crat. He was an Alchemist, a Devil, a Magician. With extraordinary speed he became notorious as a blas-phemer and satyr and inherited the mantle of Public Enemy previously worn by Caligula, Torquemada, and Gilles de Rais. In this 'Sade' were echoes of Don Juan, who challenged God, of Faust, who had signed a pact with the Prince of Darkness, and of Bluebeard, who cut up his wives. There was a sense that the butcher of Marseilles was far more than merely a criminal or a wicked aristocrat. He had escaped from some collective nightmare. He had stepped out of the world of popular tales where ogres cook children in pies. 'Sade' alarmed and disturbed.

But what is perhaps most remarkable of all is that Sade had become 'Sade' before he ever published a single word. After 1789, and still two years before the appear-ance of his first book, his image was politicized in the most extraordinary and contradictory ways. The Sade who had called to the mob from his cell became a white-haired innocent with a beard as long as his brutal sen-tence, who had been gloriously freed by the heroic people from the dank Bastille, symbol of the injustice of the *ancien régime*. An echo of this Sade is heard in Wil-liam Blake's *The French Revolution* (1791): 'the den named Horror held a Man | Chain'd hand and foot, round his neck an iron band, bound to the impregnable wall. | . . . And the man was confin'd for a writing prophetic.' Of course, Sade had not been jailed for ex-pressing freedom-loving ideas and his manacles are as much a figment of Blake's imagination as the presence 'in the Tow'r named Darkness' of the Man in the Iron Mask who had died in 1703. But in that new, blissful dawn, the details scarcely mattered.

This view of the victim of feudal injustice was to surface again in the nineteenth century. But most ob-servers in the 1790s made Sade, who now added the crime of authorship to his legendary atrocities, the representative of the perverse, cruel, feudal aristocracy which the Revolution had overturned. Yet after 1795, he was turned into the spiritual mentor of the bloodthirsty architects of the Terror who read *Justine* to excite themselves to new heights of horror. Sade thus came to symbolize the worst excesses not only of the *ancien régime* but of the Revolution too. His books fuelled the myth and he was identified with his characters. He was called evil, mad, and dangerous and by 1797 there were calls for his execrable books to be banned and for their vile author to be locked up. Reviewers asserted confidently that there was hardly a murderer abroad who had not read Sade. Restif warned that if his works were to fall into the hands of soldiers, then 20,000 women were doomed to die horrible deaths.

In the climate of moral rearmament of the early 1800s, no one spoke against his arrest and new detention. Indeed, Charenton was the right place for him. Most of those who visited the hospital grumbled about the liberal treatment he received and would have been happier if he had been left to rot while he meditated his unspeakable crimes. When Sade, still 'wrapped in the wings of evil', wrote his will, his hope that he would disappear from the minds of men was entirely misjudged. For the legend was only just beginning.

After the fall of Napoleon Sade's books were banned, but he continued to be read in progressive circles. The ban was renewed in 1825 but it was slackly enforced. In 1834 the word '*sadisme*' was officially lexicalized: in his *Dictionnaire universel*, Boiste defined it as 'A horrible, aberrant form of debauchery; a monstrous and antisocial system of ideas which revolts nature (from Sade, proper name). Little used.' The same year, Jules Janin published a widely discussed 'dissertation' on Sade which warned that reading the Marquis would endanger anyone's sanity. But it was not so much Sade's 'system' that attracted attention as his sulphurous reputation. The Romantics remade him in their own extravagant image. For them, he was an instance of the 'exceptional' figure of pure evil or pure good who transcended the petty values of their own dull, bourgeois age. As a 'Gothic' novelist he underwrote the taste for sensationalism and horror which fuelled their imaginations, and as a prisoner benefited by association with the myth of the Bastille, symbol of the repression of the individual: he was, said Pétrus Borel, 'a glory of France'. In 1843 Sainte-Beuve observed that the two presiding geniuses of Romanticism were Byron and Sade. But whereas Byron could be openly admired, 'satanic' Sade enjoyed the considerable advantage of being unnameable: he offered the attraction of the illicit. Sade's reputation, rarely hampered by knowledge of his work, continued to grow. Baudelaire noted that any study of natural man must start with Sade who was clearly a flower of evil, and Flaubert admired 'le grand Sade' who offered such 'brilliant insights into philosophy and history'. Maupassant was introduced to him during a brief encounter with Algernon Swinburne in 1868 and the meeting gave a shape to his own sense of horror and coloured the unblinking cruelty of his tales.

But Sade was not allowed to remain a purely literary figure. In 1876 Krafft-Ebing's *Psychopathia sexualis* linked 'sadism' and 'masochism' and Sade became the property of the new psychoanalysis. *The 120 Days of Sodom* was published in 1904 by Iwan Bloch, one of the leading German exponents of the new science of sexual pathology. His lead was followed in France by another medical man, Maurice Heine, who from the 1920s onwards edited unpublished manuscripts (including all the tales in this volume) and first compiled Sade's biography. Yet Sade's appeal to the imagination was not to be denied. In 1909 Apollinaire called him 'the freest spirit' and after the Great War the Surrealists adopted him as an ancestor who had destroyed bourgeois conformity and reunited man with his primitive instincts. Antonin Artaud rooted his 'Theatre of Cruelty' in Sadean soil and progressive film-makers, like Buñuel, translated Sadean shocks to the screen. In the graphic arts he proved to be a rich source of visual imagery, and painters, from André Masson to Clovis Trouille and beyond, exploited his cruelty and iconoclasm. Georges Bataille, the guru of modern French intellectualism, was fascinated by horror which he believed could be used to free the mind, and viewed Sade as an uncompromisingly honest exploder of social and moral taboos, and as the fearless proclaimer of total experience. Existentialists like Camus recognized him as a rebel against the absurd, and by the 1960s the *Tel Quel* group of radical Paris intellectuals saw him as the universal subversive. Roland Barthes saluted him not for his ideas but for creating a revolutionary language capable of communicating them. Sade, a key figure in modernism and post-modernism, has a permanent place in the French avant-garde.

In Britain, Sade has always had a lower profile. After his death, his works continued to be reprinted through-out Europe and copies were available in London in the 1820s, though only those with enough French could read him. The market was large enough, however, to tempt the publisher George Cannon to issue *Juliette* in French in 1830. Cannon was prosecuted and jailed for six months. Thereafter Sadophiles relied on smuggled imports, a constraint which only served to add the glamour of forbidden fruit to his growing reputation. The Marquis became 'Divine' not because he was Blake's victim of feudal oppression nor a philosopher of liberty nor yet a flower of evil. He was a hot-house bloom and occupied a privileged place in the library of the mid-Victorian sexual underworld: he was a spanker. In polite society, his name was unknown. Henry James recalled attending a luncheon party given by Tennyson. When one of his guests, Mrs Greville, mentioned that she was related to Sade's ancestress, Petrarch's Laura, the Poet Laureate began talking about Sade, mentioning titles of books but not their author, with the air of one who was reciting 'useful information'. No one but James knew to whom he was alluding.

It was through the Pre-Raphaelite network that Swinburne was introduced to Sade. A friend, William Hardman, met him at Rossetti's and reported that, at 24, the young poet 'upholds the Marquis de Sade as the acme and apostle of perfection, without (as he says) having read a word of his works'. In Hardman's view, 'the Marquis de Sade was a most filthy, horrible and disgusting rascal, a disgrace to humanity', but Swinburne was not to be denied. A reading of *Justine* was arranged in August 1862, but the occasion broke up in hoots of laughter. Swinburne had looked for 'some sharp and subtle analysis of lust' but found that Sade's weakness for 'bulk and number', not to mention the cruelty and coprophilia, gave the most ludicrous results: altogether 'an ingenious acrobatic performance' but no more. In his correspondence, he used 'Sadique language' when he wished to talk dirty but took the view that a 'swished youth' who had spent five years being flogged at Eton had little to learn from the 'Titanic flagellations' of the 'Divine Marquis' who, to boot, could not spell. Even so, he found supporting arguments for his antitheism in Sade who, 'a greater than Byron', 'saw to the bottom of gods and men', an unfortunate phrase given Sade's proclivities.

Although decadents and aesthetes enrolled under his banner, Sade's influence on the nineteenth century in England was less intellectual than in France and his impact was mainly restricted to providing titillation for the naughtier Victorians. By the 1890s there was a steady if 'specialized' market for pornographic pastiches of Sade. He also found his way into the drawings of Aubrey Bearsdley and Beresford Egan and subsequently into the brutal sexploitational images, especially of women, which have turned Sadean obscenities into popular icons. His books continued to be banned as obscene, but as numbers capable of reading him in French dwindled, informed opinion declined and his reputation as a mere pornographer gained ground. Even after the Second World War, American translations, though they were severely bowdlerized, were refused entry. Only in 1983 did HM Customs and Excise, using the discretion allowed by the Customs Laws Consolidation Act of 1876 (which prohibited the importation of matter defined as obscene according to the terms of Lord Campbell's Act of 1857), permit the entry of Grove Press titles hitherto unavailable in the UK. Even so, publishers and booksellers continue to tread warily.

In the United States, however, Sade has never provoked the same intensity of reaction. American Federal Law, which until the mid-twentieth century used the British definition of obscenity as printed matter likely 'to deprave and corrupt', has been altogether less stringent than in either France or the UK where, in principle, Sade is still a banned author. A revision of the Tariff Act in 1930 gave the American Secretary of the Treasury discretion to admit the classics or books of established intellectual worth, even if obscene. The celebrated judgment given in favour of the publication of James Joyce's *Ulysses* in 1934 further benefited Sade who subsequently became more easily available in the United States than in Europe. His influence, however, remained small, though even American expatriates in France could read him in the translations published by Maurice Gerodias's Olympia Press in Paris. No major nineteenth-century American intellectual had expressed more than a passing interest in Sade and few twentieth-century writers and artists have gone as far as Henry Miller who in 1952 called him 'one of the most maligned, defamed, misunderstood—deliberately and wilfully misunderstood—figures in all literature'. Even so, Sade's name has been revived by post-modernists who admire his daring, by feminists who denounce him, and by the entertainment industry which finds in him a convenient superlative for their 'adult' products. Sade refuses to go away.

For, since the War, he has continued to be what Apollinaire predicted: one of the forces which have shaped our century. Nazi and other atrocities have been re-examined in the light of the sadistic impulse, and Western societies, for the first time in history, are now required to find better answers to the collective savagery which, first catalogued by Sade, has produced holocausts and torture on a massive scale. In the area of private morality, too, Sade is regularly used to test the law and define the limits of tolerable behaviour. In 1966, during the sensational British 'Moors Murders' trial, excerpts from his books were read out and it was alleged that his ideas had contributed directly to the savage child-killings for which the accused were convicted. In Britain in 1991 a nice point of law surfaced around practices to which, though he did not invent them, Sade clearly holds the world rights: does the liberty of consenting individuals include a licence to inflict and receive acts of cruelty and perverted gratification?

In both private and public life, then, Sade continues to be perceived as a threat to the whole social fabric: in this sense, he is more profoundly revolutionary than either Freud or Marx. To interfere with established sexual practices (marriage, censorship, or arrangements for prostitution and homosexuality) is to undermine the very basis on which all societies are built. In this sense, all obscenity trials are political. Jean-Jacques Pauvert was successfully prosecuted in 1957 for bringing out a scholarly edition of Sade's complete works, yet the public debate which followed the proceedings led to a relaxation of the constraints faced by writers and artists, just as the Lady Chatterley trial did in Britain in 1961. But Sade, pressed by the permissive 1960s into the service of modern eroticism, has continued to be traduced. Pasolini made a valid point by setting his film adaptation of *The 120 Days of Sodom* in the last days of the Fascist domination of Italy, but the usual run of films which use his name simply exploit his reputation and encourage the voyeurism of audiences. Even Peter Weiss's accomplished play, *The Persecution and Assassination of Marat as Performed by the Inmates of the Asylum of Charenton under the Direction of the Marquis de Sade* (1964), projects a venerable view of the 'libertarian' Sade by contrasting

Marat's fiery idealism with the sardonic scepticism of the Marquis. The name of Sade, which cannot be kept out of the courts, has many times been used to explain extremes of private and public conduct, to test the limits of authority, and to push back the boundaries of what may be legitimately discussed in a free society.

Of course, Sade still has many enemies. Some merely wish to keep the stopper in the bottle to prevent an evil genie escaping. Others argue that the fact that he has always been a rallying point for those who oppose bourgeois order and received morality is in itself a good enough reason for resisting pleas for his unconditional rehabilitation. That he was, during his lifetime, when his familiars and judges did not have the benefit of our hindsight, locked up in turn by monarchical, Republican, and imperial order, argues that there is probably no regime which could ever allow him to walk free. But more particularly, many women, from Simone de Beauvoir via Kate Millett to Angela Carter have regarded him as the ultimate misogynist and the symbol of male contempt for women. In his books women are maimed, raped, and eviscerated to serve the pleasures of men. Both by example and precept Sade is the arch apostle of female abjection. There is certainly no denying that what Sade has come to represent is profoundly and murderously anti-feminist: Justine and her sisters in agony are mere objects in the Marquis's house of pain. Yet his philosophical position was much less clear-cut. If Justine is abused, it is for persisting with her policy of virtue, not for her gender. Her sister proved to have no such illusions when Sade told *The History of Juliette* in 1797. There she not only prospers in vice but becomes one of his greatest fiends. In Sade's world, obscenity and cruelty are the prerogative of the strong, irrespective of gender.

During his lifetime Sade was more diabolical than 'Divine', a Wizard and Magician. We should not dismiss this 'Sade' too easily as the product of a primitive society which was afraid of the dark and still believed in goblins, for a goblin is what he remains in the late twentieth century. The 'Sade' who still murders and rapes in popular magazines and the cinema has not ceased to wear the face of those same fears. He is more than just another ghoul with box-office appeal like Dracula: he walks abroad in the extermination camps and torture chambers of the world and is always ready to answer the call. 'Sade' still produces a *frisson* of horror because he is likely to invade real life at any moment. We may rationalize and define him as a subversive and a pathological archetype. But a bogeyman he remains.

The unreadability of Sade's most uncompromising books is as great an obstacle to an understanding of his purposes as his notoriety. Yet he took his literary vocation with the greatest seriousness. At first, his ambitions were limited to the theatre, but he was also an avid reader of novels. He surrendered to the sentimental charms of Samuel Richardson and the 'sublime' Rousseau. He was sufficiently well read to preface *The Crimes of Love* (1800) with an elegant essay on the novel. The first requirement of a novelist, he said, was a profound knowledge of the human heart which was to be obtained through suffering or travel. Travel, of course, was hardly an option for Sade and his sufferings as a prisoner were of an unvarying kind. His own novels are singularly lacking in the effusive emotions and the lyrical appreciation of nature which Rousseau had made fashionable. The world of his imagination is, on the contrary, closed and windowless, a zone of dungeons, labyrinths, and inaccessible eyries. Having acquired the vision of a prisoner, he never lost it, for his later fictions, written during the 1790s when he was at liberty, are even more claustrophobic and are written with considerably more rage.

But the early Sade is revealed in many moods—from the philosophical in the 'Dialogue between a Priest and a Dying Man' and *Aline and Valcour* to the comprehensively sadistic in *The 120 Days of Sodom*, surely the most

gruesome book ever written. His tales also display considerable literary skills which are much less in evidence
in his later books where the ratio of narrative to philos-
ophizing is altered in favour of the latter. *The Misfortunes
of Virtue* (1787) is a sprightly, intellectually challenging
story in the manner of Voltaire's *Candide*, whereas its
two reworkings (*Justine* (1791) and *The New Justine*
(1797)) add verbiage and horror but obscure the point.
It is the first of these three distinct versions of the history
of Justine which has been translated here. Though written quickly, it was carefully planned around ten incidents which demonstrate that chastity, piety, charity,
compassion, prudence, the refusal to do evil, and the
love of goodness and truth—in a word, virtue—are punished while a succession of brutal and ruthless villains
are seen to prosper in vice. 'From start to finish', he
wrote in 1788, 'vice triumphs and virtue is humiliated,
and only at the end is virtue raised to its rightful pinnacle; there will be no one who, on finishing this tale,
will not detest the false triumph of crime and cherish the
humiliations and misfortunes which virtue undergoes.'
If Sade had written nothing else, then his philosophical
tale might well be taken as a sharply satirical warning
against over-niceness in moral scruples. After all, life
would be impossible if, like Justine, we flatly refused to
compromise or never told white lies. Yet his verdict is
disingenuous. It is not that the odds are loaded on the
side of evil or that evil is shown in such a brutal form,
but rather that the ending does not point up his message.
Justine's death is particularly horrible and seems less a
vindication, more a judgement. And readers who doubt
the plausibility of Juliette's conversion will have their
suspicions confirmed in the sequel of 1797 where, with
the full trappings of sadism, she exults in the prosperities
of vice.

Sade's later books are black and relentlessly monot-
one, but his early stories, which he intended to publish
as *Tales and 'Fabliaux' of the Eighteenth Century, by a
Provençal Troubadour*, of which a selection is offered

here, are written in several different kinds of ink. The description of Du Harpin in *The Misfortunes of Virtue* has a Dickensian ring and there are Defoe-ish moments in Justine's adventures which relieve the stifling atmosphere of her ordeals. Sade's satire of lawyers and the Parlements—and he rarely misses an opportunity to score points off the legal system which he had good reason to loathe—is not simply personal but expresses wider liberal principles. And in the shorter tales, he inserts himself comfortably into the tradition of honest bawdy. He had ambitions to be the 'French Boccaccio' and stories like 'The Law of Talion' or 'The Windbags of Provence' handle gross rudery with considerable skill and panache. The humour, which features faithless wives and cuckolds (always more obvious figures of fun in the culture of Latin than of Anglo-Saxon peoples), may be of the schoolboy variety, but Sade spans the range from crude farce to the sophisticated comedy of 'Augustine'. Some tales, like 'The Self-Made Cuckold', work on the principle of 'the biter bit'. Others, like 'The Prude', are examples of the fashionable 'moral' story. 'The Confidence Men' is a cautionary tale written in a vein of documentary realism, while mysteries are related in a variety of registers, from the teasing understatement of 'The Pimp Well Served' to the supernatural: Sade even manages to breathe new life into the Faust legend by neatly condemning the indignant Devil of 'An Inexplicable Affair' to the role of chastiser of wickedness. One of the most accomplished tales, 'Émilie de Tourville', is not only a tense psychological drama but looks forward to the sensationalism which was to be the stuff of Romantic literature. By any standards, Sade was a gifted teller of tales (some delightfully tall) who renewed old traditions in the most inventive way.

The Misfortunes of Virtue revives the theme of persecuted beauty which had its immediate roots in Samuel Richardson and was to become immensely popular in the Gothic novels of Mrs Radcliffe and Matthew Lewis. Indeed, Sade is sometimes thought of as the most radical of the Gothic novelists. Yet it is clear that his ambitions lay elsewhere and that he used fiction not merely as a convenient vehicle for ideas but as a stimulus for his own physical and intellectual self-arousal. For during his early years in prison he had also acquired an interest in philosophy, as one of his earliest surviving texts, 'The Dialogue between a Priest and a Dying Man' (1782), serves to show. 'I am a philosopher,' he wrote to his wife. 'Those who are acquainted with me can have no doubt that I am proud to be known to profess as much.' He admired Rousseau's effusions and Voltaire's sharp good sense but was much more taken with the writings of materialistic philosophers such as La Mettrie and Diderot, though, as he wrote to his wife in 1783, D'Holbach was 'the basis of my philosophy'. Sade's philosophy is also the basis of his books.

The orthodox philosophical tradition had assumed the existence of two substances: gross matter, which was the stuff of the physical world, and spirit, the force, generally assumed to be divine, by which it was powered and directed. The best evidence for the existence of spirit was the human soul while the marvels of external nature revealed the presence of a benevolent creator. Since the universe and all that it contained were God's handiwork, it followed that His creatures were morally obliged to their creator and this, in practical terms, meant following God's law as revealed in the Scriptures and as codified by the Church. All ethical, social, and political behaviour was determined by God's authority.

As scientific knowledge spread, many found difficulty in accepting the traditional view of man's place in the cosmos, but none were so categorical as the materialists who argued that the universe is composed solely of matter organized by physical laws. Like them, Sade argued that life is the perpetual rearrangement of molecules by the unstoppable forces of Nature. Matter was not created but is eternal and therefore finite in quantity and indestructible in essence. The entire universe is ruled by Nature's urge to create. It is a self-perpetuating cosmic

workshop and God is an irrelevant hypothesis. A moral
system based on the supposed goodness of a non-exist-
ent being is clearly a nonsense. Individual will and actions count for nothing against Nature's insistence on
reusing molecules as quickly as possible, for all that
counts is the continuation of life and not how it is lived.
Moreover, Nature's perpetual re-creations assume destruction since new forms cannot emerge until more
matter becomes available. Far from underwriting conventional morality, Nature is supremely indifferent to
anything which does not directly contribute to the re-
newal of the material universe. Murder, war, and violent
death in all its forms serve Nature's ends since they
accelerate the release of reusable matter. Mercy, charity,
and anything that qualifies as 'goodness' are unnatural
since helping the weak to survive beyond their time
merely slows the process. It follows therefore that it is
not in Nature's interest that there should be more good
people than wicked people, since goodness clogs the
machinery and restricts the flow of the raw molecular
material. On the contrary, it is to her advantage that the
wicked should prosper, and crime and cruelty are admir-
ably suited to this purpose.

Individuals are so much matter organized by a nervous
system driven by an 'electrical fluid' which responds to
sensual stimuli. Odour, for instance, is an effect of the
extreme divisibility of atoms which float in the orbit of
objects, and desire 'is nothing more than the effect of
the irritation caused by the impact of atoms of beauty
on the animal spirits'. Reactions to these stimuli vary
according to physical constitution, being stronger in
some than in others, but the thrill is experienced as pain
or pleasure. In the weakly organized, the reaction is
feeble and controllable: the search for moderate pleasure
and the refusal to inflict pain on others are classed by
moralists as 'virtue'. In the strong, who are unable to
resist the strength of their desires, the result is classed
as 'vice'. Society rewards goodness and punishes evil,
whereas in reality both are merely natural expressions of

the same physical determinants. By imposing constraints on behaviour, society is seen to be no more than a conspiracy by the weak to obstruct not simply the strong but the march of Nature herself. Fortunately, social and moral restraint can never get the better of the vicious who, as efficient reprocessors of matter, are persistently favoured by Nature. Advantaged by a lack of feeling for others and an absence of moral conscience, they go like wolves among lambs. In practice, human existence is a tension between the balanced forces of hunter and hunted, the issue being decided by the skill of the participants who, since they have not consciously chosen their pre-determined roles but were given them, cannot be praised for their virtues nor censured for their vices, but can merely be acknowledged for being what they are. The urge to tyranny and torture is natural and should not be resisted. Indeed, it is a philosophical absurdity to want to behave 'well' unless there is pleasure to be got from doing so.

Sade contributed no new philosophical principles to this line of argument. His originality lies rather in pushing the ethical implications of materialism to their logical conclusion. Society is an unnatural construct designed to thwart Nature. What is called 'evil' is no concern of Nature which regards war, persecution, and tyranny with a benevolent eye. Blasphemy is absurd since there is no God. There is no property in Nature; theft is therefore no crime. There is no difference between a murder and a death by natural causes, save that the molecules of a prematurely terminated life are returned more quickly to the common pool. Whether we eat pork or human flesh is a matter of indifference, for both adequately sustain life. Once Sade's vision of Nature as a single-minded reprocessing factory is accepted, all moral values fall: ethics become redundant.

Others before him had used similar arguments to deny Church and State the right to oppose what Nature decrees. Echoes of the debate had long since been heard even in the theatre on both sides of the Channel. Sade would doubtless have approved the sentiments of Mill-wood, the predatory fiend of Lillo's *The London Merchant* (1731): 'I have done nothing that I am sorry for; I followed my inclinations, and that the best of you does every day. All actions are alike and indifferent to man and beast, who devour, or are devoured, as they meet with others weaker or stronger than themselves' (IV, sc. xviii). Nor was Sade unusual in writing pornography, for there was a ready market for classics of the genre, the abbé Du Prat's *Venus in the Cloister* (1682), say, or the Marquis d'Argens's *Thérèse the Philosopher* (1748), or Cleland's *Fanny Hill* (1748–9). Indeed, by the 1780s authors like Laclos, Nerciat, and Mirabeau had pushed back the boundaries of decency and lent force to the view that the French Revolution was sexual long before it became political. But Sade parts company with his philosophical and literary predecessors by his uncompromising application of his principles to sex.

If pity is weakness, love is pride, an illusion, for desire is the effect of sensual stimulation. Individuals can love each other only in the sense that they love raspberries. Sex is an appetite and an end in itself. Procreation is not a priority of Nature. If it were, women would not live past child-bearing age. Moreover, if all the seeds that are planted were to grow, far too many molecules would be removed from Nature's reprocessing requirements. Nature thus assumes a level of wastage and Sade was able to argue that lesbianism and homosexuality are crimes only in a social sense, as indeed are incest, prostitution, and perversions of all kinds. They are natural phenomena and have physical causes and a prior cosmic justification.

But even this does not exhaust Sade's originality. If desire is its own object, the limit upon gratification is set solely by the capacities of the desirer who is therefore justified in perpetrating any action which stimulates his priapic urges. In *The 120 Days of Sodom*, Sade enumerates a 'menu' of 600 'passions' which run from the 'simple', which are merely shocking, to the 'murderous' which require the death of the partner: satisfaction comes through the hanging, drowning, boiling, evisceration, and decapitation of 'the weak'. Sade's tormentors are invariably rich and they use their wealth to ensure that they can maim, torture, and kill with impunity: there is no escape for their victims. In other words, sexual gratification is rooted in power. Power dehumanizes the victim who becomes as much an object in the torturer's cell as the prey of a lion in the jungle. Sade's ultimate achievement was to make sex the choicest expression of obscene cruelty and absolute, despotic power.

None of Sade's philosophical predecessors made this link and not even Freudians are prepared to go as far. Nor have pornographers ever ventured so boldly into such murky regions where they are likely to sicken the readers they set out to titillate. Indeed, it has been asked whether Sade was altogether serious. His views are so grotesque that perhaps he intended them as ironical, as a means of drawing attention to the contradictions or injustices of society, a not unfamiliar shock tactic along the lines of Swift's *Modest Proposal* (1729) which suggested that the best solution to Irish famine was that the starving should eat their babies. In Samuel Butler's *Erewhon* (1872), society reinforces the penalties inflicted by Nature, and misfortunes like illness are severely punished. André Breton included Sade in his anthology of black humour in 1939, and his place there seems reasonable enough when we recall the close of Evelyn Waugh's *Black Mischief* (1932), where Basil Seal eats a stew the main ingredient of which is his mistress. Yet none of these instances of 'sadistic' humour depend for their effect on gloating sexual brutality, and they fail to shock as Sade does: the suffering and the blood in Sade is too real. Moreover, although his tales show a talent for the comic, the hypothesis is not borne out by the novels which are written from conviction and with onanistic relish. Even in *The Misfortunes of Virtue*, there is no comic point to the treatment of Justine at Sainte-Marie-des-Bois. If Sade's books are the kind which the French inelegantly describe as needing to be read with one hand, it is a sensible precaution to hold a sick-bowl in the other.

It has been argued that his target was not Providence but its perversion by the Church which used it to brain-wash suffering humanity into accepting their misery by holding out hope of bliss in the world to come. But this is to overlook the sacrilegious venom with which he ridicules all aspects of belief. It has been suggested too that his purpose was to show the emptiness of the bour-geois values of his century. The torturers of even the relatively inoffensive *Misfortunes of Virtue* are wealthy bourgeois individualists, for even Bressac, though a noble, loves money. The decent Roland who succeeds Dalville is 'promptly crushed' and his fate at Sade's hands demonstrates that it is impossible to be both hon-est and bourgeois. Clearly, then, money corrupts and capitalism is power of darkness—so different from the cleaner, healthier lines of the feudalism which Sade wished to restore. Yet none of these interpretations sur-vive a reading of *The 120 Days of Sodom* or *Juliette* which are clearly intended to be taken literally. From one furi-ous psychodrama to the next, Sade repeated his recipe for the total liberation of the self which not only took eighteenth-century materialism to its furthest conclusion but also established a kind of social Darwinism which allowed the fittest to survive on a diet of theft, murder, rape, and domination, the only bar to their progress being the ability of their victims to stop them. No one is accountable for his drives and all are free to follow them: Sade's goal is freedom without responsibility.

Yet this philosophy of anarchic individualism is flawed. Sade's model for human nature was solitary, natural man who is defined solely in terms of pathologi-cal drives. It did not occur to him that human beings are social animals and that the concern for others is no less natural than love of self. Nature may well be a blind, amoral power, but man, far from being a lone wolf, is a gregarious, feeling, and reasoning being. Devising social arrangements to protect persons and property is therefore perfectly consistent with Nature's grand design. Society provides comforts and freedoms which are necessary to the human economy which Sade defines exclusively in terms of imperious urges. He has nothing to offer the weak, and the strong can look forward only to enslavement by the tyranny of licence. For the true Sadean exists in isolation, sealed in a world bereft of all feelings save ecstatic gratification and terror. There is no evidence to suggest that even Sade was freed by sadism. He spent many years alone, felt the absence of human warmth keenly, and found release in private hallucinations which compensated him with an illusion of power. It may be that there is no God to punish his priapic monsters. But others who have announced the death of God have always found something else to put in His place as a basis for moral authority and a standard by which conduct is measured: the Existentialists, for instance, and Sartre most notably, recommended forms of political commitment which assumed that it is possible to make arrangements for human beings to live orderly collective lives. Sade offers us merely the law of the jungle, which is no law at all.

Sade was probably not mad, but neither was he entirely sane. The nature and intensity of his compulsions are the pathological rather than the logical extension of philosophical principles. His contemporary William Blake also wished to liberate instinct but believed that the way to freeing human beings was through innocence, not through destruction and cruelty. There is nothing innocent in Sade who concentrates on our baser urges and simply skips the rest. Yet he has been annexed by psychoanalysts, philosophers, libertarians, writers, and artists and by anyone who has a grudge against bourgeois values. He still retains the power to shock.

That he should still do so in the late twentieth century is remarkable. Have not all the holocausts and horrors of our age sufficiently thickened our skins to see his brutal universe for the denial of the human that it is? Thus far, opposition and time have seen off tyrants like Hitler and Stalin, and virtue has triumphed over vice to prove him wrong. There is some small comfort to be taken from history which shows that torture and terrorism cannot be sustained indefinitely. Great Dictators have always been mass torturers and Sade's books do not weigh heavily against their very real atrocities. But by defining obscene sexual cruelty as the only true standard of personal behaviour, Sade sweeps away all ethical values as illusions, focuses attention on the beast in man to the exclusion of all else, and in so doing insinuates that the Great Butchers are merely our more honest brothers who do what we do not dare to attempt. Sade is the terrorist of the psyche.

Modern psychoanalysis defines three levels of sadism which run from pathological barbarity to harmless fantasy. The active sadist, who forms a tiny minority, performs acts of perverse atrocity; the sublimated sadist needs authorization or some justification before he will maim and kill (the torturer, for instance, who is ordered to obtain vital information); and the vicarious sadist merely dreams of terrible things to do to his enemies. Sade brushes away such distinctions and would have us accept that only lack of courage and intellectual clarity prevent us all from being true to our base, despotic, obscene, natures. The early Sade who speaks in the following pages may charm us, for he rarely bares his teeth. Yet *The Misfortunes of Virtue* gives a clear signal of the horrors to come. Sade was not the Great Liberator so many have seen in him but the creator of a terrible, horrific vision which is the death of hope, of history, of civilization itself.

SELECT BIBLIOGRAPHY

THE French texts on which this translation is based appear in the still standard reference edition of Sade's writings: the *Œuvres complètes* (16 vols., Paris, 1966–7). The *Historiettes, contes et fabliaux* were first published in 1926 by Maurice Heine. The French text of *The Misfortunes of Virtue* was established by Heine in 1930, and has been edited, with useful introductions, by Jean-Marie Goulemot (Paris, 1969) and Béatrice Didier (Paris, 1977). The major novels have been scrupulously edited in the Pléiade series (3 vols., Paris, 1990–2) by Michel Delon.

Among English translations of the major works are: Pieralessandro Cassavini's version of *120 Days of Sodom* (Paris, 1954); *The Complete Justine, Philosophy in the Bedroom and other writings*, trans. Richard Seaver and Austryn Wainhouse (New York, 1965); *Juliette*, trans. Austryn Wainhouse (New York, 1968). For selections of Sade's tales, see Margaret Crosland's *De Sade Quartet* (London, 1954) and *The Gothic Tales of the Marquis de Sade* (London, 1965). An expanded version of the 'first' Justine appears in Alan Hull Walton's composite *Justine, or the Misfortunes of Virtue* (London, 1964).

Current knowledge of Sade derives largely from the pioneering work of Maurice Heine. His *Le Marquis de Sade* (Paris, 1950) was the starting-point for Gilbert Lély's standard *Vie du Marquis de Sade* (Paris, 1952, several times revised and expanded) and translated as *The Marquis de Sade: A Biography* (London, 1961). Among the best of recent French studies are J.-J. Pauvert's *Sade Vivant* (Paris, 1986–90, 3 vols.) and Maurice Lever's *Donatien Alphonse François, Marquis de Sade* (Paris, 1991). Alice M. Laborde's *le Mariage du Marquis de Sade* (Paris–Geneva, 1988) is the first of a series of re-evaluations of biographical problems.

For feminist views of Sade, see Simone de Beauvoir's essay, 'Faut-il brûler Sade?', in *Privilèges* (Paris, 1955), translated as *Must We Burn Sade?, with selections from his writings* chosen by Paul Dinnage (London, 1962); Kate Millett, *Sexual Politics* (London, 1971); and especially Angela Carter, *The Sadean Woman* (London, 1979). The best general books in English are Ronald Hayman's *De Sade: A Critical Biography* (London, 1978), and Donald Thomas's sensible and good-humoured *The Marquis de Sade* (London, 1976).

A CHRONOLOGY OF THE
MARQUIS DE SADE

1740 2 June: birth of Donatien-Alphonse-François de Sade in Paris. He was raised with the Prince de Condé, four years his elder.

1746 Sent to live with his uncle, the abbé de Sade, at Saumane, in Provence.

1750 Attends the Jesuit college of Louis-le-Grand in Paris.

1755 Becomes a sub-lieutenant in an infantry regiment. Sees active service in the Seven Years War which he ended with the rank of Captain.

1763 17 May: marriage of Sade and Renée-Pélagie de Montreuil. 28 October: gaoled briefly at Vincennes for beating Jeanne Testard.

1764 Inherits his father's office as one of the King's provincial Lieutenant-Governors and addresses the Parlement of Dijon. Liaison with Mademoiselle Colet, an actress.

1765 Liaison with Mademoiselle de Beauvoisin, an actress, and others.

1767 Death of Sade's father who leaves him with considerable debts. 27 August: birth of his son Louis-Marie.

1768 3 April: the Rose Keller affair causes a considerable scandal. Detained in the prison of Pierre-Encise near Lyons between May and 16 November.

1769 27 June: birth of his second son, Donatien-Claude-Armand. September–October: travels in the Low Countries.

1770 Attempts to take up his military career are compromised by his unsavoury reputation.

1771 17 April: birth of daughter, Madeleine-Laure. Imprisoned briefly for debt.

1772 Liaison with Anne-Prospère de Launay, his sister-in-law. 17 June: the Marseilles affair. Sade flees to Italy. 3 September: Sade and his valet sentenced to death *in absentia* as poisoners and sodomites and their effigies are publicly burned at Aix. 8 December: gaoled at Miolans in Piedmont.

1773   30 April: escapes and eventually returns to La Coste.

1774   Evades police searches at La Coste.

1775   The affair of the servants at Lacoste. Again Sade flees to Italy and gathers materials for his *Travels through Italy*.

1777   After a further series of debauches at La Coste, one irate father seeks out Sade with a gun. 13 February: arriving in Paris too late to see his mother before her death, Sade is arrested and imprisoned at Vincennes.

1778   Though the sentence of death is lifted, Sade is detained at His Majesty's pleasure by *lettre de cachet*. Escapes but is promptly recaptured and returned to Vincennes.

1781   Composition of *The Inconstant*, the first of a number of plays, few of which have survived.

1782   Writes the 'Dialogue between a Priest and a Dying Man'. Begins writing *The 120 Days of Sodom*.

1784   29 February: is transferred from Vincennes to the Bastille.

1786   Writes the bulk of his 'philosophical' novel, *Aline and Valcour*.

1787   Late June–early July: composition of *The Misfortunes of Virtue*. Begins work on his *Tales and 'Fabliaux' of the Eighteenth Century, by a Provençal Troubadour*.

1788   Finally loses the battle to retain control of his affairs. October: draws up a list of his writings.

1789   2 July: from his cell window in the Bastille, using an extemporized loud-hailer, Sade calls for help, saying that prisoners are being murdered. 4 July: is transferred to the lunatic asylum at Charenton, leaving behind his furniture and a number of manuscripts. 14 July: the fall of the Bastille signals the start of the Revolution.

1790   2 April: following the abolition of the *lettre de cachet*,
        Sade is released. 9 June: Madame de Sade's request
        for a separation is granted—a preliminary to di-
        vorce. Summer: continues with his efforts to get his
        plays performed and frequents circles favourable to
        the principle of constitutional monarchy. Start of his
        liaison with Marie-Constance Quesnet which lasts
        until his death.

1791   June: anonymous publication of *Justine, or the Mis-
        fortunes of Virtue*. 22 October: performance of *The
        Comte d'Oxtiern, or the Effects of Libertinism*. Shows
        moderate sympathy for the new regime. To his law-
        yer he writes: 'What am I now? Aristocrat or demo-
        crat? You had better tell me for I myself have no
        idea.'

1792   Increasingly short of money, serves the Revolution
        as secretary to his District, the Section des Piques.
        17–21 September: the château of La Coste is sacked
        by what Sade calls 'brigands' and 'thieves'.

1793   Appointed a member of the committee investigating
        fraud and, on the murder of Marat, publishes a
        suitable pamphlet in his honour. August: the Mon-
        treuils are suspected of wishing to emigrate, at the
        time a capital offence. Sade ensures that their name
        does not appear on the list of suspects. His leniency
        in this and other matters does not endear him to
        extremists. December: the printer of *Aline and Val-
        cour* is arrested and the half-printed sheets are con-
        fiscated. 1 December: arrested as a 'suspect', he is
        accused of 'intelligence and correspondence with
        the enemies of the Republic' and gaoled.

1794   26 July: sentence of death passed on Sade and 27
        others. 28 July: death of Robespierre and the end of
        the Terror. 15 October: Sade released.

1795   Now destitute, tries to stage more plays. Publication
        of *Aline and Valcour*, attributed to 'Citizen S★★★'.
        The Philosopher in the Bedroom published anony-
        mously.

1796   13 October: sells La Coste.

1797   Continuing efforts to remove his name from the list
        of *émigrés* published in his province. Until his name

is cleared, he has no legal access to his private finances. Sade's name was never taken off the register. Publication of *The New Justine, or the Misfortunes of Virtue, followed by the History of Juliette, her Sister, or the Prosperities of Vice.*

1799   13 February: to avoid starvation, works in a theatre at Versailles for 40 sous a day. 29 August: a newspaper reports Sade's death. 13 December: new production of *Oxtiern* in which Sade plays the role of Fabrice.

1800   18 August: in the new moral climate, the police seize a new edition of *Justine*. 22 October: Villeterque, reviewing the newly published *The Crimes of Love: Heroic and Tragic Tales*, calls Sade a menace to public morals. Sade publishes a reply.

1801   March: further seizures of Sade's 'obscene' writings. 3 April: Gaoled at Sainte-Pélagie.

1803   14 March: after attempting to seduce fellow prisoners, is transferred to Bicêtre and thence, on 27 April, to Charenton.

1804   8 September: an official enquiry concludes that Sade is 'unreformable' and characterizes his mental condition as 'a permanent state of libertine dementia'.

1805   Easter Day: helps to serve communion.

1807   5 June: the authorities confiscate *The Days of Florbelle, or Nature unveiled*, begun in 1804. After his death, the manuscript was destroyed by his son.

1808   Organizes theatrical performances for the inmates of Charenton. 2 August: the new governor affirms that Sade is not mad and that he would be better detained in a secure prison than in a hospital.

1810   7 July: death of Madame de Sade.

1812   September–October: writes *Adelaide of Brunswick, Princess of Saxony*. 6 June: once more, Napoleon refuses to grant Sade's request to be freed.

1813   Sade's last affair, with the 16-year-old Madeleine Leclerc. Composition of *The Secret History of Isabelle of Bavaria* and *The Marquise de Gange*.

1814   2 December: death of Sade. He is given a religious burial in an unmarked grave.

1815   *Justine* and other works banned.

1834   The word '*sadisme*' is formally lexicalized in Boiste's *Dictionnaire universel*.

1876   Publication of Krafft-Ebing's *Psychopathia sexualis* where, together with 'masochism', the word 'sadism' acquires authority as a scientific term.

1904   Publication by Eugene Dühren (Iwan Bloch) of the newly discovered *120 Days of Sodom*.

1909   Apollinaire publishes a selection of Sade's works and predicts that he will dominate the twentieth century.

1957   Judgement against Jean-Jacques Pauvert, publisher of various works by Sade.

1983   HM Customs, using the discretion allowed under the 1876 Act, allows works by Sade, previously unobtainable in the UK, to be imported.

A NOTE ON MONEY

1 liard = 3 deniers
1 sou = 4 liards (later 6)
1 livre = 20 sous
1 écu = 3 livres
1 louis = 8 écus

The smaller coins were widely current at the poorest levels of society, but were very small change to the cultivated classes. An insight into the cost of living is provided by the Reverend William Cole (*A Journal of my Journey to France in 1765*, ed. F. G. Stokes, London, 1931) who reckoned one louis as the equivalent of an English guinea, the écu at half a crown, and the livre at tenpence or a shilling. It cost him 150 livres to travel by post from Calais to Paris. There, he gave a guinea a week for a hotel room, though could have had full board in the house of a printseller for a guinea and a half. Firewood cost one livre 'a hundred of dry Billets'. For about 5 livres or 4s. 6d., he and two servants (whom he paid 20 sous a day) ate very well. 'The wine they chiefly drink at Paris is Burgundy: that which I drank commonly, mixed with water, was at 1 *livre* 10 *sous* per Bottle: a smaller wine for my servant cost 12 *sous* the quart: I gave for incomparable Champaign, sparkling, or as the French call it, *Moussir* [sic], also for the non-Moussir Champaign, or what did not sparkle in the glass, for each 3 *livres* a Bottle.' The bill for 'my Dozen of Shirts & 6 Cravatts' came to 214 livres, or £9. 14s. 0d. and he paid 'Mr Armand for my Coat of Cotton Velvet, & black Velvet flowered waistcoat 176 *livres* 15 *sous*, which is near 8 Guineas.' For a coat and waistcoat for his servant, he paid £3. 10s. 0d. or about 80 livres.

*The Misfortunes of
Virtue and Other
Early Tales*

The Misfortunes of Virtue

THE ultimate triumph of philosophy would be to cast light upon the mysterious ways in which Providence moves to achieve the designs it has for man, and then to deduce therefrom some plan of conduct which would enable that two-legged wretch, forever buffeted by the whims of the Supreme Being who is said to direct his steps no less despotically, to know how to interpret what Providence decrees for him and to select a path to follow which would forestall the bizarre caprices of the Fate to which a score of different names are given but whose nature is still uncertain.

For if, taking social conventions as our starting-point and remaining faithful to the respect for them which education has bred in us, it should by mischance occur that through the perversity of others we encounter only thorns while evil persons gather nothing but roses, then will not a man, possessed of a stock of virtue insufficient to allow him to rise above the thoughts inspired by these unhappy circumstances, calculate that he would do as well to swim with the torrent as against it? And will he not say that when virtue, however fine a thing it be, unhappily proves too weak to resist evil, then virtue becomes the worst path he can follow, and will he not conclude that in an age that is utterly corrupt, the best policy is to do as others do? Or if you prefer, let the man have a degree of learning and allow him to abuse the knowledge he has acquired: will he not then say, like the angel Jesrad in Voltaire's *Zadig*,* that there is no evil from which some good does not flow? And will he not add of his own accord that, since in the imperfect fabric of this corrupt world of ours there is a sum of evil equal to the sum of good, the continuing equilibrium of the world requires that there be as many good people as wicked people, and that it follows that in the general scheme of things it matters not if such and such a man be good or wicked; that since misfortune persecutes virtue, and prosperity is the almost invariable accompaniment of vice (a matter of complete indifference to Nature), then is it not infinitely better to side with the wicked who prosper than with the good who perish? It is therefore important to guard against the dangerous sophisms of philosophy, and essential to show that when examples of suffering virtue are thrust before a corrupt soul in which principles of goodness are not entirely extinct, then even that straying soul may be returned to goodness as surely as if the road to virtue were littered with the most glittering prizes and the most flattering rewards. It is of course a cruel thing to have to depict the heap of misfortunes which overwhelms the sweet, feeling woman whose respect for virtue is unmatched, and on the other hand to portray the sparkling good fortune of her sister who scorned virtue all her life. And yet if some good should come from our sketching of these two pictures, shall we take ourselves to task for laying them before the public? Shall we feel remorse for establishing an exact account which will enable the wise man, who reads with profit and draws the ineffable lesson of submission to the will of Providence, to answer part of his secret stock of unanswered questions and heed the fatal warning that it is often to redirect our steps to the path of duty that Heaven strikes those next to us who best appear to have discharged theirs?

Such are the sentiments which led us to take up our pen, and it is in deference to their unimpeachable sincerity that we ask of our readers a modicum of attention and sympathy for the misfortunes of unhappy, wretched Justine.

*   *   *

The Comtesse de Lorsange was one of those votaries of Venus who owe their fortune to a bewitching face and a generous measure of loose conduct and underhand dealing, and whose letters patent of nobility, however imposing, being concocted out of the impertinence of those who seek them and the stupid credulity of those who

issue them, exist only in the archives of Cythera.* She
had dark hair, a vivacious manner, a fine figure, marvellously expressive black eyes, much wit, and above all
that fashionable lack of religious belief which, lending
extra savour to passion, makes the woman suspected of
harbouring it a special object of attraction. She had
nevertheless been given the finest of educations.
Daughter of a merchant in a large way of business in the
rue Saint-Honoré, she was brought up with her sister
three years her junior in one of the best convents in Paris
where, until the age of 15, she was never denied good
counsel or teachers nor good books or talents. At an age
which can prove fatal to the virtue of any young woman,
she lost everything in a single day. Cruel bankruptcy
brought her father to so ruinous a pass that his only
means of escaping the most dreadful fate was to flee in
haste to England, leaving his daughters in the care of his
wife who died of grief within the space of one week after
his departure. The one or two relatives who remained
deliberated on what was to be done with the girls. Their
inheritance amounting to about a hundred écus apiece,
it was decided that the convent doors be thrown open
to them, that they be given their due and allowed to
make their own way. Mme de Lorsange, then known as
Juliette, was already to all intents and purposes as mature in character and mind as she was to be at 30, which
was her age at the time we tell this story. She seemed
alive only to the sensation of being free and did not
pause for a moment to reflect upon the cruel reverses
which had snapped the chains which had bound her. But
her sister Justine, who had just turned 12, gloomy and
melancholic by disposition yet blessed with surprising
gentleness and sensitivity, having none of her sister's
artfulness and guile but the ingenuousness, candour,
and honesty which were to make her stumble into many
traps, Justine felt the full horror of her situation. Her
face was quite unlike Juliette's. Where the features of the
one were all artifice, cunning, and coquetry, the other's
were remarkable for their modesty, refinement, and shy-

ness. A virginal air, large, engaging blue eyes, dazzling skin, a slender, well-shaped figure, a voice to move the heart, teeth of ivory, and beautiful fair hair—so much, in outline sketch, for the younger sister whose simple grace and delightful expression were of too fine, too delicate a stamp not to elude the brush which would capture them entire.

Both were given twenty-four hours to quit the convent and complete freedom to fend for themselves with their hundred écus. Overjoyed to be her own mistress, Juliette attempted briefly to dry Justine's tears, but seeing that she would not succeed, left off comforting her and fell to scolding. She told her she was a foolish girl and said that given their ages and pretty faces, it was unheard of for girls to starve to death. She quoted the instance of one of their neighbour's daughters who had escaped from her father's house and was now sumptuously kept by a tax-farmer* and lived in great style in Paris. Justine was horrified by this pernicious example. She said she would die rather than follow her lead and categorically refused to share a lodging with her sister Juliette once she saw that she had set her mind on the kind of abominable life she had commended so warmly.

And so the moment it was clear that their intentions were so different, the sisters went their separate ways, making no promises to meet again. Would Juliette, who, she claimed, would become a great lady, ever agree to have anything more to do with the foolish girl whose *virtuous*, squeamish inclinations would dishonour her? And for her part would Justine put her moral purity at risk by associating with a perverse creature who would surely be a victim of lewdness and public debauchery? And so each made provision for their money to be paid and left the convent the next day as arranged.

As a little girl, Justine had been coddled by her mother's seamstress and, thinking that this woman would be moved by her plight, sought her out, told her of her distressed circumstances, asked for work, and was sent away with harsh words . . .

'Great Heaven!' said the poor creature, 'must the first steps I take in the world come so soon and so surely to grief? This woman loved me once. Why then does she turn me away now? Because, alas, I am an orphan and penniless, because I no longer have means to call on and because people are valued only in terms of the help or profit that may be got out of them.'

When she realized this, Justine called on her parish priest and asked him for advice. But the charitable churchman answered ambiguously, saying that the parish was overburdened and that it was not possible for her to receive a portion of the poor-box, but that if she were prepared to work for him he would gladly give her lodging in his house. But as, in so saying, the holy man had placed his hand beneath her chin and gave her far too worldly a kiss for a man of the cloth, Justine, understanding his meaning only too well, pulled back sharply and said:

'Sir, I do not ask for charity or a position as servant. Too little time has gone by since my station in life was far above the lowly circumstances in which such favours have to be begged for, for me to be reduced to soliciting them now! I asked you for the guidance I need in my youth and misfortune, and you would have me purchase it with a crime.'

Angered by this word, the priest showed her the door and callously turned her out. Justine, twice spurned on the very day she was sentenced to a life of isolation, entered a house with a notice in the window, took a small furnished room which she paid for in advance, and was now at least able to surrender undisturbed to the mortification engendered by her circumstances and the cruelty of the few people to whom her unlucky star had led her.

The reader will allow us to leave her in her dark coop for a while and return to Juliette so that we may tell as briefly as possible how, from her unremarkable beginnings on leaving the convent, she became within the space of fifteen years a lady possessing a title, an income

of 30,000 livres, gorgeous jewels, two or three houses in
Paris and in the country, plus, for the time being, the
heart, purse, and confidence of Monsieur de Corville, a
Councillor of State, a man enjoying the highest credit
and poised to become a Minister of the Crown. Her path
had been thorny. Of this there can be no doubt: it is only
by serving the most shameful, bitter apprenticeship that
girls of her sort make their way. The woman who today
occupies the bed of a prince may well still bear upon her
person the humiliating marks of the brutality of the
depraved libertines into whose hands she was thrown by
her tentative first steps, her youth, and her inexperience.

On leaving the convent, Juliette had promptly gone off
in search of a woman she had heard mentioned by her
friend, the former neighbour who had taken to debauchery. She had kept the address and appeared shame-
lessly on the doorstep with her bundle under her arm,
her plain dress in disarray and with the prettiest face that
ever was and the air of one who was only too willing to
learn. She told her story to the woman and pleaded with
her to grant her the same protection that she had be-
stowed on her friend a few years earlier.

'How old are you, child?' asked Madame Du Buisson.
'I shall be 15 in a few days.'
'And has any man or woman . . . ?'
'O no, Madame, I swear.'
'But sometimes, you know, in convents—an almoner?
a nun? a friend? I shall need proof.'
'Pray proceed as you think fit, Madame, and you will
have all the proof you want.'

Madame Du Buisson perched a pair of spectacles on
her nose and, after satisfying herself of the exact state of
things, said to Juliette:

'Well, child, you may stay here. Follow my advice
strictly, be accommodating in observing my rules, be
clean and thrifty, behave candidly with me, courteously
with your companions and deceitfully with men, and
under my direction you shall be in a position a few years
hence to withdraw from this place to a room of your own

with a chest for your clothes, a pier-glass, and a maid, and the art which you acquire in my house will provide you with the means of procuring the rest.'

Madame Du Buisson took charge of Juliette's little bundle and asked if she had any money about her. Juliette having volunteered too promptly that she had a hundred écus, her dear Mama pocketed that too, telling her young pupil that she would invest it for her, for young ladies should not be allowed to have money, since money provided the means for wrong-doing and, in so corrupt a century, a girl of good character and family should take care to avoid anything that might cause her to stumble and topple into a snare. Once this sermon was done, the newcomer was presented to her companions, she was shown to her chamber in the house and the very next day her virginity was put up for sale. Within a space of four months, the same merchandise was sold in turn to eighty persons who each paid as though for unused goods, and it was only at the expiry of her thorny novitiate that Juliette was granted entry to the sisterhood. From that moment on, she was truly acknowledged as a full daughter of the nunnery and bore her share of its lewd and exhausting labours—in effect a further novitiate. If during the first, Juliette, apart from a few lapses, had served nature, she now neglected nature's laws during the second and submitted to criminal refinements, loathsome pleasures, secret, filthy debauches, shocking, bizarre tastes, humiliating fancies, all of which were born, first, of the search for pleasures free of all risk to health* and, second, of pernicious Surfeit which blunts the imagination and leaves it no scope or room except through excess and no means of satisfaction save in depravity. Juliette's morals were totally corrupted in her new school and her soul was thoroughly depraved by the victories she observed borne off by vice. She felt that since she was made for crime, then at the very least she should set her sights on the highest peak and refuse to languish in her present lowly condition which required her to commit the same foul acts and be no less

degraded, but brought her nothing like the same profit.
She took the fancy of an old, thoroughly depraved nobleman who at first had singled her out for a mere quarter
of an hour's amusement. She managed to beguile him
into keeping her in the most opulent manner and at last
she began to be seen in theatres and in the fashionable
walks on an equal footing with the luminaries of the
Order of Cythera. She was looked at, her words were
repeated, she was an object of envy, and the jade went
about her business so well that in four years she ruined
three men, the poorest of whom had an income of
100,000 écus. It was enough to make her reputation.
Such is the blindness of people nowadays that the more
impure one of these unfortunates shows herself to be,
the keener they are to be on her list. It is as though the
depth of her depravity and corruption is the only yard-
stick by which the feelings which they lavish so shame-
lessly on her in public are to be measured.

Juliette had just turned 20 when a certain Count de
Lorsange, a nobleman from the province of Anjou aged
about 40, became so smitten with her that he resolved
upon making her his wife since he had not fortune
enough to keep her as his mistress. He made over an
income of 12,000 livres to her, and arranged that the
remainder of his fortune, a further 8,000, would be hers
should he die before she did; he gave her a house, servants, and a retinue and conferred on her a degree of
respectability in society which ensured that within two
or three years her beginnings were forgotten. It was then
that the wretched Juliette, oblivious to all the decent
promptings of her birth and sound education, corrupted
by evil books and evil counsel, impatient to enjoy her
advantages alone, to have a name and to be rid of all
chains, dared yield to the culpable notion of abridging
her husband's life . . . She conceived her plan and,
regrettably, executed it with such stealth that she was
able both to elude the arm of the law and to bury all
traces of her abominable crime along with her hindrance
of a husband.

Once more in possession of her freedom and now a Countess, Madame de Lorsange took up her old habits, but thinking that she cut some figure in the world, she put a measure of decency into her proceedings. She was no longer a kept woman but a rich widow who gave gay supper-parties to which the ornaments of town and court were only too happy to be admitted—yet she could be bedded for 200 louis and bought for 500 a month.* Until she was 26, she continued to make brilliant conquests, ruined three ambassadors, four tax-farmers, two bishops, and three Knights of Royal Orders and, since it is rare to stop at one crime especially when it has turned out successfully, Juliette, the wretched, culpable Juliette sank ever deeper into the mire with two more crimes of the same kind as the first; one, that she might rob one of her lovers of a sum of money put into her keeping by him without his family's knowing which she sequestered to her own profit by means of her odious crime, the other, that she might the sooner receive a bequest of 100,000 livres which one of her admirers had written into his will in the name of a third party who was appointed to hand the money over to her against a small consideration. To these horrors, Madame de Lorsange added two or three infanticides: considerations of all kinds—fear of spoiling her pretty figure or a need to safeguard twin amours running in tandem—led her to resort on several occasions to abortion.* These crimes, like the others, went undetected and did nothing to prevent this scheming and ambitious woman from finding new dupes daily and swelling her fortune at every turn as her crimes accumulated. It is regrettably only too true that prosperity may accompany crime and that even in the most freely embraced state of depravity and corruption the thread of life may be gilded by what men call happiness. But let not this cruel and unavoidable reality be a cause for dismay. Let not the truth (of which we shall presently furnish an example) that it is on the contrary vice which everywhere pursues and attacks virtue, trouble the hearts of honest, decent persons. The

prosperity of crime is more apparent than real. Independently of Providence which of necessity punishes his
ostensible success, a guilty man harbours in the recesses
of his heart a worm which gnaws at him unceasingly,
makes it impossible for him to bask in the felicity which
bathes his existence, and leaves him instead with only
the grievous memory of the crimes by which he came by
it. And against the misfortunes which snap at virtue's
heels, the unhappy man who is persecuted by Fate has
the consolation of a clear conscience and the inner joy
which comes from the purity of his soul: together these
are a prompt compensation for the injustice of men.*

The affairs of Madame de Lorsange had reached this
pitch when Monsieur de Corville who, at 50, enjoyed the
credit which we have already mentioned, resolved to
devote himself entirely to her and to keep her for himself
alone. What with thoughtfulness or attentions on his
part and discretion on hers, he had succeeded and had
been living with her for four years together on exactly
the same footing as if she were his legally married wife,
when a superb estate which he had just bought for her
near Montargis prompted in both the desire to spend a
few months of the summer there. One June evening, the
fine weather tempted them to push on by foot as far as
the town and, feeling too weary to return in the manner
in which they had come, they entered the inn which
serves as a staging-post for the Lyons coach, thinking to
send a rider thence to fetch them a carriage from their
château. They were resting in a cool, low-ceilinged room
which looked out on to the courtyard when the coach
we have mentioned drove in. Observing travellers is a
natural pastime; anyone with an idle moment to spare
will gladly occupy it in this way when the occasion arises.
Madame de Lorsange stood up, her lover did likewise,
and both watched as the passengers entered the inn. It
appeared that no one was left on board when a constable, leaping down from the jump-seat, helped to hand
down from one of his colleagues who had been riding
next to him a young woman of about 26 or 27 with a

cheap calico shawl about her person and her hands tied together like a criminal's. At a cry of horror and astonishment which escaped from Madame de Lorsange, the young woman turned, revealing features so sweet and delicate and so fine and shapely a figure that Monsieur de Corville and his mistress could not restrain a desire to intervene on behalf of so wretched a creature. Monsieur de Corville approached and asked one of the constables what the unhappy creature had done.

'Well sir,' replied the gendarme, 'she is accused of committing three or four major crimes, to wit, theft, murder, and arson, but I don't mind admitting that neither my colleague here nor myself ever had less stomach for an escort detail. She is the sweetest creature and I'd say the straightest too.'

'Is that so?' said Monsieur de Corville. 'Perhaps she has been the victim of some mistake. Mistakes are not unknown in magistrates' courts.* Where were the crimes committed?'

'At an inn three leagues outside Lyons. She was tried at Lyons and is on her way to Paris for confirmation of sentence. Then she'll travel back to Lyons and be executed there.'

Madame de Lorsange had drawn near, overheard what was said, and now whispered to Monsieur de Corville that she would very much like to hear the story of the young woman's misfortunes from her own lips. Monsieur de Corville, sharing her wish, spoke of it to her escort and made himself known. They raised no objection. Madame de Lorsange and Monsieur de Corville now resolved to spend the night at Montargis and asked to be given a suitable apartment with an adjacent room for the constables. Monsieur de Corville took full responsibility for the prisoner. Her hands were untied and she was shown into the room of Madame de Lorsange and Monsieur de Corville. Her guards dined and went to bed in the adjoining chamber. When the poor unfortunate had been persuaded to take a little sustenance, Madame de Lorsange, who could not prevent herself from feeling the keenest interest in her and doubtless was telling herself: 'This wretched and perhaps innocent creature is treated like a criminal while everything I touch turns to gold—and I am assuredly far guiltier than she.'—Madame de Lorsange, I say, the moment she saw that the young woman was a little recovered and in some measure consoled by the attentions shown to her and the concern displayed on her behalf, persuaded her to relate the circumstances which had, notwithstanding her air of honesty and goodness, brought her to so terrible a pass.

*   *   *

The story of my life, Madame (said the beautiful, unhappy creature to the Countess), would furnish you with the most striking example of the misfortunes of innocence. To tell it would be to accuse Providence and complain of its workings. It would be a sin of a kind and I cannot bring myself to . . .

Tears then streamed from the eyes of the unfortunate young woman, but after letting them flow freely for a moment, she began her story in these terms.

With your leave, I shall withhold my name. I come of a family which, though undistinguished, Madame, was respectable, and I was not born to the mortifications which have been the source of the larger part of my misfortunes.* I lost both my parents when very young. With the modest means they left at my disposal, I had thought to obtain an honest situation, but constantly rejecting offers which were far from honest, I exhausted my small inheritance more quickly than I realized. The poorer I grew, the more reviled I was. The more I stood in need of help, the smaller grew my hopes of finding it or the more frequently was it held out to me in unworthy and shameful forms. Of all the hardships which I endured in my distressed condition, of all the horrid propositions that were made to me, I shall mention only what befell me in the house of Monsieur Dubourg, one of the richest merchants in the capital. I had been directed to him as the kind of man whose wealth and credit were most suited and best able to alleviate my fate. But those who had advised me thus either sought to deceive me or else were unaware of the hardness of the man's heart or the depravity of his morals. After waiting two hours in his antechamber, I was shown into his presence. Monsieur Dubourg, who was about 45 years of age, had just risen from his bed and was wearing a loose-fitting robe which barely covered his state of undress. Being about to have his peruke arranged upon his head, he dismissed his valet and asked me what I wanted.

'Alas, Monsieur,' I answered, 'I am a poor orphan who, though not yet 14, nevertheless am acquainted with all the degrees of misfortune.' I then told him of my setbacks, my difficulties in finding a situation, the unhappy circumstance of my having spent the little money I had in seeking a place, the rejections I had met with, even the difficulties I had encountered in finding needlework to do either in a dressmaker's shop or in my own room, and I spoke of the hopes I had conceived of his helping me to find a means of earning a living.

After listening to me most attentively, Monsieur Dubourg asked me if I had always been a good girl.

'I should neither be so poor nor have fallen so low, Monsieur,' I said, 'had I ever wanted to be otherwise.'

At this, he said: 'My child, on what grounds do you believe that Wealth should extend a helping hand seeing that you serve its purposes in no way whatsoever?'

'Serve, Monsieur? But I ask only to be of service.'

'The services which a child like you can contribute to the running of a house are of no great weight, though I was not thinking of those services. You are neither old enough nor sufficiently presentable for me to find you a position as you ask. But if you were to adopt a less ludicrously strict attitude, you might aspire to a modest future in any libertine circle. And it is in that direction that you had now best move. The virtue of which you make so much serves no useful purpose in the real world. You can tout it around as much as you like, but you will find that it won't even buy you a glass of water. Those of us who actually dole out charity, which is something we do as little as possible and then only with the greatest reluctance, want to be compensated for the money which is taken out of our pockets. Now, what can a little girl like you do to repay the help she receives, if not to agree to whatever is asked of her?'

'O sir, so there are neither philanthropy nor decent feelings in men's hearts?'

'No, not a great deal, my child. The mania for obliging others without asking anything in return is now a thing of the past. It flattered one's pride momentarily, of course. But since there is nothing so illusory and so quickly dispelled as pleasure, people have begun demanding more palpable gratifications. They felt that in the case of a girl like yourself, for example, it was far more worth while to take a return on the moneys advanced in the form of the pleasures afforded by libertinage than to take pride in having acted charitably. The reputation of a liberal, charitable, generous man is, to my way of thinking, as nothing compared to the smallest hint of the pleasure you could give me. In consideration of which—and here my views are those of almost everyone of my tastes and age—you will understand, child, that any help I give you will be proportionate to your agreeing to do whatever it pleases me to ask of you.'

'What hardness of heart, sir! Do you imagine that Heaven will not punish you for your callousness?'

'You are young and know nothing, but hear this: Heaven is the last thing in the world which interests us. Whether what we do on earth pleases Heaven or not is the last thing which gives us pause. Being only too aware of how little power Heaven has over men, we defy it daily without a qualm. Indeed, our passions acquire true enchantment only when they transgress Heaven's designs most outrageously, or at least what simpletons assure us are its designs, though in reality they form the illusory chain by which hypocrites and impostors have always set out to deceive and subjugate the strong.'

'But sir, do not such principles mean that the unfortunate man is doomed to perish?'

'What does that signify? France has more subjects than it needs. The Government sees everything in broad terms and is not overly concerned with individuals provided that the machinery runs smoothly overall.'

'But do you think that children respect their fathers when they are badly treated?'

'What does the love of children who serve no useful purpose matter to a father who already has far too many?'

'So it would have been better if we had been strangled at birth?'

'Probably. But enough of politics which you cannot possibly understand. Why do you complain of your fate when you could so easily change it?'

'But Heavens, at what cost!'

'The cost merely of an idle fancy, of a thing which has no value beyond the price which your pride sets upon it. But let us leave aside this question too and simply keep to what concerns us both at this juncture. You lay great store by this idle fancy, don't you, while I attach very little importance to it and so shall not fight you for it. The duties which I should expect of you, and for which you will be reasonably, but not excessively paid, will be of a quite different order. I shall give you into my housekeeper's charge. You will answer to her and each morning, in my presence, either this woman or my valet will subject you to . . .'

O Madame, how shall I convey this execrable proposition to you? I was too humiliated to take it in as it was being made, and my head spun, so to speak, as the words were said . . . Being too ashamed to repeat them now, I beg you to be good enough to imagine the rest . . . The cruel man spoke the names of high-ranking churchmen and I was to be their victim.

'That is as much as I can do for you, my child,' the wicked man went on as he stood up with no thought for decency, 'and even so all I can promise you for the

duration of these proceedings, which will be always pro-
tracted and painful, is to support you for two years. You
are now 14. At 16 you will be free to seek your fortune
elsewhere. Until then, you will be clothed and fed and
will receive one louis each month. It is a very fair offer:
I have not been giving as much to the girl you will
replace. Of course, she did not possess intact the virtue
by which you set such great store and which I reckon to
be worth, as you see, about 50 écus a year, a rather larger
sum than was given to your predecessor. Think it over
carefully, pay special attention to the poverty from which
I should save you, and reflect that in this unjust society
of which you are part, those who do not have enough to
live on must suffer if they are to earn enough to get by.
Like them you will suffer too, I grant, but you will earn
far more than the vast majority of them.'

The monster's appalling words had inflamed his passions. He seized me by the collar of my dress and told
me that on this first occasion he himself would show me
what was involved . . . But my plight gave me courage
and strength, I managed to struggle free and, as I rushed
to the door:

'Loathsome man!' I cried as I fled, 'may Heaven which
you offend so cruelly punish you one day as you deserve
for your odious barbarity. You are not worthy of the
wealth which you abuse so vilely, nor even of the air you
breathe in a world made foul by your brutal ways.'

I was returning dejectedly to my lodging plunged
into the black, depressing thoughts to which the cruelty
and corruption of men inevitably give rise, when my
eye seemed for a moment to catch a glimpse of fair
weather. The woman with whom I lodged was acquainted with my distress. She now came up to me and said
that she had at last discovered a house where I would be
gladly received, provided my behaviour was beyond
reproach.

'O Heavens, Madame,' I said, embracing her ecstatically, 'that is a condition I should myself insist upon! I
accept most gladly!'

The man I was to serve was an elderly money-lender who, it was said, had grown rich not only by lending against pledges but by robbing all and sundry with impunity each time he saw it was safe for him to do so. He lived in a first-floor apartment in the rue Quincampoix* with an aged mistress he called his wife who was as least as spiteful as he.

'Sophie,' the miser said to me, 'Sophie' (this was the name I had taken to conceal my own), 'the foremost virtue which I require in my house is honesty. If ever even the tenth part of a denier* should find its way into your pocket, I shall have you hanged, do you hear Sophie? hanged beyond reviving. If my wife and I enjoy a few comforts in our old age, they are the fruit of our unending labours and extreme abstemiousness. Do you eat a great deal, my child?'

'A few ounces of bread a day, sir,' I replied, 'some water and a little soup when I am fortunate enough to have it.'

'Soup! Good God! Soup! Look at her, my dear,' the old miser said to his wife, 'and see to what a pass the taste for luxury has brought us! Here's a slavey who has been looking for a place for a year, starving for a twelve-month, and she asks for soup! Soup is something we hardly ever make, just once, on Sundays, and we have been working like Turks these forty years. You will make do with three ounces of bread a day, my girl, half a bottle of river water, one of my wife's cast-off dresses every eighteen months for you to turn into petticoats, and three écus for your pay at the end of the year if we are happy with the work you do, if you are as economical as we are and, finally, if, by your orderliness and good husbandry, you help the business to prosper. We do not require much in the way of attendance and there is no servant but you. All you have to do is to polish and clean the six rooms in the apartment three times a week, make my wife's bed and mine, answer the door, powder my wig, dress my wife's hair, look after the dog, the cat, and the parrot, attend to the kitchen, shine the pans whether they have been used or not, help my wife when she makes us a bite to eat, and spend the rest of the day washing, darning stockings, trimming hats, and making other household oddments. As you see, there's not much to it, Sophie. You'll have plenty of time to yourself and we shall not stand in your way if you wish to use it for your private purposes and also to do your personal washing and make whatever clothes you may need.'

You will have no difficulty in imagining, Madame, that only one in circumstances as reduced as those in which I now found myself would ever accept such a place. Not only was there infinitely more work than my age and strength allowed me to undertake, but would I be able to live on what I had been offered? I took care, however, to avoid making difficulties and moved in that same evening.

If in the parlous circumstances I now find myself at this moment, Madame, I had half a mind to afford you a moment's amusement, though by rights I should have no thought but to interest your heart in my favour, I think I can say I should entertain you royally with some account of the miserly habits I was witness to in that house. But a calamity so terrible in its consequences for me stood waiting at the finish of my second year there that it is with no little difficulty, when I think back, that I now bring myself to relate a few humorous details before telling you of the setback I mentioned. So let me say, Madame, that no lights were ever lit in that house. Fortunately, the apartment of my master and mistress looked on to the street lamp outside and this freed them of the need to have any other glim: no lamp of any other kind served to light them to bed. They made no use of linen. My master's coat, like my mistress's dress, was furnished with a pair of cuffs stitched to the cloth at the sleeve-ends and these I washed each Saturday evening so that they were presentable of a Sunday; there were no sheets or table napkins, to save on laundry-work, always a costly item in any household according to Monsieur Du Harpin, my respected master. No wine was served, water being, as Madame Du Harpin held, the natural drink of the first men on earth and the only drink prescribed by Nature. Whenever bread was cut, a basket was placed beneath to catch the crumbs that fell, and to them anything left over from meals was carefully added, the whole being fried together on Sundays with a little rancid butter, this constituting festive fare for the day of rest. Clothes and upholstery were not to be beaten, for fear of wearing them out, but were to be lightly switched with a feather duster. The shoes worn by my master and mistress were bottomed with iron, and both husband and wife still clung reverently to the footwear which had served them on their wedding-day. But there was one practice, odder still by far, which I was required to follow regularly once a week. The apartment boasted one room of fair size whose walls were unpapered; with a knife, I was required to scrape a quantity of plaster from them which I then passed through a fine sieve, what remained from this operation being employed as the powder with which I dressed my master's wig and my mistress's hair each morning. But would to God that these shameful practices were the only ones to which these dreadful people subscribed. Nothing is more natural than the wish to preserve what one has, but what is rather less so is the desire to double one's property by adding to it property belonging to other people, and it was not long before I perceived that it was in this manner, and this manner alone, that Monsieur Du Harpin had grown so rich. Living on the floor above was a gentleman with a decent competency, being possessed of rather fine jewels. Now perhaps because he lived so near or perhaps because his effects had already passed through his hands, the extent of his wealth was well known to my master. I often heard him and his wife say how much they regretted a particular gold casket worth 30 or 40 louis which would certainly have remained in his possession had the attorney he employed known his business better; to make up the loss of the returned casket, the honest Monsieur Du Harpin now proposed to steal it and I was charged with the business.

After reading me a long lesson on the trivial nature of stealing and on the useful role it plays in society where theft redresses a balance destroyed by inequalities in the distribution of wealth, Monsieur Du Harpin gave me a counterfeit key and assured me that it fitted the door to his neighbour's apartment; that I should find the casket in a cabinet which was never locked; that I could purloin it without running any kind of risk; and that for rendering such an important service, I should have an extra écu on my wages for the next two years.

'O sir!' I cried, 'is it possible that a master should seek to corrupt his servant so? What is there to prevent me from turning against you the same weapons which you place in my hand, for what reasonable objection could you make were I to rob you according to your own principles?'

Monsieur Du Harpin, much taken aback by my answer, did not dare insist further but, nursing a secret rancour against me, said that what he had done was intended to test me, that it was fortunate indeed that I had not agreed to his insidious scheme, for had I succumbed then I would have been as good as hanged. I settled for this reply but from that time forward I was aware both of the misfortunes which hung over my head as a result of such a proposition and of my error in answering him so categorically. But there was no middle path: I had either to commit the crime he spoke of or to reject what he proposed out of hand. Had I then had a little more experience of the world, I should have quitted the house at once. But it was already written in the book of my destiny that each honest prompting of my nature would be repaid by misfortune. I was therefore forced to submit to fate, it being impossible that I should ever escape it.*

Monsieur Du Harpin allowed close upon a month to pass, that is until about the time of my completing a second year in his household, without mentioning or giving the slightest sign of ill will towards me for having refused his bidding, when one evening, withdrawing to my chamber after my work was done, there to enjoy a few hours of calm, I suddenly heard my door broken down and not without fright observed Monsieur Du Harpin leading a police officer and four men of the watch to my bedside.*

'Do your duty, constable,' said he to the officer of the law, 'the hussy has robbed me of a diamond worth a thousand écus. You will find it in her room or about her person. It's here all right.'

'I, sir, steal from you!' said I dismayed, throwing myself to the foot of my bed. 'Ah, who better than you knows how offensive I find the very thought of such things and how impossible it would be for me to have stooped so low!'

But Monsieur Du Harpin, who made a great deal of noise so that my words should go unheard, continued to oversee the search and the wretched ring was found in one of my mattresses. Against evidence so incontrovertible there was no reply. I was immediately seized, bound, and led to the Palace prison,* during which time I could not gain the smallest hearing for anything I might have said in my defence.

The trial of any hapless person who lacks credit or protection is a quickly expedited business in France where virtue is thought incompatible with poverty and the ill fortune of the accused is proof sufficient of guilt in the eyes of magistrates. An unjust assumption persuades courts that whoever was most likely to have perpetrated the crime is in fact the person who committed it; sentiments are gauged by the state in which the accused appears and the moment he is seen to have neither title nor wealth to prove that he is honest, it becomes self-evident that he is not.

In vain did I try to defend myself and provide the court advocate I was briefly allowed to have with the best arguments: my master accused me, the diamond had been found in my chamber, and it was obvious that I had stolen it. When I attempted to raise the matter of Monsieur Du Harpin's dishonest scheme and prove that

the misfortune which had befallen me was no more than
an effect of his revenge and his wish to be rid of a
creature who, knowing his secret, had power to ruin his
reputation, my counter-complaints were dismissed as
mere recriminations. I was told that for forty years Monsieur Du Harpin had been known for an honest man and
was quite incapable of such villainy, and I believed that
I was about to pay with my life for my refusal to take
part in a crime,* when an unexpected turn of events
intervened and I was freed only to be thrust once more
into the new calamities which still awaited me in this
vale of tears.

A woman of 40 years called Dubois, notorious for
abominable actions of every kind, was also on the point
of having sentence of death carried out on her, her
sentence at least being better deserved than mine since
the case against her was fully attested, whereas it was
impossible to find any crime that could be laid at my
door. I had aroused the interest of this woman. One
evening, only a few days before we were both to forfeit
our lives, she told me that I should not go to bed but,
doing nothing to attract attention, should stay by her
side and keep as close to the gates of the prison as could
be managed.

'Between midnight and one o'clock,' said the enter-
prising jade, 'the building will catch fire.* It will be my
handiwork. It is possible that someone may well be
burned to death, but no matter, for what is uppermost
is that you and I shall escape. Three men, who are my
accomplices and friends, will meet us and I shall answer
for your freedom.'

The hand of Heaven which a short space before had
punished innocence in my person now served crime in
that of my protectress. The flames caught, the confla-
gration was horrible to see, ten people were burned to
death, but we made off safely. That same day we reached
a cottage in the forest of Bondy* belonging to a poacher,
a different kind of criminal from the others but a close
associate of our gang.

'Now you are free, my dear Sophie,' Dubois said to me, 'you are at liberty to choose whatever kind of life you please. But a word of counsel: give up your virtuous ways which as you can see have never helped you prosper. Misplaced delicacy brought you to the foot of the gallows while a gruesome crime enabled me to escape the rope: ask yourself what purpose goodness serves in the world and consider whether there is any profit to be gained by sacrificing yourself for it. You are young and pretty. I shall answer for making your fortune in Brussels, if you wish. I am bound there now, for I was born in that city. Within two years, I shall raise you to untold heights, but I warn you now that it is not along the narrow paths of virtue that I shall lead you to fortune. Anyone of your age who wants to get on quickly in life must be prepared to undertake more than one trade and be adept at managing more than one intrigue at a time. Do you hear me, Sophie, do you catch my drift? Make up your mind quickly. We must leave this place, for we shall be safe here for a few hours only.'

'O Madame,' said I to my benefactress, 'I am deeply in your debt, for you saved my life. But I am also appalled that I should owe my life to a crime and you may be assured that if I had been given any choice in the matter, I would sooner have perished than set my hand to it. I am only too sensible of the dangers I have run by committing myself to those feelings of decency which will ever grow in my heart. But whatever the thorns of virtue, I shall always prefer them to the false beams that shine on prosperity, for these are dangerous marks of favour and the fleeting accompaniment of crime. I carry within me notions of religion which, thanks be to God, will never desert me. If Providence makes my course in life arduous, it is only so that I shall be the more amply rewarded in a better world. This hope is my consolation: it is balm to my sorrows and quiets my murmuring soul, it gives me strength in adversity and helps me to face whatever ills it is pleased to set in my path. It is a joy which would be soon extinguished in my heart were I to desecrate it with criminal actions and, being then filled with the fear of tribulations yet to come in this world, more terrible by far, I should also have in view the dreadful prospect of the punishments which heavenly justice reserves in the next for those who offend against it.'

'Your principles are absurd and they will lead you straight to prison, my girl, take it from me,' said Dubois with a frown. 'Forget heavenly justice, your punishments and your rewards to come. Such talk is fit only for leaving in the schoolroom or, once you have left it and entered the world, for enabling you to starve to death, should you be foolish enough to believe it. The callousness of the rich justifies the knavery of the poor, my child. If their purses would open to satisfy our needs and if humanity reigned in their hearts, then virtue would take root in ours. But as long as our distress, the patience with which we bear it, our honesty and our subjection serve merely to add weight to our chains, our misdemeanours are their handiwork and we should be dupes indeed to reject crime as a means of lightening a yoke which they fasten around our necks. We were all born equal in the eyes of Nature, Sophie. If fate chooses to disturb the original disposition of Nature's general laws, it is for us to correct departures therefrom and by our artfulness repair the depradations of the strong. How I love hearing rich people, the judges, and the magistrates, oh, how I love seeing them preaching virtue at us! Oh, how difficult it must be for them to refrain from theft when they have three times as much as they need to live on, how difficult never to think of murder when they are surrounded only by admirers and submissive slaves, how exceedingly painful indeed to be temperate and sober when they are intoxicated by sensuality and the most succulent dishes are set before them—and they must find it trying indeed to be frank and honest when the need to lie scarcely ever arises. But the likes of us, Sophie, have been condemned to crawl on the earth, like the serpent upon its belly, by that same barbaric Providence which in your folly you have made your idol. We are looked on with scorn because we are poor, humiliated because we are weak, and in every part of the globe find nothing but gall and thorns—and yet you believe that we should deny ourselves the uses of Crime, though Crime alone opens the door to life which it sustains, preserves, and prevents from losing altogether. You would have us be eternally subject and humiliated while the class* which dominates us has on its side the advantage of fortune's endless favours! You would wish upon us only toil, despair and suffering, poverty and tears, odium and the gallows! No, Sophie, no! Either the Providence which you revere was made only to deserve our contempt, or else its intentions were quite different. Learn to know Providence better, Sophie, acquaint yourself with its ways and be persuaded that if Providence places us in situations where acting wickedly becomes necessary and at the same time allows us to choose to be wicked, then its laws are served no less well by evil than by good and Providence thus gains as much by the one as by the other. The state into which we were born at her behest is a state of equality.* Whoever disturbs that state is no more guilty than anyone who seeks to restore it, for both parties act upon impulses implanted in them, and have no choice but to act upon them, clap a blindfold to their eyes, and enjoy the result.'

I confess that if ever I wavered it was as I listened to the tempting arguments put by this artful woman. But in my heart a stronger voice than hers fought against her sophisms. I heard her out and then declared for the last time that I was resolved never to allow myself to succumb to corruption.

'In that case,' Dubois told me, 'do as you please. I leave you to your wretched fate. But if they ever hang you, as will surely happen given the fatality which saves crime and inevitably punishes virtue, at least remember to say nothing of us.'

While we had been discoursing thus, Dubois's three companions had been drinking with the poacher, and since wine commonly has the effect of making the criminal forget his old crimes and of prompting him to commit new ones while still teetering on the brink of the precipice from which he has just escaped, the villains were not content to observe my resolve to flee their clutches without wishing some entertainment at my expense. Their principles and customs, the gloomy place where we had halted, the degree of safety they believed they enjoyed, their drunkenness, my youth, innocence, and appearance—all served to encourage them. They left the table where they had been sitting, talked among themselves, and consulted Dubois. The mystery of these proceedings made me tremble with horror. The final upshot was that before I departed I should have to make up my mind to pass through the hands of all four, either with good grace or by force; that if I accepted with good grace they would each give me one écu to see me to whichever destination I chose, since I refused to go with them; that if force was needed to make my mind up for me, the result would be the same; but that in order that their secret be not betrayed, the last of the four who had his way with me would plunge a dagger into my heart and then bury me at the foot of a tree. I leave you to imagine, Madame, the effect this execrable proposition made upon me. I flung myself at Dubois's feet and begged her to protect me a second time. But the jade merely laughed at a predicament which to me was appalling but which to her seemed a matter of small consequence.

'Mercy,' said she, 'what a pretty pickle! Here you are, required to oblige four lusty lads like these! There are ten thousand women in Paris, my girl, who would pay out good money to be in your shoes just now. Listen,' she said, however, after a moment's thought, 'I have enough influence over these clods to get you out of this—if you are prepared to earn it.'

'Alas, Madame! What must I do?' I cried through my tears. 'Say the word and I shall be ready!'

'You must come with us, become one of us, do exactly

as we do and do it willingly. If you are prepared to pay this price, I guarantee the rest.'

I did not believe I had any choice. By accepting, I should be courting new perils, I own, but they were less pressing than those I faced at that moment. I might be able to avoid those which still lay in the future but there was nothing to preserve me from the danger now threatening me.

'I shall go anywhere, Madame,' I told Dubois, 'anywhere, I promise. Save me from these brutal men and I shall never leave you.'

'Lads,' said Dubois to the four bandits, 'the girl is now one of our gang. I have just admitted her as a full member. I order you not to do her any violence: she must not be sickened of the business on her very first day. You can see for yourselves how useful her youth and that pretty face are going to be to us. We must use her to further our interests and not sacrifice her to our pleasures.'*

But the passions can have such power over man that no words can tame them. The men I now faced were in no mood to listen to reason. All four advanced towards me together in a state which was hardly calculated to allow me flattering hopes of being preserved, and with one voice declared to Dubois that even if there had been a gallows on the spot, I should still be their prey.

'She's mine first,' said one of them, seizing me by the waist.

'Who says you can start?' said another, as he drove his comrade off and snatched me roughly from his grasp.

'By God, your turn's after mine,' said a third.

And the quarrel growing warm, all four champions grabbed each other by the hair and let fly with their fists, brawling amongst themselves and knocking each other to the ground. Meanwhile, only too happy with this turn of events which gave me time to make good my escape, and with Dubois being occupied in trying to separate them, I made a run for it, reached the forest, and the hut was soon lost from view.

'O Supreme Being!' said I, throwing myself on to my knees the instant I felt I was safe, 'Supreme Being who art my true protector and guide, take pity on my plight. Thou seest my weakness and my innocence, and knowest the trust with which I place all my hopes in Thee. Preserve me from the dangers which beset me, or by a death less ignominious than that which I have escaped, grant at least that I be recalled promptly to Thy eternal bosom.'

Prayer is the sweetest consolation of the unfortunate. He is stronger who has prayed. I stood up fortified by courage and, since it was now beginning to grow dark, I crept into a thicket where I could spend the night with the smallest risk of discovery. The sense of security I felt, my exhausted state, and the small measure of relief which I had lately tasted, all contributed to my passing a good night. The sun was already high when my eyes opened once more upon a new day. The moment of waking is the most critical time for the unfortunate: their senses are in repose, their minds are at peace, their misfortunes are temporarily forgotten— and all this reminds them of their misery with interest and makes the weight of their wretchedness even harder to bear.

'Ah, it is true then,' said I to myself, 'there are indeed human beings who are intended by Nature to share the state of wild animals! I crouch in their lair and hide myself from men just as they do. What difference is there now between them and me? What was the point of being born to suffer so pitiable a fate?' And my tears flowed liberally as I formulated these bleak reflections. I was scarcely done when I heard a sound nearby. For a moment I thought it was some beast of the forest but gradually I made out the voices of two men.

'Come on, over here,' said one, 'it's the ideal place for us. Here at least the spoiling presence of my interfering mother will not cheat me of a brief moment's enjoyment of those pleasures which are sweetest of all to me.'

They drew near and halted so exactly opposite me that nothing of what they said, nothing of what they did escaped me and I saw . . .

'Great Heavens, Madame,' said Sophie, breaking off her tale, 'can it be possible that fate has always placed me in such uniformly parlous situations for it to be as testing to ordinary decency to hear of them as it is for me to describe them? The horrible offence which outrages both Nature and established law, the heinous crime upon which the heavy hand of God has so often descended, I mean that infamy which was so new to me that I could scarcely conceive of it, was there, before my very eyes, consummated with all the impure refinements and dreadful proceedings which the most considered depravity could inject into it.'

One of the men, the dominant partner, was aged 24, wore a green coat and was sufficiently well turned out to suggest that he came of good family. The other appeared to be a young domestic in his service. He was 17 or 18 years old and very pretty. The spectacle was as lengthy as it was scandalous, and to me the time seemed to hang all the more cruelly since I dared not move for fear of giving myself away.

Finally, the felonious players who had enacted these criminal scenes, doubtless being sated, stood up and were about to rejoin the path which led them home when the master drew near to the bush which hid me to satisfy a need. My tall bonnet gave me away. He saw it.

'Jasmine, dear boy,' he called to his young Adonis, 'we are betrayed. Our mysteries have been observed by the uninitiate, to wit, a girl. Come here and we shall winkle the hussy out and discover what the devil she is doing here.'

I did not put them to the trouble of helping me to leave my shelter. Dragging myself out, I collapsed at their feet.

'O sirs!' I cried, holding my arms out to them, 'have mercy on an unfortunate creature whose fate is more to

be pitied than you can think. Few have suffered calamities equal to mine. I beg you, do not allow the
predicament in which you discovered me to start suspicions of me in your mind, for my situation is the result
of misfortune and not of any wrongs that I have done.
Do not increase the sum of the ills which lie heavy upon
me, but on the contrary, I beseech you, kindly furnish
me with some means of escaping the rigours by which I
am pursued.'

Monsieur de Bressac (such was the name of the young
man into whose clutches I had fallen) had a mind well
stocked with licentiousness but a heart which was not
over-generously endowed with compassion. It is regrettably only too commonly observed that sensual excess
drives out pity in man. Its ordinary effect is to harden
the heart. Whether this is because most carnal excesses
require a kind of apathy of soul or whether the violent
effect they produce on the nervous system weakens the
sensitivity by which it operates, it nevertheless remains
a fact that a professional libertine is rarely a compassionate man.* But to the natural cruelty entrenches in the
minds of the type of person whose character I have here
described, there was further in Monsieur de Bressac's
case an aversion so marked for our sex, a hatred so
inveterate for everything which characterizes the human
female, that I saw I should have the greatest difficulty in
firing his soul with the sentiments through which I
hoped to gain his sympathy.

'What are you doing here, my turtle-dove?' was the
only answer, pretty harshly spoken, which I was given
by this man whose heart I wished to soften. 'The truth
now: you saw everything which passed between this
young man and myself, did you not?'

'O no, sir!' I said quickly, believing that I should do
no harm in disguising the truth on this particular score.
'I assure you, what I saw was quite unremarkable. I
observed you both, this other gentleman and you, sitting
on the grass, and I believe I noticed that you stayed there
a while talking. That is all, I do assure you.'

'I'll take your word for it—for your sake,' answered Monsieur de Bressac. 'For if I thought for a moment that you had seen anything else you would not leave this thicket alive. Come, Jasmine. It is still early. We have time enough to listen to the tale of this whore's adventures. She can start telling us all about them now, and when she's finished we shall tie her to that great oak there and try out our hunting-knives on her.'

The two young men sat down, ordered me to sit next to them and there, without art, I gave them a plain account of everything that had happened to me since the time of my birth.

'Come, Jasmine,' said Monsieur de Bressac getting up the instant I had done, 'for once in our lives, let us be just. All-seeing Themis* has pronounced the slut guilty. We cannot stand by and see the goddess's designs frustrated, so we two shall proceed to carry out on a proven criminal the punishment which she was about to undergo. What we are about to do is no crime, my friend, but virtue. It will be a restoration of the moral order of things, and since there are times when we ourselves unfortunately upset that balance, we should have the courage to redress it whenever the occasion arises.'

And the two cruel men having pulled me to my feet began dragging me towards the appointed tree, as insensible to my moans as they were to my tears.

'Tie her to it this way on,' said Bressac to his valet as he pushed me face-forward against the tree.

They used their braces, handkerchiefs, anything that came to hand, and in a trice I was bound so cruelly tight that I found it impossible to move hand or foot. When this operation was completed, the blackguards removed my skirts, raised my petticoats above my head and took out their hunting-knives. I fully believed that they were about to hack and slash my hindquarters which in their ferocity they had bared completely.

'That will do,' said Bressac before I had felt a single

thrust of his knife. 'That should be enough for her to know what we are like, to understand what we can do to her, and to ensure that she remains subservient to our will. Sophie,' he went on, releasing my bonds, 'get dressed, keep your counsel, and come with us. Serve me well and you will not have cause to regret it, my child. My mother needs a second waiting-maid. I shall present you to her. On the strength of what you have told us of your adventures, I shall make myself answerable for your behaviour. But should you take advantage of my kindness or betray my trust . . . Look closely at the oak which was to have been your hanging-tree. Never forget that it is not a league from the château where I shall now take you and that at the first offence, however trivial, you will be brought back here.'

Fully dressed once more and scarce able to find words to thank my benefactor, I threw myself at his feet. I kissed his knees and swore in every way I could think of that my conduct would be beyond reproach. But as untouched by my happiness as he had been by my distress, Monsieur de Bressac said:

'Let us be gone. Your conduct will speak for you and your conduct alone will decide your fate.'

We set off, Jasmine and his master conversing together and I meekly following in silence. Less than an hour's walk brought us to the château of the Countess de Bressac. Its magnificent appointments informed me that whatever position I was to have in this household, it would surely be better remunerated than that of head-housekeeper to Monsieur and Madame Du Harpin. I was shown into a servants' hall where Jasmine served me a very decent dinner. Meanwhile, Monsieur de Bressac went upstairs to see his mother, explained about me, and a half-hour later came to fetch me and presented me to her.

Madame de Bressac was a woman of 45, very beautiful still, who seemed to me highly respectable and, even more to the point, exceedingly considerate, though her words and principles were not unmixed with a certain asperity. She was two years the widow of a man of the highest rank who had brought her in marriage no fortune other than the noble name which he had conferred upon her. The expectations of the young Marquis de Bressac thus centred on his mother, for what his father had left him was barely adequate for his ordinary needs. Madame de Bressac swelled the sum by making him a generous allowance, but even so it was far from enough to meet her son's expenditure which was as large as it was irregular. The estate was worth at least 60,000 livres a year and Monsieur de Bressac had neither brothers nor sisters. He could never be prevailed upon to enter the army, for anything which took him away from his choicest pleasures was so unbearable to him that he refused categorically to submit to constraints of any sort. The Countess and her son spent three months of the year on their estate and the rest of the time in Paris, and those three months which she insisted that her son spend with her were torture to a man who could never absent himself from the centre of his pleasures without lapsing into despair.

The Marquis de Bressac commanded me to relate to his mother the same tale which I had already told him. When I had finished my story, Madame de Bressac said: 'Your candour and sincerity seem to me to put your innocence beyond doubt. I shall institute no enquiries about you beyond satisfying myself that you are, as you say, the daughter of the man you mentioned. If indeed you are, then I knew your father, a circumstance which will be an added reason for my interesting myself in your welfare. As for your difficulties with Du Harpin, I shall make it my business to settle matters with a couple of visits to the Chancellor who has been a friend of mine for many years. He is the most upright man in France. All that is required to overturn the charges against you so that you may return to Paris without fear is to prove your innocence to him. But you must bear in mind, Sophie, that what I promise you now is conditional upon irreproachable conduct on your part. In this way you can see that the pledges which I ask from you will not fail to turn to your advantage.'

I threw myself at Madame de Bressac's feet, assured her that she would never have reason but to be satisfied with me, and was immediately installed in the house as second chambermaid. Within three days, the information requested from Paris by Madame de Bressac arrived and proved to be all I could have wished for. All my thoughts of misfortune faded at last from my mind, their place being taken by hopes of the sweetest consolations to which I now felt justified in looking forward. But it was not written by Heaven that poor Sophie would ever be happy, for should a few instants of peace chance to settle upon her, they would only serve to make her feel more bitterly still the moments of horror which would surely follow.

We were hardly arrived in Paris when Madame de Bressac began to busy herself on my behalf. The First President of the Court asked to see me. He listened with interest to my tale of woe, and Du Harpin's villainy, being investigated, was acknowledged. It was recognized that if I had taken advantage of the fire in the Palace prison, I had taken no part in causing it and I was assured that all proceedings against me were quashed by the magistrates appointed to examine the matter without their having need to resort to further formalities.

It may easily be imagined how closely such good offices bound me to Madame de Bressac: even had she not further shown me kindnesses of every description, how could the steps she had taken on my behalf have failed to endear me eternally to such a precious protectress? However, it did not enter into the intentions of the young Marquis de Bressac to have me draw so close to his mother. Independently of the appalling lewdness of the kind I have described to you into which the young man threw himself blindly and even more wildly in Paris than in the country, it was not long before I perceived that he hated the Countess with all his being. In truth, she did all she could to put an end to his debauches or at least to curb them, but she perhaps being over-harsh in her manner of proceeding, the Marquis, further inflamed by the effects of her strictness, plunged with renewed vigour into his excesses, and all the profit the poor Countess derived from her persecution of him was to be heartily detested.

'Do not imagine,' the Marquis would often tell me, 'that my mother acts unprompted in what she does for you. Believe me, Sophie, if I did not badger her at every turn she would probably forget what promises she gave to take care of you. She makes much of all the steps she takes, but they have all been my handiwork. I think I can fairly say therefore that if you feel grateful to anyone, it should be to me, and the return I ask of you will seem all the more disinterested in your eyes since you know enough of me to be quite certain that, however pretty your face, it is not your favours that I seek. No, Sophie, the services I expect from you are of a different order, and when you are quite convinced by all I have done for you, I trust you will find it in your heart to give me everything I am entitled to expect in return.'

Such words seemed so cloudy to me that I never knew what to answer. But answer I did, saying whatever came into my head and without giving sufficient thought to my replies.

The moment has come, Madame, when I must tell you of the only real wrong I ever did in my life for which I reproach myself. Wrong is perhaps not the word, more an unparalleled extravagance, but certainly not a crime. It was simply an error which rebounded against myself alone and which I do not believe was an instrument wielded by the equitable hand of Heaven to plunge me into the abyss which was secretly opening beneath my feet. I had been unable to see the Marquis de Bressac without feeling drawn to him by sentiments of tenderness which, try as I might, I could not overcome. Whatever thoughts I had about his aversion to women, the depravity of his tastes, and the moral distance which separated us, there was nothing on earth I could do to

drench the flames of my dawning passion, and if the
Marquis had asked me to lay down my life, I should
gladly have sacrificed it for his sake and thought I had
done little enough to oblige him. He had no inkling of
my feelings which I kept very carefully locked in my
heart, no inkling, the ungrateful wretch, of the cause of
the tears shed daily by the unhappy Sophie for the
shameful excesses which were like to be his undoing. Yet
he could not but be sensible of my eagerness to anticipate and undertake anything which might please him,
nor was it possible that he could remain ignorant of my
attentions which, in my blindness, extended to second-
ing his waywardness at least in so far as decency permitted, and to hiding them from his mother. My manner
of proceeding had to some extent earned me his trust
and, anything coming from him being precious to me, I
so chose not to see how little his heart offered me that
at times I was vain enough to believe that he was not
indifferent towards me. But how promptly was I disa-
bused by the extravagance of his carnal lusts! They were
pitched at such a level that not only was the inside of
the house staffed by servants, maintained on this execrable footing, whom I could not avoid, but also he kept
a host of ne'er-do-wells outside too, he going sometimes
to them and they calling on him every day. Since his
tastes, odious though they are, rank with the most expensive, the Marquis made prodigious inroads into his
fortune. Occasionally, I took the liberty to point out the
disadvantages of his conduct. He would hear me out
willingly enough and then say that no one had the power
to correct the kind of vice which drove him; that it took
countless different forms and had for each age of a man's
life divers branches which, spawning ever new sensations
with each decade that passed, were enough to see those
unfortunate to worship at that particular shrine clear
through to the grave. But if I tried to speak to him of
his mother and the grief he caused her, all I obtained in
return was resentment, ill temper, anger, impatience at
seeing a fortune which should already be his remaining

so long in her hands, the most inveterate hatred for a respectable mother, and the most brazen rebellion against the sentiments of Nature. Can it then truly follow in the case of a man who, indulging his tastes, has so categorically infringed the sacred laws of Nature that the necessary consequence of his first transgression is the appalling ease with which he goes on to commit all other crimes with impunity?

Sometimes I resorted to persuasion through religion in which I have almost invariably found consolation. I endeavoured to open the heart of this perverse man to its balm, being almost certain that I should hold him in a net of faith if I could succeed in communicating its charms to him. But the Marquis gave me little time to employ these means of persuading him. As a declared enemy of our sacred mysteries, a stubborn kicker against the purity of our doctrine, and a furious opponent of the existence of a Supreme Being, the Marquis, instead of allowing me to convert him, sought rather to corrupt me. 'All religions start from a false premiss, Sophie,' he would say. 'Each one assumes the need for belief in a Creator. Now if this everlasting world of ours, like all the others which hang in the infinite plains of space, had no beginning and can never have an end; if all the products of nature are the consequential effects of laws by which Nature herself is bound; if her perpetual actions and reactions presuppose the movement which is an integral part of her essence,* then what role is left for the prime mover which you gratuitously impute to it? Believe me, Sophie, the God you admit to is nothing but the fruit on the one hand of ignorance and on the other of tyranny. When the strong first set out to enslave the weak, they convinced their victims that God sanctified the chains that bound them, and the weak, their wits crushed by poverty, believed what they were told. All religions are the destructive consequences of this first fiction and merit the same contempt as its source deserves. There is not one of these fairy-tales which does not march under the banner of imposture and stupidity. In all these mysteries which stagger human reason, I see only dogmas which outrage Nature and grotesque ceremonials which warrant nothing but derision. From the moment my eyes were opened, Sophie, I loathed all these disgusting shams. I vowed I should trample them beneath my feet and never return to the fold as long as I lived. If you wish to be a rational being, follow my lead.'

'O sir,' I answered the Marquis, 'you will rob an unfortunate creature of her sweetest hope if you deprive her of the religion which consoles her. Firmly attached to what it teaches, fervently believing that all the kicks that come my way are no more than the effects of libertinism and the passions, shall I sacrifice the sweetest thoughts I know in life to sophisms which make me tremble?'

To this, I added countless other arguments dictated by my head and watered by my heart, but all the Marquis did was laugh, and his captious principles, enhanced by a more virile eloquence and backed by reference to books that I am glad to say I had never read, always got the better of mine. Madame de Bressac, a woman of virtue and piety, was not unaware that her son justified his wayward conduct by using all the paradoxes of the unbeliever. Oftentimes she communicated her grief to me and, being of a mind to think me possessed of a little more good sense than the other women who attended her, she took a fancy to confiding her sorrows to me.

However, she was increasingly exposed to her son's evil ways. He reached the stage where he no longer hid them from her. Not only did he surround his mother with the dangerous rabble who served his pleasures but he went so far in his insolence as to tell her, within my hearing, that if she tried to interfere with his tastes once more, then he would convince her of their power to charm by demonstrations thereof in her presence. Such talk and his behaviour cut me to the quick, and I did all in my power to summon from deep within me reasons for stifling the wretched passion which consumed me. But is love a sickness which can be cured? Every argument I put up against it served only to stoke it higher, and the perfidious Bressac never seemed to me more alluring than when I had assembled in my mind all the reasons that should have led me to hate him.

I had been in that house for four years, still persecuted by the same sorrows, still solaced by the same sweet consolations, when the ghastly reason for the Marquis's exploiting his seductive power over me was made plain in all its horror. At the time, we were in the country and I was the Countess's sole attendant, her first chambermaid having obtained leave to remain in Paris on account of some business of her husband's. One evening, shortly after quitting my mistress, I was taking the air on the balcony of my chamber, unable to make up my mind to go to bed, it being excessively warm, when the Marquis knocked unexpectedly on my door and begged me to give him leave to talk with me for part of the night. Alas, every moment granted me by the cruel architect of my unhappiness seemed so precious that I dared not pass up the chance of a single instant with him. He entered, closed the door carefully and, flinging himself on to a chair next to me, said in a slightly embarrassed way:

'Listen, Sophie, I have something of the greatest consequence to tell you. Swear now that you will never reveal anything of what I am about to say.'

'O sir, how can you think me capable of betraying your confidence?'

'You have no idea what you would be risking if you ever showed me that I was mistaken in placing my trust in you.'

'The greatest of my regrets would be to forfeit it. That is threat enough for me.'

'Well then, Sophie, I am hatching a plot against my mother's life and it is your hand that I have chosen to serve me.'

'I, sir?' I cried, recoiling in horror, 'how could you ever

have imagined two such horrible ideas? Take my life, sir, it is yours, I owe it to you. But you must never think that you will prevail upon me to be a party to a crime the very idea of which my heart could never countenance.'

'Listen, Sophie,' said Monsieur de Bressac, calmly quieting my agitation, 'I suspected you might be reluctant, but since you are a quick-witted girl, I flattered myself I could overcome your resistance by proving to your satisfaction that the crime which you think so monstrous is really a quite simple thing. To your unphilosophical eye, two crimes are involved: the destruction of a fellow human being and the circumstance that the deed is compounded by the fact that the death concerned is that of one's own mother. As far as the destruction of a fellow being is concerned, Sophie, you can be clear in your own mind that it is an illusion. The power to destroy life is not given to man who at most has the power to change its forms, but not the ability to obliterate it. Now, all forms are equal in the eyes of Nature. Nothing is lost in the immense melting-pot where endless variations are produced. Each quantity of matter thrown into it is continually renewed and given a new shape. Whatever part we play in the process cannot offend directly against the whole. Nothing we can do outrages Nature directly. Our acts of destruction give her new vigour and feed her energy, but none of our wreckings can weaken her power. So of what concern is it to Nature, endlessly creating, if a mound of flesh which today has the shape of a woman, should reproduce itself tomorrow as countless insects of different types? Have you courage enough to assert that it requires more effort on her part to construct an individual such as we are than to make a worm and that therefore Nature should logically take a greater interest in us? Or if her degree of concern, or rather unconcern, is the same in both cases, what can it matter to Nature if, through what we call the crime of one individual, another is changed into a fly or a lettuce? Even if it were proved to me that the human species is Nature's most sublime handiwork, and were I to be shown beyond doubt that humankind is so important to her that her laws are necessarily thrown into confusion by its being prematurely destroyed, then I might think that such destruction was a crime. But if the most careful study of Nature should prove to my satisfaction that everything which flourishes on this earth, even the least perfect of her works, is of equal importance in her eyes, I should never imagine that the transformation of one of these beings into a thousand others could ever infringe her laws. I should say to myself: all men, all plants, and all animals which grow, flourish and destroy each other in similar ways, never truly dying but simply reappearing as variants through the process which modifies them—all forms of life, I should further say, growing, destroying, reproducing themselves mechanically, taking now one form and now another, have the ability, if it pleases the Being who alone has the will and the power to actuate them, to change many, many times within the space of a single day without affecting a single law of Nature.

'But the being I propose to strike is my mother, she who bore me in her womb. But why should this footling consideration give me pause? On what grounds should it stay my hand? Was she thinking of me when lubricity drove her to conceive the foetus from which I grew? Should I be grateful to her for thinking of her pleasure? In any case, it is not the blood of the mother which shapes the child, but the blood of the father only. The female womb fructifies, preserves, and amplifies, but does not of itself contribute any vivifying ingredient.* Since this is so, I could never have raised my hand against my father, whereas I view the idea of abbreviating my mother's life as a quite straightforward matter. If it is nevertheless possible for a child's heart to be justifiably moved by feelings of gratitude towards its mother, it can only be by reason of the manner in which she treated us from the time we were old enough to appreciate it.* If she dealt with us kindly, we can love her, indeed perhaps we should. But if she showed us acts of unkindness linked to no law of Nature, then not only do we owe her nothing, but everything tells us we should be rid of her: it is a consequence of the egoism which naturally and irresistibly leads man to rid himself of everything which gives him pain.'*

'O sir,' I replied in alarm to the Marquis, 'the indifference you impute to Nature is yet another effect of your passions. Just for an instant, I beg you, heed your heart and ignore their clamour, and you will see that it reproves the arrogant reasoning prompted by your libertinism! Is not your heart, that judge before whom I ask you to stand, the temple where Nature, which you outrage, demands to be heard and obeyed? If Nature there inscribes the greatest horror for the crime you are planning, will you not concede that it is indeed reprehensible? If you answer that the heat of passion will destroy the horror of it in a twinkling, you will scarcely have time to take satisfaction from its being extinguished before it catches fire again, prompted by the imperious voice of Remorse. The more sensitive you are, the more agonizing its call will be. Each day, every moment, you will see before your eyes the tender mother whom your brutal hand dispatched to her grave. You will hear her plaintive voice still speaking the sweet name which was the delight of your childish years. She will appear in your waking nights, she will rack your dreams, she will reach out with bloody hands to reopen the wounds with which you savaged her. From that moment on, you would not know a single glimmer of happiness on earth, all your pleasures would be poisoned and all your ideas overcast. A heavenly hand whose power you underestimate will avenge the life you destroyed by turning yours to ashes and, without ever enjoying the fruits of your crimes, you will perish a victim of the mortal regret that you ever dared commit them!'

My tears flowed freely as I pronounced these last words. I threw myself at the feet of the Marquis, implored him by whatever he held most dear to put out of his mind all thought of an infamous deed which I swore I would keep secret all my days. But I did not know the heart of the man I tried to disarm: it might beat strongly still, but crime had snapped its springs and the passions in all their fiery heat had melted all save evil-doing. The Marquis stood up coldly.

'I see clearly that I was mistaken, Sophie,' said he. 'I am perhaps as sorry for it for your sake as for mine. But no matter, I shall find other ways and you will have lost much in my eyes while your mistress will have gained nothing.'

This threat changed all my ideas. By not agreeing to the crime as put to me, I should place myself at considerable risk and my mistress would surely die; by consenting to be an accessory, I should be safe from my young master's anger and would necessarily save his mother. This thought, which with me was the work of a moment, prompted me to change sides at once. But since so sudden a shift might seem suspect, I made my defeat a lengthy business, forced the Marquis to repeat his sophisms many times, and gave the impression of not quite knowing how to answer them. The Marquis believed I was beaten, I justified my weakness by acknowledging his persuasive powers, made out at the last that I had capitulated, and the Marquis threw his arms about me. How happy his doing so would have made me had not his barbarous plans cast out all the feelings which my vulnerable heart had conceived for him. Had it been possible for me to love him still .

'You are the first woman I ever kissed,' the Marquis said to me, 'and in truth I do so now with all my heart. You are delicious, child. A ray of philosophy has lit up your mind. How is it possible that such a pretty face could have dwelt so long in darkness?'

And thereupon we agreed our plans. To ensure that the Marquis was firmly snared in the trap, I kept up a certain show of reluctance each time he outlined more of his scheme or explained by what means he intended to carry it off, and it was by this deception, which my unhappy plight fully justified, that I succeeded in fooling him completely. We arranged that some two or three days hence, depending on the opportunities which came my way, I should, without attracting attention, empty the small sachet of poison the Marquis gave me into the cup of chocolate which the Countess was in the habit of taking each morning. The Marquis answered for what would happen next and promised me 2,000 écus annually for the rest of my life which would be mine to spend either in his entourage or in some other place which I should be free to choose. He signed this contract but without specifying in it what I was to do to earn his bounty and then we parted.

In the mean time, there occurred something too singular and too revealing of the character of the man with whom I had to deal for me not to pause at this point in my account, which you are doubtless anticipating, of the manner in which the cruel adventure I was embarked upon was concluded. Two days after our interview, the Marquis received news that an uncle, of whom he had entertained no expectations whatsoever, had died leaving him 80,000 livres a year. 'Sweet Heaven,' I asked myself when I was told the news, 'is it thus that celestial justice punishes those who plot treasons? I believed that by refusing to commit an infinitely smaller crime, I should forfeit my life. And now this man, for devising a scheme of appalling proportions, is set high upon a pinnacle!' But instantly repenting of this blasphemy against Providence, I fell to my knees, asked pardon of God, and took heart from the thought that this unexpected legacy would at least lead to a change in the Marquis's plans. Great God, how mistaken I was!

'O my dear Sophie,' Monsieur de Bressac said to me as he burst into my chamber that same evening, 'prosperity positively showers me with favours! How often have I told you that there is nothing better guaranteed to bring happiness than conceiving a crime—indeed, the road to happiness seems to be made easiest for the wrong-doer. Eighty plus sixty, child, makes 140,000 livres to spend annually on my pleasures.'

'But sir,' I replied, with a surprise modified by the circumstances by which I was bound fast, 'given this unexpected piece of good fortune, will you not now wait patiently for the death which you are intent on hastening?'

'Wait? I do not intend waiting two minutes, child. I am 28 now and waiting is hard at my age. I beg you, do not allow what has happened to alter our plans. Let us take satisfaction in finishing our business before the time comes for us to return to Paris. Try and see to it that the deed is done tomorrow or the next day at the latest. I am already looking forward to paying your first quarter's allowance and then of making over the full sum to you.'

I did my best to disguise the fear which such fervent pursuit of crime inspired in me. I resumed the role I had been playing, but all my feeling for him now being finally quenched, I believed that so hardened and villainous a man was deserving only of my horror.

But my position was extremely delicate. If I did not do what he wanted, the Marquis would soon realize that I had tricked him. If I warned Madame de Bressac, then whatever action she took as a result of my telling her, the young man would still know that he had been deceived and would perhaps resort to surer methods which would not only bring about the death of the mother but also leave me exposed to the vengeance of the son. There remained the law, but I was absolutely determined not to go down that road. I resolved therefore, come what may, to warn the Countess. Of all the avenues open to me, this seemed the best and I now stepped out boldly upon it.

'Madame,' I said to her the day after my latest interview with the Marquis, 'I have something of the greatest consequence to reveal to you. But though it affects you closely, I am determined to say nothing unless you first give me your word of honour that you will not give your son the smallest mark of your displeasure at what he has been rash enough to plan. You will act, Madame, you will do what you think best, but say nothing. You must grant what I ask or I shall remain silent.'

Madame de Bressac, thinking that the matter consisted of no more than new instances of her son's ordinary excesses, readily agreed to the promise I asked of her and I told her everything. When that unhappy mother learned of such infamy, she burst into tears.

'The wretch!' she cried, 'What did I ever do that was not for his good? If I tried to curb his vices or correct them, what motives could ever make me act with such severity but his happiness and tranquillity? To whom does he owe the fortune he has lately inherited if not to me and my efforts on his behalf? If I did not mention them to him, it was to spare his feelings. The monster! O Sophie, show me how black the scheme he has formed, paint every corner of the picture so that I have no room left to doubt, for I need to hear anything that will finally silence the voice of Nature in my heart.'

I then showed the Countess the sachet of poison which had been given into my keeping. We gave a little of it to a dog which we then shut up. It died two hours later in the throes of the most agonized convulsions. The Countess, doubting no longer and quickly determining upon the course she would follow, bade me hand over the rest of the poison and immediately dispatched a courier with a letter to her relative, the Duke de Sonzeval, asking him to call secretly on the Minister; to let him have the fullest account of the black-hearted villainy of which she was soon to be the victim; to obtain a *lettre de cachet** against her son; to proceed with all convenient speed to her estate with the letter and an officer of the law; and to deliver her without delay from the monster who plotted against her life. But it was written in Heaven that the abominable crime would be committed and that virtue brought low would succumb to the stratagems of the wicked.

The wretched dog upon which we had performed our experiment revealed all to the Marquis. He heard it howling and knowing his mother to be passing fond of it, anxiously asked what was the matter with the dog and where it was. Since those of whom he enquired knew nothing of the matter, they could not answer. It was doubtless at this point that he began to suspect. He said nothing, but I could see that he was worried, uneasy, and watchful all day long. I mentioned this to the Countess, but there was no choice: all we could do was to impress the courier with the need for haste while concealing the object of his mission. The Countess told her son that she was sending the man to Paris to request the Duke de Sonzeval to take personal charge of the affairs of the lately testate uncle, for unless an authorized signature appeared on the papers, there was every risk of lawsuits ensuing. She added that she had invited the Duke to come in person to lay the whole matter before her so that she could know whether or not, if the business required it, to go up to town taking her son with her. The Marquis, too skilled in physiognomy* not to read the embarrassment on his mother's face nor to mistake the hints of confusion in mine, took all this in but was now even more on his guard than before. Using the pretext of a walk with his *mignons*, he left the château and waited for the courier at a spot where he must surely pass. This messenger, who answered more willingly to him than to his mother, made no difficulties in handing over his dispatches and the Marquis, convinced of what he no doubt called my 'treachery', gave the man 100 louis, told him never to show his face at the house again, and returned with rage in his heart. But controlling himself as best he could, he met up with me, teased me in his usual manner, asked me if the deed was fixed for the morrow, added that it was vital it should be done before the Duke arrived, and went off to bed calmly enough and without a sign that anything was amiss. If the dreadful crime was committed—and the Marquis informed me soon afterwards that it was—it could only

have happened in the manner which I shall now set
down . . .

The next morning Madame took her chocolate according to her custom and, since no one had touched it
but me, I am certain that nothing had been put into it.
But at about ten o'clock the Marquis, entering the kitchen and finding there only the cook, commanded the
man to go into the garden at once and pick peaches for
him. The man protested, saying that he could not leave
his viands, but the Marquis insisted on his pressing fancy
to eat peaches, saying he would stay and watch over the
stove. The cook went, the Marquis inspected the viands
destined for dinner and in all likelihood dropped the
fatal drug which was to snap her life's thread into the
chards of which Madame was passionately fond. Dinner
was served, the Countess probably ate from the lethal
dish, and the crime was perpetrated. What I have told
you is conjecture only: during the unhappy aftermath of
the event, Monsieur de Bressac told me that the deed
was done, and my best guesses have yielded this as the
only explanation of the manner in which he managed it.
But let us leave these horrid speculations and turn now
to the cruel way in which I was punished for having
refused to have any hand in so dreadful a business and
for having divulged it.

As soon as dinner was over, the Marquis came up to me:
'Listen, Sophie,' he said, with the outward coolness of
a tranquil mind, 'I have hit upon a safer way of achieving
my ends than the one I put to you, but it requires
detailed work. I dare not appear in your chamber as
frequently as I have of late, for I fear everyone's prying
eyes. Be at the corner of the park at five o'clock. I shall
collect you there and during a long walk I shall explain
it all to you.'

Whether it was by the express leave of Providence or
the fault of too much innocence or blindness on my part,
I own there was nothing to forewarn me of the misfortune which lay in wait. I so believed the secret was safe
and was so confident of the Countess's arrangements

that I never imagined that the Marquis might have found them out. However, I confess to feeling a certain little awkwardness in my heart. One of our tragic poets has remarked that:

> He perjures not but virtue furthers
> Who betrays a trust to punish murthers.*

And yet perjury must always be repellent to persons of a nice and feeling disposition who find that they are driven to stoop to it. My role went somewhat against the grain though my doubts did not last long. The Marquis's odious proceedings were to give me fresh cause for distress and my initial scruples were soon silenced.

He came up to me as gaily and as openly as could be and together we walked into the forest without his doing anything more than laughing and bantering as was his habit when he was with me. When I attempted to direct the conversation towards the matter about which he wished to speak to me, he told me to wait a little longer, saying that he feared that we were observed and that we were not yet in a safe place. Imperceptibly, we drew near to the thicket and the oak where he had first encountered me. I could not suppress a shudder on seeing the place, and at that moment the full extent of my imprudence and the true horror of my fate seemed to loom up before my eyes. You may judge if my fears multiplied when I saw, seated at the foot of the fatal tree where I had undergone so ghastly a trial, two of the Marquis's young *mignons* who were thought to be those he liked best. They stood up when we approached and into the grass let fall ropes, bludgeons, and other instruments which made me quake. Then the Marquis, addressing me now only with the crudest and foulest epithets, turned to me:

'You b–ch,' he said, while we were still out of earshot of his young men, 'do you recognize this thicket from which I dragged you like a beast of the forest and saved your life which you had richly deserved to lose? Do you recognize this tree to which I threatened to return you if you ever gave me cause to regret my generosity? Why

did you agree to perform the actions against my mother
I asked you to undertake if you were bent on betraying
me? And what made you think you could serve virtue by
putting at risk the life of a man to whom you owed your
own? Placed of necessity between two crimes, why did
you choose the more abominable? You should have simply refused what I asked, not agreed to it the better to
betray me.'

Then the Marquis told me of the manner of his inter-
cepting the courier's dispatches and of the suspicions
which had led him to take such a step.

'What have you achieved by your duplicity, you lying
b—ch?' he went on. 'You risked your life without saving
my mother's, for that deed is done, and when I return
to the house I expect to see my labours amply rewarded.
But I must punish you, I must teach you to see that the
path of virtue is not always the best and that there are
times when to connive at a crime is preferable to exposing it. Knowing me as you must, how did you ever dare
think you could play games with me? Did you imagine
that the feeling of pity which my heart has never admitted except in so far as it furthers my pleasures, or
perhaps one or two principles of religion which I have
always trampled underfoot, would be enough to stay my
hand? Or perhaps you were relying upon your beauty?'
he added, in the most cruelly bantering tone. 'Ha! I shall
now prove to you that your beauty, even when stripped
of the last concealing veil, can never be more than the
brand which kindles my vengeance!'

And without giving me time to reply, and showing not
the slightest emotion on seeing the torrent of tears which
flowed from me, he grasped my arm as in a vice and
dragged me across to his henchmen.

'Here she is,' said he. 'This is the jade who set out to
poison my mother and, in spite of my best efforts to stop
her, has perhaps already succeeded in committing her
foul crime. It might have been better if I had handed her
over to the law, but then she would simply have forfeited
her life whereas I prefer to let her live so that she may

have more time to feel her sufferings. Strip her quickly
and tie her with her face to that tree so that I may
chastise her as she deserves.'

The order was no sooner given than executed. A handkerchief was thrust into my mouth, I was made to clasp
the tree in a tight embrace and was bound at the shoulders and legs, which left the rest of my body free of ropes
so that I should have no protection against the beating
which I was about to receive. The Marquis, marvellously
excited, seized a thong. Before striking me, he was cruel
enough to wish to observe my face, and it was as though
he was feasting his eyes not only on my tears but also
on the expressions of pain and fear with which my countenance was suffused.* He then placed himself behind
me at a distance of about three feet and I immediately
felt, from the middle of my back to the top of my legs,
the stroke of the lash which he applied with all the
strength he could muster. My tormentor paused for a
moment and ran his hands roughly over the areas which
he had just beaten black and blue. I did not catch what
he said to one of his satellites but a handkerchief was
immediately thrown over my head so that I was deprived
of the power to see anything of their movements. However, I heard them moving about behind me before the
resumption of the bloody scenes in which I was destined
to play a further part. 'Oh yes, that's good,' the Marquis
said before striking me anew. But hardly were these
words, of which I understood nothing, out of his mouth
when the beating began again with increased violence.
There was another interval, hands again explored my
lacerated flesh and there was more muttering. One of
the young men said, 'Am I better this way?' and these
new words, which made as little sense to me but to
which the Marquis replied, 'Closer, closer', were followed by a third assault which was even more vigorously
delivered than the others. While it lasted, Bressac said
the following words two or three times in rapid succession, seasoning them with appalling curses: 'Go to it,
both of you. Don't you understand? I intend her to die

by my hand here and now?'* These words, spoken in a graded crescendo of pitch and volume, brought the murderous onslaught to a close. For a few moments more, I caught the sound of whispering, heard them moving around, and felt the ropes being untied. It was then that I saw my blood on the grass and realized the state I must be in. The Marquis was alone. His aides had disappeared.

'Well now, whore,' he said, looking at me with the distaste which comes when passion is spent, 'don't you think virtue is a rather expensive calling? Were not 2,000 écus a year a better bargain than a hundred strokes of the lash?'

I collapsed at the foot of the tree, almost fainting away. The unfeeling blackguard, still not sated by the horrors by which he had been transported and cruelly excited by the spectacle of my suffering, trampled me beneath his feet, pressing me into the earth as though he would choke me.

'I am more than generous, for I have spared your life,' he repeated twice or thrice. 'You would be well advised to think seriously of the use to which you intend to put this new instance of my charity.'

Then he ordered me to my feet and told me to dress. Since there was blood everywhere, I dazedly gathered handfuls of grass and cleaned myself so that my clothes, which were the only ones I had, would not be stained with it. Meanwhile, he paced up and down, paying me no attention, concerned more with his thoughts than with me. My swollen flesh, the still flowing blood, the pain I was suffering—all made the business of dressing virtually impossible. But not once did the brutal man with whom I had to deal, the monster who had reduced me to this pitiful state and for whom, only days before, I should gladly have given my life, not once was he moved by the slightest feeling of commiseration to extend a helping hand. When I was ready, he came up to me.

'Go where you will,' said he. 'You must have money

left in your purse. I shall not take it from you. But have a care never to come anywhere near me again, either in Paris or here in the country. I warn you, word will go out that you murdered my mother. If she is not dead yet, I shall tell her it was you who did for her so that she may carry the thought with her to the grave. The entire household will be told. I shall inform the authorities to that effect. As a result, you will find Paris even more uninhabitable than before, for you should bear in mind that the previous case against you was never officially closed but, take note, simply adjourned. You were told that the matter had been dropped, but you were misled. Your sentence has neither been served nor cancelled and it was decided to let you carry on in this footing to see how you would behave. So now you face not one charge but two, and have as your adversary not a common money-lender but a rich and powerful man determined to follow you to hell if, by making slanderous complaints, you should abuse the life which I have been generous enough to let you keep.'

'O sir,' I answered, 'though you have used me cruelly, you need fear nothing from me. I believed I had no choice but to act as I did when your mother's life was at stake. But I shall never lift a finger against you if Sophie's interests alone are uppermost. Goodbye, sir. May your crimes make you as happy as your cruelties have caused me pain. Whatever fate Heaven has in store for you, then as long as that same Heaven chooses to prolong my deplorable life, so long shall I use it solely to pray for you.'

The Marquis looked up and could not help but stare as I said these words. Seeing me bathed in tears and scarce able to stand, the heartless man, fearing no doubt to give way to his feelings, walked away and did not look back once in my direction. As soon as he had gone, I sank to the ground and there, surrendering to my distress, rent the air with my groans and watered the earth with my tears:

'O God!' I exclaimed, 'Thou hast worked Thy purpose

out. It was by Thy will that innocence has fallen prey to
the guilty once more. Do with me, O Lord, as it pleaseth
Thee, for the pain I have suffered is as nothing beside
the pain Thou once didst bear for us! May the suffering
which I endure as I praise Thee render me worthy one
day of the rewards which Thou hast promised the weak
who keep Thee as a beacon in their time of trouble and
glorify Thee in the midst of their travails!'

Night was falling. I was in no fit state to venture any
further, indeed I was barely able to stand. I recollected
the thicket where I had spent that night four years before, my situation being rather less wretched then than
now, and dragged myself into it as best I could. Lodged
in that same place, enduring agonies from my wounds
which still bled, stricken by the grief of my thoughts and
the sorrows of my heart, I spent the cruellest night that
can be imagined. The resilience of my youth and my
constitution both gave me a little strength as the new
day dawned and, filled with dread by the proximity of
that cruel château, I made off promptly, left the forest
and, resolving to strike out at random for the first dwell-
ings which I should meet with, entered the little town of
Claye,* some six leagues distant from Paris. I asked to
be directed to the surgeon's house and I was shown the
way. I begged him to bind my wounds, saying that
fleeing my mother's house in Paris as the result of some
affair of the heart, I had unfortunately fetched up in the
forest of Bondy where wicked men had reduced me to
the state he saw me in. He tended me, on the condition
that I should swear out an affidavit to the Clerk of
Justice in the village. I agreed. It seems that the matter
was looked into though I never heard what came of it.
The surgeon, agreeing to keep me in his house until such
time as I should be well again, set about his business
with such skill that within a month I was completely
recovered.

As soon as my condition allowed me to take the air,
my first thought was to find some village girl sufficiently
shrewd and intelligent to be sent to the Château de

Bressac to discover what had transpired since my departure. Curiosity was not my only motive in taking this step. Indeed, curiosity might have been dangerous and was certainly out of place. But I had left in my chamber there the little money I had earned while in the service of the Countess and I had barely 6 louis to hand, whereas I had 30 in the château. I did not imagine that the Marquis would be so cruel as to refuse me what was mine by right and was convinced that once his first anger had passed, he would not inflict a second injustice upon me. I wrote the most affecting letter I could. Alas, it was perhaps too affecting, for in it, despite my better judgement, my sorrowing heart spoke out in favour of that false-hearted man. I carefully hid the place of my confinement from him and entreated him to send me my effects and the small sum of my money which was in my chamber. A peasant girl aged between 20 and 25, brisk-mannered and with all her wits about her, promised to carry my letter and to make such discreet enquiries as would satisfy me on her return as to the various matters on which I informed her she would be questioned. I enjoined her expressly to withhold the name of the place whence she came, on no account to speak of me, but to say that she had got the letter from a man who had brought it from another town more than fifteen leagues distant. Jeannette set off (such was the name of my messenger) and four and twenty hours later brought me my answer. It is indispensable, Madame, for me to relate to you now what had happened in the residence of the Marquis de Bressac before I allow you to see the letter which I received from him.

The Countess de Bressac, falling gravely ill on the day I left the château, had died suddenly during that night. No one had arrived at the château from Paris and the Marquis, plunged into the deepest affliction (the hypocrite!), claimed that his mother had been poisoned by a chambermaid who had run off that same day and whose name was Sophie. A search was instituted for this maid, the intention being that if found she should be sent to the gallows. Besides this, the Marquis, now succeeding to his estate, had found himself far richer than he had thought, for Madame de Bressac's strong-boxes and gems, of which little had been known, made him master, independently of his own fortune, of 600,000 francs in property and ready cash. It was said that, sorely afflicted though he was, he had great difficulty in hiding his jubilation. The relatives who had been summoned for the post-mortem examination he had insisted on had duly lamented the fate of the unhappy Countess and sworn to avenge her if the maid who had committed so heinous a crime should ever fall into their hands. Then they left the young man in complete, undisturbed possession of the fruit of his villainy. Monsieur de Bressac himself had spoken to Jeannette and had asked her divers questions which the girl had answered with such firmness and candour that he had resolved to write a reply for her without pressing her further.

'This is the fatal letter,' said Sophie, taking it from her pocket. 'I have it here, Madame. There are times when my heart has need of it and I shall keep it until my dying breath. Read it, if you can do so without revulsion.'

Taking the note from the hand of our fair adventurer, Madame de Lorsange read the following words:

'A slut capable of poisoning my mother is bold indeed who dares write to me after committing so foul a mischief. She does well to conceal her whereabouts, for she may rest assured that if discovered she will be seriously incommoded. But what does she ask? Why does she speak of money and effects? Is not what she left behind the equivalent of what she stole during both her sojourn and her committing of her late crime? She is well advised never to send here again as she now does, for she should know that her messenger would be detained until the secret of her hiding-place was known to the authorities.'

'Pray continue, my child,' said Madame de Lorsange, returning the letter to Sophie. 'These proceedings fill me with the deepest horror. To be rolling in wealth and to withhold from an unfortunate girl who refused to abet a crime the little money which she honestly came by, is an act of unprecedented infamy!'

'Alas, Madame,' continued Sophie, taking up the thread of her tale, 'I was two days weeping over his cruel letter, bitterly lamenting the base dealing it revealed far more than the refusal which it contained. I am guilty, then, I cried, I am denounced to the law of men for having too earnestly respected Justice. So be it! But I do not repent of my conduct. Whatever befalls me, I shall always remain beyond the reach of spiritual torment and remorse as long as my heart remains pure and my wrongs run to nothing more than my having too well heeded those sentiments of even-handedness and virtue which will never desert me.'

Yet I could not believe that the searches the Marquis had spoken of had any substance to them. They seemed most unlikely for there would have been such danger to him of his bringing me before the Justices that I reasoned that he must secretly have been more frightened at the prospect of coming face to face with me, if he were ever to discover my hiding-place, than I was of his threats. This reflection determined my resolve to stay in the place where I then was and, if possible, to find employment there until my funds swelled sufficiently to enable me to leave. Monsieur Rodin (this was the name of the surgeon with whom I was lodged) himself suggested that I should enter his service. He was a man of 35 years of age, of a callous, abrupt, and brutal character, but nevertheless enjoying an excellent reputation throughout the whole of the surrounding country. He was totally wedded to his doctoring and as he employed no woman in his service, was only too pleased, on his returning home each day, to find one there to attend to the needs of his house and his person. He offered me 200 francs annually and a small share of the revenue from his practice, and I accepted what he proposed. Monsieur Rodin had too exact a knowledge of my person to be ignorant of the fact that I had never known a man. He was also aware of my extreme desire to keep myself always pure and promised he would never trouble me on that score. As a result, our mutually agreeable arrangement was quickly settled. But I did not tell my new master everything and he never knew who I was.

I had been two years in his house, and though I did not fail to have a great deal of hard labour to do in it, yet the kind of peace of mind I enjoyed there had almost driven my sorrows from my mind, when Heaven, resolved never to allow one single virtue to go forth from my heart without immediately burdening me with misfortune, intervened once more to wrench me from the cheerless felicity I fleetingly tasted and plunge me into new calamities.

One day, finding myself alone in the house and passing through various parts of it as and where my duties beckoned, I thought I heard groans coming from the depths of a cellar. I approached, the sounds grew clearer, and I made out the cries of a girl. But a securely locked door separated her from me and I was quite unable to open up the place where she was held. Countless thoughts crowded into my mind. What was the poor creature doing there? Monsieur Rodin was childless and to my knowledge had neither sisters nor nieces in whom he might profess an interest. The perfect regularity of the life I had observed him lead ruled out the possibility that the young woman was intended for his debauches. For what reason, then, had he locked her away? Exceeding curious to resolve these difficulties, I dared question the child, asking her what she did there and who she was.

'Alas, Mademoiselle,' the hapless creature replied through her tears, 'I am the daughter of a woodcutter who lives in the forest. I am but 12. The gentleman who lives here, aided by a friend, carried me off yesterday at a moment when my father was absent. Together they bound me, threw me into a bag of sawdust which prevented my crying out, put me over the back of a horse, and smuggled me into this house late last night, bringing me directly to this cellar. I do not know what they want of me but on reaching this place they stripped

me naked, inspected my person, asked my age, and then
the gentleman who seemed to be master of the house
told the other that the operation would have to be post-
poned until the evening of the day after next on account
of my being afraid; that the experiment would pass off
all the better for my being a little calmer; and that
otherwise I answered fully to the conditions required in
a *subject*.'

After pronouncing these words, the girl fell silent and
began weeping again more bitterly than before. I persuaded her to calm herself and promised to help. I found
it exceeding difficult to understand what Monsieur
Rodin and his friend, also a surgeon, were intending to
do with this hapless girl. However, the word *subject*,
which I had heard them use on other occasions, immediately prompted the suspicion that it was more than
likely that they were planning to perform some ghastly
anatomical dissection on the wretched child. But before
fixing myself in this cruel opinion, I resolved to make
further enquiries. Rodin returned with his friend and
they supped together and dismissed me. With a show of
obedience, I hid myself, and their conversation convinced me only too well that they were indeed hatching
a horrible plan.

'It is a part of the anatomy,' said one, 'which will never
be properly understood until it has been examined with
the greatest exactness in a subject aged 12 or 13 who is
cut open at the precise moment pain makes contact with
the nerves. It is odious that considerations of a piddling
sort should impede the progress of science the way they
do. She would be one subject sacrificed to save millions:
can we afford to wonder whether we should pay such a
price? Is the murder which is sanctioned by law of a
different nature to the kind which we are about to commit in our operation? Is not the whole point of the wise
laws which permit capital punishment that one life
should be sacrificed to save a thousand others? So let no
such reservations stand in our way.'

'As far as I am concerned,' the other went on, 'I am

clear in my own mind. I should have done it long ago if I had dared to do it alone.'

I shall not report to you the rest of this conversation. It ran solely upon medical matters and I took in little of it. But from that moment I set the whole of my mind, whatever the cost might be, to the task of rescuing this wretched victim from an art which, though precious no doubt from every point of view, bought its progress at too high a price when that price was the immolation of innocence. The two friends parted and Rodin went to bed without speaking a word to me. The following day, which was the day appointed for the sacrifice, he left the house in the usual way, saying that he would not return till supper which he would, as on the previous evening, take with his friend. He was hardly out of the house when I began busying myself with my own scheme. Heaven gave its blessing, but whether this was to succour innocence sacrificed or with a view to punish wretched Sophie for her act of compassion, I dare not say. I shall relate the matter as it happened, and you will be the judge, Madame, for I am brought so low by the hand of impenetrable Providence that I cannot ever fathom what it has in store for me. Endeavouring always to promote its designs, I have been barbarously punished for doing so and can say no more than that.

I went down to the cellar and again questioned the girl who repeated the same talk and the same fears. I asked her if she knew where her captors left the key when they closed her prison door on her. 'I don't know,' she answered, 'but I believe they take it with them.' Determined to leave no avenue unexplored, I was casting around me when I felt something in the dirt at my feet. I bent down. It was the key! I opened the door. The poor little creature threw herself at my feet and watered my hands with the tears of her gratitude. Without pausing to wonder what risk I ran, without reflecting on the fate which must await me, I thought of nothing but of ways of helping the child to escape. I succeeded in getting her out of the village without our meeting anyone and set her down on the forest path, kissed her, and rejoiced as much as she both in her present happiness and in the good cheer she would bring to her father when she reappeared before him. Then I promptly returned to the house.

Our two surgeons returned at the hour appointed in eager anticipation of executing their odious plans. They supped with as much good humour as haste and went down into the cellar the moment they had finished. The only precaution I had taken to conceal what I had done was to break the lock and return the key to the place where I had found it, so as to suggest that the girl had escaped unaided. But the men I hoped thus to deceive were not the kind to let themselves be so easily duped. Rodin came back up fuming, leaped upon me and, in a welter of blows, demanded to know what I had done with the girl he had locked up. I began by denying all knowledge of it, but my wretched honesty led me in the end to admit everything.* There is nothing that can match the callous, wild rantings which these two blackguards then uttered. One proposed that I should take the place of the child I had saved, the other that I should be subjected to tortures even more appalling. All these proposals and ravings were interspersed with blows which sent me reeling from the one to the other and soon I was so dazed that I fell to the ground unconscious. Their fury was then quieted. Rodin brought me round and as soon as I had recovered my wits, they ordered me to strip. I obeyed tremblingly. When I was as they wanted, one of them held me while the other operated: they cut a toe from each of my feet then, sitting me down, they pulled out one of my back teeth apiece.

'But that's not the finish of it,' said Rodin, putting an iron into the fire. 'She came to me with the stripes of the whip on her. I intend to send her away otherwise marked.'

And so saying, the unspeakable wretch applied to the back of my shoulder the red-hot iron with which thieves are branded* while his colleague held me fast.

'Now let the whore try and make trouble, just let her try,' said Rodin furiously and, pointing to the shameful brand, added: 'I shall have no trouble now explaining my reasons for dismissing her from my service with such secrecy and such dispatch.'

This said, the two friends laid hold of me. It was night. They took me to the edge of the forest and callously left me there, but not without a reminder of how dangerous it would be for me in my present disreputable state to lodge any kind of complaint against them.

Anyone else but I would have paid little heed to this threat: the moment it was shown that the treatment I had received was not the work of any established court of law, what had I to fear? But my weakness, my ingrained lack of guile, the alarms which arose out of my unfortunate adventures in Paris and at the Château de Bressac, all these things numbed my wits and made me fearful and I had now only one thought, which was to flee from that dreadful place as soon as my sufferings had eased a little. Since they had carefully bound the hurts they had inflicted on me, the pain had subsided by the next morning and, after spending one of the most dreadful nights of my life under a tree, I set off at first light. The injuries to my feet prevented my walking very quickly but, anxious to be well clear of the forest which was so full of danger for me, I nevertheless made four leagues that first day and as many again the next and the day following. But having no directions and not daring to enquire my way, I simply went in circles around Paris, and by the evening of the fourth day of my perambulation, I found I had got no further than Lieusaint.* Knowing that this road would carry me to the cities of southern France, I resolved to follow it and make my way as best I could to those distant places, believing that the peace and safe haven which were so cruelly denied me in my native land stood waiting for me perhaps at the other end of the globe.

O fatal error! O, how numerous the trials I had yet to endure! My funds, swelling more modestly in my service with Rodin than during the time I had spent with the

Marquis de Bressac, were not so large that I had needed
to set a proportion aside for safe-keeping, and fortunately I had the entire sum with me, which is to say about
10 louis, this sum being made up of what I had salvaged
from my Bressac service and what I had earned in the
house of the surgeon. Although excessively weighed
down by my sorrows, I could yet rejoice that this money
had not been taken from me and I flattered myself that
it would at least last me until I was able to find a
situation. As the infamies which had been inflicted upon
me did not show outside my clothes, I fancied I should
always be able to hide them and their stigma would not
be a bar to my earning a living. I was 22 and enjoyed
rude good health in spite of my being slight in build and
slenderly made; I was possessed of a face which, to my
cost, others praised too well, and a handful of virtues
which, though they had never borne me but misfortune,
nevertheless afforded me inward consolations and
allowed me to hope that in the end Providence would
grant them if not some measure of reward then at least
some suspension of the ills which they had brought upon
my head. Taking heart and full of hope, I continued on
my way as far as Sens. But my badly healed feet caused
me considerable pain and I resolved to rest up there for
a few days. Not daring to expose the cause of my sufferings to any person and recalling the drugs which I had
seen Rodin employ in similar cases, I bought quantities
of the same and treated myself. A week's rest set me
completely to rights. I might perhaps have found myself
employment at Sens, but only too sensible of the need
to get away I did not even think to ask. I went on my
way with an idea that I might seek my fortune in the
Dauphiné region.* I had heard a great deal about this
part of France during my childhood and fancied happiness was to be had there. We shall see if I succeeded in
finding it.

Whatever the circumstances of my life, the feeling for
religion had never deserted me. Scorning the sophisms
of clever men which I believed to stem much more from

libertinism than from true conviction, I always counter-
ed them with my heart and my conscience, finding in
both sufficient weapons to combat them. Forced on
occasions by my misfortunes to neglect the duties of
religion, I made good my deficiencies whenever I could.
I had just left Auxerre on 7 June—I shall never forget
that time—and had proceeded for about two leagues.
The heat was beginning to tell on me and I resolved to
climb a low hill topped by a spinney to my left which
was somewhat out of my way, with a notion of finding
a little coolness and of sleeping a couple of hours there,
which I could do at a cheaper cost than at an inn and in
greater safety than on the high road. I made my way up
and settled at the foot of an oak where, after partaking
of a frugal meal of a crust of bread and water, I surrendered to the charms of Morpheus. I slumbered peace-
fully for above two hours. On waking, I feasted my eyes
on the landscape spread out before me, still to the left
of the road. In the middle of a forest which stretched
away endlessly, I could make out, more than three
leagues off, a small steeple rising modestly into the air.
   'Sweet solitude!' said I, 'how dearly I long to dwell in
thy midst! Here must be the retreat of solitary nuns or
saintly men, with thoughts only for their duties, wholly
devoted to religion, far removed from pernicious society
where crime, ceaselessly doing battle with innocence,
invariably gains the upper hand. I feel sure that all the
virtues reside behind those walls.'
   I was musing thus when a young woman of my age,
shepherding a few sheep on this higher ground, suddenly
came into view. I enquired of her what the buildings
were and she said that what I could see was a house of
Recollet Friars* which was occupied by four solitary
Brethren whose religion, abstinence, and sobriety were
without equal.
   'It is,' said she, 'a place of pilgrimage where once a
year people go to see a miraculous Virgin who grants the
truly pious whatever they ask.'
   Filled with an immediate desire to go and solicit help

at the feet of the Holy Mother of God, I asked the girl
if she would come with me. She said that she could not,
that her mother was waiting even then for her at home,
but that the way was easy. She pointed it out to me,
adding that the Father Superior, who was the most respectable and holy of men, would not only receive me
warmly but extend a helping hand should I be in need
of one.

'He is called the Reverend Father Raphael,' the girl
went on. 'He is Italian but has lived all his life in France.
He is happy in this solitary place and has several times
refused excellent offers of advancement from the Pope
to whom he is related. He is a man of high family,
mild-mannered, obliging, full of zeal and piety, aged
about 50, and considered by everyone hereabouts to be
a saint.'

The words of the shepherdess inflaming me further, I
found it quite impossible now to ignore the desire I had
formed to undertake a pilgrimage to the monastery and,
by as many pious acts as I was capable of, to make
amends for all the neglected observance of which I was
guilty. Although I myself stood in need of alms, I gave
the girl of my charity and without more ado was embarked upon the road to Sainte-Marie-des-Bois (this was
the name of the monastery towards which I was headed).
Down on the plain once more, I lost sight of the steeple
and my only guide was now the forest itself. I had not
asked my informant how many leagues it was from the
place where I had encountered her to the monastery,
and soon I discovered that the distance was in fact much
greater than the idea I had formed of it. But I was in no
whit discouraged. I reached the edge of the forest and,
observing that there was ample daylight left, I decided
to press on into it, being virtually assured of getting to
the monastery before nightfall. However, my eyes met
with no sign of human activity, not a house even, and
the only way forward was a little-used path which I
followed as best I could. I had come at least five leagues
from the hill where I had thought that three at most

would see me to my destination, and could still make out nothing of it. The sun was about to desert me when at last I heard the sound of a bell less than a league from where I was. I turned towards the sound, I quickened my steps, the path widened a little, and after an hour's walking from the time I heard the bell, I finally made out some hedges and shortly after that the monastery itself. Nothing could be more rural than this deserted spot. There were no other buildings close by, the nearest being more than six leagues off, and in every direction the forest extended for at least three leagues. The monastery being in a hollow, I had been obliged to make a considerable descent to get to it: this explained why I had lost sight of the steeple the moment I was down on the plain. The hut occupied by one of the Brothers who tended the garden was built against the wall of the inner refuge, and it was here that the traveller applied before gaining entry. I asked the saintly hermit if it was allowed to speak to the Father Superior. He asked me what I wanted of him. I gave him to understand that a matter of religious observance, a vow, had drawn me to this pious retreat and that I should be thoroughly consoled for all the trouble I had taken to reach the place if I could, just for a moment, prostrate myself before the Virgin and kneel at the feet of the holy director of the house where her miraculous statue resided.* After showing me where I could rest, the Brother disappeared into the monastery and, since it was already night and the friars were, said he, at supper, it was some time before he returned. Finally, he reappeared accompanied by a friar:

'This is Father Clement, Mademoiselle,' said the Brother. 'He is the steward of our House and he has come to determine whether what you desire is sufficiently grave to warrant disturbing the Superior.'

Father Clement was a man of 45, enormously stout and colossally tall. His eyes were wild and dark, his voice rough and hard, and his manner made me tremble far more than it consoled. An involuntary shudder seized me and, powerless to prevent it, the recollection of all my past misfortunes swam up into my memory.

'What do you want?' the friar said very sternly. 'What time is this to be coming to church? You have the look of an adventuress about you.'

'Holy Man,' said I, flinging myself to the ground, 'I thought there was never a wrong time to appear in the house of God, and to enter it I have travelled far, full of fervour and devotion. I ask to be confessed if that is possible, and when the secrets of my heart are known to you, you will see whether or not I am worthy to prostrate myself at the feet of the miraculous Virgin which you care for in your saintly house.'

'But it is not the hour for confession,' said the friar in a kindlier tone. 'Where will you spend the night? We have nowhere to accommodate you. Morning was the time to come.'

Against this I set out for him all the reasons which had prevented my doing so and, without giving me any further answer, he went off to report to the Superior. A few moments later, I heard the church doors opening and then saw the Father Superior himself, striding towards the gardener's hut where I was. He invited me to go with him into the temple. Father Raphael, of whom I should give you some idea before proceeding further, was as old as I had been given to believe but looked a man of not above 40 years. He was slim, quite tall, and his face was intelligent and kindly. He spoke French extremely well though with a slight Italian accent, and was as outwardly genteel and considerate as he was inwardly saturnine and fierce, of which I shall presently have only too much occasion to persuade you.

'My child,' this man of God said graciously, 'for all that the hour is quite unseemly and although it is not our custom to welcome callers so late, I shall nevertheless hear your confession. We shall then consider what arrangements can be made for you to spend the night with respect to the decencies until tomorrow when you will bow down to the holy statue which we have in our care.'

So saying, he lit a number of lamps around the confessional, bade me go inside and, sending the Brother away and shutting all the doors, urged me to confide fully and freely in him. In the presence of so kindly-seeming a man, I felt perfectly recovered from the fears which Father Clement had started in me. After humbling myself at my confessor's feet, I opened my heart fully to him and, with my habitual candour and trust, left him in ignorance of nothing which concerned me. I confessed all my faults and confided all my misfortunes ever to him: nothing was omitted, not even the shameful mark with which the execrable Rodin had branded me.

Father Raphael listened with the closest attention, and even asked me to repeat a number of details which he heard with an air of compassion and concern. His chief questions at various times concerned the following points:

1. Was it quite true that I was an orphan and hailed from Paris?
2. Was it really the case that I had no family or friends or protectors or anyone with whom I corresponded?
3. Had I told anyone other than the shepherdess of my design to come to the monastery, and had I arranged to meet her on my return?
4. Was it a fact that I was a virgin and that I was but 22 years of age?
5. Was it absolutely certain that I had not been followed and that no one had observed my entering the monastery?

When I had given him full satisfaction on these matters and answered each question in the most candid fashion, the Superior rose to his feet and, taking me by the hand, said:

'Come, my child. The hour is too late for you to kneel to the Virgin this evening. But I shall see to it that tomorrow you will have the sweet comfort of hearing mass at the foot of her statue. But first let us think of how we shall arrange for you to sup and sleep tonight.'

And so saying, he led me towards the sacristy.

'But Father,' said I with a hint of unease which I felt was beyond my control, 'am I then to be lodged inside your house?'

'But where else, fair pilgrim?' he replied, opening the doors of the cloister which, giving on to the sacristy, gave me entry to the main body of the building. 'Come now! Are you afraid to spend the night with four men of God? Oh, you will discover, my angel, that we are not really as sanctimonious as we appear and that we know how to take our pleasure with a pretty girl.'

These words made me quake. 'O, just Heaven!' said I to myself. 'Am I once more to be the victim of my righteous sentiments? Will the desire which I felt to draw near to what is most respectable in religion meet with the same punishment as a crime?' Meanwhile we continued to advance through the darkness until at last, at the end of one of the sides of the cloister, there appeared a stairway. The Superior indicated that I should precede him and, observing that I was somewhat reluctant to do so, turned to me:

'Twice a whore!' he said angrily and, immediately exchanging his smooth tone for the most sneering of manners, went on: 'Don't think you can turn back now! God's blood, you will soon learn that you had done better to tumble into a robbers' lair than fall into a company of four Recollets!'

Causes for my fears increased and multiplied so rapidly before my very eyes that I had no time to be alarmed by these words which had no sooner registered when new subjects of alarm assailed my senses. The door opened and seated at a table I saw three friars and three girls, all six in the most indecent state imaginable. Two of the girls were completely naked and the third was in the process of being undressed. The friars were more or less in the same condition.

'My friends,' said Raphael as he entered the room, 'we were one short: now we have her! Allow me to present to you a genuine phenomenon. Here is a Lucretia* who bears on her shoulder the mark of the whore and here,' he went on with a gesture as clear as it was indecent, 'here, proof certain of an authentic virginity.'

Great hoots of laughter from every corner of the room greeted this singular welcoming address and Clement, the friar I had met first, already half drunk, immediately shouted for the facts to be checked at once. Given the obligation on me to paint a picture for you of the people in whose midst I now found myself, I shall interrupt my tale here—but shall leave you in suspense with regard to my situation for the shortest time possible.

You are already sufficiently acquainted with Raphael and Clement for me to come directly to the others. Antonin, the third of the friars in the monastery, was a small man of 40, spare, slight, with a temperament of fire and the face of a satyr, hairy as a bear, a man of unbridled lechery, mettlesome and nasty beyond example. Father Jerome, the senior man, was an old libertine of 60, as hard and as brutal as Clement but the greater drunkard of the two. Being indifferent to ordinary pleasures, he was obliged, if he was to feel any glimmer of sensuality, to have recourse to tastes as depraved as they were revolting.

Florette was the youngest of the women. She was a native of Dijon, aged about 14, the daughter of a prosperous merchant of that town. She had been abducted by agents of Raphael who, wealthy and enjoying great credit in his Order, was prepared to spare no pains in the pursuit of his pleasures. She was dark, had very pretty eyes and an exceedingly alluring and provocative face. Cornélie was about 16, blonde and comely in appearance. She had beautiful hair, dazzling skin, and the finest of figures; she was from Auxerre, the daughter of a wine-merchant, and had been seduced by Raphael himself who had covertly lured her into his snares. Omphale was a woman of 30, very tall, with a very sweet and pleasing face, an extremely full figure, superb hair, the most handsome bosom conceivable, and the tenderest eyes you could ever hope to see. She was the daughter of a well-to-do vine-grower from Joigny* and had been on the point of marrying a man who would have made her fortune when Jerome detached her from her family at the age of 16 by decoying her with the most extraordinary enticements. Such was the company in which I was to live, such the sink of foulness and filth, whereas I had fancied I would find virtues there fully consonant with all that may be assumed of a respectable place of retreat.

The moment I joined this fearsome group, I was given to understand that I should be well advised to imitate the submissiveness of my companions.

'You can easily imagine,' said Raphael, 'how futile it would be to put up any resistance in this inaccessible fastness to which your unlucky star has brought you. You say you have endured many misfortunes and, judging by your tale, that is quite true. Yet you will note that the greatest mishap of all for a virtuous maid is still missing from the catalogue of your misfortunes. Is it natural for a girl to be a virgin at your age? And is not being so a kind of miracle which could not be prolonged indefinitely? Like you, your companions were extremely put out when they realized they had no choice but to serve our desires and, as you will wisely do, they submitted at the last when they saw that failure to do so would lead only to harsh treatment. In your present circumstances, Sophie, how can you possibly hope to defend yourself? Give a thought to how alone you are in the world. On your own admission you have neither relatives nor friends remaining. Think of your situation here in this sequestered place far from help, forgotten by the outside world, in the clutches of four libertines who certainly have no wish to spare you. To whom will you turn ? Will it be to the God whose help you implored with such fervour only moments since, who takes advantage of your zeal to push you a little more firmly into the trap? You must see that there is no power human or divine capable of plucking you from our grasp, nothing in the realm of physical possibilities or in the class of miracles, nothing in short which can succeed in further preserving the virtue of which you are so proud, nothing which will prevent your becoming in every sense and in all conceivable ways the prey of the foul excesses which all four of us are about to indulge in at your expense. So remove your clothes, Sophie, and may your most total resignation earn our leniency which, however, if you do not submit, will be instantly replaced by the harshest treatment which will, in turn, serve only to inflame us further without shielding you from our intemperance and brutal appetites.'

I was only too aware that this terrible haranguing left me without expedient. But would I not have been indeed guilty not to resort to the shift which my heart now prompted me to take and which Nature still left open to me? I threw myself at Raphael's feet and, deploying all the forces of my moral being, implored him not to take advantage of my predicament. The bitterest of salty drops bedewed his knees and everything my heart could furnish by way of pathos I dared try upon him as I wept—but having yet to learn that tears are but an added attraction in the eyes of crime and debauchery, I did not know that everything I did in my efforts to move the hearts of these monsters would simply have the effect of inflaming them further. Raphael got to his feet in a fury:

'Take the slut, Antonin,' he said, frowning ominously, 'and as you strip her and we look on, teach her that compassion has no claim upon men like us.'

Antonin seized me in his spare, wiry arms and, spicing word and action with appalling oaths, took less than two minutes to throw off my clothes and expose my nakedness to the gaze of the assembled company.

'Such a beautiful creature!' said Jerome. 'May the monastery walls fall on me if I ever saw such loveliness these thirty years past!'

'One moment,' said the Superior, 'let us put a little

order into our dealings. You are all aware, my friends, of our customary procedures with new acquisitions. She must undergo them all, without exception, and meanwhile let these three other women remain at hand to attend to or stimulate our needs.'

Immediately, a circle was formed and I was placed in the centre. There, for above two hours, I was inspected, scrutinized, probed by all four libertines, the object in turn of their praise and censure. You will permit me, Madame (said the beautiful prisoner blushing furiously at this juncture), to draw a veil over a part of the obscene details which were observed at this first ceremony. Let your imagination picture every outrage to which the spirit of debauchery is like to incite lecherous men to perform in such circumstances. Let it observe them as they pass in turn from my companions to me, comparing, contrasting, juxtaposing, discoursing—and you will have only the palest notion of what was perpetrated during the course of those first orgies which, however, were tepid affairs compared with the horrors of which I was shortly to be the victim.

'Come,' said Raphael whose desires had reached a prodigious pitch of excitement which he seemed incapable of containing any longer, 'the time has come to sacrifice the victim. Let each of us prepare to make her undergo our chosen pleasures.'

And the wicked man, placing me on a couch in an attitude propitious to his execrable pleasures and ordering Antonin and Clement to hold me fast, this Raphael, who was Italian, a friar and thoroughly depraved, satisfied his impure desires but left me still a maid. Was there ever such frenzy? It was as though each of these crapulous men gloried in denying Nature in the choice of their ignoble pleasures. Clement stepped forward, excited by the sight of the infamies committed by Raphael, and made more furious still by what he had been engaged in as he watched. He declared that he would be no more dangerous to me than his Superior and that the altar on which he paid his homage would similarly leave my virtue unthreatened. He ordered me to kneel and, clasping me close as I crouched, assuaged his perfidious passions in such a way that during the sacrifice I was denied the power of protesting at the irregularity of his procedure. Jerome followed, choosing the temple favoured by Raphael, but without attempting to reach the sanctuary; content to observe the portals from without and excited by preliminary, quite indescribable obscenities, he achieved the full satisfaction of his desires only by employing the same barbarous means of which Dubourg almost made me the victim and which I suffered entire at the hands of Bressac.

'The preparations have begun well,' said Antonin as he seized me. 'Come, my sweet, come that I may make up for the irregularity of my brothers and pick the flower which their intemperance has left for me . . .'

The details . . . O God! . . . I cannot find words to paint them. It was as if the villain, the most libertine of the four, though seemingly the least removed from the views of Nature, was prepared to tread her path and put a smaller degree of nonconformity into his order of worship, only by compensating for a semblance of lesser depravity by inflicting the highest degree of outrage upon my person . . . Alas, if in imagination I had on occasion strayed to thoughts of such pleasures, I always believed them to be as chaste as the God who inspired them: they were given to humankind by Nature as a consolation and were born of love and decency. Foreign to me was the notion that man, like the beasts of the field, could pleasure himself only by making his partners suffer. But this I now discovered, and with such a degree of violence that the natural pain of the loss of my virginity was the least of the agonies which I was required to bear during his terrifying onslaught. But Antonin marked the moment of paroxysm with such furious whoopings and bellowings, with such murderous assaults on every part of my body, and not least with bites which were like the tiger's bloody caress, that for a moment I believed I had fallen prey to some wild animal which would not be sated until it had devoured me whole. When these horrors ended, I collapsed upon the altar where I had been sacrificed, motionless and almost unconscious.

Raphael ordered the women to care for me and give me food, but a fit of rage and sorrow mixed assailed my soul at this cruel moment. I could not bear the horrible idea that I had now at last lost the treasure of my maidenhood for which I would have sacrificed my life a hundred times over, nor the thought that I had been defiled by the very men from whom I had every reason on the contrary to expect to receive most help and the highest spiritual consolation. My tears flowed freely, my screams reverberated around the room, I rolled upon the ground, tore my hair and begged my tormentors to make an end of me. But though the blackguards, far too hardened to such displays, busied themselves more with tasting new pleasures with my companions than with easing my sufferings or comforting my hurts, yet nevertheless being inconvenienced by my wailing, they resolved to send me away to rest in a place where I could not be heard. Omphale was about to lead me off when the perfidious Raphael, casting another lubricious glance upon me notwithstanding the cruel state to which I had been reduced, declared that he would not allow me to be dismissed without making me his victim one more time. No sooner was the scheme conceived than it was carried out. But since his desires now required an extra degree of stimulation, it was not until he had fully employed the cruel expedients favoured by Jerome that he succeeded in finding the powers necessary for the execution of his latest crime. What new heights of debauchery were there scaled! Great God, how was it that these lechers could be so savage as to choose an instant of agonizing spiritual crisis such as the one through which I was then passing to inflict upon me its barbarous physical counterpart?

'By God!' said Antonin as he too resumed with me, 'there is nothing finer than to follow the example set by a Superior, and nothing spicier than to repeat a crime. They say that pain is conducive to pleasure,* and I am persuaded that this delicious child will make me the happiest of mortals.'

And notwithstanding my struggles, my screams, and my supplications, I became once more the hapless butt of the wretch's outrageous urges . . . Finally, I was allowed to quit the room.

'If,' said Clement, 'I had not been quite so premature when our beautiful princess first arrived, she would not leave the room without serving my passions a second time. But she will lose nothing by waiting.'

'I can promise her as much,' said Jerome, and as I passed by him he let me feel the weight of his arm. 'But for tonight, let us retire to our beds.'

Raphael being of the same mind, the orgies ceased. He kept Florette by him—and doubtless she remained there the whole night—while the rest of the company went their several ways. I was given into the keeping of Omphale, a sort of Sultaness who, being older than the others, appeared to me to have charge of the sisters. She led me into our common apartment in a kind of square tower with a bed in each corner for each of the four of us. By custom, one of the friars always followed their women as they retired, securing the door with two or three bolts. It was Clement who carried out this duty. Once inside, it was impossible to get out again, there being no other exit apart from a small adjoining closet designed for our ease and our toilets, which had a window as closely barred as the one in the chamber where we slept. The place was, furthermore, sparsely furnished: a chair and bedside table curtained off by a piece of cheap calico, one or two wooden chests in the closet, close-stools, bidets, and a dressing-table for our common use. It was not until the next morning that I observed these things, for during that initial instant I had no thought but for my sufferings. 'O just Heaven!' said I to myself, 'so it is indeed written that no act of virtue shall go forth from my heart but that it is immediately

followed by its punishment! What wrong did I commit,
my God, by wishing to call on this house and follow
some slight religious observance? Did I offend against
Heaven by wishing so to do and was this my reward for
making the attempt? O incomprehensible decrees of
Providence, grant me, I beg, a moment's clear view of
your laws if it is not your design to drive me to revolt
against them!' Bitter tears followed these reflections and
I was still wet with them when Omphale drew near to
my bed as day was about to break.

'Dear sister,' said she, 'I come to urge you to take
heart. During my first days here, I wept as you do, but
now habit prevails and you will get used to things as I
have. The first times are horrible. It is not simply that
we are endlessly forced to satisfy the unbridled lust of
debauched men which makes our life such torture: it is
the loss of liberty and the brutal way we are treated in
this infamous place. Those who are wretched are consoled when they see those around them suffer;* however
much my wounds smarted, I soothed them by asking one
of my companions to acquaint me with the further ills
which lay in wait for me. 'Listen,' said Omphale, sitting
at the head of my bed, 'I am going to speak to you in all
honesty, but remember: you must never abuse my trust.
The most cruel of our sufferings, my dear, is not knowing what our fate will be: we have no way of knowing
what will happen to us when we leave here. We have as
much evidence as our solitude allows us to acquire that
girls dismissed from this place are never seen again in
the world outside. The friars themselves give us notice
of this, for they do not hide from us that this retreat is
also our grave. Even so, hardly a year goes by but that
two or three girls leave. What happens to them? Do the
friars make an end of them? At times they claim that
they do and at other times they say that they don't, but
none of those who have gone away, however sincerely
they swore to lodge a formal complaint against the monastery and to work for our release, not one I say has ever
kept her word. Do the friars see to it that the complaints

are hushed up or do they ensure that the girls are in no state to make them? When we ask new arrivals for news of those who have left, they invariably know nothing about them. So what happens to the poor creatures? That is what makes us sick with worry, Sophie, that is the fatal uncertainty which makes our lives so anguished and wretched. I have been in this house for fourteen years and I have seen above fifty girls go hence. Where are they now? Why, since all gave their oath to help us, why has none ever been true to her word? Our number is fixed at four, at least as regards this chamber, for we are all convinced that there is another tower corresponding to ours where they keep a similar contingent. All manner of things the friars do and say have persuaded us that this is so. But if these fellow-sufferers do indeed exist, we have never seen them. One of the strongest pieces of evidence we have for their presence is that we are never on duty on succeeding days. We were required yesterday; so today we rest. For it is quite clear that our lechers never allow themselves a single day's abstinence. In practice, no known principles determine the moment of our superannuation, not age, nor fading charms, nor on their part lassitude or revulsion, nothing save their whim decides when they give us the fatal quietus and we have no means of telling if our dismissal is to benefit us or not. I have known here an inmate aged 70; she left just last summer, having been in this place for sixty years. Whereas they kept her on, I saw a good dozen sent away, none being aged above 16. Some I have seen leave three days after their arrival, some within a month, and others besides at the end of several years: in this matter there is no rule beyond their will, or rather their caprice. Nor does our conduct enter into it: I have known some girls prepared to go more than half-way to anticipate their desires who were dismissed after six weeks while others who were surly and temperamental were kept on for many years. It is therefore but a waste of breath to prescribe to a new arrival the kind of conduct she should observe, for our masters' fantastical whims overturn all laws and there is no logic in them. The friars do not vary a great deal. Raphael arrived fifteen years ago, Clement has lived in this place for sixteen years, Jerome has been here for thirty and Antonin for ten: he has been the only one to come in my time. He took the place of a friar aged 60 who died in the course of one particularly frenzied orgy. Raphael, a Florentine by birth, is a close relative of the Pope with whom he is on the best of terms. It is only since his coming that the miraculous Virgin has brought the house a measure of reputation which prevents prying eyes from taking too close an interest in what goes on here, but the monastery was as you see it now when he first arrived. It has been, so it is said, on the same footing for almost eighty years and all the Superiors appointed have continued to run its affairs in a way entirely favourable to their pleasures. Raphael, one of the most depraved churchmen of the century, arranged to be sent here only because he already knew what it was like and his intention is to preserve its secret privileges for as long as he can. We are part of the diocese of Auxerre but whether the bishop has knowledge of what transpires here or not, we never see him within these walls. Indeed, few visitors ever appear here. Except during the time of the matronal festival at the end of August, scarcely ten persons come throughout the whole of the year. But when outsiders do appear, the Superior is most careful to receive them well and to impress them with an infinite show of austerity and piety; they go away content and speak warmly of the monastery, and in this way the impunity enjoyed by these scoundrels has become rooted in the good faith of the people and the credulity of the faithful. Yet there are no stricter rules than those which govern our conduct and nothing more dangerous to us than to breach them in the smallest particular. It is vital that I should go into this matter with you in some detail,' continued my instructress, 'for it is no excuse here to say: "Do not punish me for breaking such and such a law for I did not know it existed." It is for each newcomer to seek instruction from her companions or else to work it out for herself: no one is informed about anything but every infringement is punished.* The only form of correction allowed is the Lash, for it was logical that a rite which forms part of the pleasures of these wicked men should become their favoured form of punishment. You felt its bite yesterday having done no wrong; you will feel it again soon enough for committing some fault. All four are obsessed by this barbarous flagellating mania and each takes turns to act as chastiser. Each day there is one who is named Regent-in-Charge. He receives the reports submitted by the Doyenne of the inmates, has the running of the seraglio, makes all the arrangements for the suppers to which we are admitted, and frames accusations of misconduct which he himself then punishes. But let us look more closely at each of these heads. We are all required to be up and dressed by nine in the morning.* At ten we are brought bread and water for luncheon. At two, dinner is served: it generally consists of a quite acceptable potage, a piece of boiled meat, a dish of vegetables, sometimes a little fruit, and a bottle of wine which we share. Punctually each day, winter and summer, the Regent calls on us at five o'clock. It is then that he hears the Doyenne who informs on her companions. The only complaints she is authorized to make concern the behaviour of the girls in her chamber: whether any words of ill humour or sedition have been spoken; whether all rose at the appointed time; whether face and hair were carefully groomed and hygiene thoroughly attended to; whether all have eaten properly; and whether any have talked of escape. The Doyenne is required to render an exact account of all these matters, for we ourselves run the risk of punishment if we are remiss. Next, the Regent goes into our closet where he inspects divers objects. When he has done, it is rare that he leaves without taking his pleasure with one of us, and frequent that he does so with all four. Once he has gone, unless it be our Supper Day, we are free to read or chat, amuse ourselves as we choose and retire to bed when we will. But if we are to sup that evening with the friars, a bell is rung which tells us that it is time to prepare. The Regent himself comes to fetch us, we go down to the room where you first saw us, and the first thing to be done is the reading out of the catalogue of faults committed by us since our last appearance. First come infractions committed during the previous supper: examples of remissness, instances of cool responses to the friars at those moments when we serve their desires, plus any failure of attentiveness, submission, or cleanliness. To this is added the list of offences committed in our chamber in the space of the intervening two days as recorded by the Doyenne. The delinquents advance in turn to the middle of the room. The Regent states the charge and confronts the accused with their crime. They are then stripped naked by the Doyenne (or the vice-Doyenne in cases where the Doyenne is at fault), and the Regent administers the prescribed punishment in a manner so energetic that they find it difficult to forget. So skilled at the business are these awful men that it is virtually impossible for there to be a single day when one or two chastisements are not administered. Once these matters are over, the orgies begin. It would be quite impossible for me to list all the variants in detail: could such bizarre whims ever be catalogued?* Our prime objective is never to refuse them anything . . . and always to anticipate. But even when we observe this rule, however sound it may be, we are still sometimes none too safely off. Half-way through the orgies, supper is served. We are permitted to share the meal which is always finer and more sumptuous than those which we are served. The bacchanalia resumes when the friars are half-drunk. At midnight, they disperse, but each has the right to keep one of us by him through the night, the chosen favourite sleeping in the cell of the friar who selected her, being restored to us on the morrow. The rest retire and on returning find the chamber cleaned, the beds made, and our clothes-boxes tidied. Sometimes of a morning, as soon as we are up and about, before luncheon, it may occur that a friar will send for one of us to go to his cell. The Brother who sees to our menial needs then comes to fetch us and escorts us to the friar who desires us; the friar either brings us back himself or has it done by the same Brother the moment he tires of us. The Cerberus who cleans our apartments and occasionally escorts us is an aged monk whom you will see presently. He is 70 years old, has one eye, limps, and is dumb. Responsible for the running of the entire establishment, he is aided by three other monks: one to prepare the food, one to clean the cells of the friars, sweep all through the buildings and help in the kitchen, and lastly the porter whom you encountered when you arrived. Of these, we see only the Brother who serves us; the briefest word to him would count as one of our most serious offences. The Superior occasionally comes to call on us. At these times, there are a number of ceremonial customs which you will learn by practice: failure to observe them is a crime, for the desire the friars have to seek out infractions so that they might have the pleasure of punishing them leads them to find more and more faults daily. It is rarely without some scheme in mind that Raphael pays us a visit and his schemes are unfailingly cruel or lewd as you have had ample opportunity to learn for yourself. For the rest, being securely shut up always, there is no occasion during the year when we are allowed to take the air; though there is a very large garden, yet there are no gates to it for they fear an escape which would be highly dangerous since by information laid before the Justices and Mother Church regarding all the crimes which are committed in this place, matters here would soon be set to rights. We never practise the least religious observance; we are as forbidden to think of it as to speak thereof: any such talk is one of the wrongs which most surely receives punishment. And that is the sum of what I can tell you, my dear,' added our Doyenne. 'Experience will teach you the rest. Take heart if you can, but give up all thought of escape, for there has never been a girl yet who left this prison and saw the outside world again.'

This last comment making me horribly uneasy, I asked Omphale what she really thought had become of the girls who had been sent away.

'What sort of answer do you expect me to give you?' said she, 'for hope springs up eternally to contradict my dismal opinion. Everything tells me beyond doubting that a grave is their final refuge—yet every instant brings a crowd of thoughts born of hope to overturn my all too fatal conviction. We are not informed,' Omphale went on, 'until the morning of the day they intend to be rid of us. The Regent comes before our luncheon is served, saying, as I imagine: "Omphale, pack your bag, the monastery is sending you away. I shall come for you when it gets dark", and then he goes out. The girl who has been dismissed embraces her companions and promises over and over to help them, to lodge complaints, to raise a clamour about what goes on here. The hour tolls, the friar comes, the girl goes . . . and is never heard of again. Yet if it is a Supper Day, then everything carries on as usual. All we have noted on those days is that the friars exert themselves much less, drink a great deal more, send us away much earlier, and take no one into their beds.'

'Dear Omphale,' said I to the Doyenne as I thanked her for instructing me, 'perhaps you never had to deal before except with children who had not strength enough to keep their word. Are you willing to make that same mutual promise with me? I shall begin by swearing in advance upon everything I hold most sacred that I shall make an end of these infamies or die in the attempt. Do you promise me as much on your side?'

'With all my heart,' said Omphale, 'but you must appreciate that such promises are quite futile. Girls older than you, and more outraged too if that is possible, who belonged to the best families in the province and were therefore far better armed, the kind of girls who would have given their life's blood for me, have broken the self-same oaths before. Please understand therefore if my cruel experience leads me to consider the pledge we have just sworn to be meaningless and to say that I do not place more hope in it than in the others.'

We then talked of the characters of the friars and of our companions.

'There are no men in Europe', said Omphale, 'more dangerous than Raphael and Antonin. Their natural qualities are duplicity, villainy, spite, nastiness, cruelty, and irreligion. Joy never sparkles in their eyes except when they are most fully launched upon their vices. Clement who appears to be the gruffest of the four is in fact the best of them, for he is to be feared only when in his cups; but when he is, you must take great care not to cross him, for doing so can often be a highly risky affair. As to Jerome, he is naturally brutal, and cuffs, kicks, and punches are common coin with him, though when his passions are spent he becomes as gentle as a lamb, which is an important difference between him and the first two who revive their flagging desires only by committing the most perfidious and appalling actions. Turning to the girls,' the Doyenne went on, 'there is really very little to say. Florette is a child who is none too intelligent and can be twisted around anyone's little finger. Cornélie has a good heart and a fund of fine feelings: she is utterly inconsolable and cannot be reconciled to her fate.'

When I had noted all this information, I asked my companion if it were indeed quite impossible to discover whether there was or not a second tower containing other unfortunates besides ourselves.

'If they exist, and I am virtually certain they do,' said Omphale, 'we shall never know unless it be through some indiscretion on the part of the friars or the mute Brother who serves us and doubtless attends to their needs also. But such knowledge would be a source of great danger. For what purpose would be served by knowing whether we are alone here or not, since we have no means of helping each other? If you ask what grounds I have for saying that their existence is more than likely, then I shall tell you: a number of remarks the friars have

let slip without thinking are more than enough to persuade us that such is the case. Moreover, I was once
leaving Raphael's cell in the morning after a night spent
there, and was stepping through his door and he was
about to follow me and bring me back here himself,
when I saw without his noticing the mute Brother going
into Antonin's with a very pretty girl aged about 17 or
18 who was certainly not one of us. Seeing that he was
observed, the Brother pushed her hurriedly into
Antonin's cell—but not before I got a clear view of her.
He did not report me and the matter was left there. Had
it been made public, I might perhaps have bought my
knowledge dear. So it is quite certain that there are
women here other than ourselves, and since we sup with
the friars every two days, they must sup with them on
the intervening days, and most likely are as many as we
are.'

Omphale had scarcely finished speaking when Florette
returned from Raphael's cell where she had spent the
night. It was expressly forbidden for girls to tell each
other what had happened when they had been chosen
and, seeing that we were awake, she simply murmured
a 'good-morning' and threw herself exhausted on to her
bed where she remained until nine o'clock, which was
our time for getting up. The tender Cornélie then came
up to me and, weeping as she looked at me, said:

'Oh, my dear mademoiselle! What wretched creatures
we are!'

Luncheon was brought, my companions forced me to
take a little nourishment and I ate something for their
sakes. The day passed quietly enough. At five, as Omphale had said, the Regent for that day entered: it was
Antonin. With a laugh he asked me how I was after my
adventure and, since the only answer I could give him
was to lower my tear-filled eyes, he said sneeringly:

'She'll learn. There is not a convent in the whole of
France where girls get a better education than they are
given here.'

He completed his inspection and took the list of offences from the Doyenne who, being too good-hearted to overfill it, very often said that there was nothing to report. Before leaving us, Antonin came up to me. I shuddered, for I believed I was about to become the monster's victim once more—though since I might be at any time, what did it matter if the thing happened then or the next day? However, I was let off with some rough fondling and he leaped instead upon Cornélie and, busying himself with her, ordered all of us present to help stimulate his passions. Already replete with sensuality, the beast, grudging himself no form of voluptuousness, ended his business with the hapless creature exactly as he had with me the evening before, which is to say with the most considered excesses of brutality and lewdness. Group enactments of this kind were a pretty regular occurrence. It was more or less customary that when a friar took his pleasure with one of us sisters, the other three should gather round and stimulate his senses in every manner conceivable so that he should be aware of his sensuality through each and every one of his organs. I set down these loathsome details here so that I shall not have to return to them again, it not being my purpose to dwell further on the obscenity of these occasions. To describe one is to describe them all and, of my long sojourn in that place, my design is to speak to you only of happenings of any significance and not to appal you further with the details. As it was not a Supper Day for us, we were left quite to ourselves. My companions consoled me as best they could, but nothing could assuage sorrows as deep as mine. They strove in vain, for the more they spoke of my misfortunes, the more desperate those misfortunes seemed.

The following morning at nine o'clock, the Superior came to see me, though it was not his day to do so, and asked Omphale if I was beginning to set my mind to make the best of my plight. Without waiting for a reply, he opened one of the chests in our closet and took several women's garments from it:

'Since you brought no raiment with you,' said he, 'we

must give some thought to what you shall wear, a little more perhaps for our sake than for yours. There is no need therefore to be grateful. I am not myself in favour of all this pointless dressing up. If we were to allow the girls who serve our needs to go about as naked as the beasts of the field, it strikes me that the drawbacks of such a proceeding would be of little consequence. But the friars are men of the world and demand luxury and finery, and they must be satisfied.'

On to the bed he tossed a number of dishabilles together with a half-dozen shifts, several bonnets, stockings, and shoes, and bade me try them all. He watched as I put them on and did not miss a single opportunity for indecent fondlings which the situation gave rise to. There were two or three loose gowns of taffeta and one of India cotton which all fitted me tolerably well. These he allowed me to keep and told me to suit myself as to the remainder, reminding me however that they were all House Property and saying that they were to be returned if I should chance to leave before wearing any of them out. These various proceedings affording a number of spectacles which raised him to boiling pitch, he ordered me to adopt the attitude which I knew suited him best. I was minded to entreat for mercy but seeing the rage and anger already ashine in his eyes, I judged that the speediest issue was through obedience and I took up my position . . . The libertine, abetted by the three other women, took his pleasure as was his wont at the cost of morality, religion, and Nature. I had roused him to a fever. At supper, he made much of me and I was designated to spend the night with him. My companions withdrew and I passed into his apartment. I shall say no more of my loathing or my sufferings, Madame, for you can doubtless picture both to be extreme, and my monotonous retailing of them would perhaps blunt the edge of what I have yet to tell. Raphael occupied a very pretty cell which had been furnished voluptuously and in the finest taste: nothing was lacking which could render this private place as pleasant as it was purpose-made for pleasure. When we were inside, Raphael, stripping naked and bidding me to do likewise, took a good long time to be brought to a peak of excitement by the self-same methods with which, as the active agent in the business, he next inflamed his own passions. I can state here that during that night I followed as complete a course of lewd conduct as any supplied to the best taught harlot who has been schooled in these foul exercises. From being the mistress, I soon passed to the status of pupil once more, but durst not treat as I was treated, and though I was never asked to stay my hand I was quickly reduced to pleading, weeping hot tears, that he stayed his. But my entreaties were met with scoffing, my attempts at evading him were nullified by the most barbarous counters and, once he observed that I was mastered, I was subjected to unparalleled brutality for two hours and more. He did not limit himself to the bodily parts reserved for such matters but wandered everywhere without distinction: the most contrary places, the most delicate globes, nothing escaped the fury of my tormentor whose *frissons* of sensuality received their impetus from the symptoms of pain upon which his hungry eyes feasted.

'And now to bed,' said he at the last. 'Perhaps you have had enough, but I certainly have not. I never weary of this most holy order of worship, and all we have done thus far is no more than a faint image of pleasure as it might really be.'

We got into the bed. There, Raphael, his lasciviousness as unabated as his depravity, held me all night, the slave of his criminal desires. Thinking him momentarily assuaged, I took advantage of a brief interval of calm in these debauches to beseech him to tell me if I could ever hope to quit the house one day.

'Most certainly,' Raphael answered, 'you were allowed entry only on that basis. When all four of us are agreed that you should be permitted to leave, then leave you most certainly shall.'

'But,' said I, thinking to extract something more definite from him, 'do you not fear that girls who are younger and far less discreet than I swear to be all my life, might not on occasion make disclosures about what is done here?'

'That would be impossible,' said the Superior.

'Impossible?'

'Absolutely.'

'Perhaps you would explain . . . .'.

'No. It's our secret. All I can tell you is that, discreet or not discreet, once you are outside it will be quite impossible for you ever to reveal anything of what goes on within these walls.'

And so saying, he ordered me roughly to speak of other things and I dared not enquire further. At seven in the morning, he ordered the Brother to escort me back and, putting what he had said to me together with what I had learned from Omphale, I convinced myself, over-pessimistically perhaps, that it was only too plain that the most violent measures were taken against girls who left the house, and that if they never raised a hue and cry, it was because they were prevented from doing so by being shut up in a coffin. I remained all atremble at this terrible thought for some time until, managing at the last to overcome it by the force of hope, I fell into the same dull state as my companions.

Within the space of a week, I had done the rounds of the four friars and during this time had ample opportunity to observe the various aberrant and infamous practices perpetrated in turn by each of them. But with them as with Raphael, the torch of libertinage was lit only by excesses of brutality. It was as though this vice of their corrupt hearts was the organ which stimulated all the rest, and it seemed that only by giving vent to it could their efforts be crowned with pleasure.

Antonin was the friar at whose hands I suffered most. It is impossible to imagine how far the wretch carried cruelty in the course of his ecstatic frenzies. He was unfailingly guided by his sombre urges: they were the true masters of his pleasure, they continued to fuel his desire even at the peak of his enjoyment, and they alone revived it when his passion was near to being spent. Given all this, I was amazed that the methods he used, for all the severity of their application, never ended with the impregnation of any of his victims. I asked our Doyenne by what means he managed to avoid such an eventuality.

'By immediately destroying,' Omphale told me, 'any consequence of his ardour. As soon as he has an indication of its early progress, he forces us on three days running to swallow six large glasses of a certain tea or infusion which, by the fourth day, leaves no trace of his intemperance.* Cornélie has just had it happen to her. It has happened to me on three occasions. There is no adverse effect on our health. Indeed, it appears that we all feel much the better for it. But as you will have observed, he is the only one of the four with whom we need anticipate this danger. The irregular desires of each of the others leave us nothing to fear from them on that score.'

Then Omphale asked me if it were not true that of all the friars Clement was the one of whom I had least to complain.

'Alas,' said I, 'surrounded as I am by horrors and obscenities which both sicken and revolt me, I should have the greatest difficulty in saying which one wearies me least. They all exhaust me and I wish I were already free of this place, whatever fate awaits me.'

'But it is possible that you will have your wish soon,' Omphale went on. 'You came here quite by chance, and they had not counted on your coming. A week before you arrived, a girl had just been sent away, and they never send anyone away unless they are quite sure of having a replacement. They are not always the ones who select new recruits. They have well-paid agents who serve them zealously. I am pretty certain that a new girl will be coming at any moment and your wish might well be granted. Moreover, the matronal festival is almost upon us. It is rare that the event passes without bringing

them some advantage: either they use the confessional
to seduce a few young girls or else they shut one of them
up here, but it is most unusual that the occasion passes
without some tasty morsel being snapped up.'

The great day finally arrived. Would you believe, Madame, to what depths of monstrous impiety the friars
sank during the festival? They fancied that a visible miracle would considerably enhance their good name and
consequently dressed Florette, who was the youngest
and smallest of us, in all the Virgin's finery, secured her
fast around the waist by ropes which could not be seen,
and ordered her to raise her arms solemnly heavenwards
when the host was lifted up. Since the unhappy creature
was threatened with the most cruel treatment if she
uttered a single word or failed to carry out her role, she
performed to the best of her ability and the fraud was
every whit as successful as could have been wished for.
The congregation acclaimed a miracle, gave rich offerings to the Virgin, and went away more convinced than
ever of the mercy of the Heavenly Mother.

To crown their impiety, the libertines required Florette to appear at supper dressed in the costume which
had brought her such homage, and each inflamed his
odious desires by subjecting her, she still wearing the
same vestments, to his lewd whims. Excited by this
initial crime, the monsters did not stop there. They then
made her lie face down, unclothed, upon a large table,
lit candles, placed a figure of Our Lord next her head,
and dared celebrate the most awful of our mysteries
upon her bare back. I fainted at the horrible sight of it,
being unable to bear the spectacle. Seeing this, Raphael
declared that, to break me to their ways, I should serve
as altar in my turn. I was seized and placed where Florette had been and the foul Italian, enacting much cruel-
ler and infinitely more sacrilegious rites, consummated
over me the same horror which he had the moment
before performed over my companion. I was dragged
from there unconscious and had to be carried back to
the chamber where for three days I wept the bitterest

tears over the hideous crime in which I had, though
against my will, participated. The memory of it still
racks my heart, Madame, and I cannot think of it without weeping. In me, religion is a function of my sensibility and anything which offends or outrages my faith
makes the blood drain from my heart.

Meanwhile, it did not seem to us that the new companion we were expecting had been taken from among
the vast concourse of people who had been drawn by the
festival. A new recruit might have been made to the
other seraglio, but no one came to ours. And so everything continued in the same manner for two weeks more.
I had been in that hateful place for six weeks when
Raphael came to our tower one morning at about nine
o'clock. He appeared to be very restive and a kind of
madness gleamed in his eyes. He examined each of us,
made us adopt his favoured position one after the other,
and came to a noticeable halt at Omphale. He stood
there for several minutes gazing at her in that posture,
exciting himself quietly, trying out one of his choicest
fantasies, but without consummation. Then, ordering
her to her feet, he stared at her very sternly for a while
and, with ferocity painted upon every feature of his face,
said:

'You have served us long enough. Our fraternity hereby dismisses you and I have come to give you notice of
it. Make ready. I shall come for you myself as darkness
falls.'

So saying, he examined her once more with the same
severe look in his eye and left the chamber abruptly.

The instant he had gone, Omphale threw herself into
my arms.

'Oh, the moment has come,' said she through her
tears, 'which I have been both dreading and longing for.
O God! What will become of me?'

I did all I could to calm her, but without success. She
swore by the most expressive oaths that she would stint
no effort to see that we were delivered and to lay information against our perfidious captors, if she were given

the opportunity to do so, and her manner of giving me these pledges left me not an instant's doubt that either she would do it or else the thing could not be done at all. The day passed like any other and at about six o'clock, Raphael himself returned.

'Come,' he said sharply to Omphale, 'are you ready?'

'Yes, Father.'

'Let us go then, and go quickly.'

'Will you allow me to embrace my companions?'

'That is quite unnecessary,' said the friar, pulling her away by the arm. 'You are stayed for. Follow me.'

Then she asked whether she was to bring her bundle with her.

'Bring nothing, nothing at all,' said Raphael. 'Is not everything here House Property? You will have no further need of these things.'

Then correcting himself like someone who has said too much, he added:

'These clothes will be of no further use to you. You will have others made to measure which will suit you better.'

I asked the friar if he would permit me to accompany Omphale as far as the monastery gate, but he answered with so savage, so wild a look that I recoiled in fear and dared not repeat my request. Our hapless companion left us, casting me a glance as she went which brimmed with disquiet and tears, and the moment she was gone all three of us gave way to the sorrow of the parting. A half-hour later, Antonin came to fetch us to supper. Raphael did not appear until about an hour after we had gone down. He looked extremely agitated, whispered much to the others, and yet everything passed off much as usual. However, I noticed, as Omphale had led me to expect, that we were sent to our chambers much earlier and that the monks, who drank vaster quantities than was their wont, made do with stimulating their desires without ever permitting their consummation. What could be deduced from these observations? I remarked all these things because everything is noticed in such circumstances, but as to telling what followed from them, I had not wit enough to see and perhaps I should not bother to tell you now of these circumstances had they not made such a singular impact upon me.

We spent four days waiting for news of Omphale, one moment not doubting but that she would without fail honour the pledge she had given, and the next quite convinced that the cruel measures taken against her would make it impossible for her to serve us in any way. We despaired then and our anxieties reached a new pitch. The fourth day after Omphale's departure, we were escorted down to supper in accordance with the normal state of affairs, but what was our surprise when all three of us beheld a new companion enter from an outside door at the very moment when we appeared through ours!

'Mesdemoiselles, this is the recruit our fraternity has chosen to replace the girl who has lately left us,' declared Raphael. 'Pray have a thought to live with her as with a sister and to ease her passage in those matters which are yours to decide. Sophie,' said the Superior, turning to me, 'you are the oldest in the class and I hereby raise you to the position of Doyenne. You are acquainted with the duties of the post. Take care to carry them out punctually.'

I sorely wanted to refuse, but it was impossible for me to do so, for I was eternally obliged to sacrifice my own wishes and desires to those of my evil captors. I bowed my head and promised to see to everything in a way which would content him.

Then, from the head and shoulders of our new companion were removed the mantles and veils which hid her face and figure, and we beheld a girl of 15 years endowed with the most expressive and delicate physiognomy. Her eyes, though wet with tears, seemed to us quite magnificent: she raised them with such grace to each one of us that I can state now that never did I see a look more touching in all my life. She had long fair hair which cascaded over her shoulders in natural curls, and a fresh, rosy mouth. She carried her head nobly and there was something so attractive in her general bearing that it was impossible to see her without feeling drawn towards her. We learned soon enough from her own lips (and I include it here so that I may make one piece of all that concerns her) that her name was Octavie, that she was the daughter of a prosperous merchant at Lyons, that she had just finished her education in Paris, that she had been returning thence to her parents' house in the company of a governess when, being attacked at night on the road between Auxerre and Vermenton,* she had been abducted against her will and brought to the monastery, and that she had been unable to discover news of the coach in which she had ridden or of the woman who had accompanied her. She had been kept locked up by herself in a confined cell for above an hour where she had surrendered to her despair, and then had been fetched away to join our company without any of the friars having yet spoken one word to her.

The four libertines, momentarily struck with ecstasy at the spectacle of so many charms, had strength only to admire. The power of beauty imposes respect, and the most corrupt of scoundrels cannot help but pay a kind of worshipful tribute which cannot be transgressed without feelings of remorse. But monsters such as those with whom we had to deal do not allow such a brake to check their course for long.

'Come, Mademoiselle,' said the Superior, 'pray show us if the remainder of your charms answer those which Nature has so liberally scattered upon your face.'

And as the beautiful creature grew uneasy and blushed, not understanding what was meant, the brutal Antonin seized her by the arm and shouted curses and reprimands at her far too indecent for me to repeat:

'Don't you understand, little Miss Prig, that what you are being told to do is to strip naked as quick as you like!'

There followed more tears and further efforts at resistance. But Clement immediately took hold of her and within one minute had sent flying off everything which had veiled the alluring creature's maidenly modesty. The charms which decency normally required Octavie to keep hidden could not have been a better riposte to the delights which usage allowed her to display. It is unlikely that a whiter skin or more pleasing forms were ever seen, and yet so much freshness and innocence and delicacy were about to fall to these barbarous men. It was only to be defiled by them, it seemed, that Nature had showered her with so many advantages. The circle formed around her and, exactly as had happened with me, she was passed round in all directions. Antonin, in a fury, had not strength enough to resist: a cruel on- slaught upon Octavie's budding charms decided the homage to be paid and incense smoked at the feet of the god. Raphael, of a mind to think of more serious mat- ters, but in no state to be patient, seized the victim and positioned her according to his desires. Since she did nothing to accommodate him, he beseeched Clement to hold her for him. Octavie wept but her wailings went unheard. Fire blazed in the eyes of the execrable Italian. Master of the fortress which he was about to take by storm, it was as if he paused to examine his ways forward the better to overcome all resistance: he neither em- ployed ruse nor lingered over preparations. However great the disproportion between attacker and defender, the former did not hesitate to launch his onslaught. A heart-rending scream from the victim announced her final capitulation. But nothing could move the heart of her proud conqueror. The more she seemed to beg for mercy, the more ferociously he pressed her and, follow- ing my example, the hapless girl was ignominiously defiled while never ceasing to be a maid.

'Never was a prize more difficult to win,' said Raphael, regaining his composure. 'For the first time in my life, I thought I would fail in my attempt.'

'Let me take it from here,' said Antonin, preventing her from rising, 'there is more than one breach in the rampart and you have taken only one of them.'

So saying, he advanced proudly to do battle and a

moment later was master of the field. More groans were heard . . .

'God be praised!' said the horrid ghoul, 'I should have been uncertain of the completeness of the defeat but for the squawking of the vanquished. I value my triumphs only when it has cost tears.'

'In truth,' said Jerome, advancing with a bundle of wands in his hand, 'I shall not disturb her pleasant pose either, for it could not be better suited to what I have in mind.'

He gazed, touched, and felt, and then all at once the air was filled with a hideous swishing sound. The beautiful flesh changed colour, brightest crimson mingling with the whiteness of the lily. But what might on another occasion have afforded Love a moment of innocent diversion had moderation directed this maniacal practice, now turned instantly into a criminal act. No consideration stayed the hand of the heartless friar: the more the pupil moaned, the more strictly the master applied himself. Every part received equal treatment and none obtained grace in his sight. Soon there was not a single part of that beautiful body but bore the mark of his barbarity and it was over the bloody remnants of his odious pleasures that the perfidious friar finally quenched his burning fires.

'I shall be gentler by far than all that has gone before,' said Clement, taking the girl in his arms and planting an impure kiss upon her coral lips. 'Here is the altar on which I shall make my sacrifice.'

A few kisses more on those adorable lips, made by Venus herself, served to stoke him to new heights. He forced upon the unhappy girl the infamies which were his delectation and the sweetest refuge of love was befouled by horror.

The rest of the evening proved to be much like what you know of those occasions, with this difference, viz., that the beauty and touching youth of the girl inflamed the barbarians more effectively, so that their savagery was increased several fold and it was satiety rather than compassion which, having first sent her off to our chamber, restored to her, at least for a few hours, the calm of which she stood in such need. I should have liked to have been able to comfort her, at least on that first night, but, being required to spend it with Antonin, it was on the contrary I who might well have been reduced to needing succour. I had had the misfortune not to please, the word is quite unsuitable, but to excite more ardently than any of my companions the lecher's foul desires, and for a long time past very few weeks had gone by when I did not spend five or six nights in his room. When I got back the next morning, I found the new inmate in tears. I told her what I had formerly been told to calm me, but I had no more success with her than had been obtained with me. It is no easy thing to find solace for such an abrupt change in one's circumstances. Moreover, the girl had a great fund of piety, virtue, honour, and fine feeling, and in consequence her present state seemed all the more cruel to her. Raphael, who had taken a great fancy to her, kept her by him several nights running, and little by little she did as the rest did: she found consolation for her misfortunes in the hope of seeing them ended one day. Omphale had been right to say that seniority had no effect upon our being sent away, for the matter being dictated solely by the friars' whims or perhaps by subsequent girl-hunts outside, it could as well come after a week as after twenty years. Octavie had been with us for less than six weeks when Raphael came one day and told her she was to leave. She made us the same promises as Omphale had given and disappeared just as she had without our ever hearing what became of her.

We remained for about a month without seeing a new face arrive to take her place. It was during this interval that I, like Omphale, had occasion to be convinced that we were not the only women to live in the monastery and that there was another building which doubtless contained the same complement as ours. But Omphale had been able to do no more than surmise; my adventure, being much more conclusive, confirmed my own suspicions fully. This is how it came about. I had just spent the night with Raphael and was leaving his cell according to the customary practice at about seven in the morning when a Brother, as old and repulsive as ours, whom I had never seen before, suddenly debouched into the corridor with a tall girl of 18 or 20 who struck me as being beautiful enough to have sat for a painter. Raphael, who was to escort me back to our chamber, kept me waiting. He emerged as I came positively face to face with the girl; the Brother did not know what to do with her to get her out of my sight.

'Where are you taking that creature?' shouted the Superior in a fury.

'I'm bringing her to you, Reverend Father,' said the ghoulish go-between. 'Your Grace has perhaps forgotten that you gave me the order last night.'

'I said nine o'clock.'

'Seven, Monsignor. You told me you wanted to see her before you said mass.'

All this time, I stood gazing at this companion who stared back with the same astonishment.

'Come, the matter is of no importance,' said Raphael, ushering me back into his cell and bringing the other girl in too. 'Look here, Sophie,' said he, shutting the door, 'this girl holds the same position in another tower as you hold in yours: she too is a Doyenne. No harm will be done by allowing both our Doyennes to meet and, that you may know her thoroughly, Sophie, I shall now show you Marianne undressed.'

This Marianne, who appeared to me to be a very forward sort of girl, disrobed in a twinkling and Raphael, bidding me stimulate his desires, subjected her to his choicest pleasures as I looked on.

'That is what I wanted with her,' the blackguard declared when he was satisfied. 'Spending the night with one woman always makes me want another in the morning. Nothing is quite as insatiable as our urges; the greater the offerings we make to them, the hotter they burn. Of course, the outcome is always pretty much the same, yet we always imagine that there is better just around the corner. The instant our thirst for one woman is slaked is also the moment when the same drives kindle our desire for another. You both hold positions of trust and you must remain silent. Go now, Sophie, go, the Brother will take you back. I have a new mystery to celebrate with your companion here.'

I promised to say nothing as I was bid and went, absolutely certain now that we were not alone in serving the monstrous pleasures of these unbridled libertines.

But Octavie was replaced immediately. A young peasant girl of 12, fresh-faced and pretty but very inferior in beauty to her predecessor, was chosen to fill her shoes. Within two years, I had become the longest server. Florette and Cornélie duly left, both swearing like Omphale that I should hear news of them and neither succeeding any better than she. Both had just been replaced, Florette by a 15-year-old from Dijon, a plump, fat-cheeked creature who had in her favour only the bloom of youth, Cornélie by a girl from Autun, a real beauty, who came of a very upright family. Fortunately the latter, who was 16, had ousted me from my place in Antonin's affections. But then I realized that if I had been expunged from the lecher's good graces, I was also in immediate danger of losing my credit with all the others. The fickleness of all four made me tremble for my fate, for I was aware that it signalled my dismissal, and I was only too clear in my mind that my cruel superannuation was tantamount to a sentence of death, not to feel a moment of great alarm. A moment, did I say? Unhappy that I was, could I then still cling on to life? Should not my greatest happiness then be to have had that life ended? These reflections comforted me and helped me await my fate with such resignation that I made no effort to restore my credit. I felt the weight of the friars' spiteful dealings; hardly a moment went by when they did not find me at fault, scarcely a day when I was not punished. I prayed to Heaven and awaited the sentence. I was perhaps about to be given it when the hand of Providence, wearying of torturing me in the same continuing way, plucked me from my present abyss only to hurl me headlong into another. But let us not anticipate events. Allow me to begin by recounting the circumstances which finally delivered us from the clutches of these arrant libertines.

Of course, the same principle of vice rewarded was to dictate the course of events just as, to my eye, it always had at each crisis of my life. It was written that those who had tortured, humiliated, and chained me would receive, promptly and plain for me to see, high wages for their crimes, as though Providence was bent upon showing me the futility of virtue—a hard lesson which did not alter my ways and which, if I escape the sword which even at this instant hangs over me, shall never prevent my being the eternal slave of the deity which rules my heart.

Quite unexpectedly one morning, Antonin appeared in our chamber and announced that the Reverend Father Raphael, a relative and protégé of the Pope, had just been named Vicar-General of the Order of St Francis* by His Holiness.

'And I, my children,' he said, 'am to be Superior of the community of Lyons. Two new friars will soon be here to replace us. Indeed they may come before the day is over. We do not know them and it is as likely that they will send you all to your homes as it is that they will keep you here. But whatever your fate, I advise you for your own sakes and for the honour of the two brother friars we leave behind us to conceal all details of our proceedings and to admit only those things which cannot be gainsaid.'

News so flattering to our hopes prevented our denying the friar anything he appeared to desire, and we promised everything he asked yet still the wretch insisted on taking his leave of all four of us together. The end of our misfortunes now half-glimpsed, we had strength enough to bear this final onslaught without complaint. We refused him nothing and he left, never to set eyes on us again. We were served our dinner in the usual way. About two hours after this, Clement came to our chamber with two monks both venerable in age and features.

'You must confess, Father,' one of them said to Clement, 'you must confess that all your debauches have been quite disgraceful and that it is curious indeed that Heaven should have suffered them to continue for so long.'

Clement meekly agreed upon every head, apologizing for the failure of himself and his brother friars to introduce changes and saying that all four of them had found everything in exactly the same state as they now left it, that in truth inmates had come and gone but that, likewise finding the system of rotation in place, they had therefore done no more than follow custom as laid down by their predecessors.

'Very well,' resumed the same friar whom I took to be the new Superior, which indeed he was, 'but let us make an end at once to this execrable debauchery, Father. It would be sickening in men of the world, so I leave you to think how it would be viewed in men of the cloth.'

He next asked us what we wanted to become of us. Each of us answered that she would like to go back whence she had come or to be returned to her family.

'And so it shall be, my daughters,' said the friar, 'and I shall give each of you what money you require to go hence. But it is indispensable that you leave one after the other, at intervals of two days, that you go alone and on foot, and that you say nothing of what has happened in this place.'

We pledged ourselves to abide by these conditions. But the Superior was not satisfied by our word and urged us to partake of the Sacrament. None of us refused and there, kneeling at the altar, he made us swear that we should keep forever secret the things which had happened in the monastery. I did as the others and if, in your hearing, Madame, I now break that promise, it is because I respect the spirit rather than the letter of what the good priest then asked of me. His intention was

that no official complaint should ever be made and I am
quite certain that my relating of my adventures to you
could never possibly result in any unpleasantness for the
Order to which the friars belonged. My companions left
first and since we were absolutely forbidden to arrange
to meet anywhere and had been separated at the time of
the arrival of the new Superior, we never saw each other
again. I had asked to go to Grenoble and I was given 2
louis to see me there. Donning the clothes I had been
wearing on the day I arrived at the monastery, I found
the 8 louis which I had with me at that time and, buoyed
up with relief that I was forever fleeing that terrifying
refuge of vice and that I was leaving it in so easy and so
unexpected a manner, I struck out into the forest from
which I emerged on the Auxerre road at the same spot
where I had left it to walk of my own free will into the
trap. It was just three years after I had committed my
folly, that is, I was now 25 years old, or a few weeks off
it. My first thought was to throw myself on to my knees
and ask God to grant me new pardons for the involuntary offences which I had committed. I did so with even
greater compunction than when prostrate before the
fouled altars of the ignoble monastery which I had left
with such joy in my heart. Tears of regret flowed from
my eyes. 'Alas,' said I, 'I was pure when long ago I
turned off this very road, being guided by a principle of
faith which was so cruelly abused. But in what sorry state
do I now find myself!' These bitter reflections being
modified somewhat by my pleasure on finding myself
free, I went on my way. To avoid boring you further,
Madame, with details which I fear would try your patience, I shall henceforward dwell, if you approve, only
on those incidents which either taught me important
lessons or which further changed the course of my life.
After resting for a few days at Lyons, I chanced one day
to glance at a foreign gazette belonging to the woman in
whose house I lodged. Imagine my surprise on finding
therein crime once more rewarded and one of the principal authors of my misfortunes raised to a pinnacle!

Rodin, the ignoble doctor who had so cruelly punished me for preventing his committing a murder and had been forced to flee from France no doubt for committing others, had just, according to my news-sheet, been appointed Surgeon-in-Chief to the King of Sweden, a post carrying rich emoluments. 'Let the scoundrel prosper,' said I, 'let him enjoy the fruits, if Providence so wishes, while you, wretch that you are, must go on suffering alone and without complaint since it is written that gall and tribulation are the grim wages of virtue!'

I left Lyons after sojourning three days there and set out on the Dauphiné road, full of wild hope that some small measure of prosperity lay waiting for me in that province. I had scarcely gone two leagues from Lyons, still journeying by foot as was my custom, having a couple of shifts and handkerchiefs in my pouches, when I met an old woman who seemed to be distressed. She came up to me and begged me to give her alms. Being naturally compassionate and knowing no charm on earth comparable to that of helping a fellow human being, I instantly got out my purse intending to take a few coins from it to give to the woman.* But the unworthy creature, who was nimbler than I was, though I had at first taken her to be old and broken-winded, adroitly snatched my purse and sent me sprawling with a hefty punch to my stomach. When I next saw her, which was not until I was on my feet again, she was standing a hundred paces off in the company of four rough men who made threatening gestures in my direction each time I tried to approach them. 'O just Heaven!' I cried bitterly, 'so it really is impossible for a virtuous impulse to start within me without its being instantly punished by the cruellest misfortunes I have to fear in the whole universe!' In that dreadful moment, all my courage was on the point of deserting me. Today I entreat Heaven to forgive me, but at that moment rebellion was not far from my heart. Two appalling courses of action now presented themselves to me: I was of a mind either to join up with these footpads who had cruelly wronged me the moment before, or else to go back to Lyons and take to a life of vice. God granted that I did not succumb to either and although the light of hope which He lit once more in my heart was to prove no more than the dawn of more terrible adversities yet to come, I nevertheless give Him thanks for being my prop and my sustainer. The chain of misfortunes which has led me to the scaffold, though I am innocent, will bring me no end but death. Other expedients I might have tried would have brought me shame, remorse, and infamy, and death is less cruel in my eyes than all of these.

I continued on my way, resolving to sell the few effects I had with me when I reached Vienne* and thence to strike out for Grenoble. I was walking along dejectedly and was within a quarter of a league from the town when, on a piece of level ground away to the right of the road, I saw two mounted men trampling a third beneath the hooves of their horses. Leaving him for dead, they galloped off at high speed. This savage spectacle moved me to tears. 'Alas!' said I, 'here is someone even more unfortunate than I. I at least still have my health and my strength, I am able to earn my living and if he is not rich and in the same pass as myself, then he will be a cripple for the rest of his life. And what will become of him then?' However much I ought to have been on my guard against such feelings of compassion, and though the punishment to which they had recently led me was cruel indeed, I could not refrain from heeding them once more. I went up to the dying man. I had with me a little smelling-water which I made him inhale. He opened his eyes to the light, and his first reactions being of gratitude I was prompted to persist in caring for him. I tore one of my shifts for a bandage; it was one of my few remaining effects and I had counted on it to prolong my life, yet I rent it into strips for this man, staunched the blood which flowed from numerous wounds, made him drink a little of the small quantity of wine which I carried in a bottle to revive my faltering steps at weary moments, and used the rest to bathe his bruises. In the end, the unfortunate man suddenly regained both strength and heart. Although he was not mounted and was somewhat casually dressed, he did not appear to be without means, having a few costly items on him, viz., rings, a watch, and other pieces of finery, though his mishap had left them in a sorry state. When at last he was able to speak, he asked me who was the angel of mercy who had helped him and enquired what he could do to show his gratitude. Being guileless enough to believe that a heart bound by gratitude must be mine forever, I believed I could quite safely enjoy the sweet pleasure of sharing my own tears with a man who had the moment before himself been weeping in my arms. I related all my adventures to him. He listened with interest and when I ended with an account of the latest catastrophe to befall me, the telling of which opened his eyes to the cruel state of destitution I was then in, he declared:

'How happy I am at least to be able to say how grateful I feel for everything you have done for me! My name is Dalville,' my adventurer went on, 'and I own a château, a rather fine one, in the mountains fifteen leagues from here. I should very much like to invite you to stay with me there if you would care to come—and lest the invitation should alarm your modesty, allow me to explain at once exactly how you could be useful to me. I am married and my wife needs at her side a woman she can depend upon. We lately dismissed a woman who turned out to be a bad lot. I should like you to take her place.'

I thanked my protector humbly and asked how it chanced that a man such as I took him to be had ventured forth unaccompanied on his travels, thus leaving himself vulnerable to attacks by footpads in the manner he had just experienced.

'Being strong, young, and active,' said Dalville, 'I have long been in the habit of travelling in this fashion from my home to Vienne: both my health and my purse are the better for it. Not that my circumstances are such that I need to worry about expense, for I am rich, thank God, and you should see how rich for yourself by being good enough to accept my offer to come home with me. The two men you saw me fall foul of are a couple of down-at-heel gentlemen who live in the district. They have nothing but a name and a sword, one being a soldier of the Guards and the other a Musketeer, which is to say they are a pair of rogues and cheats. Last week I won a hundred louis from them in a gaming-house at Vienne. Since they were nowhere near having even a fraction of the money between them, I agreed to take their note for the sum. I met up with them today and asked them for what they owe me. You saw for yourself the manner in which they paid me.'

I was commiserating with my honest gentleman over the double misfortune which had befallen him when he proposed that we should make a start.

'Thanks to your attentions, I feel somewhat recovered,' said Dalville. 'It will soon be dark. Let us make for a hostelry I know of about two leagues distant. From there, with horses we can get in the morning, perhaps we might be able to reach home by evening.'

Fully determined to take advantage of the helping hand which Heaven seemed to have extended to me, I helped Dalville to get to his feet and start walking. I gave him my support along the way and, carefully avoiding all known roads, we proceeded as the crow flies towards the Alps along small side-tracks. We found the hostelry of which Dalville had spoken about two leagues further on and ate a decent dinner there in good spirits. When the meal was over, he commended me to the mistress of the hostelry who let me sleep in her bed and in the morning, mounted on two hired mules and accompanied on foot by one of the inn's stable-lads, we reached the border of Dauphiné, still set on our course for the mountains. Dalville, having received a thorough drubbing, was incapable of completing the journey without interruption and I was not sorry for this on my own account for, little used to this mode of travel, I was no less discomfited than he. We halted at Virieu* where I was shown the same honest attentions by my protector, and the next morning we went on our way again, still heading in the same direction. At about four o'clock in the afternoon, we reached the foot of the mountains. Our way now becoming virtually impassable, Dalville ordered the stable-boy to stay close by me for fear of accidents and we picked our way through the gorges. Constantly turning and climbing, we made no more than four leagues, by which time we had left all human habitation and frequented roads so far behind us that I believed I had got to the end of the world. Despite myself, I was gripped by a slight feeling of unease. As I strayed further into this inaccessible rocky fastness, I was reminded of the twisting paths of the forest surrounding the monastery of Sainte-Marie-des-Bois, and the dislike I had conceived of all solitary places made me shudder at my present environs.* At last, we saw a château teetering on the very edge of an awesome precipice. It seemed to hang suspended atop a sheer rock face and looked more like the lair of ghostly spirits than a dwelling-place intended for humankind. We could see the château but no visible path that led up to it. The track we were following, used only by goats and littered with stones, took us there, however, though in an endless upward spiral. 'That is where I live,' said Dalville when he judged I had seen the château, and on my expressing my surprise at his living in such an out of the way place, he replied with extreme tartness that one lived where one could. I was as much shocked as frightened by his tone. Nothing escapes our attention when misfortune threatens, and the slightest inflexion of the voice of those on whose mercies we depend will strangle or revive our hopes. But since it was now too late to go back, I gave no outward sign of any misgivings. At length, after we had ridden round and round the ancient pile, it suddenly loomed up before us. Dalville got down from his mule and bidding me do likewise returned them both to the stable-lad, paid him, and ordered him to return whence he came—another piece of business which I found exceeding distasteful. Dalville noticed my unease.

'What is it, Sophie?' said he, as we walked towards his house. 'You have not left France. My château is on the borders of Dauphiné, but is still on French territory.'

'That may be so, sir,' I replied, 'but whatever made you decide to settle in such a bandits' lair?'

'It's no bandits' lair,' said Dalville, glancing slyly at me as we proceeded. 'It is not quite the lair of bandits, my dear, but neither is it a place where very honest folk live.'

'O sir,' I replied, 'you are frightening me. Where are you taking me?'

'I am taking you, whore, where you will be set to work for coiners,'* said Dalville and, seizing me by the arm, he dragged me by force across a drawbridge which, being let down at our approach, was now immediately raised once we were inside. 'Here you are,' he added when we reached the courtyard. 'Do you see this well?' he went on, pointing to a wide-mouthed, deep pit close by the gate where two naked women in chains were turning the wheel which raised the water which flowed into a storage cistern.* 'These are your companions and this your task. You will toil twelve hours each day keeping the wheel turning and, like your companions, you will be duly and roundly beaten each time you slacken your efforts. In return, you will be allowed six ounces of black bread and a dish of beans each day. As to freedom, give up all thought of it, for you will never see the sky above your head again. You will die in harness and be thrown down that shaft which you see next to the well, to join the thirty or forty who are there already, and then you will be replaced by another like you.'

'Just Heaven, sir,' I cried, throwing myself at Dalville's feet. 'Be so good as to recall that I saved your life, that being momentarily moved by gratitude you appeared bent on making me happy, and that my rightful expectation was not to be reduced to this.'

'What do you mean, pray, by this sense of "gratitude"

with which you imagine you hold me fast?' said Dalville. 'Come, you must think straighter, you witless creature. What exactly did you do when you came to my aid? You had the choice of continuing on your way or of helping me, and you chose the latter because your heart prompted you to do so. Which means that you did what gave you pleasure. Now how the devil can you say I should be under any obligation to reward you for giving yourself pleasure?* How can it enter your head to imagine that a man such as myself, rolling in gold and wealth, with an income of a million a year and ready to travel as far as Venice to enjoy what it can buy him, should ever allow himself to be indebted to a nobody such as you? Had you raised me from the dead, I should still owe you nothing since what you did was for your own benefit. To work, slave, to work! Know this: though civilization has upset the established order of Nature, it has nevertheless not deprived Nature of her rights. In the beginning, she created strong and weak, her intention being that the latter be eternally subordinate to the former as the lamb still is to the lion or the insect to the elephant. The adroitness and wit of humankind determined the relative positions of individuals, for soon it was not physical strength which decided rank but the strength a man acquired through wealth. The richest man was the strongest man, the poorest was the weakest. But in spite of this change in the manner by which an individual came by his power, the superiority of the strong over the weak remained fundamental to the laws of Nature, according to which it mattered not if the rope which secured the weak was held by a man who was rich or a man who was strong, or whether its coils weighed heaviest on the weakest or the poorest.* Now this sense of gratitude on which you stake your claims on me, Sophie, is not recognized by Nature. It was never a part of her laws that the pleasure one person took in obliging another should be a reason for the recipient to abandon his rights over his benefactor. Are these sentiments in which you take such pride to be found among animals which are examples to us all? If I dominate you by my wealth or strength, is it natural that I should have to give up my rights because in helping me you either self-servingly got the satisfaction you wanted or else consciously set out to help yourself? But even if the helping hand were extended by one equal to another, the self-respect of a lofty soul would never permit itself to be debased by gratitude. The man who receives is always a man humiliated, and is not the humiliation he feels a sufficient return for the person who obliged him? Is it not balm to our pride to rise above our neighbour? Does the obliger need anything more? And if the obligation which humbles the pride of the obliged is burdensome to him, by what right shall he be bound to tolerate it? Why should I consent to be humiliated each time my benefactor looks at me? Ingratitude, far from being a vice, is therefore the virtue of proud souls as surely as charity is the virtue merely of faint hearts. The slave talks of gratitude to his master because he stands in need of it, but the master, guided by his passions and by Nature, must yield only to what promotes his interest or flatters him. Oblige whomever you like if you find pleasure in it, but do not expect rewards for enjoying the experience.'

At these words, which Dalville gave me no time to answer, two underlings, acting upon his orders, seized me, stripped off my clothes, chained me to my companions, and put me to work alongside them that same evening, no opportunity being given me to rest after the wearisome journey I had made. I had been toiling at the loathsome wheel for less than a quarter of an hour when the full company of coiners, having ended their labours for the day, crowded round, with their leader at their head, and proceeded to inspect me. They all heaped sarcastic, rude remarks upon me on account of the mark of shame which, though innocent, I bore upon my hapless body. They drew close, feeling me roughly all over and casting aspersions spiced with pungent pleasantries upon everything which, despite myself, I exposed to their view. This painful scene being over, they retreated a few paces. Thereupon Dalville, picking up a horsewhip which was always conveniently kept nearby, struck me with it all over five or six times with all his strength.

'That, you slut, is what you will get,' said he as he applied the lash, 'each time you are unfortunate enough to fail in your duty. This time it was not for shirking, but just to give you an idea of how I deal with anyone who does shirk.'

Each stroke broke the skin and, never having felt such intense pain at the hands of either Bressac or the brutal friars, I shrieked and struggled against my chains. My contortions and my screams were a matter of great mirth for the monsters who looked on and I was given the cruel satisfaction of learning that if there are men who, whether moved by vengeance or by ignoble sensuality, can take pleasure from the pain of others, then there are others barbaric enough to enjoy the same delights for no other motive than to feel their power or indulge the most ghoulish curiosity. Man is thus naturally evil. He is only a whit less evil when driven by his passions as when he is not, and in both cases the ills which befall his fellows are like to make execrable sport for him.

Three dank pens, each separate from the other and all barred and bolted like prison cells, stood around the well. One of the men who had chained me showed me which was mine and I withdrew into it after first receiving from him the ration of water, beans, and bread which was intended for me. It was there that I was at last able to contemplate undisturbed the full horror of my plight. 'Is it possible,' thought I, 'that there are men barbaric enough to smother their feelings of gratitude and the virtue to which I for my part will gladly yield whenever the plight of some honest person furnishes me with an opportunity to feel it warm within me? Can virtue then be so little esteemed by men? And can the man who smothers it with so much inhumanity be anything other than a monster?' My mind was occupied with these reflections which I watered with my tears, when suddenly the door of my cell was flung open: it was Dalville.

Without a word, without uttering a sound, he set down the candle which had lit his way, leaped upon me like a savage beast, forced me to submit to his desires, using his fists to repulse the resistance I tried to put up against him and scornfully brushing aside the protests which sprang from my wits, took his brutal pleasure, picked up his glim, went out and bolted the door. 'O mercy!' thought I, 'is it possible that indecency could ever be carried further than this? What difference can there be between a man such as this and the least savage creature of the forest?'

The sun came up before I had enjoyed a single instant's repose. Our cells were opened, we were chained once more, and we resumed our grim task. My companions were both aged between 25 and 30 years. Although they had been drained by wretchedness and crippled by physical overwork, they still exhibited a few remnants of their beauty; their figures were handsome and their waists small and one of the two still had magnificent hair. A dismal conversation with them informed me that both, at different times, were former mistresses of Dalville, one in Lyons and the other in Grenoble; that he had brought them to this hideous place where they had lived on the same footing with him for a few years; and that to reward them for pleasures they had afforded him, he had sentenced both to this humiliating drudgery. From them, I further learned that he currently had a charming mistress but that she, more fortunate than they, would in all likelihood follow him to Venice, where he was then about to go, if the considerable coinage which he had lately shipped to Spain resulted in his getting the letters of change he was waiting for before embarking on his Italian venture, since he did not wish to travel with his counterfeit gold to Venice. He never sent any there; it was always to his agents in countries other than the one he was shortly to visit that he expedited his false coin. As he never as a consequence had any money in the place where he wished to stay except for paper wealth drawn upon a different nation, his operations could never be found out and his fortune remained upon solid ground. But the structure might come crashing about his ears at any moment and the decampment he was planning was entirely dependent upon the success of this latest negotiation in which the larger part of his funds was engaged. If Cadiz accepted his piastres and louis d'or and in return sent him unimpeachable bills drawn on Venice, he would be set up for the rest of his life. But if his knavery were discovered, then he stood in danger of being denounced and hanged as he deserved. 'Alas!' said I on learning these particulars, 'Providence must for once be just. It will not permit a monster like this to succeed and we shall all three of us be revenged.' At noon, we were given two hours rest which we used, each going her separate way, to catch our breath and eat in our cells. At two, we were chained again and forced to turn the wheel until nightfall. We were never permitted to go inside the château. The reason for our being kept naked for five months of the year was the unbearable heat and the excessive work which we did, but also (as my companions assured me) so that we were more vulnerable to the beatings which our fierce master administered from time to time. In winter, we were given trousers and a waistcoat which fitted like a second skin, a type of garment which, enclosing us pretty tightly, similarly made our bodies easy of access to the beatings of our tormentor. Dalville did not make an appearance on that first day, but about midnight he repeated what he had done the night preceding. I tried to use the occasion to entreat him to mitigate my fate. 'And by what right do you ask this?' said the barbarian. 'Because I care to indulge a whim with you? Am I then to kneel down and beg your favour which, when granted, would entitle you to ask for something in return? I ask nothing of you: I take. I do not see that because I exercise a right over you once it must necessarily follow that I should therefore abstain from doing so twice. There is no love in what I do. Love is a sentiment which was ever a stranger to my heart. I make use of a woman out of necessity, just as a man might use a pisspot for another kind of need. But I never bestow upon her, subject as she is to my money and my authority, either esteem or affection and, owing what I take solely to my own efforts and requiring nothing from her but submission, I fail to see why, given all this, I should have to show her any gratitude. Such would be tantamount to saying that the thief who robs a man of his purse in a wood because he is the stronger, should show his gratitude for the wrong he has done him. The same holds true for a violence performed upon a woman: it may entitle a man to repeat the violation but can never be an adequate reason why he should grant her any form of compensation.'

So saying, Dalville, having taken his pleasure, quitted me abruptly and left me deep in further thoughts which, as you might imagine, were not to his credit. In the evening, he came to watch us at work and finding that we had not supplied the regular daily quantity of water, he took down his cruel horsewhip and beat all three of us bloody. This did not prevent his coming to me that night (though I had been as little spared as the others) and behaving towards me as he had on the previous night. I showed him the weals he had raised on me and was bold enough again to remind him of the time I tore my shift to bind his wounds. But, preoccupied with his pleasure, the only answer Dalville gave my recriminations was a dozen cuffs interspersed with divers curses, and the moment he was satisfied he simply got up and went out as was his wont. This state of affairs lasted a month, after which time I at least obtained from my tormentor the relief of not being exposed at night to the dreadful anguish of seeing him take what he was so unworthy to have. Yet my life did not change one whit. I received neither more nor less kindness nor was I treated more or less harshly than before.

A year went by and still I was in this cruel pass when news finally spread throughout the house that not only was Dalville's fortune made and not only was he now in receipt of the vast sums in paper bills for Venice which he had wanted, but he had been asked to supply several further millions in false coin, payment for which would be made in the form of whatever bills drawn on Venice he cared to ask for. The villain could not possibly have made a larger and more unexpected fortune: when he left, he would have an annual revenue of more than a million, and that was to reckon without his further expectations. Such was the latest example which Providence thrust before me, such her freshest manner of seeking to persuade me that prosperity was the wages of crime and misfortune the reward of virtue.

Dalville made ready to leave but on the eve came to me at midnight, though he had not done so in a very long time. It was he himself who told me about his fortune and announced his imminent departure. I threw myself at his feet and beseeched him in the most earnest terms to restore me to liberty and to furnish me with as little money as he thought fit to see me to Grenoble.

'When you got to Grenoble, you would denounce me.'

'O sir,' I said, leaving his knees moist with my tears, 'Then I give you my oath that I shall never set foot there. But to make you quite easy on this score, there is something you could do: take me with you to Venice. Perhaps there I should find hearts less hard than they are in my own country, and if you were to carry me hence, I swear on everything I hold most sacred that I should never bother you again.'

'You will get no help and no money from me,' the arch-blackguard replied harshly. 'Anything which savours of alms or charity is so repugnant to my character that had I three times the gold I presently have, I still should not give a farthing to a beggar-man. I have considered principles on this question and I shall never stray from them. The poor man is part of the natural order. By creating men unequal in strength, Nature has clearly shown us her wish that inequality be preserved, even though civilization should alter natural laws. The poor have replaced the weak, as I have already explained. To ease their plight would mean overturning the established order, opposing the natural order, and destroying the balance which underpins Nature's sublime arrangement of things. It would mean striving for equality which would be fatal to society and encouraging idleness and sloth. It would teach the poor to pick the pocket of any rich man who chose not to give them charity, a lesson the more easily learnt from the habit they would acquire of expecting to have money without working for it.'*

'O sir! How harsh your principles are! Would you say the same things if you had not always been rich?'

'I was not always rich, far from it. But I got the better of fate. I stamped on the mirage of virtue which invariably leads a man to gaol or the hangman's noose. I realized very early on that religion, philanthropy, and charity were sure stumbling-blocks placed in the path of anyone who aspired to wealth and success and I have built my fortune on the ruins of human misconceptions. It was by mocking the laws of God and man, running roughshod over the weak who barred my way, abusing the good faith and gullibility of other people, and ruining the poor and robbing the rich that I have made my steep way up to the temple of the god to whom I kneeled. Why did you not do likewise? Your fortune was in your own hands to make. Has the imaginary virtue which you chose instead consoled you for the sacrifices which you have made in its name? But it is too late, you miserable creature, too late. Shed tears for your mistakes, suffer and, if you can, try and find in your cherished illusions those things which your gullibility has prevented you from enjoying.'

With these last cruel words, Dalville leaped upon me. But he was now so odious to me and his atrocious ideas inspired such hatred in my heart that I fought him off roughly. He attempted to use force but did not succeed. He made good his defeat with cruelties: I was beaten almost senseless but still victory was denied him. His fires, having burned to no purpose, died down and the tears shed by the rabid wretch, which were quite wasted on me, were my revenge at last for the outrages he had committed against me.

Before setting out the next day, the blackguard subjected us to a fresh scene of cruelty and barbarity of which there is no equal in the annals of the Andronici or the reigns of Nero, Tiberius, and Wenceslas.* It was generally believed that his mistress was to go with him and he had bade her deck herself out accordingly. But when he was about to mount his horse, he brought her to where we were.

'Here is your billet, you vile minx,' he barked at her, and thereupon ordered her to strip to the skin. 'I should like my comrades to have something to remember me by, and so, as a token of my esteem, I shall leave them the woman they believe I am most fond of. But since only three are needed here and since I am about to set out on a dangerous road where my weapons will prove their worth, I shall try out my pistols on one of you.'

So saying, he cocked one, aimed it at the breast of each of us as we turned the wheel and finally, turning to one of his former mistresses:

'Go,' said he, blowing her brains out, 'go and tell news of me in the other world! Go tell the Devil that it is Dalville, the richest rogue on earth, who thus defies both his hand and the hand of Heaven with such insolence!'

His hapless victim had not been killed outright and struggled for some time in her chains. It was a horrid sight and the vile monster feasted his eyes on it with intense delight. In the end, he ordered the chains to be taken off her and put on to his mistress. He insisted on watching her push the wheel around three or four times and on personally administering a dozen lashes with the horsewhip. Then, when these barbaric acts were over, the fiend got on his horse and, accompanied by two men, rode out of our sight for ever.

The day after Dalville went away, everything became different. His successor, a mild, right-thinking man, ordered our immediate release.

'This is no fit employment for the gentle, weaker sex,'

he told us kindly, 'but the work of animals to serve the wheel. The business on which we are engaged is already crime enough. We should not outrage the Supreme Being further with gratuitous acts of cruelty.'

He installed us in the château, disinterestedly reinstated Dalville's mistress to all the domestic functions of which she previously had charge, and employed my companion and myself in the workshop where we stamped out the coins—a much less tiring occupation certainly and one for which we were recompensed with very good rooms to sleep in and excellent eating. After a space of two months, Dalville's successor, who was named Roland, informed us of the safe arrival of his colleague at Venice. He had settled there, had turned his bills into money, and was enjoying his prosperity exactly as he had flattered himself he would.

The fate of his successor was very different. The luckless Roland was an honest man: it took no more than this for him to be promptly crushed. One day, when all was quiet in the château and, ruled by the laws of this good master, we were busying ourselves with our work which, though criminal, was easy and agreeable, the walls suddenly came under siege. Denied entry by the drawbridge, the attackers clambered across the moat and, before those inside had time even to think of defending themselves, the place was overrun by more than a hundred mounted officers of the constabulary. There was no course but surrender. We were chained together like animals, shackled and set upon the backs of horses, and carried off to Grenoble. 'O Heaven!' said I, as we arrived, 'here at last is the town where I was foolish enough to think that happiness would begin for me!' The trial of the coiners soon came to a judgement: all were sentenced to hang. The mark I bore being observed, my judges scarcely troubled to question me, and I was about to be sentenced along with the others when I spoke up in the hope of at last attracting a measure of compassion from the celebrated magistrate† who was a credit to the

† Monsieur Servant* [*Author's note*].

bench: an upright judge, respected citizen, and enlightened philosopher, his celebrated and glorious name will be carved in the temple of Memory by his charity and humanity. He heard me out, but more, being won over to my good faith and to the truth of my tale of misfortune, he condescended to give me the comfort of his tears. O worthy man! I owe you a homage of respect: grant my heart leave to give you this mark of my esteem. You will not find the gratitude of an unfortunate woman heavy to bear and the tribute she offers in honour of your great and noble heart will ever give hers its sweetest felicity. Monsieur S. became my personal advocate, my griefs were heard, my groans found homes in kindly souls, and my tears flowed over hearts which, not being made of flint towards me, were further softened by his generous pleading. The general statements sworn by the criminals who were to be executed, being favourable to my cause, buttressed the zeal of this man who had taken it up. I was held to have been abducted and was declared innocent. My name was cleared, the charges against me were dropped, and I was unconditionally discharged, free once more to decide my own fate. To these services, my protector added the raising of a subscription for me which brought near to a hundred pistoles to my profit. It was at last a glimpse of happiness, my best hopes seemed about to be realized, and I believed I had reached the end of my misfortunes, when it pleased Providence to teach me that I still had a long road to travel.

On leaving prison, I had taken a room at an inn opposite the bridge over the river Isère where I had been assured that I should be respectably lodged. Following the advice given to me by Monsieur S., my intention was to remain there a while and make shift to find myself a position in the town or, if I did not succeed in this, to go back to Lyons armed with letters of recommendation with which he would be kind enough to furnish me. I was eating what is called the set dinner at the inn when, on the second day, I perceived that I was being closely watched by a stout, very well dressed woman who went about under the title of Baroness. Examining her in my turn, I fancied I recognized her. Each of us stepping forward to greet the other, we embraced like two people who have met but cannot remember where. Then, taking me to one side, the ample Baroness said:

'Sophie! Surely I am not mistaken! Are you not the Sophie I rescued ten years ago from the Palace prison. Do you not know your Dubois?'

Scarcely comforted by this discovery, I nevertheless gave her a civil answer. But I was dealing with the cleverest, most cunning woman in France and I could not escape her. Dubois said the kindest, most courteous things and told me that like the rest of the town she had followed my case with interest, though she had not known that I had been the object of it. With my customary weakness, I allowed myself to be led to her chamber and there recounted my misfortunes to her.

'O my dear,' she said, embracing me again, 'if I wanted to have a quiet word with you in private, it was to tell you that I have made my fortune and that everything I possess is now yours to dispose of. Look here,' she said, and she opened caskets filled with gold and diamonds. 'This is the fruit of my industry. But had I, like you, worshipped virtue, I should have been hanged long ago or left to rot in gaol.'

'O Madame,' said I, 'if you owe these riches to crime alone, then Providence, which never fails to be just at the last, will not allow you to enjoy them for long.'

'You are mistaken,' Dubois said. 'Do not think that Providence always favours the virtuous. Take care lest a passing moment of prosperity should fill up your head with such misleading notions. It is a matter of indifference to the continued working of the laws of Providence if one man leads a life of vice while another treads the path of virtue. Providence requires equal quantities of vice and virtue, and the individual who practises either the one or the other is the smallest item in its calculations. Listen to me, Sophie, and listen well.

You have wit and sense and I should like to see you come round finally to this view. It is not the choice which a man makes between vice or virtue, my dear, which enables him to be happy, since vice, like virtue, is simply a manner of behaving towards others. It is therefore not a matter of following one rather than the other but simply of how one makes one's way along the common path. He who strays from that path is always in the wrong. In a wholly virtuous world, I should advise you to follow virtue since, all rewards being related to its practice, your happiness would be inextricably dependent upon it. And in a wholly corrupt world, I should never advise anything except the pursuit of vice. Whoever does not tread the path taken by others will surely perish, for every obstacle which bars his way will stub his foot and, since he is always the weaker of the two forces, it follows necessarily that he will come off the worse in the encounter. In vain do civil laws seek to restore order and return mankind to virtue: being too corrupt to undertake the task and too weak to bring it off, they may make men momentarily turn their backs on the common highway but will never make them wander off it for good. When the general interest of people prompts them to do evil, it follows that he who will not be corrupted along with the rest must perforce rise up against the general interest. Now what happiness can a man expect if he is perpetually at odds with the interest of others? You will say that it is vice which is hostile to the interest of men and this I should concede in a world where the vicious are equal in number to the virtuous, since in such a world the interest of the one clashes noisily with the interest of the other. But such is far from true in a society which is utterly corrupt, for there my vices, harming only the man who is vicious (there being only such), would turn his mind to other vices which would compensate him for his losses, and he and I would both be happy. There would result a general effervescence, a multiplicity of conflicts and mutually inflicted wounds, in which each person, now making good what he lost the moment before, constantly finds that he has regained the winning hand. If vice is a danger only to virtue, it is because virtue is too weak-kneed and timid to take the initiative. But if virtue be banished from the face of the earth, then vice, harming only those who are vicious, will cease to be bothersome: it will hatch further vices but will not taint virtue. "Ah," you say, "but what of the beneficial effects of virtue?" This too is a sophism: in reality, these "beneficial effects" benefit only the weak and do not profit the man whose energies make him self-sufficient, whose resourcefulness is all he requires to correct the vagaries of fate. What can you have expected all your life other than to fail, my dear, since you always chose to go in the opposite direction to everybody else? If you had decided to swim with the current, you would have reached a safe haven as I have. Does the man who journeys up a river arrive at his destination as quickly as the man who travels down it? The first goes against Nature and the second drifts with it. You speak much to me of Providence, but what proof do you have that Providence loves order and therefore virtue? Has it not given you enough examples of its inherent unfairness and arbitrariness? Is it by visiting upon mankind war, pestilence, and famine, is it by creating a universe which is vicious in every respect, that Providence, in your eyes, makes manifest its extreme love of virtue? And why should you think that vicious persons should incur its displeasure since Providence itself operates strictly through vice, both its will and its works being nothing but wickedness and corruption, crime and chaos? In any case, whence comes the impulse which leads us to do evil? Is it not implanted in us by the hand of Providence? Is there a single wish or sensation which does not come to us from the same source? Is it therefore reasonable to argue that Providence would allow us keep, or give us a taste for anything which would not further its designs? If therefore vices serve the purposes of Providence, why should we want to combat them, by what right should we strive for their destruction, and why should we turn a deaf ear to them? If the world were a little more philosophical, everything would soon be in its rightful place again, and legislators and governors would see that the vices which they denounce and punish so sternly can sometimes be much more useful than the virtues which they preach but never reward.'

'But even were I weak enough, Madame, to adopt your wicked doctrine,' I answered my corruptress, 'how would you silence the remorse which it would constantly breed in my heart?'

'Remorse is an illusion, Sophie,' Dubois went on. 'It is nothing but the witless grumbling of minds too weak to dare to stop its voice.'

'But can its voice be stopped?'

'There is nothing easier, for we repent only those things which we are not in the habit of doing. If you repeat over and over the actions which make you feel remorseful, you would quickly put out their fire. Raise the torch of passion against them, vent on them the irresistible laws of self-interest, and you will discover that they evaporate like the morning mist. Remorse is not the infallible test of crime: it is no more than the badge of a mind which is easily enslaved. If some non-sensical order were to be given which forbade you to leave this room, then however convinced you were that you would be doing no wrong by doing so, you would not go through the door without a feeling of guilt. So it is quite untrue that only criminal actions give rise to remorse. If you could bring yourself to see how meaningless crime is, or how necessary crimes are to Nature's overall scheme of things, it would be as easy for you to overcome remorse as it would be to commit criminal acts—just as easy, in fact, as it would be for you to silence the remorse which would follow your quitting this room in contravention of the illegal order you had received to stay in it. We must begin by analysing exactly what men call "crime", starting from the conviction that what they describe as such is nothing more than a want of respect for the laws and manners of their nation; that what is called crime in France ceases to be criminal a hundred leagues beyond its borders; that in practice there is no action which is universally considered to be a crime; that in consequence there is in rational terms nothing which truly warrants the name of crime; and that the whole question is no more than a matter of opinion and geography.* Given this, you will see how absurd it is to submit to practising virtues which pass for vices elsewhere, and to avoid committing crimes which under other skies are thought to be good actions. I ask you: is it possible that these conclusions, reached after mature reflection, would still breed remorse in the heart of a man who on French soil, whether for his pleasure or out of self-interest, commits an act of Chinese or Japanese virtue which would, however, incur the law's displeasure in his native land? Would he be stopped in his course by this fanciful hair-splitting? And would it have sufficient sway over him to make him feel remorse if he had something of a philosophical cast of mind? Now remorse is merely a function of a prohibition. It arises as an effect of the violation of a prohibition and not as an effect of an action: is it a wise feeling which we should allow to persist in us, or should we not do better to strangle it at birth? Let us rather acquire the habit of thinking of actions which make us remorseful as being neutral; let us judge them in the light of a serious study of the manners and customs of all the nations of the world; and then, having looked at them in this way, let us commit those actions again, whatever they may be, as often as we can. Then should we see the torch of reason put an end to remorse and dispel the gloomy mind-workings which are but the product of ignorance, cowardice, and education. For thirty years, Sophie, an unending train of vices and crimes has been leading me step by step along the road to this brink of fortune where I now stand: two or three more successful tilts and I shall have risen out of the condition of poverty and beggardom in which I was born to an estate worth

50,000 livres a year. Do you imagine that throughout my brilliant career I ever once felt the prick of remorse? You must not think so, for I never did. Even if at this stage in the game some dreadful calamity were to cast me from my pinnacle into the abyss, I still should not give remorse houseroom. I should blame other people or my own want of skill, but I should remain at peace with my conscience.'*

'That may be,' said I, 'but pray allow me to dwell a moment on the philosophical principles you have invoked. By what right do you insist that my conscience should be as firm as yours, for mine has not been accustomed from childhood to overcome the same scruples as you have? On what grounds do you say that my mind, which does not work like yours, can adapt to your way of thinking? You admit that there is a finite quantity of good and evil in Nature and that it follows therefore that there must be a certain number of people who do good and another category of persons who do evil. The policy which I have chosen is, by your own principles, natural. You cannot therefore ask me to depart from the laws which Nature prescribes for me. Furthermore, since you say you have found happiness in the career which you have followed, I should in my turn find it equally impossible to meet with felicity by departing from the course on which I am embarked. Nor should you think that the vigilance of the law will allow law-breakers to go on their way untroubled for long. Have you not just seen an example of its working for yourself? Out of fifteen wicked men whose company I was unfortunate enough to keep, fourteen have died shameful deaths.'

'Is that what you call misfortune? Tell me: how much does shame matter to a man who has abandoned all principles? When the final ditch has been crossed, when honour is no more than a quaint fancy, reputation a will-o'-the-wisp and the future a bubble, does it matter whether a man dies on the scaffold or in his bed? There are two kinds of wicked men in the world: those whom great wealth and prodigious influence put beyond the reach of so tragic an end, and those who, if apprehended, will not avoid it. The latter kind, born with nothing, if they have any wit at all, can have only two prospects in view: either Wealth or the Wheel.* If they succeed in acquiring the first, they have achieved their object; if they meet only with the second, what regrets can they have since they had nothing to lose? The law thus has no power over any wicked man. It cannot touch the scoundrel who has become powerful, for the successful rogue can always avoid its grasp, while the unsuccessful villain, who can expect nothing else from the sword of justice, can have no cause to fear it.'

'Ah! But do you not then believe that in the next world heavenly justice lies in wait for the man who has not feared to lead a life of crime in this?'

'I think that if there were a God, there would be less evil on this earth. I believe that if evil exists here below, then either it was willed by God or it was beyond His powers to prevent it.* Now I cannot bring myself to fear a God who is either spiteful or weak. I defy Him without fear and care not a fig for His thunderbolts.'

'You perturb me greatly, Madame,' said I, getting to my feet. 'You will forgive me if I listen no more to your execrable sophisms and odious blasphemies.'

'Hold hard, Sophie. If I cannot convince your reason, then let me at least try to win over your heart. I need your help: do not refuse me. See, I have a hundred louis here. I put them to one side, so, as you may observe: they will be yours once the business has been successfully concluded.'

Giving expression now only to my natural inclination to do good, I immediately asked Dubois what business she meant, so that I might do all in my power to prevent the crime which she was preparing to commit.

'This is the way of it,' said she. 'Have you remarked the young merchant from Lyons who has been dining with us downstairs for the last three days?'

'You mean Dubreuil?'

'The very same.'

'Well?'

'He is in love with you. He told me so. He has 600,000 francs in gold and paper which he keeps in a little casket next to his bed. Let me give him the idea that you would be agreeable to hearing his suit. Whether this is the case or not cannot matter to you. I shall suggest that he invites you to drive out into the country with him. I shall let him think that he will advance his cause during the drive. You will keep him amused and ensure that he stays out for as long as possible. Meanwhile, I shall be robbing him. I shall not run away, however: I shall still be here in Grenoble when his goods will be safely in Turin. We shall use all our ingenuity to prevent his suspecting us. We shall give every appearance of helping him with his enquiries. Then I shall announce my departure which will not arouse his suspicions, you will follow, and the hundred louis will be made over to you when we both arrive safely in Piedmont.'*

'Very well, Madame,' I told Dubois, quite resolved to warn the hapless Dubreuil of the callous trick which was to be played on him. And the better to deceive the jade, I added: 'But pray reflect, Madame, that if Dubreuil is in love with me, I could, by warning him or by selling him my favours, earn much more than the paltry sum which you are offering me to betray him.'

'True, true,' said Dubois. 'Indeed, I begin to think that Heaven has given greater talents for crime to you than to me. If that is the way of it,' she went on, writing a paper, 'here is my note for a thousand louis. See if you dare refuse me now!'

'I should never dream of any such thing, Madame,' said I, taking the note from her. 'But at least seek no explanation for my weakness and my wrong in accommodating your request, other than in my unhappy circumstances.'

'I thought I could give you credit for showing some wit,' said Dubois, 'but you would rather have me put the blame on your poverty. As you wish. But serve me always and you will be content.'

The plot was arranged. That same evening, I began to be a little less unyielding with regard to Dubreuil and noticed that he did indeed feel something for me.

My position was exceeding delicate. Of course, I should have been utterly opposed to being a party in the proposed crime even had there been three times the money to be got from it. But I had no stomach whatsoever for consigning to the gallows a woman to whom, ten years before, I had owed my freedom. I wished to prevent the crime without exposing it, and with anyone but a consummate scoundrel like Dubois, I should assuredly have succeeded. Such is what I resolved to do, quite unaware that the veiled manipulations of this abominable creature would not only undermine the entire structure of my honourable scheme but would bring a punishment on my head for having conceived it.

On the day appointed for the planned excursion, Dubois invited both of us to dine in her chamber. We accepted and, when the meal was over, Dubreuil and I went down to urge haste to be made with the carriage which was being got ready for us. Dubois did not go down with us and I found myself for a moment alone with Dubreuil before we climbed on board.

'Sir,' said I quickly. 'Listen to me carefully. Show no reaction and above all carry out exactly what I tell you. Do you have a friend staying at this inn on whom you can count absolutely?'

'Yes, a junior partner of mine. I trust him as I should trust myself.'

'Well, sir, you must go to him promptly and instruct him not to leave your chamber for a single instant for the whole of the time we shall be out driving.'

'But I have the key to my chamber here in my pocket. What is the meaning of this extreme precaution?'

'It is more important than you think, sir. Pray see to it, else I shall not drive out with you. The woman we have just left is a thief. She has only arranged the excursion we are about to embark upon together so that she may rob you undisturbed while we are out. Please hurry, sir, for she is watching us. She is very dangerous. It must not appear that I am giving you a warning. Give your key to your friend, urge him to keep to your chamber in the company of a few others if he can arrange it, and order the garrison not to stir out until we return. I shall explain the rest when we are in the carriage.'

Dubreuil heard me out, took my hand to thank me, and rushed away to give orders according to my recommendations. He returned, we set off and, as we drove, I revealed the whole plot to him. The young man expressed, in the most fulsome terms, his gratitude for the service which I had rendered him and then, begging me to tell him the full truth of my current situation, he declared that nothing in my account of my adventures revolted him sufficiently to prevent his making me the offer of his hand and his fortune.

'We both come of the same class,' Dubreuil said. 'My father was a merchant like yours, my affairs have prospered while yours have not. I am only too happy to be able to right the wrongs which Fortune has done you. Think, Sophie, I am my own master, I answer to no one, I am on my way to Geneva to make an excellent investment of the money which your kind intervention has prevented me losing. You will follow me there. When you arrive I shall become your husband and you will not reappear in Lyons except as my wife.'

This turn of events was altogether too flattering to my hopes for me to dare refuse. Nevertheless I felt that I could not accept without making Dubreuil understand quite clearly all the circumstances which might lead him to regret his having asked. He was grateful for my niceness of sentiment but only pressed me the harder . . . O hapless creature that I was, was it ever to be that happiness was held out to me only to make me feel more keenly the bitter pain of never being able to grasp it? Was it an inescapable arrangement of the decrees of Providence that no virtue should ever burgeon in my heart but that it should tip me over into misfortune? Our conversation had already taken us two leagues from the town and we were about to step out of the carriage to enjoy the cool of the riverside walks which border the Isère where it was our intention to stroll, when all at once Dubreuil said that he felt terribly ill. He got down from the coach and was instantly attacked by the most dreadful retching. I ordered him to be put back in the carriage and we flew back in haste to Grenoble. Dubreuil was so ill that he had to be carried to his room. His condition amazed his friends who, following his orders, had not stirred from his apartment. I did not leave his side. A leech arrived and, just Heaven, the unfortunate young man's state was diagnosed: he had been poisoned! The moment I heard this ghastly news, I ran to Dubois's apartment. The wicked woman was gone! I hurried to my chamber where I found my clothes box broken into, the little money and all the clothes I owned all spirited off and Dubois, I was told, departed post-haste three hours since in the direction of Turin . . . There was no doubt that she was the author of all these crimes. Presenting herself at Dubreuil's door and vexed to find people in it, she had taken her revenge upon me. She had poisoned Dubreuil during dinner so that, on his returning to find she had succeeded in robbing him, the luckless young man, more concerned to save his life than to pursue her, would leave her to flee in safety, but also to ensure that the accident of his death occurring so to speak in my arms, I should be more like to be suspected than she.* I ran back to Dubreuil's chamber but was not allowed to go near him: surrounded by his friends, he was expiring, but also exonerating me, assuring them I was innocent and forbidding them to bring charges. He had scarcely closed his eyes when his partner ran out to bring me the news and declared that I was to set my mind at rest. Alas, how could I? Was I not to weep bitter tears for the only man who, from the time when I first knew misfortune, had so generously proposed to rescue me from it? Was I not to lament a theft which returned me to the cruel pit of destitution out of which I seemed so incapable of climbing? I told Dubreuil's partner everything, not only what had been plotted against his friend but also what had happened to me. He pitied me, grieved bitterly for his partner, and reproved me for the excessive delicacy which had prevented my reporting the facts the moment I had learned of Dubois's scheme. We calculated that the abominable woman, who needed only four hours to see her safely to another country, would be there long before we could take steps to have her pursued; that it would be an expensive business; and that the innkeeper, closely implicated by the information I should lay before the justices, would defend himself vigorously and in the process might perhaps be the ruin of a person, namely myself, who, so it seemed, was still alive in Grenoble only because she had already survived one criminal trial, and was apparently able to subsist only on the strength of public charity. This reasoning seemed quite conclusive to me and, more, it filled me with such fear that I resolved to quit the town without taking formal leave of my protector. Monsieur S. Dubreuil's friend applauded my decision. He did not disguise from me that if the incident were to attract attention, then whatever precautions he took, I should be compromised by the depositions which he would be obliged to make, partly because of my connection with Dubois and partly because I had been with his friend on that last drive. Bearing all this in mind, he repeated his urgent advice that I should leave Grenoble at once without seeing anyone, and assured me that in the mean time I could count absolutely on his never acting in any way whatsoever which was contrary to my interests. Left alone to meditate on the whole affair, I saw that the young man's advice was all the sounder when I reflected that it was as clear that I appeared to be guilty as it was certain that I was not, and that the only aspect of the business which spoke spiritedly on my behalf—viz., my warning to Dubreuil, which he had perhaps explained none too clearly on his

death-bed—would not be such convincing evidence that
I should count absolutely on it. In the light of all this, I
made up my mind quickly. I informed Dubreuil's partner what I had resolved.

'Would that my friend had charged me,' said he, 'with
making some advantageous provision for you, for I
should have attended to the business with the best of
wills. And I wish heartily,' he added, 'that he had told
me that it was to you that he owed the warning to mount
a guard on his apartment while he went driving out with
you. But he did none of these things. He merely said
several times over that you were not guilty and that no
charges should be brought against you. I am forced
therefore to limit my role to the execution of his wishes.
The losses which you say you have incurred through
acting on his behalf are such that I should be tempted
to do a little something extra for you myself, Mademoiselle, if I could. But I am just starting out in business, I
am young and my resources are pretty slender. There is
not a penny-piece of mine amongst Dubreuil's monies,
and I must now return the entire sum to his family. Pray
therefore, Sophie, understand if I restrict my services to
the small gesture I shall now make. Here are 5 louis and
here,' he added, ushering into his room a female I had
glimpsed at the inn earlier, 'here is an honest woman of
business from Châlon-sur-Saône* which is my home
town. She will return there after stopping for four and
twenty hours in Lyons where she has affairs to settle.'

'Madame Bertrand,' said the young man as he introduced me to the woman, 'I earnestly recommend this
young person to you. She would be happy to find a
position in the provinces and I beg you, as punctually as
though you did it for me, to use every possible effort to
find her a place in our town consonant with her birth
and education. She is to pay out no money until it is
done. I shall settle with you when I see you next. Goodbye, Sophie. Madame Bertrand leaves tonight. Go with
her and may a larger measure of happiness accompany
you to a town where I may soon have the satisfaction of

seeing you again and be better able to express the deep gratitude I shall feel all my life for your honest manner of proceeding towards Dubreuil.'

The good-heartedness of this young man, who at bottom owed me nothing, made me shed a few tears despite myself. I accepted his gifts and swore that I should work solely to achieve a station in which I should be able one day to repay him. 'Alas,' said I, on leaving him, 'though the practice of virtue has plunged me into misfortune once again, then at least, for the first time in my life, a glimmer of comfort has appeared in the ghastly pit of woe into which virtue continues still to propel me.' I never saw my young benefactor again and, in accordance with what had been resolved between us, set off with Madame Bertrand the night following the terrible fate which had overtaken Dubreuil.

Madame Bertrand travelled in a small covered carriage drawn by a single horse which we took turns to drive from inside. In the carriage she carried all her effects and a good round sum in cash, together with her little daughter of 18 months who was still suckling and of whom I was soon, to my cost, to be altogether as fond as the mother who had borne her.

Madame Bertrand was a kind of fish-wife, having neither education nor wit, suspicious, garrulous, gossipy, tiresome, narrow-minded and, as such, more or less indistinguishable from any woman of the common people. Each evening, we regularly carried her goods into inns and we slept in the same chamber. We reached Lyons without any new incident arising, but during the two days which the woman needed to attend to her business, I had a singular encounter in the town. I was strolling on the bank of the Rhône with one of the servants from the inn whom I had asked to go with me, when suddenly I saw walking towards me the Reverend Father Antonin, now Superior of the Recollets of that place, the despoiler of my virginity whom I had known, as you will recall, Madame, at the little monastery of Sainte-Marie-des-Bois where my evil star had led me.

Antonin came up to me in the most casual manner and, though the serving-girl was there, asked me if I would care to call on him in his new abode where we might resume the pleasures we had known before.

'But here is a buxom wench,' said he, alluding to the girl who was with me, 'who would be very welcome too. In our abbey, there are a number of stout fellows more than capable of holding their own against a brace of pretty women.'

I blushed prodigiously at his words and for a moment attempted to make him believe that he was mistaken in thinking he knew me. But not succeeding, I tried by signs to persuade him at least to restrain himself in the presence of my guide. But nothing could check his impudent flow and his solicitations simply became all the more pressing. In the end, upon our refusing repeatedly to go off with him, he insisted upon knowing our addresses. To rid myself of his importunities, I immediately thought to give him a false one. He wrote it down in his notebook and left us, promising that he would surely see us again soon. We returned to the inn. On the way, I imparted as well as I could to the serving-girl who was with me the history of my unfortunate acquaintance with the man. But either she was not satisfied by my account or else, being as indiscreet as her female sort always are by nature, I judged by what Madame Bertrand later said after the sorry adventure which befell me in her company, that the chit had fully apprised her of my knowing the abominable friar. However, he did not come and we went our way. We left Lyons rather late and on that first day got no further than Villefranche.*
It was there, Madame, that I suffered the dreadful calamity which has led me to appear before you as a criminal—without my being any guiltier in this latest pass in my life than in any of the others in which you have observed me so unjustly smitten by the cruel blows of fate, and without there having been any reason for my being plunged into the pit of woes other than the charitable impulses which I was utterly unable to eradicate

from my heart.

On arriving in Villefranche at about six o'clock on a February evening, my companion and I had made haste to sup and go up early to bed so that we should make a longer day of it on the morrow. We had been sleeping for under two hours when a frightful quantity of smoke filled our chamber and made us both wake with a start. We could not but doubt that there was fire raging close at hand. Just Heaven! The speed with which the flames were spreading was already only too alarming. Half-dressed, we opened our door, but all we heard around us was the roar of walls collapsing, the ghastly noise of roof-timbers giving way, and the hideous screams of poor wretches as they fell into the fire below. A tongue of devouring flame reached up towards us, leaving us hardly time enough to hurry out of our room. However, we managed to scramble through the door and found ourselves commingled with the crowd of sorry folk who, half-naked as we were and some half-scorched too, were seeking safety in flight. At that instant, I recalled that Madame Bertrand, more concerned for herself than for her daughter, had given no thought to preserving her from certain death. Without a word to her, I ran back into our chamber through flames which blinded my eyes and burned me on several parts of my body, seized the poor little thing, and sprang up intending to return her to her mother. Trusting to a beam which was already partly burned through, I lost my footing and my first instinct was to put my arms out in front of me. Thus prompted by Nature, I was obliged to let go the precious burden I carried and the hapless infant fell into the flames as her mother looked on. This abominable woman, not pausing to think either of the object of the action I had tried to take, which was to save her child, or of the state to which the child's falling while she watched had reduced me, and hysterical with grief, now accused me of killing her daughter, leaped wildly upon me, and attacked me with her fists. Meanwhile the fire abated and the multitude of helpers managed to save

half the inn. Madame Bertrand's first thought was to
return to her chamber, which was one of the least dam-
aged of all. There she repeated her charges, saying that
I ought to have let her daughter be, that no harm would
have come to her.* But she became quite beside herself
when, searching about for her goods, she discovered that
she had been comprehensively robbed! Then, heeding
only her despair and her anger, she screamed at me,
accusing me of being the cause of the fire which I had
started so that I could rob her more easily. She said she
would report me, and straightway matching the threat
to the deed, demanded to speak to the Justice of the
place. In vain did I plead my innocence: she would not
listen. The magistrate she had asked to see was not far
away, having himself supervised the rescue work, and he
appeared in answer to the summons of the loathsome
woman. She stated her charge against me, shoring it up
with anything that came into her head to give it greater
force and legitimacy, and painted me in the colours of a
common streetwalker who had escaped a hanging in
Grenoble, as a baggage whom a young man, doubtless
her lover, had given into her keeping against her better
judgement, and she spoke too of the Recollet in Lyons.
In short, nothing was omitted from the most emphatic
performance which slander envenomed by grief and
revenge could inspire. The judge received her statement
and then the building was examined. It transpired that
the fire had begun in a loft full of hay where several
persons swore they had seen me go the previous evening,
which was quite true. While looking for a water-closet
to which I had been misdirected by the tavern servants
whom I had asked, I had gone into this hay-loft and had
remained there long enough to start a suspicion that I
had done what I was accused of. And so my arraignment
got under way, all the rules of procedure being strictly
observed:* the witnesses were all in agreement, nothing
I alleged in my defence was even listened to, it was
demonstrated that I was the arsonist, it was proved that
I had accomplices who, while I busied myself here, were

busying themselves committing thefts there, and, next morning at first light, without any further enquiry being made, I was taken back to Lyons, to the prison there, and was committed for arson, child-murder, and robbery.

Long grown accustomed to slander, injustice, and misfortune, and used since childhood to the idea that I never could yield to any virtuous impulse without being certain to find thorns somewhere in it, my affliction made me feel more bewildered than anguished, and I wept more than I bewailed my fate. However, it being natural for any suffering creature to grasp at every possible means by which he might climb out of the abyss into which misfortune has cast him, I thought of Father Antonin. However small the help I could hope for from that quarter, I did not reject out of hand my wish to see him and requested that he be fetched. Not knowing who could be asking for him, he came, but then affected not to recognize me. I told the gaoler that it was possible he could not place me because he had been my director of conscience only when I was very young, but on these grounds I requested a private interview with him. This was agreed by both parties. When I was alone with the friar, I threw myself at his feet and beseeched him to save me from the cruel pass I had come to. I proved my innocence to him and did nothing to disguise the fact that the crude suggestions he had made to me two days before had antagonized the person to whom I had been recommended, she now being my chief accuser. The friar listened to me very attentively and hardly had I finished my tale when he said:

'Listen, Sophie, and do not fly into a passion as you usually do when anyone contradicts your cursed principles. You see where your notions have brought you, for now you have adequate leisure to convince yourself that they have served no purpose but to tip you into one abyss after another. So if you wish your neck to be saved, abandon them for once in your life. I can see only one way of managing it. One of the holy Brothers here in

Lyons is a close relative of both the Governor and the King's Intendant; I shall inform him of your plight. Say you are his niece and as such he will call for your release. By promising to pack you off to a convent for the rest of your life, I am certain that he will prevent matters being taken any further. In the event, you will disappear; he will hand you into my keeping and I will undertake to hide you until such time as a change of circumstances enables me to restore your freedom. But during your detention, you will belong to me. I make no bones of it: you will be a slave and subject to my whims which you will satisfy without demur. You understand me, Sophie, for you know me well enough. Come, choose now between this course and the scaffold—and do not make me wait for an answer.'

'O Reverend Father!' I replied in horror, 'But you are a monster to take such cruel advantage of my situation to force me thus to choose between death and dishonour! Leave this place! I shall die innocent, but I shall at least die without remorse!'

My resistance excited the villain who thereupon was bold enough to show me just how inflamed his passions were. The vile man had the gall to think of the rites of love in that place of dread and chains beneath the sword of justice which was waiting to strike me down. I tried to escape his embrace, but he came after me and knocked me down on to the miserable straw pallet which did service as a bed, and if he did not quite consummate his crime, then at least he left me bearing marks so unambiguous that I could have no possible doubts as to the abhorrent nature of his intentions.

'Listen,' he said, brushing himself down, 'you clearly do not want my help. Very well, I shall leave you to it. I shall neither help nor hinder, but if you take it into your pretty head to breathe a single word against me, then I shall charge you with crimes so heinous that I shall ensure that you will be left with no means of ever defending yourself again. Think hard before you answer and try to grasp the meaning of what I shall tell the gaoler. Or else I shall put the final touches to your downfall.'

He knocked on the cell door and the gaoler appeared:
'Sir,' the villain said, 'this good woman was mistaken. She wished to speak to a Father Antonin who is now at Bordeaux. I neither know her nor have I ever known her. She asked me to hear her confession and this I have done. You are acquainted with the law which respects the confessional and I have therefore nothing to say of what passed in confidence between us. I give you both good-day. I shall always be ready to present myself here should my holy ministrations be judged necessary.'

So saying, Antonin went out, leaving me as disconcerted by his double-dealing as I was dumbfounded by his sheer impudence and licentiousness.

The lower courts have no equal in the speedy dispatch of their work. As they are almost invariably composed of fools, cloddish martinets, or brutal fanatics, whose inane judgements will almost certainly later be reviewed and corrected by more intelligent eyes, there is nothing to restrain them whenever they have an opportunity to show their stupidity. I was thus unanimously sentenced to death by the eight or ten shop-keepers who sat on the worthy bench in this town of bankrupts,* and was immediately transported to Paris for my conviction to be confirmed. The bitterest and most anguished thoughts rose up in me to finish off my much battered heart.

'Under what fatal star was I then born,' I asked myself, 'for it now to be impossible for me even to think of following the smallest inclination to virtue without its being immediately washed away by a tide of woe! And how can it be that enlightened Providence, whose justice I willingly adore, punishing me for my virtues, simultaneously offers me the spectacle of those whose vices brought me low being raised on high to pinnacles? When I was very young, a money-lender attempted to persuade me to commit a theft: I refused, he grew rich, and I came close to hanging. Convicted robbers tried to ravish me in a forest because I would not join them: they prospered while I fell into the clutches of a lewd Marquis who gave me a hundred lashes because I would not poison his mother. Next, I went to the house of a surgeon: I saved him from committing an execrable crime which the brute repaid by butchering, branding, and ejecting me; he doubtless went on to complete further crimes and made his fortune while I was forced to beg for bread. I was then of a mind to partake of the sacrament and to offer fervent prayers to the Supreme Being who had visited as much misfortune upon me as these men had done. The august tribunal which I hoped would purify me through the workings of one of its holiest mysteries, viz., confession, became instead the ghastly scene of my undoing and my dishonour: the monster who defiled and befouled me was thereupon raised to the highest honours while I fell back into the dismal pit of my wretchedness. I gave money to alleviate the sufferings of a poor woman who promptly robbed me. I went to the aid of an unconscious man, and the scoundrel set me turning a wheel like some beast of burden and beat me mercilessly when my strength gave out: yet all of fortune's favours were showered on him while I came near to forfeiting my life for having been forced to work in his service. An abominable woman sought to involve me in another crime: but, for a second time, I lost everything I possessed because I tried to protect her victim's money and keep him safe from harm; the luckless man offered to reward me with marriage but died in my arms before we could be betrothed. I risked my life in a fire to save a child who was not mine: for doing as much I found myself a third time with head bowed before the sword of Themis. I begged protection of a cur who had dishonoured me, hoping to find him sympathetic to the extent of my misfortunes; yet it was at the cost of my being further dishonoured that the ogre offered to help me. O Providence! am I finally to doubt of your justice? Or what even greater horrors would have scourged me had I always, like those who have persecuted me, paid homage to vice?'

Such, Madame, were the imprecations which, against my better self—their being torn from deep inside me by dread of my impending fate—I had the temerity to utter. And then you had the kindness to turn a glance of pity and compassion upon me. Pray forgive me, Madame, for having presumed so long on your patience. I have reopened my wounds and I have troubled your peace of mind, and these are the only fruits which we both have picked out of the sorry tale of my adventures. The sun is rising, my guards will come for me, let me go now to meet my death. I no longer fear it, for it will abridge my sufferings, nay will end them. Death is to be feared only by those fortunate enough to lead pure, cloudless lives. But the wretched creature who has trodden on serpents, whose bleeding feet have stepped only on thorns, who has become acquainted with human nature only to learn how to hate humankind, who has seen the sun rise only to loathe its rising, whose cruel reverses have separated her from parents, fortune, help, protection, and friends, who in the great wide world has only tears for drink and tribulations for meat, a wretched creature such as this, I say, sees death draw near without fear, welcomes it as a safe haven where she will once more know peace in the bosom of a God too just to allow innocence, blighted and persecuted on this earth, to be denied some day the reward of its tears in heaven.

*   *   *

The honest Monsieur de Corville had not sat through this tale without being prodigiously moved by it. As for Madame de Lorsange, whose sensibility, as we have said, had not been blunted by the monstrous errors of her youth, she was almost reduced to a swooning state.

'Mademoiselle,' she said to Sophie, 'it is difficult to hear you and not be moved to feel the keenest interest in your case. But I must confess, a sentiment which I cannot explain, keener still than that interest I defined a moment since, draws me irresistibly to you and makes your misfortunes mine. You have kept your name from

me, Sophie, you have concealed the truth of your birth.
Tell me the secret, I beg you. Do not think it is idle
curiosity which prompts me to ask this of you. If what I
suspect should be true . . . O Justine! If only you were
my sister!'

'Justine! Madame, what name . . .?'

'She would be your age now.'

'O Juliette, is that you whose voice I hear?' said the
ill-starred prisoner throwing herself into the arms of
Madame de Lorsange. 'You! My sister! Great God! But
what blasphemy have I committed in doubting Providence! Ah! I shall die less wretched now that I have
been allowed to embrace you once more!'

And the two sisters, their arms tightly encircling each
other, spoke only through sobs and heard each other
only in their tears. Monsieur de Corville, incapable of
stopping up his eyes and perceiving that he could not
but take the most pressing interest in these events, immediately left the chamber and entered an adjacent
room. There he wrote to the Lord Chancellor, painting
the wretched Justine's ghastly fate in strokes of blood
and offering to stand as guarantor for her innocence. He
petitioned that until a full investigation into her trial was
complete, the alleged criminal be detained in his château
and nowhere else, and signed an undertaking to give her
up immediately on receipt of his Lordship's order requiring him to do so. Having written his letter, he gave
it into the keeping of the two escorts, made himself
known to them, ordered them to deliver it immediately
to its destination and to return. Then, if the Chief
Magistrate gave his authorization, they were to carry the
prisoner to his residence. The two men, seeing that they
were dealing with a person of consequence, did not fear
that they would be compromised by obeying his instructions. In the mean time, a carriage drew up at the ready.

'So beautiful and so ill-used!' said Monsieur de Corville to Justine who was still locked in her sister's arms.
'Come. The past quarter of an hour has wrought a
transformation in your affairs. It must not be said that

your virtues will never find their reward on this earth, nor that you met only with hearts of flint. Come, follow me. You are my prisoner. Henceforth I alone shall answer for you.'

Then Monsieur de Corville spoke briefly of what he had just arranged.

'Dear, worthy man!' said Madame de Lorsange, throwing herself to the ground at her lover's feet, 'this is the finest thing you ever did in your life! He alone can avenge the innocent oppressed and succour the unfortunate undone by fate who truly understands both the hearts of men and the spirit of the law. See now your prisoner stand before you! Come, Justine, come! Make haste to kiss the feet of this even-handed protector who, unlike the others you have known, will never desert you! O sir! If the chains of my love were dear to me before, how much more precious will they be henceforth now that they are bedecked by Nature's garlands and drawn tighter by my affection and esteem!'

And both women vied with each other to kiss the feet of so generous a benefactor and moistened them with their tears. Then they made their departure. Monsieur de Corville and Madame de Lorsange took the greatest pleasure in guiding Justine's passage from the depths of misfortune to the heights of ease and prosperity. They took delight in feeding her the most succulent dishes, they gave her the softest beds to sleep in, they urged her to use what was theirs as though it were her own: in short, they used her with as much niceness of feeling as could possibly be expected of any two sensitive spirits. During those first days, she was given the attentions of a physician. She was bathed, given fine clothes to wear, and made to appear to advantage. She was worshipped by the two lovers who competed in the race to make her forget her trials. A skilled practitioner undertook to remove all trace of the ignominious brand, cruel legacy of Rodin's villainy. Everything proceeded as Madame de Lorsange and her delicate lover wished. Already the furrows etched by misfortune were fading from gentle

Justine's exquisite brow whose smoothness was being repaired by the graces; the ghastly white of her alabaster cheeks was ousted by the roses of spring; the smile long since wiped from her lips now returned on the wings of pleasure. The news from Paris could not have been better, for Monsieur de Corville had roused the whole of France and fanned the zeal of Monsieur S. who now worked with him to make Justine's misfortunes known and restore to her the tranquillity which was also her due. Finally, there came letters from the King which overturned all the verdicts unjustly made against her since childhood, restored her to full citizenship, silenced in perpetuity all the courts of his Kingdom which had plotted against an unfortunate, and granted her a pension of 1,200 livres to be paid for out of the monies seized in the coiners' eyrie in the Dauphiné. She almost died of joy on learning of such flattering developments. For several days together she wept the sweetest tears in the home of her protectors and then, so unaccountably that the cause of it was not to be discovered, her mood changed. She became sad, troubled, dreamy. Sometimes she wept in her friends' company, and could not herself have said what was the reason for her tears.

'I was not born to be so deliriously happy,' she would sometimes say to Madame de Lorsange. 'O dear sister! Such felicity is not made to last!'

Vainly was it put to her that, her tribulations now being over, she now had no further cause for anxiety of any sort. In drawing up the statements made on her behalf, the care which had been taken to avoid mention of any of the persons with whom she had been implicated, whose influence was still to be feared, was another reason for her being easy in her mind. Yet she was not to be persuaded. It was as though the poor girl, destined to know nothing but unhappiness and eternally sensing the hand of misfortune poised above her ready to strike, had some intimation of the final blow by which she was to be cut down.

Madame de Lorsange was still in residence in the

country. It was the end of summer. A stroll was mooted which was made doubtful by the gathering of a violent storm. The heat being extreme, every window in the drawing room was open. The lightning flashed, hail fell, the wind howled and shrieked, and the thunder roared alarmingly. Madame de Lorsange quaked. Always terrified by thunder, Madame de Lorsange beseeched her sister to close up all the windows as quickly as she could. Monsieur de Corville came into the room just at this moment. Bent on allaying her sister's fears without delay, Justine flew to a window where she struggled for a whole minute against the wind which resisted her efforts. Suddenly, a bolt of lightning struck her and hurled her clear to the middle of the room where she lay lifeless on the floor.

Madame de Lorsange uttered a piteous cry, then fainted. Monsieur de Corville summoned help which was divided between the two casualties. Madame de Lorsange was revived but the hapless Justine had been so comprehensively struck down that there was not even the smallest hope remaining for her. The bolt had entered by her right breast, had blasted her thorax and come out again through her mouth, so disfiguring her face that she was hideous to look at. Monsieur de Corville thought it best that she be carried off without delay, but Madame de Lorsange, with an air of the greatest calm, rose to her feet and countermanded the order.

'No,' said she to her lover. 'No, leave her a moment where I may see her. I need her there to gaze upon so that I may be confirmed in the resolve which I have this moment made. Pray hear me out, sir, and do not obstruct the course I propose to follow, for nothing now shall deter me from it. The unprecedented misfortunes experienced by this benighted creature, though she ever respected virtue, are far too removed from the ordinary run not to open my eyes upon my own case. Do not think, sir, that I am blinded by the glimpses of that sham of happiness which, throughout all her adventures, we have observed to be the lot of the wicked men who plagued her. They are whims of fate, puzzles invented by Providence which it is not for us to try to penetrate nor should they ever tempt us. The prosperity enjoyed by wicked men is a test which Providence sets us. It is as the lightning whose beguiling flashes lend momentary beauty to the air before hurling headlong into death's chasm the unhappy man who is dazzled by its brilliance. We have before us an example of it. The chain of calamities, the dreadful, uninterrupted misfortunes of this poor girl are a warning which Almighty God has given me to repent of my ways, to heed the voice of remorse and fly at last to His bosom. How much must I fear at His hands, I whose crimes would appal you if you ever came to know them, I, whose lewdness, irreligion, and rejection of all decent principles have marked each step I have taken in life. What should I expect, then, if one such as this, who never once in her life knowingly committed a blameworthy act, has been so categorically treated? Let us part, sir; the time is ripe. There being no tie that binds us, forget me and allow me to go to a place where, repenting eternally at the feet of God Almighty, I may abjure the wicked actions by which I have debased myself. This catastrophe, though so dreadful for me, was nevertheless necessary for my redemption in this life and for the happiness for which I hope in the life that is to come. Farewell, sir, you will never see me more. The last gesture of friendship I ask of you is to promise you will never undertake any kind of investigation with the object of discovering what has become of me. I shall await you in a better world, for your virtues will assuredly bring you to it. May the mortifications in which I shall spend such wretched years as are left me in expiation of my crimes allow me indeed to see you there some day.'

Madame de Lorsange left the house at once, ordered a carriage to be made ready, took some small provision of her money with her, leaving the rest for Monsieur de Corville to whom she gave directions concerning pious bequests to be made, and drove in haste to Paris where she entered the Carmelite Convent* there. Within the space of a few years, she had become its model and example, known not only for her deep piety but also for the serenity of her spirit and the unimpeachable propriety of her morals.

Monsieur de Corville, a man deserving of the highest offices in his native land, was honoured to obtain them and accepted with the sole object of working for the happiness of the people, the glory of his sovereign, and the fortune of his friends.

And now, reader, having read this tale, may you extract the same profit from it as this reformed woman of the world. May you, like her, be persuaded that true happiness lies in virtue alone and that, though God allows goodness to be persecuted on earth, it is with no other end in view than to prepare for us a better reward in heaven.

Written in the space of two weeks,
this eighth day of July 1787.

Dialogue between a Priest
and a Dying Man

PRIEST. Now that the fatal hour is upon you wherein the
veil of illusion is torn aside only to confront every
deluded man with the cruel tally of his errors and
vices, do you, my son, earnestly repent of the many
sins to which you were led by weakness and human
frailty?

DYING MAN. Yes, I do so repent.

PRIEST. Then in the short space you have left, profit from
such timely remorse to ask that you be given general
absolution of your sins, believing that only by considering the reverence of the most comfortable and
holy sacrament of penitence may you hope for forgiveness at the hand of Almighty God our Eternal
Father.

DYING MAN. I understand you no better than you have
understood me.

PRIEST. What's that?

DYING MAN. I said I repented.

PRIEST. I heard you.

DYING MAN. Yes, but you did not understand what I
meant.

PRIEST. But what other interpretation . . . ?

DYING MAN. The one I shall now give. I was created by
Nature with the keenest appetites and the strongest
of passions and was put on this earth with the sole
purpose of placating both by surrendering to them.
They are components of my created self and are no
more than mechanical parts necessary to the function-
ing of Nature's basic purposes. Or if you prefer, they
are incidental effects essential to her designs for me
and conform entirely to her laws. I repent only that I
never sufficiently acknowledged the omnipotence of
Nature and my remorse is directed solely against the
modest use I made of those faculties, criminal in your

eyes but perfectly straightforward in mine, which she
gave me to use in her service. I did at times resist her,
and am heartily sorry for it. I was blinded by the
absurdity of your doctrines to which I resorted to fight
the violence of desires planted in me by a power more
divinely inspired by far, and I now repent of having
done so. I picked only flowers when I could have
gathered in a much greater harvest of ripe fruits. Such
is the proper cause of my regret; respect me enough
to impute no other to me.

PRIEST. To what a pass have you been brought by your
errors! How misled you have been by such sophisms!
You attribute to the created world all the power of
the Creator! Do you not see that the lamentable tendencies which have misdirected your steps are themselves no more than effects of that same corrupt
Nature to which you attribute omnipotence?

DYING MAN. It seems to me that your reasoning is as
empty as your head. I wish that you would argue more
rationally or else just let me alone to die in peace.
What do you mean by 'Creator'? What do you understand by 'corrupt Nature'?

PRIEST. The Creator is the Master of the Universe. All
that was created was created by Him, everything was
made by His hand, and His creation is maintained as
a simple effect of His omnipotence.

DYING MAN. Well now, He must be a very great man
indeed! In which case, tell me why this man of yours,
who is so powerful, nevertheless made Nature 'corrupt', as you put it.

PRIEST. But what merit would men have had if God had
not given them free will? What merit would there be
in its exercise if, in this life, it were not as possible to
choose good as it were to avoid evil?

DYING MAN. So your God proceeded to make the world
askew simply to tempt and test man. Did He then not
know His creature? And did He not know the outcome?

PRIEST. Of course He knew His creature but, in addition, He wished to leave him the merit of choosing wisely.

DYING MAN. But what for? He knew all along what His creature would choose and it was within His power— for you say that He is all-powerful—well within His power, say I, to see to it that he chose correctly?

PRIEST. Who can comprehend the vast and infinite purpose which God has for man? Where is even the man who understands all things visible?

DYING MAN. Anyone who sees things simply, and especially the man who does not go looking for a multiplicity of causes with which to obscure the effects. Why do you need a second difficulty when you cannot explain the first? If we admit it is possible that Nature alone is responsible for creating what you attribute to your God, why do you insist on looking for a master hand? The cause of what you do not comprehend may be the simplest thing there is. Study physics and you will understand Nature better; learn to think clearly, cast out your preconceived ideas and you will have no need of this God of yours.

PRIEST. Miserable sinner! I understood you were no more than a Socinian* and came armed with weapons to fight you. But since I see now that you are an atheist whose heart is closed to the authentic and innumerable proofs which are daily given us of the existence of the Creator, there is no point in my saying anything more. Sight cannot be restored to a blind man.

DYING MAN. Admit one thing: is not the blinder of two men surely he who puts a blindfold on his eyes, not he who removes it? You edify, you fabricate reasons, you multiply explanations, whereas I destroy and simplify the issues. You pile error on error, and I challenge all errors. So which of us is blind?

PRIEST. So you do not believe in God?

DYING MAN. No, and for a very simple reason: it is impossible to believe what one does not understand. There must always be an obvious connection between understanding and belief. Understanding is the prime condition of faith. Where there is no understanding, faith dies and those who do not understand yet say they believe are hypocrites. I defy you to say that you believe in the God whose praises you sing, because you cannot demonstrate His existence nor is it within your capacities to define His nature, which means that you do not understand Him and since you do not understand you are incapable of furnishing me with reasoned arguments. In other words, anything which is beyond the limits of human reason is either illusion or idle fancy, and since your God must be either one or the other, I should be mad to believe in the first and stupid to believe in the second.

Prove to me that matter is inert, and I shall grant you a Creator.* Show me that Nature is not sufficient unto herself, and I shall gladly allow you to give her a Master. But until you can do this, I shall not yield one inch. I am convinced only by evidence, and evidence is provided by my senses alone.* Beyond their limits, I am powerless to believe in anything. I believe the sun exists because I can see it: I take it to be the centre where all of Nature's flammable matter is gathered together and I am charmed but in no wise astonished by its regular courses. It is a phenomenon of physics, perhaps no more complex than the workings of electricity, which it is not given to us to understand. Need I say more? You can construct your God and set Him above such phenomena, but does that take me any further forward? Am I not required to make as much effort to understand the workman as to define His handiwork?

Consequently, you have done me no service by erecting this illusion of yours. You have confused but not enlightened my mind and I owe you not gratitude but hatred. Your God is a machine which you have built to serve your own passions and you have set it to run according to their requirements. But you must see that I had no choice but to jettison your model the instant it fell out of step with my passions? At this moment, my weak soul stands in need of peace and philosophy: why do you now try to alarm it with your sophistry which will strike it with terror but not convert it, inflame it without making it better? My soul is what it pleased Nature to be, which is to say a consequence of the organs which Nature thought fit to implant in me in accordance with her purposes and needs. Now, since Nature needs vice as much as she needs virtue, she directed me towards the first when she found it expedient, and when she had need of the second, she filled me with the appropriate desires to which I surrendered equally promptly. Do not seek further than her laws for the cause of our human inconsistency, and to explain her laws look not beyond her will and her needs.

PRIEST. And so everything in the world is necessary?

DYING MAN. Of course.

PRIEST. But if all is necessary, there must be order in everything?

DYING MAN. Who argues that there is not?

PRIEST. But who or what is capable of creating the order that exists if not an all-powerful, supremely wise hand?

DYING MAN. Will not gunpowder explode of necessity when lit by a match?

PRIEST. Yes.

DYING MAN. And where is the wisdom in that?

PRIEST. There isn't any.

DYING MAN. So you see it is possible that there are things which are necessary but were not wisely made, and it follows that it is equally possible that everything derives from a first cause in which there may be neither reason nor wisdom.

PRIEST. What are you driving at?

DYING MAN. I want to prove to you that it is possible that everything is simply what it is and what you see it to be, without its being the effect of some cause which was reasonable and wisely directed; that natural effects must have natural causes without there being

any need to suppose that they had a non-natural
origin such as your God who, as I have already observed, would require a good deal of explaining but
would not of Himself explain anything; that therefore
once it is conceded that God serves no useful purpose, He becomes completely irrelevant; that there is
every likelihood that what is irrelevant is of no account and what is of no account is as nought. So, to
convince myself that your God is an illusion, I need
no other argument than that which is supplied by my
certain knowledge that He serves no useful purpose.

PRIEST. If that is your attitude, I cannot think that there
is any reason why I should discuss religion with you.

DYING MAN. Why ever not? I know nothing more entertaining than seeing for myself to what extravagant
lengths men have taken fanaticism and imbecility in
religious matters—excesses so unspeakable that the
catalogue of aberrations, though ghastly, is, I always
think, invariably fascinating to contemplate. Answer
me this frankly, and above all, do not give self-interested responses! If I were to be weak enough to let
myself be talked into believing your ludicrous doctrines which prove the incredible existence of a being
who makes religion necessary, which form of worship
would you advise me to offer up to Him? Would you
have me incline towards the idle fancies of Confucius
or the nonsense of Brahma? Should I bow down before the Great Serpent of the Negro, the Moon and
Stars of the Peruvian, or the God of Moses' armies?
Which of the sects of Muhammad would you suggest
I join? Or which particular Christian heresy would
you say was preferable to all the others? Think carefully before you answer.

PRIEST. Can there be any doubt about my reply?

DYING MAN. But that is a self-interested answer.

PRIEST. Not at all. In recommending my own beliefs to
you, I love you as much as I love myself.

DYING MAN. By heeding such errors, you show little
enough love for either of us.

PRIEST. But who can be blind enough not to see the miracles of our Divine Redeemer?

DYING MAN. He who sees through Him as the most transparent of swindlers and the most tiresome of humbugs.

PRIEST. *O Lord, thou hearest but speakest not with a voice of thunder!* *

DYING MAN. Quite so, and no voice is heard for the simple reason that your God, perhaps because He cannot or because He has too much sense or for whatever other reason you care to impute to a being whose existence I acknowledge only out of politeness or, if you prefer, to be as accommodating as I can to your petty views, no voice, I say, is heard because this God, if He exists as you are mad enough to believe, cannot possibly have set out to convince us by using means as ludicrous as those employed by your Jesus.

PRIEST. But what of the prophets, the miracles, the martyrs? Are not all these proofs?

DYING MAN. How, in terms of strict logic, can you expect me to accept as proof something which itself first needs to be proved? For a prophecy to be a proof, I must first be completely convinced that what was foretold was in fact fulfilled. Now since prophecies are part of history, they can have no more force in my mind than all other historical facts, of which three-quarters are highly dubious. If to this I were to add further the possibility, or rather the likelihood, that they were transmitted to me solely by historians with a vested interest, I should be, as you see, more than entitled to be sceptical.* Moreover, who will reassure me that such and such a prophecy was not made after the event, or that it was not just politically or self-fulfillingly contrived, like the prediction which foretells a prosperous reign under a just king or forecasts frost in winter? If all this is in fact the case, how can you argue that prophecies, which stand in dire need of proof, can themselves ever become a proof?

As for your miracles, I am no more impressed by

them than by prophecies. All swindlers have worked miracles and the stupid have believed in them. To be convinced of the truth of a miracle, I should have to be quite certain that the event which you would call miraculous ran absolutely counter to the laws of Nature, since only events occurring outside Nature can be deemed a miracle. But there, who is so learned in her ways to dare state at what point Nature ends and at what precise moment Nature is violated? Only two things are required to accredit an alleged miracle: a mountebank and a crowd of spineless lookers-on. There is absolutely no point looking for any other kind of origin for your miracles. All founders of new sects have been miracle-workers and, what is decidedly odder, they have always found imbeciles who believed them. Your Jesus never managed anything more prodigious than Apollonius of Tyana,* and it would never enter anyone's head to claim that he was a god. As to your martyrs, they are by far the weakest of all your arguments. Zeal and obstinacy are all it takes to make a martyr and if an alternative cause were to furnish me with as many martyred saints as you claim for yours, I should never have proper grounds for believing the one to be any better than the other but, on the contrary, should be very inclined to think that both were woefully inadequate.

My dear fellow, if it were true that the God you preach really existed, would He need miracles, martyrs, and prophecies to establish His kingdom? And if, as you say, the heart of man is God's handiwork, would not men's hearts have been the temple He chose for His law? Surely this equitable law, since it emanates from a just God, would be equally and irresistibly imprinted in all of us, from one end of the universe to the other. All men, having in common this same delicate, sensitive organ, would also adopt a common approach to praising the God from whom they had received it. They would all have the same way of loving Him, the same way of adoring and serving Him, and it would be as impossible for them to mistake His nature as to resist the secret bidding of their hearts to praise Him. But instead of which, what do I find throughout the whole universe? As many gods as there are nations, as many ways of serving them as there are brains and fertile imaginations. Now, do you seriously believe that this multiplicity of opinions, among which I find it physically impossible to choose, is really the handiwork of a just God?

No, preacher, you offend your God by showing Him to me in this light. Allow me to deny Him altogether, for if He exists, I should offend Him much less by my unbelief than you by your blasphemies.* Think, preacher! Your Jesus was no better than Muhammad, Muhammad was no better than Moses, and none of these three was superior to Confucius, though Confucius did set down a number of perfectly valid principles whereas the others talked nonsense.* But they and their ilk are mountebanks who have been mocked by thinking men, believed by the rabble, and should have been strung up by due process of law.

PRIEST. Alas, such was only too true in the case of one of the four.

DYING MAN. Yes, He who deserved it most. He was a seditious influence, an agitator, a bearer of false witness, a scoundrel, a lecher, a showman who performed crude tricks, a wicked and dangerous man. He knew exactly how to set about hoodwinking the public and was therefore eminently punishable in the type of kingdom and state of which Jerusalem was then a part. It was a very sound decision to remove Him and it is perhaps the only case in which my principles, which are incidentally very mild and tolerant, could ever admit the application of the full rigour of Themis. I forgive all errors save those which may imperil the government under which we live; kings and their majesty are the only things that I take on trust and respect. The man who does not love his country and his King does not deserve to live.*

PRIEST. But you do admit, do you not, that there is something after this life? It hardly seems possible that your mind has not on occasion turned to piercing the mystery of the fate which awaits us. What concept have you found to be more convincing than that of a multitude of punishments for the man who has lived badly and an eternity of rewards for the man who has lived well?

DYING MAN. Why, my dear fellow, the concept of nothingness! The idea never frightened me; it strikes me as consoling and simple. All other answers are the handiwork of pride, but mine is the product of reason. In any case, nothingness is neither ghastly nor absolute. Is not Nature's never-ending process of generation and regeneration plain for my eyes to see? Nothing perishes, nothing on this earth is destroyed. Today a man, tomorrow a worm, the day after a fly—what is this if not eternal life?* And why do you believe that I should be rewarded for virtues I possess through no merit of my own, and punished for criminal acts over which I have no control? How can you reconcile the goodness of your alleged God with this principle? Can He have created me solely in order to enjoy punishing me—and punish me for choosing wrongly while denying me the freedom to choose well?

PRIEST. But you are free to choose.

DYING MAN. I am—but only according to your assumptions which do not withstand examination by reason. The doctrine of free will was invented solely so that you could devise the principle of Divine Grace which validated your garbled presuppositions. Is there a man alive who, seeing the scaffold standing next to his crime, would willingly commit a crime if he were free not to commit it? We are impelled by an irresistible power and are never, not for a single instant, in a position to steer a course in any direction except down the slope on which our feet are set. There are no virtues save those which are necessary to Nature's ends and, reciprocally, no crime which she does not need for her purposes. Nature's mastery lies precisely in the perfect balance which she maintains between virtue and crime. But can we be guilty if we move in the direction in which she pushes us? No more than the wasp which punctures your skin with its sting.*

PRIEST. So it follows that even the greatest crimes should not give us cause to fear anything?

DYING MAN. I did not say that. It is enough that the law condemns and the sword of justice punishes for us to feel aversion or terror for such crimes. But once they have, regrettably, been committed, we must accept the inevitable and not surrender to remorse which is pointless. Remorse is null since it did not prevent us from committing the crime, and void since it does not enable us to make amends: it would be absurd to surrender to it and absurder still to fear punishment in the next world if we have been fortunate enough to escape it in this. God forbid that anyone should think that in saying this I seek to give enouragement to crime! Of course we must do everything we can to avoid criminal acts*—but we must learn to shun them through reason and not out of unfounded fears which lead nowhere, the effects of which are in any case neutralized in anyone endowed with strength of mind. Reason, yes reason alone must alert us to the fact that doing harm to others can never make us happy, and our hearts must make us feel that making others happy is the greatest joy which Nature grants us on this earth. All human morality is contained in these words: *make others as happy as you yourself would be,** and never serve them more ill than you would yourself be served. These, my dear fellow, are the only principles which we should follow. There is no need of religion or God to appreciate and act upon them: the sole requirement is a good heart.

But, preacher, I feel my strength abandon me. Put aside your prejudices, be a man, be human, have no

fear and no hope. Abandon your divinities and your
creeds which have never served any purpose save to
put a sword into the hand of man. The mere names
of horrible gods and hideous faiths have caused more
blood to be shed than all other wars and scourges on
earth.* Give up the idea of another world, for there
is none. But do not turn your back on the pleasure in
this of being happy yourself and of making others
happy. It is the only means Nature affords you of
enlarging and extending your capacity for life. My
dear fellow, sensuality was ever the dearest to me of
all my possessions. All my life, I have bowed down
before its idols and always wished to end my days in
its arms. My time draws near. Six women more beautiful than sunlight are in the room adjoining. I was
keeping them all for this moment. Take your share of
them and, pillowed on their bosoms, try to forget, as
I do, the vain sophisms of superstition and the stupid
errors of hypocrisy.

NOTE

*The Dying Man rang, the women entered the room, and in
their arms the priest became a man corrupted by Nature—
and all because he had been unable to explain what he meant
by Corrupted Nature.*

The Successful Ruse

THERE are many, many foolish wives who imagine that—provided they do not go all the way with a man—they may indulge at least a certain level of genteel dalliance without offence to their husbands. It is a point of view which not infrequently gives rise to consequences far more dangerous than if their fall were to be complete and utter. The case of the Marquise de Guissac, a lady of quality from Nîmes in Languedoc, furnishes the clearest proof of the proposition which we have expressed in the form of a general truth.

Giddy, scatter-brained, vivacious, having a fair turn of wit and pretty ways, Madame de Guissac believed that a handful of gallant letters, written and received between herself and the Baron d'Aumelas, would have no untoward consequences, firstly because no one would know about them and secondly, because if by some mischance they were to be discovered, she could prove her innocence, since she had done nothing to incur her husband's displeasure. But she was mistaken. Monsieur de Guissac, being an exceedingly jealous man, suspected that a correspondence was being carried on, questioned a chamber-maid, and got hold of a letter. There was nothing ostensible in it to justify his fears outright, though it contained infinitely more than was required to feed his suspicions. Caught in a cruel state of uncertainty, he armed himself with a pistol and a glass of lemonade and burst angrily into his wife's bedroom.

'I am betrayed, Madame,' he cried in a rage. 'Read this note. It tells me all I need to know. The time for wavering is past. I leave you to decide the manner of your death.'

The Marquise spoke up in her defence. She swore to her husband that he was mistaken, saying that it was true that she might perhaps have been guilty of imprudence but was absolutely innocent of any crime.

'Faithless woman, I have been deceived by you for the last time,' replied her furious husband. 'But I shall not be taken in ever again. Come, decide quickly, or else this pistol will make a speedy end of you!'

Poor Madame de Guissac, frightened out of her wits, opted for the poison, picked up the glass and drank.

'Stop!' ordered her husband when she had swallowed part of its contents. 'You shall not die alone. Hated by you, deceived by you, what do you imagine will become of me now?'

And so saying, he drained what was left of the cup.

'O sir!' exclaimed Madame de Guissac. 'In this dreadful pass to which you have brought us both, you will not deny me a confessor nor will you refuse to allow me to embrace my father and mother for the very last time!'

Word having at once been sent to the persons the hapless woman had asked for, she threw herself into the arms of the parents who had brought her into the world and protested once more that she was not guilty. But what words of reproach could be spoken against a husband who believed that he had been deceived and, in punishing his wife so cruelly, had meted out the same sentence to himself? The only path left open now was to surrender to despair and tears flowed on all sides.

Meanwhile, the confessor arrived.

'At this cruel moment of my life,' the Marquise said, 'it is my wish, both for the consolation of my parents and the honour of my memory, to make a public confession.'

And she proceeded, aloud, to tax herself with everything which had lain on her conscience since the day she was born.

Her husband, listening attentively and hearing no mention of the Baron d'Aumelas, and being quite certain in his mind that his wife was unlikely to resort to deceit at such a juncture, stood up, overcome with delight.

'My dear, dear parents,' he cried, clasping his mother-in-law and father-in-law in a single embrace, 'take heart!

And may your daughter forgive me the fright I have given her. She gave me enough cause for worry to justify my giving her a few moments' anxiety in return. There was no poison in the cup from which we both drank. So she may set her mind at rest and so may you all. And let her remember this at least, that not only should a truly good wife never do wrong: she should never do anything which might suggest that she has.'

It was only with the greatest difficulty that the Marquise recovered from the state to which she had been reduced. So utterly had she believed the cup was adulterated that in the heat of her imagination she had already begun to feel the agonizing symptoms which herald death by poison. Tremblingly, she stood up and kissed her husband. Relief replaced suffering, and the young woman, having thoroughly absorbed the lesson of the whole dreadful episode, sincerely vowed that she would henceforth avoid doing anything at all which might be construed as wrong. And she was true to her word. She lived with her husband for thirty years, and during all that time he never had cause to reproach her for anything she did.

The Pimp Well Served

DURING the Regency,* there occurred in Paris an adventure so extraordinary that it still bears repeating even today. In the first place, it tells of furtive lewdness, the precise nature of which was never fully made clear; and in the second, it is a story with three brutal murders, the perpetrator of which was never caught. [We shall summarize]* the theories of what probably happened before relating how it actually ended and shall show how events were fully justified by what led up to the climax. In this way, the ending will perhaps be less frightening.

It is said that Monsieur de Savari, an elderly bachelor who, though badly served by Nature,† was a man of wit and good company and regularly entertained the very best people in his house in the rue des Déjeûneurs,* had taken it into his head to turn his premises into the setting for a bizarre kind of prostitution. Ladies of quality exclusively, both of the married and unmarried kind, who wished with impunity to enjoy voluptuous pleasure under a cloak of the deepest secrecy, could call on him and find a number of partners ready and able to accommodate them—and nothing would ever come of their passing conjunctions which allowed a woman to gather roses without the least risk from the thorns to which arrangements of this sort are all too prone should they become public knowledge and acquire the character of regular liaisons. At some social gathering the next day, the lady, married or unmarried, might well meet up again with the man she had encountered the evening before and give no sign that she knew him, nor would he seem to mark her out from all the other women there, the upshot being no jealousy within marriages, no apoplectic fathers, no separations, no wives or daughters shut up in convents, in short, none of the disagreeable consequences which normally follow affairs of this kind.

† He was a legless cripple. [*Author's note*]

A more satisfactory arrangement could not have been easily imagined, though in all likelihood it would be dangerous to operate a similar scheme nowadays. Indeed, in our own age, when the depravity of both sexes has exceeded all known bounds, it would unquestionably be a matter for legitimate concern that our making it public might itself give people the idea of reintroducing the model if we did not at the same time tell of the cruel fate which befell the man who invented it.

Though he was a wealthy man, Monsieur de Savari, who both devised and managed the scheme, restricted his household to just one servant and a cook so as to avoid having unnecessary witnesses to what went on under his roof. One morning, a man he knew was shown in who had come to ask if he could be given luncheon.

'But of course, you are most welcome,' replied Monsieur de Savari. 'And to show just how delighted I am to accommodate you, sir, I shall get my man to fetch up the very best wine from my cellar . . .'

'One moment,' the friend said after the servant had been given the order, 'I should like to see for myself if La Brie tries to cheat us. I know which barrels are which. I should like to follow him down and watch if he really brings up the best.'

'Very well,' said the master of the house, entering into the spirit of the thing. 'If I were able-bodied, I'd come with you. But I should be most happy if you could make sure the knave does not get up to any tricks.'

The friend left the room, went down to the cellar, picked up a crowbar and brained the servant. Then he went back up to the kitchen, left the cook for dead on the floor, and even killed a dog and a cat which got in his way, before returning to the apartment of Monsieur de Savari who, his handicap leaving him in no position to defend himself, was helplessly slaughtered like his servants. The pitiless butcher, quite unruffled and without feeling the least tinge of remorse for what he had just done, calmly used a blank page of a book he found lying on the table to write down the manner in which he had proceeded, touched nothing, took nothing away, left the house which he locked behind him, and disappeared.

Too many people were in the habit of coming to Monsieur de Savari's house for these horrible murders to remained undiscovered for long. Callers knocked and, on obtaining no answer and being certain that the master could not be out, broke down the doors, whereupon they beheld the horrible state of affairs inside the poor man's house. Not content with leaving a public statement of the details of his actions, the murderer had, over a clock decorated with a death's head and bearing this device, *Look upon this and regulate your life,* had, I said, coolly pinned over this pronouncement a paper which read, *Look at his life and you will not be surprised by his death.*

Such an occurrence could not but attract a great deal of attention. The premises were thoroughly searched but the only item found which had a bearing on the whole ghastly business was an unsigned letter, written by a woman, addressed to Monsieur de Savari, which ran as follows:

'We are lost! My husband has discovered all! You must look for a way out. Only Paparel can talk him round. Get him to speak. Otherwise, there is no hope of salvation.'

A man named Paparel, who worked as a paymaster extraordinary at the War Office, a kindly man of excellent background, was summoned before the Justices. He admitted to knowing Monsieur de Savari but declared that of more than a hundred personages of court and town who had called on the dead man regularly—and the most prominent of these could be named as the Duke de Vendôme*—he himself was one of those with whom Monsieur de Savari was the least acquainted.

Several people were arrested and then freed again almost at once. In the end, enough was learned for it to be clear that there were endless ramifications to the affair which, highly compromising to the honour of half the fathers and husbands in the capital, would also trumpet abroad the names of a very large number of people of the highest rank. For the first time in their lives, prudence replaced severity in the minds of the magistrates. And so the affair ended there. As a result, the death of this unfortunate man, who was of course too guilty to be mourned by honest citizens, called forth no avenger. But if his loss did nothing to increase the stock of Virtue, there is good reason to believe that Vice had cause to grieve for him long and hard, and that independently of the eager rakes who had found so many of Love's blossoms for the picking in the house of that sweet son of Epicurus, the pretty votaries of Venus who had come daily to burn incense upon the altars of love must surely have shed bitter tears over the demolition of their temple.

Everything is measured out thus. On reading this tale, a philosopher would say: if, out of a thousand persons implicated in this adventure, 500 were made happy and the other 500 unhappy, the act which produced the effect is neutral. But if unfortunately the calculation were to give 800 made unhappy through deprivation of pleasure occasioned by the calamity against only 200 who gained by it, then Monsieur de Savari did much more good than evil and the only guilty party was the man who sacrificed him to his wrath. I shall leave you to decide the matter and now turn to another subject.

The Windbags of Provence

IT is well known that there appeared in France, during the reign of Louis XIV, an Ambassador from Persia.* The French King delighted in welcoming to his court strangers from every nation who would admire his greatness and carry home with them a few stray beams of that radiant glory which he made to shine on the furthest-flung corners of the earth. Travelling by way of Marseilles, the Ambassador was received magnificently by its inhabitants. On learning of this, the honourable magistrates of the Parlement at Aix* resolved that when he came to them, they should not be outdone by a city above which, though for no very good reason, they rated their own much more highly. Accordingly, the principal plank in their planning was a ceremonial eulogy of the Persian. It would have been a small matter to deliver an oration in Provençal, but the Ambassador would not have understood it: this problem gave them considerable pause. The Council sat and deliberated. It has never required much for it to sit and deliberate—a peasant wrangle, some fuss or other at the theatre, and especially any case involving whores: matters of this sort have been subjects of great moment for these indolent magistrates ever since the days when they lost the right, fully exercised under François I,* to put the province to fire and sword, and water it with the gushing blood of the unfortunate people who live there.

And so they met and deliberated. But how were they to have the address translated? They deliberated in vain, for they could not see how it was to be done. Was there perhaps in the Worshipful Company of Fishmongers, whose livery conveniently happened to be black, was there perhaps a member of the guild who could speak Persian (though there was not a man among them who was much of a hand at even French)? For the address was written: three celebrated lawyers had laboured over it for six weeks. In the end, either in the ranks of the corporation or somewhere in the town, they ran to earth a sailor who had lived for many years in the Levant and who spoke Persian almost as well as his own vernacular. He was told what was required and agreed to be their man. He learned the address and translated it without difficulty. When the great day came, he was dressed in a First President's ancient black gown and was loaned the fullest wig owned by any of those appointed to the bench. Then, followed by the full complement of magistrates, he advanced to meet the Ambassador. It had been agreed between them what he should do and the orator had particularly recommended those who walked behind him not to take their eyes off him for an instant and to imitate to the very last detail his each and every action. The Ambassador halted in the middle of the mall where it had been arranged that he would be met. The sailor bowed and, unused to having such a splendid wig perched upon his head, his peruke fell off as he made his obeisance and landed at His Excellency's feet. Their honours of the bench, who had sworn to imitate everything he did, promptly shed their perukes and cringingly presented their bald (and here and there somewhat mangy) pates to the Persian. Undismayed, the sailor picked up his wig, put it back on his head, and intoned the eulogy. He spoke so well that the Ambassador was convinced that here was one of his own countrymen. This thought made him extremely angry.

'You miserable wretch!' he exclaimed, reaching for his sabre, 'there can be only one reason why you speak my tongue so well: you are an infidel renegade who has turned your coat against the Prophet. I must punish you for your faithlessness. You must pay at once with your head.'

The poor sailor made vain efforts to defend himself: his words went unheeded. He waved his arms about and swore. Yet none of his gestures was wasted. Each was repeated instantly and energetically by his areopagitic following. In the end, not knowing quite how to extricate himself, he hit upon an unanswerable stratagem, which was to undo his trouser buttons and brandish, for the benefit of the Ambassador, patent proof that he had never been circumcised in his life. This latest action was promptly imitated, and forty or fifty Provençal magistrates made bold, with buttons undone and foreskin in hand, to prove, in the manner of the sailor, that there was not a man among them who was less good a Christian man than St Christopher. It may easily be imagined that the ladies watching the ceremony from their windows were highly diverted by these antics. In the end, the ambassadorial envoy, fully persuaded by such an unambiguous argument and requiring no further convincing that the orator was not guilty and that, moreover, he was come unto a City of Trousers, went on his way with a shrug, probably saying to himself: 'It comes as no surprise to me that these people keep a gibbet in a permanent state of readiness, for a rush to harsh judgement, which is the other face of stupidity, must surely be the natural temper of these barely human creatures.'

It was felt that a painting should be made of this novel manner of professing the faith. It had already been drawn from the life by a young artist. But the Parlement banished the artist from the province and ordered his canvas to be burnt—probably not realizing that in so doing they were ordering themselves to be burnt since they were portrayed in the sketches.

'It does not bother us to be cretins,' said the grave magistrates. 'And even if it did, we have spent too long demonstrating to the whole of France just what cretins we are. But we simply cannot allow a painting to preserve our stupidity for future generations. Posterity will forget this trivial episode and will remember it no more than it remembers Mérindol and Cabrières.* For the honour of the bench, it is much, much better to be assassins than asses.

An Inexplicable Affair Vouched for by an Entire Province

NOT two hundred years ago, there were still parts of France where people were feeble-minded enough to believe that they had only to give their souls to the Devil, in ceremonies featuring rites as cruel as they were fanatical, and everything they asked would be granted by the Prince of Darkness. And not a century has passed since the adventure I am about to relate occurred in one of our southern provinces where it is confirmed today by the still extant public records of two towns and supported by evidence of the kind which would convince even the most hardened sceptic. The reader may be reassured that we speak only after a great deal of thorough checking. Naturally, we cannot give an absolute guarantee that the episode actually happened, but we can and do certify that more than a hundred thousand souls believed that it did, and that there are fifty thousand alive today who will vouch for the authenticity of the entries which record it in official and quite unimpeachable registers. If the reader permits, we shall not say which province and we shall change the names.

Since early youth, the Baron de Vaujour had combined the most appalling libertinism with a taste for all the sciences, especially those which regularly lead Man into error and encourage him to waste on idle fancies and illusions time which could be infinitely better spent in other ways. He was an alchemist, an astrologer, a sorcerer, a necromancer, a quite capable astronomer for all that, and a moderate doctor. At the age of 25, master of his fortune and his actions, the Baron claimed to have discovered in his books that, by sacrificing a child to the Devil in an execrable ceremony involving certain incantations and bodily contortions, the Demon himself could be conjured and, being summoned, would grant your every wish, provided you promised him your soul. He resolved to carry out the hideous ritual, the sole contractual clauses being that he would live happily until his sixtieth year, that he would never want for money, and that, until the age specified, his faculties would also be teemingly productive and function at the highest pitch of their power.

The ghastly deed was done and the bargain was solemnized: this is what happened.

Until he was 60, the Baron, who had an income of no more than 15,000 livres a year, regularly spent 200,000, and never incurred a pennyworth of debt. As far as his sexual prowess is concerned, he could still, at this same age, pleasure a woman fifteen or twenty times in a single night and when he was 45 won a wager of 100 louis against friends who bet him he could not satisfy twenty-five women one after the other in quick succession. He managed it and gave the 100 louis to the women. After another supper party, when a card-game got under way, the Baron arrived and declared that he could not sit in on it as he had no money. Offers of cash were made to him, but he refused. He then walked around the room two or three times while the others played, then rejoined them, asked for a place at the table, and on a single card bet 10,000 louis which he produced in rouleaux in ten or twelve separate raids on his pockets. The bet not being accepted, the Baron asked the reason why. When one of his friends said ironically that the card was not sufficiently covered, the Baron promptly staked another 10,000 louis on it. All these particulars are set out in the archives of two highly respected town halls and we have read them for ourselves.

When he was 50, the Baron decided he would marry. He took to wife a charming young woman from his province and lived equably and happily with her, notwithstanding various infidelities which, given his character, were far too predictable to be held against him. By this woman, he had seven children and for some considerable time the charms of his wife had kept him at home much more than formerly. He lived with his family in the château where, as a young man, he had taken the dreadful vow of which we have spoken, and was in the habit of inviting men of letters to visit him, for he was fond of their company and loved their conversation. Yet as he drew near to the end of his threescore years, recalling his wretched pact and not knowing whether the Devil would now settle for stripping him of his powers or deprive him of his life, his mood changed completely. He became pensive and morose and hardly ever went out any more.

On the appointed day, at the very instant when the Baron became 60 years of age, a servant announced a stranger who, having heard of his talents, craved the honour of being allowed to converse with him. Not thinking just then, as it happened, of those matters which however had constantly preyed on his mind for some years past, the Baron ordered that the man be shown up to his study. He climbed the stairs that led to it and beheld a stranger who, by his speech, seemed to him to be from Paris, a well-dressed man of extremely handsome countenance who immediately began discussing high scientific matters with him. The Baron answered all his questions, the conversation got seriously under way, Monsieur de Vaujour suggested a walk to his guest, the guest agreed and our two philosophers strode out of the château. It was one of the labouring seasons of the year, when the peasants are all out in the fields. Some, seeing Monsieur de Vaujour gesticulating and talking to himself, thought his wits had turned and went off to inform Madame. But getting no reply from the château, these good people returned whence they came and went on staring at their Lord who, imagining that he was conversing with a real person, waved his arms about as people do at such moments. At length, the two learned men set their feet upon an avenue ending in a cul-de-sac from which they could not escape except by returning the way they had come. Upwards of thirty peasants watched them: thirty were later questioned and thirty answered that Monsieur de Vaujour, waving his arms about wildly, had been alone when he entered what was in effect a bower.

After an hour had gone by, the man he believed he was with said:

'So, Baron. You do not recognize me. Do you not remember the promise you made in your youth? Have you forgotten how I have kept my side of the bargain?'

The Baron turned pale.

'Don't be afraid,' said the shade he was conversing with, 'I have no power over your life, but I can take back my gifts and everything that you hold dear. Go back to your house: you shall see what state it is in and shall confront the just punishment of your imprudence and your crimes. I love crime, Baron, I yearn for crime, and yet it is my fate to have to punish criminal actions. Go to your house, I say, and see the error of your ways. You have another five years to live, five years before you die, yet the hope of being some day united with God need not be dashed if only you mend your ways. Farewell.'

Then the Baron, finding himself alone though he had not seen anyone leave his presence, hurriedly retraced his steps, and asked all the peasants he met if they had not observed him go into the bower accompanied by a man of such and such an appearance. Every one of them said that he had been alone and being frightened when they saw him wave his arms about thus, they had even run off to inform Madame. But there was no one in the château.

'No one?' cried the Baron, greatly alarmed. 'But I left six servants, seven children, and my wife there.'

'There is no one at home, sir,' was the answer.

With mounting fear, he ran home and knocked loudly. There was no reply. He broke down a door and went inside. Blood streaming down the stairs proclaimed the catastrophe which was about to strike him down. He opened the door to a large room and there saw his wife, his seven children, and his six servants, all with their throats cut, littering the floor, each in a different pose, lying in pools of their own blood. He fell to the ground unconscious. A handful of peasants, whose statements

are still extant, entered the room and saw the same sight.
They went to the aid of their master who, gradually
recovering his wits, begged them to attend to the last
rites for his wretched family and without more ado made
his way on foot to the Grande Chartreuse* where he
died five years later, having continued during this time
in the exercise of the most pious devotions.

We shall refrain from offering any comment on this
incomprehensible affair. It happened. It cannot be called
into question. But it is inexplicable. Of course, we
should always be on our guard against the belief in
spirits, but when something happens which is universally
authenticated and of the same singular variety as this,
then we must bow our heads, close our eyes, and say: 'I
do not understand how the planets float in space: it
follows that there may well be things on earth which are
beyond my comprehension.'

The Prude, or the Unexpected Encounter

MONSIEUR DE SERNENVAL, who was about 40 years old and in receipt of an annual income of 12,000 or 15,000 livres which he got through quite happily in Paris, had ceased to be active in the business which had once occupied him and wanted for no other distinction but that of burgher of Paris and perhaps a seat on the magistrates' bench. He had been married for only a year or two now to the daughter, then aged 24, of one of his former associates. No one could have been fresher-faced, rosier-cheeked, plumper, more buxom, or milkier-white than Madame de Sernenval. She might not have been built like the Graces, but she was more luscious than the mother of all the Cupids. She might not have had the bearing of a queen, but she exuded such sensuality in every department—eyes so tender and languid, such a pretty mouth, a bosom so firm and shapely, and the remainder designed to provoke such desire—that there were very few beautiful women in all Paris more capable of appealing to a man. But Madame de Sernenval for all her physical attractions had a capital moral failing: insupportable prudery, tiresome devoutness, and such a ridiculously exaggerated brand of maidenly modesty that her husband found it quite impossible to persuade her to appear in the circles he frequented. Taking bigotry to an extreme, Madame de Sernenval was rarely willing to spend a whole night with her husband and even in those moments she deigned to grant him, she did so only with excessive reservations and a night-gown which was not to be raised. A buckler of sorts tastefully positioned at the portals of the temple allowed access thereto only on the express condition that all unseemly gestures not to mention carnal conjoining were forbidden. Madame de Sernenval would have been raised to a pitch of fury if any attempt had been made to broach the limits set by her modesty, and the husband who tried it was likely to run the risk of never regaining the good graces of this chaste and virtuous woman. Monsieur de Sernenval made light of such flummery but, since he adored his wife, felt he should respect her little failings. However, on occasion he did try to talk sense to her. He proved to her in the clearest manner possible that it is not by spending her life in churches and in the company of priests that a good wife properly discharges her duties; that the most important of these are her household responsibilities which any woman with her mind on Heaven will neglect of necessity; that she would do infinitely more honour to the wishes of the Almighty by living respectably among other people than by burying herself in convent gloom; and that there was far more danger in consorting with 'exemplars of the Virgin' than in mixing with those trusty friends whose company she ridiculously refused to keep.

'It is as well I know you and love you as I do,' Monsieur de Sernenval added further, 'otherwise I should be extremely concerned for your welfare when you are at your frequent devotions. How am I to know that if you sometimes forget yourself it is not on some cleric's soft couch rather than kneeling at the altars of the Lord? There is nothing more dangerous than all these villainous priests. It is invariably with their talk of God that they seduce our wives and daughters. It is unfailingly in His name that they dishonour and deceive us. Take it from me, my dear, people may be good anywhere. It is not in the cell of the Buddhist priest nor in the niche of some graven idol that Virtue builds its temple, but in the heart of an honest woman. There is nothing in the respectable company I invite you to keep which runs counter to your duty to worship Virtue. You are generally thought of as being one of her most faithful handmaidens, and I genuinely believe that you are. But what proof do I have that you really deserve your reputation? I should be more convinced if I were to see you resisting the attacks of guileful men. The woman whose virtue is most clearly established is not she who always goes out

of her way to avoid a seducer but she who is sufficiently
sure of herself to face any situation without fear.'

To this, Madame de Sernenval usually said nothing,
for in truth the argument was unanswerable. But she
would weep tears, which is the common way with weak,
fallen, or false women, and her husband did not dare
press the lesson home.

Things had reached this pass when an old friend of
Sernenval named Desportes arrived from Nancy to see
him and at the same time to settle some business which
he had in the capital. Desportes was a man who enjoyed
life, was about the same age as his friend, and in no wise
averse to any of the pleasures which Nature in her ben-
evolence has made available for man's use to help him
forget the ills which she heaps on his head. He did not
demur when Sernenval offered him the hospitality of his
house, was overjoyed to see him again but was at the
same time somewhat taken aback by the strictness of his
wife's behaviour. For, the moment she was aware of the
presence of a stranger in the house, she categorically
refused to put in an appearance and did not even come
down to meals. Desportes felt that he was in the way
and suggested that he should stay somewhere else. But
Sernenval would not hear of it and in the end told him
all about his dear wife's little absurdities.

'You must excuse her,' said the gullible husband. 'She
makes up for these little wrongs with so many virtues
that she has earned my indulgence, and I hope that you
will grant her yours.'

'But of course,' answered Desportes. 'As long as none
of it is directed at me personally, I absolve her entirely.
The shortcomings of the wife of the man who is my
friend shall, to my eye, never be more than commend-
able qualities.'

Sernenval embraced his friend and their thoughts then
turned to pleasure.

If the staggering ineptitude of the two or three dim-
witted officials responsible for keeping the prostitutes of
Paris in order these last fifty years (and notably the

stupidity of one thoroughly dishonest Spaniard who
earned 100,000 écus a year during the last reign by
organizing the kind of inquisition we shall shortly describe), if, I say, the petty puritanism of these numskulls
had not led them to the unimaginably idiotic notion that
one of the most illustrious methods of managing the
State, one of the surest techniques of government, one
of the foundations in short upon which public morality
is built, was to order these unfortunate females to give
an exact account of whichever part of their bodies best
entertained the individual who paid them court, on the
grounds that between the man who ogles a breast and
the man who dotes on bottoms there is incontrovertibly
the same difference as exists between an honest citizen
and a scoundrel, and that when a man falls into one or
other of these categories (and his choice is dictated by
fashion), he must of necessity be the State's greatest
enemy—then, I repeat, had it not been for these despicable platitudes, it is certain that two honourable bur-
ghers, the one having a sanctimonious wife and the other
being a bachelor, could have quite lawfully spent an
hour or two in the company of the aforementioned
young ladies. But because these absurd and infamous
rulings* throw cold water over the pleasures of citizens,
it did not enter Sernenval's head even to let Desportes
suspect that he had this kind of dissipation in mind. But
his friend, observing his reticence and not knowing what
reasons there could be for it, asked him why, having
suggested all the pleasures the capital could offer, he had
not mentioned that one. Sernenval raised the objection
of the stupid inquisition. But Desportes made light of it
and, notwithstanding the official register of keepers of
bawdy-houses, the reports written by police inspectors,
the statements filed by their deputies together with all
the other ramifications of the vile system set up by the
government to keep a check on the pleasures of the
denizens of Paris, he told his friend that he had every
intention of supping with whores.

'Listen,' said Sernenval, 'you can count on me. And

to prove that I take a strictly philosophical point of view
of the whole business, I shall even see to the introductions. But I plead a certain delicacy of sentiment which
I hope you will not hold against me, I mean those feelings I owe to my wife which I cannot find it in me to
overcome. I trust that you will understand if I do not
share your pleasures. I shall procure them for you but
that is as far as I will go.'

Desportes quibbled for a moment, but seeing that his
friend was determined not to budge on this point, he
agreed and they set off together.

The celebrated S. J.* was high priestess of the temple
where Sernenval thought his friend should make his
sacrificial offering.

'What we need is a reliable girl,' said Sernenval, 'a
decent girl. I want you to take special care of my friend
here. He is up from the country, just passing through
Paris. He doesn't want to be going home with an unwanted present, the sort of thing that could ruin your
reputation where he comes from. Just say if you can
supply the necessary and you can name your price for
seeing to his needs.'

'Listen,' said S. J., 'I can see what kind of gentleman
I have the honour of addressing. You aren't the sort I
lead up the garden path. So I'll make you an honest offer
as you will see for yourselves by what I am prepared to
do for you. I've got the very thing. All that needs doing
is for us to agree a price. She's a ravishing creature and
from the minute you hear that voice you'll be absolutely
delighted with her. She's what we call in the trade "a
church belle" because, as you know, my very best customers are clerical gentlemen and I don't serve them up
with just anything. Why, not three days since, the Bishop
of M. gave me 20 louis for her, the Archbishop of R. put
50 her way yesterday, and just this morning she brought
me in another 30 from the Coadjutor of the see of . . .
But I'll let you gentlemen have her for 10, the reason
being that I value your goodwill. But you'll have to keep
strictly to the day and the time. She has a husband, a

jealous husband who has eyes only for her. Since she can
only get away at certain times, you must come punctually at the hour we agree on.'

Desportes haggled for a while, for no whore in the
whole of Lorraine ever fetched 10 louis. But the more
he tried to beat her down, the more she inflated the
quality of the merchandise. In the end, they settled on
the following morning, and ten o'clock sharp was the
hour appointed for the rendezvous. Since Sernenval had
no wish to join the party, the matter of a supper did not
now arise. On this basis Desportes's assignation was
agreed, he being only too glad to get the business out of
the way early so that he would have the rest of the day
free to attend to more important matters. The hour
struck. The two friends arrived at the premises of their
most accommodating bawd and were shown into a dimly
lit, sensually decorated boudoir which harboured the
goddess to whom Desportes was to make his sacrificial
offering.

'Come, o chosen child of Love!' said Sernenval, pushing him into the sanctuary. 'Fly to the voluptuous arms
which are held out to receive you—only don't forget to
come and tell me all about it later. I shall rejoice in your
happiness and my joy will be all the purer because I shall
not feel in the least jealous.'

Our initiate passed into the boudoir. Three whole
hours were barely long enough for his homage. Finally
he emerged, assuring his friend that never in his whole
life had he seen such a woman and adding that the
mother of all the cupids could not have given him so
much pleasure.

'So she really is ravishing, then?' said Sernenval, who
began to feel a certain excitement.

'Ravishing? Oh, I couldn't find words to convey what
she is really like. Even now, when the illusion should by
rights have worn off, I feel that the brush does not exist
which could paint the floods of delight into which she
plunged me. She has a sensual artistry which so enhan-
ces the graces which Nature endowed her with, and puts

such provocative, piquant touches to the pleasure she gives, that I am still reeling from it all. Why not give her a trial yourself? You really should. You may be used to Parisian beauties, but I am absolutely certain that you will readily acknowledge that not one of them was ever a match for her.'

Sernenval remained firm though he did feel a twinge of curiosity. He asked S. J. to arrange for the girl to pass close by him when she left the boudoir. This request was granted and the two friends remained standing to have a better view. At length, the Princess emerged . . .

Great Heavens! Sernenval's thoughts were sent spinning when he recognized his wife! It was she! The prude who could not bring herself to leave her room to meet her husband's friend but who had the gall to sell herself for money in a house of ill-repute!

'You wretch!' he exclaimed furiously.

But his efforts to leap on his perfidious wife were vain. She had realized who he was at exactly the same moment that he had recognized her, and was already far from the bawd's house. Sernenval, now in a state which is hard to describe, began to round on S. J. But she pleaded ignorance and told Sernenval that the young woman in question had been receiving gentlemen under her roof for more than ten years, that is, since well before the unfortunate man had married her.

'The jade!' exclaimed the despairing husband who remained immune to all attempts by his friend to comfort him. 'But no! Let that be an end of it. I owe her nothing but scorn. May she from this day hence be enveloped in my contempt—and may I learn from this bitter lesson that it is not by the hypocritical mask of women that they should be judged.'

Sernenval returned home but did not find his whore there. She had already decided on what course to follow and he did not concern himself with what had become of her. The friend, finding it impossible to remain in his company after what had happened, went his way the next day and the luckless Sernenval, alone, overcome with shame and grief, penned a large quarto volume denouncing hypocritical wives. It did not persuade any women to mend their ways and no men read it.

Émilie de Tourville, or Brotherly Cruelty

IN any family, nothing is as sacred as the honour of its members. Yet should this treasure be tarnished, pearl of great price though it be, ought those who are at pains to protect it go so far in its defence as to assume the shameful role of persecutors of any hapless female who should give them offence? Would it not be more reasonable to consider that the horrible treatment they mete out to their victims fully cancels the often unfounded injury which they complain has been done them? For who in the eyes of reason is the guiltier: some weak, deceived girl, or the relative who, setting up as the avenger of the family honour, turns into the tormentor of the unhappy creature? The drama which we shall set before the reader may help to answer this question.

The Count de Luxeuil, a provincial Lieutenant-Governor,* a man of 56 or 57, was posting home from one of his estates in Picardy one late November evening at about six o'clock when, traversing the forest of Compiègne, he heard a woman's cries which seemed to come from a bend in a road which ran close by the highway which he himself was following. He stopped and ordered his valet who was running by the side of the post-chaise to investigate. He was informed that a young woman of 16 or 17 summers, so covered in her own blood that it was impossible to tell where she was wounded, was calling for assistance. The Count immediately stepped down from his conveyance and hurried to where the distressed girl lay. It was dark and he too experienced difficulties in detecting the source of the blood she was losing. But in the end, guided by the answers to his questions, he found it in the veins in her arms which doctors normally use for bleeding their patients.

'Mademoiselle,' said he, having attended to her wounds as best he could, 'I have no power here to enquire the cause of your misfortunes, nor are you in any fit state to tell me. Pray step into my coach. Let our every thought now be on your part to set your mind at rest and on mine to offer you all the help I can.'

And so saying Monsieur de Luxeuil, assisted by his valet, carried the poor girl to his carriage and they set off.

No sooner did the delectable young woman observe that she was safe than she attempted to stammer a few words of gratitude. But the Count entreated her not to try to speak, and added:

'Tomorrow, Mademoiselle, tomorrow you will, I hope, tell me everything about yourself. But today, by the authority vested in me by age and by my good fortune in being able to serve you, I must insist that you give no other thought than to setting your mind to rest.'

They reached their destination. To avoid attracting attention, the Count ordered his charge to be wrapped in a man's cloak and be escorted by his valet to a suitable apartment in a distant wing of his house. There he called to see her after being embraced by his wife and son who had waited supper for him that evening.

When he came to see the patient, the Count brought a surgeon with him. The young woman was examined and was found to be in a state of indescribable prostration. The pallor of her face was such that it almost seemed to suggest that she had little time to live, and yet there was not a mark upon her. Her weakness, she said, was caused by the enormous amount of blood which she had been losing each day for the past three months. Just as she was about to tell the Count the unnatural cause of so prodigious a loss, she quite fainted away from weakness, and the surgeon declared that she should be allowed to rest while they for their part should be content with administering restoratives and cordials.

The unfortunate young woman passed a fairly comfortable night, but not for six days was she in a fit state to enlighten her benefactor as to the exact nature of what had happened to her. Finally, on the evening of the seventh day, when all the members of the Count's household were still in ignorance of her being hidden there and even she, as a result of the precautions which had been taken, did not know where she was, she begged the Count to hear her out and most particularly to grant his indulgence, however grievous the faults which she was about to confess. Monsieur de Luxeuil, pulling up a chair, assured her that he would never relinquish the desire to oblige her which she naturally inspired in him, and the lovely, intrepid girl began her account of her misfortunes in these terms:

Mademoiselle de Tourville's Story

I am, sir, the daughter of the President de Tourville, a man too eminent and too distinguished in his profession to be unknown to you. After leaving my convent two years since, I never set foot outside my father's house. I lost my mother when I was very young and he took personal charge of my education, and I can honestly say that he spared no effort to ensure that I was given all the graces and pleasing arts proper to my sex. Such attentiveness, my father's stated plans to arrange for me the most advantageous marriage possible, and even perhaps a hint of favouritism, all this, I say, soon awakened the jealousy of my brothers, one of whom, a President of the Parlement these last three years, has just reached the age of 26, while the other, a Councillor of more recent standing, will soon be 24.

I had no idea that I was as thoroughly hated by them as I now have good reason to know I was. Having done nothing to deserve such sentiments on their part, I lived in the sweet illusion that they reciprocated the feelings which my innocent heart conceived for them. O just Heaven! How mistaken I was! Except for the times taken up by the requirements of my education, I enjoyed the greatest freedom in my father's house. Making me and no one else responsible for my own conduct, he let me do as I pleased and for the past eighteen months I even had his permission to walk out in the mornings with my maid either along the terrace of the Tuileries or on the ramparts near which we lived, and in like manner to make calls with her, either on foot or in one of my father's carriages, on women friends or female relatives—provided that I did not do so at times when it is not suitable for a young woman to appear unescorted in social gatherings. All my misfortunes stem from this fatal liberty, which is why, sir, I speak to you of it now. Would to God I had never known such freedom.

A year ago, as I was out strolling in the manner I have described with my maid who was called Julie along a shady path in the Tuileries where I thought I should be more solitary than on the terrace and where the air I breathed seemed purer, six ill-mannered young men accosted us and made it plain by the familiarity of their language that they took us both to be what are commonly called women of the town. Horribly embarrassed by such an encounter and not knowing how to extricate myself, I was about to seek safety in flight from this cruel predicament when a young man, whom I regularly saw walking unaccompanied at more or less the same times as myself and whose appearance and manner bespoke the most proper sentiments, happened to pass by.

'O sir!' I exclaimed, beckoning to him, 'I do not have the honour of being known to you but our paths cross here virtually every morning. I flatter myself that what you have seen of me must surely have told you that I am no adventuress. I beseech you most earnestly to give me your hand, take me home, and deliver me from these ruffians!'

Monsieur de —— (with your leave I shall not reveal his name: I am pledged to silence for good reason) ran up, scattered the depraved young men who were mobbing me, convinced them of their error by the polite and respectful manner of his greeting me, took me by the arm, and led me out of the gardens without further ado.

'Mademoiselle,' said he, a little while before we reached my house, 'I think it would be prudent if I were to leave you here. If I escorted you to your door, an explanation would be called for which might give rise to

a ban on your walking out alone. So say nothing of what
has happened and continue to appear as usual in the
same avenue, since doing so pleases you and since your
parents permit it. I shall be there each day without fail
and you will ever find me prepared, if needs be, to lay
down my life to ensure that your tranquillity is not
disturbed.'

Such a wise precaution and so obliging an offer made
me look upon the young man with a more attentive eye
than I had hitherto thought to. Finding him two or three
years older than I was and with a very handsome face, I
blushed as I thanked him, and the flaming arrows of the
seductive god who is today the cause of all my troubles
struck clear to my heart before I could think of warding
them off. We separated, but I thought I detected in the
manner in which Monsieur de —— took his leave that I
had made the same impression on him that he had
produced in me. I returned to my father's house, took
care to say nothing, and the following morning returned
to the same avenue, impelled by a sentiment stronger
than myself which would have made me brave any perils
I might have encountered there, or rather, might perhaps have led me to desire such dangers to have the
pleasure of being rescued from them by the same man.
I lay bare my soul too openly perhaps, sir, but you did
promise me your indulgence. Each new twist of my tale
will show how much I stand in need of it; this is not the
only imprudent action which you will observe me commit, nor is it the only moment when I shall have occasion
to call upon your compassion.

Monsieur de —— appeared in the avenue six minutes
after I did and, approaching me the moment he saw me,
said:

'May I make so bold, Mademoiselle, to ask whether
yesterday's adventure has led to any talk and whether
you have suffered any ill effects?'

I reassured him on both scores. I said I had followed
his advice, that I was thankful to him, and that I was
confident that nothing could now spoil the pleasure I

took in coming thus to breathe the morning air.

'If you find a measure of charm in this place, Mademoiselle,' Monsieur de —— went on in the most civil tone, 'then those who are fortunate enough to meet you here must surely feel more charmed still, and if I took the liberty yesterday to advise you to say nothing which might jeopardize your walks, you have absolutely no need to be grateful. I venture to assure you, Mademoiselle, that what I did was less for you than for me.'

And as he said this, his eyes looked into mine with such an expression . . . O sir, was it to so kind a man that I should one day owe my misfortunes? I answered him candidly, a conversation started up, we walked twice round the gardens together, and Monsieur de —— did not take his leave without begging me to tell him the name of the person he had the honour of having served the previous day. I saw no reason why I should not divulge it. He told me likewise who he was and we separated. For close on a month, sir, we did not stop seeing each other in this way almost every day and that month, as you can easily imagine, did not go by without our mutually confessing the sentiments which we felt or without our swearing that we would go on feeling them without end.

Eventually, Monsieur de —— implored me to allow him to meet me in a place less cramped than a public garden.

'I dare not call on your father, fairest Émilie,' said he. 'I have never had the honour of being presented to him, and he would soon suspect what motive attracted me to his house: far from promoting our plans, such a step would perhaps harm them greatly. But if you are really sufficiently good and tender-hearted to have no wish to let me die of a broken heart by refusing to grant me what I now venture to ask, I shall tell you how it might be arranged.'

To begin with, I would not listen. But soon I was weak enough to ask him what arrangements he meant. These arrangements, sir, involved our meeting three times a week in rooms belonging to a Madame Berceil, a milliner in the rue des Arcis,* whose discretion and honesty Monsieur de —— vouched for as being the equal of his own mother's.

'Since you are allowed to see an aunt who, as you told me, lives nearby, you must pretend to be going to pay your respects to this aunt. You should really call in on her briefly, then leave, and the rest of the time you would normally spend with her you will spend at the house of the woman I have mentioned. If your aunt is questioned, she will say that she indeed saw you on the day you said you were going to call on her and all that remains is to be careful about the length of your visits— though you can be quite sure that this is something no one will ever think of doing as long as you are trusted.'

I shall not rehearse, sir, all the objections I raised against Monsieur de —— to divert him from his scheme and make him see its dangers: what purpose would be served if I were to acquaint you with my attempts to resist since in the end I succumbed? I promised Monsieur de —— everything he asked. The 20 louis which he gave Julie without my knowledge won her over entirely to his cause, while I worked conscientiously for my own downfall. To make my ruin the more complete and to gorge myself for longer and at greater leisure on the sweet venom which flowed through my heart, I deliberately misled my aunt. I informed her a young lady of my acquaintance (who had been let into the secret and would give the appropriate answers) had been kind enough to offer to take me three times a week to her box at the Théâtre-Français; that I did not dare tell my father for fear that he would not agree to it; but that I should say to him that I would be at my aunt's; and I implored her to vouch that such was the case. After making some difficulties, my aunt was unable to resist my pleadings. We agreed that Julie should come in my stead and that as I was returning from the theatre I should pick her up as I passed so that we should return home together. I showered my aunt with kisses. Oh, how fatally passion blinds us! I actually thanked her for contributing to my ruination, for opening the door to the transgressions which were to bring me to within an inch of the grave!

And so began our meetings at the house of the Berceil woman. Her shop was handsome and her house utterly respectable. She was a person of 40 or so years of age in whom I believed I could place my trust. Alas, I placed too much in both her and my lover, my false-hearted lover. For it is time, sir, that I confessed everything. By our sixth meeting in that pernicious house, he had acquired such power over me and won me over so completely that he was able to take full advantage of my weakness: in his arms I became the idol of his passion and the victim of mine. Cruel pleasures, how many tears have you cost me already? How much more remorse have you still in store to torment my heart until the day I die?

Twelve months went by in this fatal illusion, sir, and took me to my seventeenth year. Each day now my father would speak of finding me a husband and, as you may imagine, I shuddered at the prospect. And then there occurred a baneful event which finally tipped me into the bottomless pit into which I was only too eager to fall. It was surely with the grim permission of Providence that an incident in which I was innocent should be the means by which I was punished for the crimes of which I was guilty, with the express intent of making plain that we can never escape its long arm, that it dogs the transgressor's every step, and that it is out of the most harmless circumstances that Providence fashions the event which becomes the instrument of its vengeance.

One day, I was forewarned by Monsieur de —— that some unavoidable affair of business would rob him of the pleasure of my company for the whole of the full three hours which we were in the habit of spending together; that he would nevertheless drop by a few minutes before our assignation ended; that furthermore, so that nothing be allowed to interfere with our regular practice, I should still come and pass at Madame Berceil's the time I normally spent there; and that in reality, for an hour or two, I should be as amused by the company of the milliner and her shop-girls as I would be by myself at home. I believed I could place sufficient trust in this woman to feel no objection to what my lover proposed. Accordingly, I promised that I should go but begged him not to be too long in coming. He assured me that he would settle his affair as quickly he could. And so I went. O, how ruinously was that day to turn out for me!

Madame Berceil met me at the entrance to her shop but would not suffer me to go up to her quarters as she usually did.

'Mademoiselle,' she said the moment she saw me, 'I am delighted Monsieur de —— is unable to come early today, for I have something to say to you which I dare not tell him, something which requires us both to step outside at once, just for a moment. We could not very well do so if he were here.'

'But what can it be, Madame,' said I, already a little frightened by this beginning.

'A trifle, Mademoiselle, a mere bagatelle,' Madame Berceil went on, 'so pray begin by composing yourself. It is the most trivial matter, I assure you: your affair has come to the attention of my mother. Now, she is an old harridan and as strait-laced as any Father Confessor and I humour her because she has money. But she is quite set against my letting you come here any more. I dare not tell Monsieur de —— but I have thought of a way out. I shall take you off at once to see a colleague of mine, a woman of my age who is every whit as reliable as I am. I shall introduce you. If you like her, you can tell Monsieur de —— that I took you to see her, that she is an honest woman, and that you think it best if your meetings should now take place in her house. If you do not like her, which I do not think for an instant will be the case, then seeing that we shall have been under her roof for only a moment or two, you need not mention anything of our little scheme to him, for I shall take it upon myself to say that I cannot lend him my house any more and the two of you can then get together and look for some other way of continuing to see each other.'

The woman's words struck me as so straightforward, her manner and the tone of voice she used appeared so natural, and my trust in her was so complete and my innocence so total, that I had not the least difficulty in agreeing to do what she asked. Indeed, the only feeling I experienced at all was one of regret at her being unable, as she said, to go on serving us. I told her how genuinely sorry I was for it and we left her shop. The house I was taken to was located in the same street, not above sixty or eighty paces further along from Madame Berceil's front door. There was nothing about the outside which made me uneasy: a carriage entrance, fine casement windows overlooking the street, and everywhere an air of respectability and neatness. And yet I seemed to hear a secret voice cry out from the innermost recesses of my heart that some singular event awaited me in that ill-fated house. I felt a kind of revulsion with each stair I climbed and everything about me seemed to murmur: 'Where do you go, wretched girl? Fly, fly this nefarious place!' But we reached the top and entered a rather fine antechamber which was deserted and from there passed into a drawing-room in which we were immediately shut up, as though there had been someone hiding in wait behind the door. I shuddered. It was dark in that drawing-room, so dark that there was barely light enough to move about in. We had scarcely gone three paces when I was seized by two women. Then the door of a small room opened and inside I saw a man of perhaps 50 years of age flanked by two other women who shouted to those who had laid hands on me: 'Strip her, strip her! Do not bring her here until she is naked!' Recovering from the surprise of being seized by the women and realizing that my salvation lay more in crying out than in being afraid, I raised a pretty hullabaloo. Madame Berceil made every effort to quieten me.

'This will take only a moment, Mademoiselle,' she said. 'Just a little compliance, I beg you, and you'll earn me 50 louis.'

'You unspeakable harridan!' I cried. 'Do not imagine that you can buy and sell my honour like this. I shall throw myself out of a window if you do not release me at once!'

'You'd only end up in a yard that belongs to us, my girl, and you'd soon be retaken,' said one of the ghastly women as she tore off my clothes. 'So believe me, your quickest way home is just to let it happen . . .'

O sir! Pray spare me the remainder of these horrible details! I was stripped bare in a trice, my screams were stopped by the most inhuman methods, and I was dragged towards the vile man who, while making sport of my tears and laughing at my attempts at resistance, gave all his attention to making the fullest use of the unhappy victim whose heart he was breaking. Two women continued to hold me fast and to force me towards the monster who, having complete power to do with me as he liked, dowsed the flames of his culpable ardour with no more than impure manipulations and embraces which left my honour intact.

I was helped to dress quickly and was given back into Madame Berceil's keeping, dazed, bewildered, and filled with a kind of dark, bitter anguish which froze the tears deep in my heart. I looked at her in a fury.

'Mademoiselle,' said she, highly alarmed, before we had even left the antechamber of that hellish house, 'I realize now the full horror of what I have done, but I beg you to forgive me—and at least to reflect a moment before you decide to make a commotion. If you tell Monsieur de —— what has happened, it will be absolutely useless to say that you were brought here against your will. This is the one sort of conduct which he will never forgive you, and you will fall out once and for all with the man whose goodwill you need above all others, since your only means of restoring your honour, which he has already made off with, is to persuade him to marry you. Now, you can be quite sure he will never agree to that if you tell him what has happened.'

'But, you dreadful woman, if that is so, why did you push me into this pit, why did you put me in the position of either deceiving the man I love or losing both my honour and him?'

'Gently, Mademoiselle! Let us say no more of what has happened, for there is no time for it. We must think now only of what needs to be done. If you tell, you are lost; if you say nothing, my house will always be at your disposal, no one will betray you, and you will remain on the same footing with your lover. You must consider if yielding to thoughts of vengeance—and I really could not care less about your revenge because now that I know your secret I shall always be able to prevent Monsieur de —— from harming me—consider, I say, whether the small pleasure of taking your revenge will be much of a compensation for all the dire effects it will bring in its train.'

Fully realizing then with what an abominable woman I was dealing and sensing the force of her arguments, however ignoble they were, I said:

'Let us go, Madame, let us quit this house. Do not leave me here a moment longer. I shall say nothing and you must do likewise. You will continue to serve me since I cannot dismiss you without uncovering infamous dealings which must remain concealed. But I shall at least have the satisfaction deep in my heart of hating and despising you as thoroughly as you deserve.'

We returned to Madame Berceil's shop . . . Just Heaven! On arriving I was assailed by new fears on being informed that Monsieur de —— had been and gone, that he had been told that Madame was out on business and that Mademoiselle was not yet come. At the same time as I learned this, one of the serving girls handed me a note which he had written me in haste. All it contained was these words: 'You are not here. I imagine that you were not able to come at the usual time. I am unable to see you today as I cannot wait. Until the day after tomorrow, without fail.'

His note did nothing to calm me, for there was a coolness about it which did not seem to augur well. Not to wait for me, and so impatient—it all made me feel agitated to a degree I find impossible to express. Might he not have observed us leave the shop and followed us? And if he had, was I not lost and dishonoured? Madame Berceil, who was as worried as I was, questioned everyone. She was told that Monsieur de —— had arrived three minutes after we left, that he had looked very anxious, that he had gone away again at once but had returned to write his note perhaps half an hour later. More alarmed than ever, I sent for a carriage . . . but would you believe, Monsieur, to what degree of effrontery that vile woman dared carry vice?

'Mademoiselle,' said she, observing that I was about to depart, 'say no word of all this: I cannot recommend you too often to keep silent. But should you have the misfortune to break with Monsieur de ——, then, believe me, you should make the most of your freedom and make up pleasure parties with elegant gentlemen—so much better than having just one lover. I know you are a very proper miss, but you are young, your people certainly do not give you much money, and being as pretty as you are, I could put you in the way of earning as much as you liked. Come, come, you're not the only one. There are plenty of fine ladies in the best circles who marry counts and marquis just as you might do some day, and yet, either of their own accord or with their governesses as go-betweens, they once passed through our hands as you could.* As you have seen for yourself, we have special customers for little dolls like you. They treat the goods like roses: they enjoy the fragrance but do not wither the flower. Farewell, my pretty miss, and be all this as it may, let there be no bad feeling between us. As you see, I may yet be able to be of use to you.'

I turned a look of horror on this wicked creature and thereupon left without answering her. I collected Julie from my aunt's as usual and returned home.

I had no means now of communicating with Monsieur de —— since, seeing each other three times every week, we were not in the habit of writing. I had therefore to wait until our next assignation. What would he say to me? What should I answer? Ought I to keep what had happened secret? Was there not the greatest danger if the truth were to be discovered? Was it not therefore much wiser to admit everything? All these different courses of action kept me in a state of indescribable anxiety. In the end, I resolved to follow Madame Berceil's advice, and being confident that secrecy was very much in her interest, I determined to follow her lead and say nothing. But just Heaven! what use to me was all this scheming, because I was never to see my lover again and the thunderbolt which was about to burst over my head was already flashing on all sides!

The day following these events, my elder brother asked me why I thought fit to go out by myself on so many days of the week and at such times.

'I spend the afternoons at my aunt's,' I said.

'That is not true, Émilie. You have not set foot there for a month.'

'O dear brother,' I replied tremblingly, 'I shall tell you everything. One of my friends, whom you know well, Mademoiselle de Saint-Clair, has been kind enough to invite me into her box at the Théâtre-Français three times a week. I did not dare say anything about it for fear that Father would disapprove. But our aunt is fully in the picture.'

'So you go to the play,' my brother said. 'You should have told me. I would have escorted you myself and the business would have been much simpler. But to go alone with a woman who is in no way connected to you and almost as young as you are . . .'

'Come, come,' said my other brother who had come up to us as we spoke, 'Our sister has her pleasures and they must not be interfered with. She is obviously scouting round for a husband and by behaving as she does she is sure to draw them in crowds.'

And with that, both abruptly turned their backs on me. This conversation alarmed me. Yet as my elder brother seemed quite satisfied with the business of the theatre box, I believed that I had succeeded in putting him off the scent and that he would let matters rest there. Moreover, even if both of them had said more, there was no power on earth that could stop me from keeping my next appointment, short of their locking me up. It had become too important to clear the air with my lover for anything to prevent my going to see him.

As for my father, he continued much the same, idolizing me, suspecting nothing of my waywardness, and never for a moment interfering with my liberties. How cruel it is to have to deceive such parents! How surely does the remorse born of such deceit set thorns among the pleasures which are bought at the cost of betrayals of this sort! May this awful example of a cruel passion preserve any young women in the same case as myself from committing my mistakes, and may the suffering which my guilty pleasures have cost me halt them at the brink of the precipice, should they ever hear my pitiful tale!

The fatal day dawned at last. Taking Julie with me, I slipped away as usual. Leaving her at my aunt's, I quickly reached Madame Berceil's street by cab. I stepped down from it. The silence and darkness which filled the house alarmed me prodigiously. No familiar face showed itself to me. The only living soul to appear was an old woman I had never seen before but of whom I was, to my cost, to see only too much. She told me to stay in the room where I was and that Monsieur de ——— —she named him—would shortly come to join me there. A comprehensive chill froze my senses and I collapsed into an armchair, not having the strength to speak a word. Hardly had I done so when my two brothers, pistol in hand, appeared before me.

'You wretch,' cried the elder, 'so this is how you play us false. If you put up the least resistance, if you utter as much as a single cry, you are dead. Come with us. We are about to teach you what it is to betray not only your family, which you dishonour, but also the lover to whom you have given yourself.'

As he spoke these last words, I completely lost consciousness. I regained my senses only to find I had been bundled into a carriage, which seemed to be travelling very fast, between my two brothers and the old woman I mentioned, with my legs bound and both hands tied together by a handkerchief. The tears, up to that moment held back by the extravagance of my despair, now flowed abundantly and for the space of an hour I was plunged into a state which, guilty though I was, would have touched the hearts of anyone else but the two tormentors in whose power I was. They did not say a word to me all the time we travelled. I imitated their silence and remained sunk in my sorrows. At last, the next morning at eleven o'clock we reached a château belonging to my elder brother situated deep in a wood, between Coucy and Noyon.* The carriage drove into the courtyard. I was ordered to stay inside it until the horses and servants were out of the way. Only then did my elder brother come for me. 'Follow me,' he said roughly when he had untied me. I obeyed tremblingly. O God! I was filled with such dread when I saw what horrible den was to serve as my place of detention! It was a low-ceilinged room, gloomy, damp, and dark, protected by iron bars on all sides and lit weakly by a single window which looked out on to a wide moat full of water.

'Here is your abode, Mademoiselle,' said my brothers. 'A daughter who brings dishonour on her family cannot rightly reside anywhere else but here. Your food will be in proportion to the rest of the treatment. This is what you will be given,' they went on, showing me a lump of bread of the kind given to animals. 'Now, though we do not wish to prolong your sufferings unduly yet on the other hand, because we intend to deny you every means of ever leaving this place, these two women,' they said, gesturing to the old woman and to another, virtually her double, whom we had encountered on arriving at the château, 'will be instructed to bleed you in both arms as many times each week as you ran off to be with Monsieur de —— at the house of the Berceil woman. Imperceptibly, at least we hope so, this treatment will lead you to your grave, and we shall not be easy in our minds until we learn that our family is rid of a monster like you.'

So saying, they ordered the women to seize me and there and then, in their presence, the villains—pray forgive my language, sir—in their presence, my heartless brothers had me bled in both arms at once, only ordering an end to the cruel operation when they saw I had lost consciousness. When I came to, I saw them congratulate themselves on their barbarity. Then, as though they were determined that all fate's blows should strike me together, as if they took great pleasure in breaking my heart at the same time as they spilled my blood, my elder brother took a letter from his pocket and, handing it to me, said:

'Read this, Mademoiselle. Read it and learn whom you have to thank for your present troubles.'

I opened it with trembling fingers; my eyes were only just strong enough for me to make out that fatal hand. Great God! It was my lover himself! He it was who had betrayed me! This is what that cruel letter said: its words are still imprinted on my heart in characters of blood:

'Sir, I was foolish enough to love your sister and rash enough to dishonour her. I was on the point of setting all to rights; consumed by remorse, I was about to throw myself at your father's feet, confess my guilt, and ask for his daughter's hand. I feel sure I would have secured my own father's permission, while my birth and background amply qualified me to be allied to your family. But just as these resolves were taking shape in my mind, my eyes, my own eyes convinced me that I was dealing with nothing less than a whore who, under the cloak of assignations motivated by a sentiment as respectable as it was pure, had the gall to go on to satisfy the ignoble desires of the most crapulous men. Do not expect from me, Sir, any further effort to make amends, since I owe you nothing. Henceforth, all my obligation is reduced to this: that I will never speak to you ever again and that I will regard her with the most inviolable hatred and the profoundest contempt. I forward herewith the address of the house which your sister chose for her debauches, so that you, Sir, may have confirmation that I do not play you false.'

No sooner had I read these fatal words when I sank back into a state of the most utter despair. 'No,' I said to myself, tearing my hair, 'no, O cruel man, you never loved me! If your heart had been warmed by the slightest flicker of true feeling, would you have condemned me without a hearing? Could you have thought me guilty of such crimes when it was you I adored? O false heart! And it was by your hand that I was betrayed, your hand that pushed me into the arms of unfeeling brutes who are determined to make me die little by little each day, die without your springing to my defence, die scorned by the man I worship, though I never knowingly of-fended him, though I have never been anything more than a dupe and a victim. O no! my plight is too cruel, it is more than my strength can bear!' And weeping, I threw myself at my brothers' feet, beseeched them either to listen to me or to let all my blood drain out of me drop by drop and put an end to me there and then.

They agreed to hear me out and I told them my tale. But they wanted me out of the way. They did not believe me and treated me even more harshly. In the end, having heaped curses on me and ordered the two women to carry out their instructions to the letter under pain of death, they left me, adding coldly that they hoped never to see me again.

When they had gone, my two keepers left me with bread and water and locked me in. But at least I was alone. I could now surrender to my unbearable anguish and afterwards felt less wretched. In the first convulsions of my despair, I was prompted to take the bandages off my arms, and thus allow myself to die by losing the rest of my blood. But the hideous thought of dying without being vindicated in the eyes of my lover struck me with such violence that I could not set myself on such a course. A moment of calm brought a gleam of hope. Hope! That comforting spirit which springs eternal in the midst of troubles, the divine gift which Nature offers us to counterbalance or calm our woes. 'No,' I told myself, 'I shall not die before I have seen him again. Let this object be uppermost in my mind. I must have no other thought but this. If he persists in believing that I am guilty, that will be time enough to die and I shall at least do so without regret, since life can have no attraction whatsoever for me if I lose his love forever!'

Having made up my mind to this, I resolved to neglect no means of extricating myself from my odious lodging. I had been comforted by these thoughts for four days when my two gaolers came to replace my provisions and, at the same time, to draw off the slender strength I derived from them. They again bled me in both arms and left me prostrate on my bed. They came again on the eighth day and, on my throwing myself at their feet and begging for mercy, they bled me in only one arm. To cut matters short, two months went by in this manner and during all this time I was bled in alternate arms every fourth day. The strength of my constitution sustained me, and my youth, the extreme desire I had to escape from my awful predicament, the amounts of bread I ate to counteract the exhaustion and stay fit enough to carry out my plans, all worked in my favour. By the beginning of the third month I had the good fortune to break through a wall, clamber through the hole I had made into an adjoining unlocked chamber, and escape at last from the château. I was attempting to reach the Paris road on foot as best I could when, as my strength gave out completely at the spot where you found me, I obtained from you, sir, the generous assistance for which my sincere gratitude is but small repayment and which I dare entreat you to continue for some while yet, so that I may be returned to the care of my father who has certainly been deceived and would never be so cruel as to pronounce me guilty before allowing me an opportunity to prove my innocence. I shall show him that I was weak, but he will see at once that I have not been as guilty as appearances seem to suggest. And thanks to your intervention, sir, you will have given a new lease of life to a poor unfortunate who will never cease to be grateful. But you will also have restored to a family the honour of which it believed itself unjustly robbed.'

'Mademoiselle,' said the Count de Luxeuil after giving his fullest attention to Émilie's tale, 'it would be hard indeed to see and hear you and not feel the keenest interest in your welfare. You have evidently not been as guilty as one might have reason to think, yet there has been in your conduct a want of prudence which you would be very hard put not to recognize yourself.'

'O sir!'

'Pray hear me out, Mademoiselle, listen to one who has a greater wish to serve you than anyone else alive. Your lover's behaviour was disgraceful. Not only was it unjust, for he should have enquired further and confronted you, but cruel too. When a man's mind is so made up against a woman that he wants no more to do with her, he may well simply drop her, but he does not denounce her to her own family, dishonour her, betray her into the hands of those who would ruin her, and encourage them to exact vengeance. I find the conduct of the man you loved infinitely reprehensible, but the way your brothers behaved was even more ignoble, indeed atrocious, from every point of view: only butchers would conduct themselves as they did. An offence like yours does not call for such strong punishment: forcible restraint is no solution. In such cases, it is best to say nothing; one certainly does not drain the blood out of the guilty nor does one deprive them of their freedom. Such odious methods bring more dishonour to those who employ them than to the person who is their victim:

they deserve that person's hatred, cause a great commotion, and set nothing to rights. However dear a sister's virtue might be to us, her life should have an entirely higher value in our eyes. Honour may be restored, but blood once shed cannot be replaced. Their behaviour is therefore so unspeakable that it would most certainly be punishable by law if an official complaint were to be laid before the authorities. But to report them would mean resorting to the tactics of your persecutors and it would only make public what we need to keep dark, and we shall not stoop to such methods. I shall therefore proceed quite differently in your interests, Mademoiselle, but I warn you that I can do so only on the following conditions: first, that you agree to give me in writing the addresses of your father, your aunt, Madame Berceil, and the man to whose house this Berceil woman took you; and second, Mademoiselle, that you make no bones about giving me the name of the man you care for. This latter clause is so vital that I make no secret of the fact that I shall be unable to help you in any way whatsoever if you persist in keeping the name I ask for from me.'

Émilie, not knowing what to do for the best, began by complying exactly with the first condition and, giving the addresses to the Count, blushed as she said:

'Do you still require me to name the man who seduced me?'

'Absolutely, Mademoiselle. Without it, I can do nothing.'

'Well, Monsieur, the man is . . . the Marquis de Luxeuil.'

'The Marquis de Luxeuil!' cried the Count who could not disguise the turmoil into which mention of his son's name had thrown him. 'What? Was he capable of stooping so low?' Then, collecting himself: 'He will atone, Mademoiselle, he will atone and you shall be avenged. You have my word on it. Farewell!'

The unexpected ferment into which Émilie's last revelation had plunged the Count de Luxeuil took the poor girl completely by surprise, for she feared she had been tactless in some way. Yet she was reassured by the words the Count had spoken as he left and, understanding nothing of the connections between all these facts which she had no means of linking, and not knowing where she was, she resolved to wait patiently to see what would come of the steps taken by her protector. Meantime, the care which continued to be lavished on her while the Count set about his task finally put her mind at rest and convinced her that her happiness was the sole object of so much concern.

She was given every reason to be fully persuaded that such was the case when, four days after the explanations she had furnished, she saw the Count enter her room holding the Marquis de Luxeuil by the arm.

'Mademoiselle,' said the Count, 'I have brought you in one person the cause of your misfortunes and their redeemer, for he comes on bended knee and begs you not to refuse him your hand.'

At these words, the Marquis threw himself at the feet of his beloved. But the surprise was too much for Émilie. Not yet strong enough to bear it, she fainted into the arms of the maid who attended her. Help, however, being at hand, she soon recovered her senses only to find herself in the arms of her lover.

'O cruel man!' she exclaimed, shedding a deluge of tears, 'what grief have you brought upon the one you loved! How could you believe her capable of the vile actions you dared suspect her of? The Émilie who loved you may have been the victim of her own weakness or of the villainy of other people, but she would never have been unfaithful to you!'

'O you whom I worship,' cried the Marquis, 'forgive a despicable fit of jealousy induced by false appearances! We are safe now from their effects but were not those appearances, alas, against you?'

'You should have had a better opinion of me, Luxeuil, and then you would not have believed me capable of deceiving you. You ought to have paid less attention to your aching heart and more to the sentiments I flattered myself I had inspired in you. Let this example teach my sex that it is almost always through excess of love, almost invariably because we give ourselves too quickly, that we lose the respect of the men we adore. O Luxeuil, you would have loved me better if I had loved you less quickly—and you punished me for my weakness. What ought to have made your love stronger is precisely what made you suspect mine.'

'Let all faults be forgotten on both sides,' broke in the Count. 'Luxeuil, your conduct has been reprehensible and if you had not immediately offered to make amends and had I not recognized the sincerity of your intentions in your heart, I should have wished never to set eyes on you again. "When love is true," as our old troubadours put it, "then, though words are said and sights are seen that bring discredit on your queen, listen not to ear and eye but only to your own heart's sigh."† Mademoiselle, I shall look forward to your complete recovery with impatience,' said the Count, turning to Émilie. 'It is my wish to return you to your family as nothing less than my son's bride-to-be, and I flatter myself that they will not refuse to join with me in mending your fortunes. If they do not, my house shall be yours, Mademoiselle. Your marriage shall be celebrated here and whether others agree to it or not, I, for my part, until my dying day, shall always consider myself honoured to have you as a cherished daughter.' Luxeuil embraced his father warmly. Mademoiselle de Tourville clasped her benefactor's hands and burst into tears, and then she was left to herself for an hour or two to recover from events which, had they been prolonged, would have delayed the recovery which was so eagerly desired by all parties.

Exactly two weeks after her return to Paris, Mademoiselle de Tourville being fit enough to get up and ride out in a carriage, the Count bade her don a white dress which matched the innocence of her heart. Nothing was omitted to heighten the bloom of her beauty which was

† So said the troubadours not of Picardy, but of Provence. [Author's note]*

further enhanced by a lingering pallor and the last of her
fatigue. Then she, the Count, and Luxeuil drove to the
house of the President de Tourville who had not been
forewarned and whose surprise on seeing his daughter
shown in was prodigious. He was with his two sons and
her unexpected entrance etched lines of anger and rage
on their faces. They knew their sister had escaped, but
they believed she lay dead in some forest glade and, as
was plain to see, had got over her loss without undue
anguish.

'Sir,' said the Count as he handed Émilie to her father,
'here is Innocence itself which I now return to your
keeping.' Émilie flung herself at her father's feet. 'I ask
forgiveness for her,' the Count went on, 'though I
should be the last to do so were I not absolutely convinced that she was deserving of it. Now sir,' he continued quickly, 'the surest proof I can give you of the
profound regard I have for your daughter is to ask her
hand in marriage for my son, which I now do. Our
respective positions in society amply justify the alliance,
sir, but were there some falling short on my part in the
matter of fortune, I should gladly sell all I possess to
provide my son with a competence worthy to be offered
to your daughter. Pray settle this matter, sir, and give
me leave not to quit you until I have your word on it.'

The elderly President de Tourville, having always
adored his dear Émilie, being at bottom goodness itself
and having these twenty years and more retired from the
active discharge of his official duties precisely on account of this very excellence of character,* the old President, as I say, liberally scattering his tears on to the
bosom of his darling girl, answered the Count saying
that he was only too delighted by the proposed match
and that he regretted only that his dear Émilie was not
more worthy of it. The Marquis de Luxeuil threw himself at the President's feet and begged forgiveness for his
errors and permission to atone for them. Pledges were
given, agreement was reached, and all concerned regained their composure. Only the brothers of our tender

heroine refused to share the general joy and pushed her away when she stepped forward to embrace them. Such behaviour made the Count very angry, and he tried to bar the way of one of them as he attempted to leave the apartment. But Monsieur de Tourville said to the Count:

'Leave them, sir, let them be. They have grossly deceived me, for if this dear girl had really been as guilty as they told me she was, would you now be so set on giving her to your son? They marred my happiness by depriving me of my Émilie. Let them be.'

Thereupon both wretches, fuming with rage, departed, after which the Count informed Monsieur de Tourville of the horrible things his sons had done and of the undoubted wrongs his daughter had committed. The President, noting the lack of proportion between her faults and the severity of their punishment, swore that he would never speak to his sons again. The Count soothed his anger and made him promise to blot from his memory everything that had happened. The marriage took place a week later. The brothers refused to attend, but their presence was not missed and they were regarded with universal contempt. Monsieur de Tourville made do with requiring them to say nothing of the matter under pain of being locked up themselves, and they kept a silence which, however, did not exclude their boasting of their ignoble behaviour by criticizing their father's leniency. Those who came to know of these unfortunate happenings were appalled by the dreadful particulars which marked them, and exclaimed:

'O just Heaven! Here is an instance of what horrible things people can do in private when they take it upon themselves to punish the crimes of others! It is rightly said that such infamy is the preserve of the crazed, half-witted devotees of Themis. Reared on a diet of pettifogging inflexibility, raised from childhood to harden their hearts to the cries of the unfortunate, having blood on their hands from the moment they leave the cradle, free with their judgements of others but allowing themselves great latitude, they are convinced that the only way of keeping their private vices hidden and their public jobbery safe from view is to adopt a policy of unbending, unyielding rigour which gives them the outward manner of the goose and the inner character of the tiger. The only purpose of this manner of proceeding, which stains their hands with crimes, is to fool the gullible and give the wise man the profoundest loathing for their odious principles, their bloodthirsty laws, and their contemptible persons.'*

Augustine de Villeblanche, or
Love's Stratagem

'OF all Nature's anomalies, the one people talk about most, the one which appears strangest of all to those pseudo-philosophers who analyse everything and understand nothing,' Mademoiselle de Villeblanche, of whom we shall presently have occasion to speak more, remarked one day to one of her closest women friends, 'is the peculiar taste which women of a particular constitution or temperament conceive for other persons of their own sex. Since long before the time of the immortal Sappho,* and of course subsequently, there has never been a single region of the globe or any city which has not furnished us with examples of women addicted to this fancy. Given such overwhelming evidence, it would seem more reasonable to arraign Nature for her eccentricity than to tax such women with unnatural crimes. Yet they have always been judged harshly and were it not for our sex's irresistibly orthodox ascendancy, who knows if a Cujas or a Bartole or a Louis IX* might not have framed laws which sent these sensitive, unfortunate females to the stake, just as they thought fit to legislate against men who, built along the same singular lines and, for equally good reasons of course, believed they could manage very well by themselves and supposed that the mingling of the sexes, though useful for the propagation of the species, did not have quite the same value from the point of view of sexual pleasure. God forbid that we should take sides on this question, but my dear, don't you agree,' went on the fair Augustine de Villeblanche, shooting kisses at her friend which seemed just a trifle suspect, 'that instead of the public burnings, the contempt, and the sarcasm which as weapons have nowadays lost their cutting edge, it would be infinitely simpler if, in a matter which does not affect society at large in any way and is of no concern whatsoever to God—though it may be rather more useful to Nature than is generally thought—it would be simpler, I say, if everyone were to be allowed to do as they pleased? What could there possibly be to fear from such depravity? It will be quite clear to anyone with common sense that impropriety of this kind may well prevent more serious evils, but I defy anyone to show how it could ever lead to more dangerous excesses. O just Heaven! who can really be afraid that such inclinations in persons of both sexes will mean the end of the world, that they will sell precious humankind short, or that their so-called crime will doom us to extinction, and all because they have not gone forth and multiplied? If you think about it, you will see that this alleged loss of population is a matter of total indifference to Nature. Not only does Nature not show her displeasure at it, but she demonstrates in countless ways that she is very much in favour and fully approves. Why, if such prevention of life really made Nature angry, does she tolerate so many instances of it? If producing offspring were really so vital to her, would she have arranged matters so that women are capable of doing so for only a third of their lives? Or that from birth half the creatures she gives life to should have tastes which run counter to the procreation on which she seems nevertheless to be so intent? Or putting it more plainly still: she may allow all species to multiply, but she certainly does not require them to do so. Knowing that there will always be far more individuals than she needs for her purposes, it would not occur to her to block the inclinations of anyone who does not have the uses of procreation in view and is revolted by the thought of it. Oh! let us admit that Mother Nature knows best! Let us remember that her powers are immense, that nothing we do could ever offend her, and that the crime that threatens her power will always be beyond our reach.'

Mademoiselle Augustine de Villeblanche, a sample of whose reasoning we have just overheard, having at 20 been left mistress of her own actions and of an annual income of 30,000 livres, had in accordance with her tastes decided that she would never marry. She was of good but not illustrious birth, the daughter of a man who had made his fortune in the Indies: he had left no other child but her and died without managing to persuade her to take a husband. Since we have no wish to mislead, it must be said that there was in Augustine's reluctance to embrace the married state a good deal of that fancy in defence of which she has just spoken so warmly. Whether it was on account of advice she had been given, her education, the way she was made or her hot blood (she was born at Madras), the promptings of Nature or for any other reason you might care to name, Mademoiselle de Villeblanche detested men and, surrendering completely to what chaste ears will understand by the word Sapphism, she found satisfaction only with members of her own sex and was compensated by the Three Graces for what she lost by her contempt for Eros.*

Augustine was a great loss to men. Tall, pretty as a picture, with the most beautiful brown hair, a slightly curved nose, dazzling teeth, eyes so expressive, so vivacious, and skin so silky, so white—in short, the whole ensemble exuded voluptuousness of so piquant a sort that it was inevitable that when men saw her so obviously made to give love but so clearly set against receiving it, many quite naturally came out with endless sarcastic comments directed against a taste which, though straightforward enough, nevertheless robbed the altars of Paphos of one of the universe's most eligible handmaidens, and consequently never failed to anger the votaries of the temples of Venus.* Mademoiselle de Villeblanche laughed heartily when these complaints and tasteless remarks reached her ears, but they did not stop her from continuing to indulge her caprices.

'It is the absolute height of folly,' she would say, 'to feel ashamed of the proclivities which Nature has implanted in us. Making mock of a person who has unusual tastes is every whit as barbarous as scoffing at a man or a woman who has been blind or lame since the womb. Yet it would be easier to stop the stars in their course than to make foolish people see the sense of such a reasonable point of view. One's pride derives no small pleasure from laughing at defects from which one is oneself free, and this pleasure gives such enjoyment to people and more particularly to stupid people that it is rare that they are observed to forgo it. All of which, furthermore, breeds spiteful comments, unfeeling witticisms, and shabby puns. Now in society, which is to say in that press of human beings brought together by boredom and made duller still by collective stupidity, it is very amusing to chat away for a couple of hours without actually saying anything, so utterly delicious to shine at the expense of others and raise with due censoriousness the issue of a vice that is quite foreign to one's own nature—and this of course amounts to a kind of indirect singing of one's own praises. Since such rewards are on offer, people are even prepared to side with others and will join forces against anyone who commits the grave sin of not thinking like the common herd. Afterwards, they go home bloated with all the clever things they have said whereas at bottom all they have demonstrated by their behaviour is their own priggishness and stupidity.'

So thought Mademoiselle de Villeblanche and, her mind quite made up to brook no constraint, paying no attention to what people said, rich enough to go her own way, having better things to do than to worry about her reputation, setting her sybaritic sights on a life of sensuous pleasure and not on heavenly bliss in which she hardly believed at all—and she believed even less in immortality which, to her way of thinking, was a highly chimerical notion—and, surrounded by a small circle of like-minded women, our dear Augustine innocently indulged every pleasure which took her fancy. She had had many suitors but all had been treated so badly that matters had almost reached the point where no one thought she would ever be conquered, when a young man named Franville, who was almost as well born and at least as rich as she, having fallen madly in love with her, not only proved to be undeterred by her unbending severity but even undertook with grim determination not to leave the field until she yielded. He informed his friends of his intention. They laughed at him. He maintained that he would succeed. He was challenged to do so. He accepted. Franville, two years younger than Mademoiselle de Villeblanche and still virtually beardless, had a trim figure, fine features, and the most beautiful hair imaginable; when he was dressed as a girl, he looked so well in female costume that he invariably deceived persons of both sexes. Some were fooled, though others knew exactly what they were about, but from them all he had received a host of declarations so unambiguous that within the space of the same day he could easily have become the Antinous of this Hadrian or Adonis to that Psyche.* It was in woman's clothing that Franville planned to win Mademoiselle de Villeblanche. We shall see how he set about it.

One of Augustine's greatest pleasures was to dress up as a man at Carnival time* and do the rounds of all the social gatherings got up in a disguise which so exactly matched her tastes. One day, Franville, who had been having her followed and until that moment had taken care not to show himself overmuch, discovered that she whom he worshipped was to be present that evening at a ball given by the Friends of the Opera, where any mask could freely enter: true to the charming girl's customary practice, she would be going as a Captain of Dragoons. He for his part disguised himself as a woman. Fitted out and dressed as prettily and as meticulously as could be, he put on a great deal of rouge but decided against using a mask. Then, accompanied by one of his sisters who was considerably less attractive then he, he took himself off to the ball where the lovely Augustine went only to prowl.

Before Franville had circled the room three times he caught Augustine's practised eye.

'Who is that pretty girl?' said Mademoiselle de Villeblanche to the woman friend she was with. 'I do not seem to recall seeing her anywhere before today. How could so ravishing a creature have escaped us?'

These words were hardly out of her mouth when she began trying every way she could to start a conversation with the counterfeit Mademoiselle de Franville who began by running away, then stopped and turned round, eluded her and ran off again in the most tantalizing manner. Finally, she was cornered and a banal conversation was struck up which gradually grew more interesting.

'It is terribly warm here in the ballroom,' said Mademoiselle de Villeblanche. 'Why don't we leave our companions to themselves and take a turn in the ante-rooms where there's gaming and we can find something to drink.'

'O sir!' said Franville to Mademoiselle de Villeblanche, still pretending to believe she was a man. 'Really, I dare not. I'm only here with my sister, but I know my mother is to bring the man I am to marry and if either of them were to see me with you, there would be the most awful fuss.'

'Come, come. You must learn to pay no attention to these childish fears. How old are you, my sweet?'

'I am 18, sir.'

'So! Well, let me tell you that if you are 18, you should be entitled to do whatever you like. Come on, follow me—and don't be afraid.'

Franville allowed himself to be led away.

'Can it be true, you fascinating creature,' went on Augustine making off with what she still assumed was a girl towards the salons adjoining the ballroom, 'that you are really going to be married? You have my sympathy. And who is this husband you are to marry? Some clod, I'll wager. He will be a very lucky man! I'd willingly change places with him! But would you rather have someone else as a husband? Me, for instance? Say, my angel. Don't be shy.'

'Alas sir, as you know, when we are young we are not free to follow our hearts.'

'Come now, turn the ghastly fellow down! We could get to know each other better and if we saw eye to eye, we could come to an . . . arrangement. I, thank God, need no one's permission. I am just 20, but I have full control of my fortune and if you could persuade your parents to turn a favourable eye in my direction, then a week from now you and I could be bound by everlasting ties.'

Chatting thus, they left the ballroom. The artful Augustine, who had no intention of making off with her to talk of sweet nothings, skilfully led her into a room set well apart from the others which, by prior arrangement with the organizers of the entertainment, she always ensured was reserved for her exclusive use.

'O dear God!' cried Franville when he saw Augustine lock the door behind them and felt himself gathered up in a close embrace, 'Just Heaven! What are you thinking of? A tête-à-tête here, sir? In so secluded a place? Unhand me! Let me go, I beseech you or I shall scream for help!'

'I shall prevent you from doing so . . . thus, you angel from heaven,' said Augustine, planting her luscious mouth on Franville's lips. 'Now scream—if you can! The pure stream of your rose-sweet breath will fan my heart into a prompter blaze!'

Franville defended himself tepidly: it is difficult to be very angry when being kissed so tenderly for the first time by the person you adore. Suitably encouraged, Augustine returned more vigorously to the attack, going to it with the zest peculiar to delicious women of her persuasion. Soon hands began to stray and Franville, counterfeiting the melting female, allowed his to roam too. Clothes were flung off and fingers ventured almost simultaneously to places where both parties hoped to find what they were seeking. Then Franville, suddenly exchanging one role for another, cried out:

'O just Heaven! But . . . but you are a woman!'

'You loathsome beast!' said Augustine, putting her hand on certain . . . endowments, the condition of which left no room for illusion. 'Have I put myself to a great deal of trouble only to land myself with an objectionable man? Oooh! I'm so unhappy!'

'No more unhappy than I,' said Franville, straightening his clothes and affecting an air of deepest contempt. 'I adopt a disguise which will attract men—I like men, I run after them—and all I come up with is a tart.'

'Tart? I'm no tart,' said Augustine sharply. 'I've never been one in my life! No one who loathes and detests men can be called a tart!'

'What? You are a woman and you hate men?'

'Yes, and for exactly the same reason that you are a man and you hate women.'

'What an extraordinary thing. What more is there to say?'

'Well, it's all dreadfully upsetting for me,' said Augustine, with all the marks of the most evident bad temper.

'To tell the truth, Mademoiselle,' said Franville bitterly, 'it has been even more tiresome for me. This means that I am now dishonoured for the next three weeks: perhaps you knew that in our Order we take a vow never to touch a woman?'

'I should have thought a man could touch a woman like me without denting your honour.'

'I can't honestly see any good reason for making an exception for you nor can I understand how owning up to a vice should make you any more deserving a case.'

'Vice! I hardly think you are in any position to hold my vices against me seeing that yours are just as depraved as mine.'

'Come now,' said Franville. 'There is no need for us to quarrel. Let's call it quits. The quickest solution would be to go our separate ways and never see each other again.'

And so saying, Franville made as if he were about to open the door.

'One moment,' said Augustine, preventing him. 'I'll wager that you intend to tell everybody about our little encounter.'

'I might, if it amuses me.'

'Still, it doesn't matter. Thank God, I am above wor-

rying about what other people say. Go, sir, go. Say
whatever you like. But,' she said, stopping him once
again, 'this whole business has been most unusual, you
know,' she went on with a smile. 'Both of us were completely taken in.'

'Ah,' said Franville, 'but the mistake was much more
painful to someone with my tastes than to anybody with
yours. The lack of . . . it was really most distasteful.'

'Now just a moment! You don't imagine that we find
what you have to offer us any less nauseating? But look
here, both of us found the experience equally repulsive.
Still, it was a most amusing incident. At least there is
nothing to stop us agreeing on that. Are you going back
to the ball?'

'I don't know.'

'I don't intend to,' said Augustine. 'You have made
me feel quite cross. I shall go to bed.'

'Capital idea.'

'But perhaps, sir, you would be civil enough to give
me your arm as far as my house—I live close by. I did
not bring my carriage. You can leave me at my door.'

'Of course, I would be only too delighted to escort
you,' said Franville. 'Our tastes need not prevent us
from being polite. Will you take my hand? Here.'

'I shall take it—but only because there's no one else
available.'

'And for my part, please believe that in giving you my
arm I wish only to appear civil.'

They reached the door of the house where Augustine
had rooms and Franville prepared to take his leave.

'Charming!' said Mademoiselle de Villeblanche.
'Surely you do not intend to leave me here in the street?'

'I'm most terribly sorry,' said Franville. 'I didn't
dare . . .'

'How churlish you men who don't like women can be!'

'The thing is, do you see,' said Franville, who nevertheless gave his arm to Mademoiselle de Villeblanche
and escorted her up to her apartment, 'to tell the truth
I should very much like to get back to the ball and try

to redeem my foolish behaviour.'

'Foolish behaviour! So you are none too pleased, then, to have met me?'

'I did not say that. But isn't it true that both of us could have done rather better for ourselves?'

'Yes, you are right,' Augustine said finally as she entered her apartment, 'absolutely right. I certainly could have. For as it is, I fear that this fateful meeting of ours will cost me my happiness for the rest of my life.'

'Really? In that case, you cannot be very certain of your feelings.'

'I was yesterday.'

'Well, if that's so, then you cannot be particularly bound by your principles.'

'I'm not bound by anything. Oh, I've no patience with you.'

'Very well, Mademoiselle, in which case I shall go. God forbid I should impose myself on you any longer.'

'No, stay. I command you. Could you, for once in your life, bring yourself to do a woman's bidding?'

'There's nothing I cannot do,' said Franville compliantly, and he sat down. 'See? I told you so. I am a very civil sort.'

'It is really quite dreadful, you know, that you should have such perverse tastes at your age.'

'Do you think it is particularly respectable to have such bizarre preferences at yours?'

'Oh, it is quite different for us. We see it as reserve, or modesty, even pride if you like. But it is also the fear of surrendering to your sex which invariably uses seduction as a means of dominating us. Still, our senses cannot be denied and we arrange matters quite nicely among ourselves. Providing we set about it discreetly, we can manage a veneer of respectability which deceives most people. As a result, Nature is happy, decency is respected, and morality is not outraged.'

'I should call that a fine collection of sophisms. Going on similar lines, anyone could justify anything. Besides, you have not said anything that could not equally be said in our favour.'

'Nonsense! Your way of thinking is quite different and you cannot possibly fear the same things as we do. What is victory to you is defeat for us. The more battles you win, the greater your reputation. If you refuse to respond to what we make you feel, then you can only do so deliberately, from sheer vice and depravity.'

'I really think you could convert me.'

'I should like to.'

'But what would you gain by converting me, so long as you yourself continue to labour under your misapprehensions?'

'My sex would have reason to be grateful to me. And since I am on the side of women, I am only too happy to do what I can for them.'

'If the miracle were to happen, its effects would not be quite so general as you seem to think. I should not want to be converted just for one woman so that she might try me.'

'But the principle is honourable.'

'Yes, and certainly making up one's mind without first exploring all the possibilities does savour rather of obstinacy.'

'What? Haven't you ever been with a woman?'

'Never. And you? Would you by any chance be as absolutely pure in that department as I am in mine?'

'I wouldn't say pure, exactly. The women we deal with tend to be so resourceful and thorough that they leave nothing intact. But I have never obliged a man in my whole life.'

'And you swear to that?'

'Yes. Nor do I ever want to see or know one with tastes as bizarre as mine.'

'I very much regret not having made the same vow myself.'

'Oooh! Was anyone ever more impertinent!'

And so saying, Mademoiselle de Villeblanche stood up and told Franville he was free to go. Our young gallant, still as cool as ever, bowed low and made ready to leave.

'So you are returning to the ball, then,' said Mademoi-selle de Villeblanche curtly, casting a look in his direction which was a mixture of contempt and the most ardent love.

'Why yes. I do believe I mentioned it.'

'In other words, you are incapable of making for me the sacrifice I have made for you.'

'I'm sorry? What sacrifice have you made for me?'

'I came home only because I did not want to stay any longer after having the misfortune of meeting you.'

'Misfortune?'

'You force me to use the word. But I could use quite a different word. It's entirely up to you.'

'And how would you reconcile that with your tastes?'

'When people are in love, they will give up anything.'

'That's quite true. But you couldn't possibly love me.'

'No I couldn't, not while you persisted with those loathsome practices I discovered in you.'

'What if I gave them up?'

'Then I should immediately sacrifice my own on the altar of love. Oh, you unfeeling wretch! Do you realize how much it hurts my pride to confess this? Do you realize what you have forced me to say?' said Augustine tearfully as she collapsed into a chair.

'I have obtained the most flattering admission I could ever hope to hear from the most beautiful lips in the whole universe!' cried Franville, throwing himself at Augustine's feet. 'Ah! dearest girl, my sweetest love! It was all a ploy! Please say you will not punish me! I beg mercy on bended knee and I shall not get up again until I am forgiven. You see before you, Mademoiselle, the most constant, the most passionate lover. I believed that my stratagem was necessary if I was to win your heart which I knew was so stern, so unbending. Have I succeeded, fair Augustine? Will you now spurn the love free of vice which you declared for a guilty lover, for one as guilty as I . . . as guilty as you thought I was? Oh, how could you have imagined that an impure passion could ever exist in the heart of one who burns only for you!'

'Of all the underhanded . . . It was all a trick! . . . but I forgive you. Still, you hypocrite, this means you have nothing to give up for me and my pride is suitably mortified. But no matter, I shall give up everything for you. To please you, I gladly renounce all the errors into which mortals are led as much by vanity as by taste. I sense that Nature, smothered beneath bad habits which I now thoroughly detest, has won. Her power is irresistible. She created us women for you and she made you men for us. Let us obey her laws. It is through love that Nature has taught me to respect them and love will make them ever more sacred in my heart. Here is my hand, sir. I believe you are an honourable man and eminently acceptable as a suitor. If I deserved to forfeit your good opinion momentarily, then perhaps I may make up for the error of my ways by my attentiveness and affection, and I shall force you to acknowledge that a wayward imagination does not necessarily debase a soul that is well-born.'

Franville, having achieved what he wanted and splashing tears of joy on to the fair hands to which his lips were still pressed, now stood up and threw himself into her arms which opened to receive him.

'This is the happiest day of my life,' he cried. 'Can there be anything to equal my victory? I have returned a straying heart to the path of virtue and in that heart I shall reign for ever!'

Franville showered kiss after kiss on his divine, his darling love, and then they parted. Next day, he informed his friends of his success. Mademoiselle de Villeblanche was far too good a match for his parents to refuse their consent, and he married her within the week. Affection, trust, the most scrupulous reserve and the strictest modesty set the seal on his marriage and, in succeeding in making himself the happiest of men, he also proved sufficiently astute to turn the most libertine of young ladies into the most chaste and virtuous of wives.

The Law of Talion*

AN upstanding burgher of the province of Picardy, a
descendant perhaps of one of those illustrious troubadours hailing from the banks of the Oise or the Somme
who were dragged from their torpid slumber in the sha-
dows some ten or a dozen years ago by one of the great
writers of our century,* an upright, respectable burgher,
as I was saying, once lived in the town of Saint-Quentin,
rightly famed for the great men it has given to Literature*—and lived there with honour too, he, his wife,
and a female cousin three times removed who was a nun
in one of the town's convents. The cousin three times
removed was small and dark, had vivacious eyes, a pert
face, a turned up nose, and a trim figure. She was afflicted with 22 years of age and had been a nun for four
of them. Sister Petronille, such was her name, had moreover an attractive voice and a temperament which inclined more to the profane than to the sacred. As for
Monsieur d'Esclaponville, which was the name of our
good bourgeois, he was easy-going, cheerful and stout,
aged about 28, extremely fond of his cousin and somewhat less of Madame d'Esclaponville, for he had been
sharing her bed for ten years—and a habit of ten years'
standing is decidedly fatal to the fires lit by Hymen.
Madame d'Esclaponville—for we must paint her to the
life: what would people think if we did not portray our
characters to the life in an age when only paintings are
called for, to the point where even tragedies are not
accepted for performance unless the art dealers can spot
at least six good subjects to be got out of them ?*—Madame d'Esclaponville, I say, had hair more like straw
than flax, a rather pallid complexion, quite pretty eyes,
a figure of the fuller sort, and the kind of chubby cheeks
which are generally said by the best people to make a
person 'look well'.

Up to this point, Madame d'Esclaponville had been
quite unaware that there is always a way of paying back

an erring husband. Virtuous like her mother who had lived with the same man for eighty-three years without once being unfaithful to him, she was still sufficiently naïve and innocent not to have any inkling of the appalling transgression which the casuists have named 'adultery' but which more accommodating persons who take an easier line with everything call simply 'dalliance'. But a wife who has been deceived quickly learns to extract counsels of vengeance from her resentment, and since no one likes to be thought neglectful, there is nothing she can do that she will not do to deny other people an opportunity of querying her conduct in such matters. In the end, Madame d'Esclaponville became aware that her dear husband was paying over-frequent visits to the cousin three times removed. The green-eyed god of jealousy took possession of her heart. She observed, made enquiries, and discovered that there was hardly any news in Saint-Quentin quite so public as her husband's affair with Sister Petronille. Finally, sure of her ground, Madame d'Esclaponville informed her husband that his behaviour wounded her through and through, and that her conduct did not warrant such treatment and she begged him to give up his wicked ways.

'Wicked ways!' her husband replied coolly. 'But don't you see, my dear, that I am working for my salvation by sleeping with my cousin? For she is a nun! The soul is cleansed by such sacred dealings, we draw close to the Supreme Being and the Holy Spirit is made flesh in us. Dearest, there is no sin in having relations with persons who have given themselves to God: they purify everything that passes between us and them and to seek their company is, in short, to unlock the gates to heavenly joy.'

Madame d'Esclaponville, thoroughly unhappy with the outcome of her remonstrations, said nothing but vowed she would find a better way which would be more eloquent and quite unanswerable. The devilish thing of it is that women always have a way ready to hand: even when they are not over-attractive, they only have to say 'yes!' and avengers come running from all directions.

Now there lived in the town a certain parish curate, the abbé du Bosquet, a man of lecherous tendencies who, at 30 or so, chased every woman in sight and was the reason why a forest of horns sprouted on the foreheads of the cuckolded husbands of Saint-Quentin. Madame d'Esclaponville got to know the curate and by degrees the curate got to know Madame d'Esclaponville. In short, both knew the other—and so intimately that they might have painted a full-length portrait of each other in such detail that there would have been no mistaking either. When a month had gone by, people began making a point of congratulating the unfortunate d'Esclaponville who regularly boasted that he alone had been preserved from the curate's formidable amorous endeavours, adding that his was the only head in the whole of Saint-Quentin which the rogue had left smooth.

'No doubt about it,' d'Esclaponville would say to people who spoke to him on the matter. 'My wife is as chaste as Lucretia*—you could tell me the opposite until you're blue in the face and I'd still never believe it.'

'Come with me,' said one of his friends, 'just you come along with me and I'll make you see for yourself. And then we'll see if you have doubts.'

D'Esclaponville allowed himself to be led off and his friend took him half a league outside the town to a deserted spot where the Somme, squeezing between two new-green hedges covered with flowers, creates a pool where the townsfolk come and bathe. But since the lovers' tryst had been fixed for a time before bathing ordinarily begins, our hapless husband suffered the vexation of seeing his honest wife and his rival arrive one after the other, with no one to disturb them.

'Well,' the friend said to d'Esclaponville, 'I imagine your forehead is beginning to itch?'

'Not at all,' said the bourgeois, though he rubbed it involuntarily. 'Perhaps she's come to be confessed.'

'In that case, we'd better stay to the end,' the friend said.

They did not have long to wait. Almost the moment

he crept into the shade of the sweet-smelling hedge, the abbé du Bosquet removed everything which stood between him and the sensual contact which he had in mind and, perhaps for the thirtieth time, piously set about the task of placing good, honest Monsieur d'Esclaponville squarely in the ranks of the rest of the town's husbands.

'Well, are you convinced now?' the friend said.

'Let's get away from here,' d'Esclaponville said bitterly. 'I'm so convinced that I could kill that swine of a priest. Still, the price I'd have to pay for doing him in would be far more than he's worth. Let's go back—and please keep quiet about this.'

D'Esclaponville returned home with his mind in a whirl. A little while later, his mild-mannered wife came and made as if to sit down to supper at his chaste side.

'One moment, my sweet,' said the bourgeois in a fury, 'ever since I was a boy, I always swore to my father that I would never sup with harlots.'

'With harlots?' Madame d'Esclaponville replied mildly. 'My dear, your words astound me. What can I have done to warrant your displeasure?'

'I'll tell you what has incurred my displeasure, you slut! It's what you went off and did this afternoon by the pool with our curate!'

'Heavens,' the sweet woman replied, 'is that all? Is that all you have to say?'

'What do you mean, dammit, is that all?'

'But, my dear, I merely took your advice. Didn't you tell me that there was no risk in sleeping with people of the cloth, that the soul is purified by such sacred relations, that we draw close to the Supreme Being, that the Holy Spirit is then made flesh in us and, in short, it is the way to unlock the gates to heavenly joy? Well, dearest, I simply did as you said, and that makes me definitely no harlot but a saint! And I can tell you that if there's one pure soul of God who has the power to unlock, to use your words, the gates to heavenly joy, then it must be the curate, for I never saw a bigger key.'

The Self-Made Cuckold, or the Unexpected Reconciliation

ONE of the greatest failings of ill-mannered people is that they are forever making indiscreet remarks, slanderous comments, and libellous statements at the expense of anyone and anything that lives and breathes. They will even do this in the hearing of people they do not know. Who can tell how much unpleasantness, duels even, have resulted from such loose talk. Indeed, is there any self-respecting man who can stand by and hear ill spoken of those he cares for and not rebuke the blockhead who spoke it? Educators do not give the principle of decent self-restraint enough importance in the training of the young who are not adequately taught to know society—the names, titles, and connections of the people with whom their station in life requires them to associate. Instead, their heads are filled with endless silly notions which are fit only to be trampled underfoot once they arrive at the age of reason. One is left with the impression that they are brought up like Capuchin monks:* bigotry, mummery, and useless knowledge at every turn, and not a useful moral maxim in sight. Go further into the matter and question any young man about his proper duties to society: ask him to say what he owes to himself and what he owes to others and how he should behave if he intends to be happy. He will tell you that he was brought up to go to mass and say the litanies but that he does not rightly understand what you mean; that he was taught how to dance and sing but not how to get on with other men. The particular incident which resulted from the failing we speak of was not serious: that is, no blood was spilt. But the outcome was in point of fact rather amusing and it is to retail it that we shall trespass for a few moments on the patience of our readers.

Monsieur de Raneville, then aged about 50, was one of those phlegmatic characters you can never come across in a social gathering without finding the experience entertaining. He did not laugh much himself but he made other people laugh a great deal, not simply with scathing, witty comments but also with the deadpan way he had of delivering them. Just by saying nothing at all or by giving his normally inexpressive face a comic twist, he found he could keep the gatherings to which he was invited much better amused than those ponderous, boring gossip-mongers who always have a story that they must tell you which has had them in stitches for an hour already but which never comes anywhere near to wiping the scowl off the face of their listeners. He was something in taxes, something rather important in fact. To console himself for a rather bad marriage which he had made some while previously at Orléans where he had abandoned his unfaithful wife, he now lived in Paris, quietly getting through 20,000 or 25,000 livres a year with the pretty woman he kept and with a small circle of friends all as congenial as himself.

Monsieur de Raneville's mistress was not exactly a courtesan but a married woman, which of course made her all the more desirable. For it cannot be denied that a small pinch of adultery often adds a great deal of spice to an affair. She was very pretty, 30 years of age, and had the most marvellous figure imaginable. Separated from her dull, boring husband, she had come to Paris from the country to seek her fortune and had not been long in finding it. Raneville, a libertine by nature, constantly on the watch for juicy morsels, made sure this one did not drop off his fork. For the last three years, by means of his highly considerate treatment of her, a great deal of wit and a considerable outlay of money, he had succeeded in blotting from the young woman's mind all the sorrows which it had pleased the god of marriage to strew on the conjugal path she had trod. Both having experienced the same fate, they consoled each other and became more convinced than ever of a great truth which, however, never changes anyone for the better: the reason why there are so many bad marriages and consequently so much unhappiness in the world is that parents, because they are miserly or just plain stupid, prefer to arrange matches between two piles of money rather than between two people. 'For,' as Raneville would often remark to his mistress, 'it is quite clear that had fate united the two of us instead of giving you to a ridiculous tyrant of a husband and me to a rutting whore of a wife, then roses would have sprung up beneath our feet instead of the briars with which we had so long to contend.'

A passing circumstance, which we need not go into, led Monsieur de Raneville one day to that miry, unwholesome village known as Versailles where Kings, who are surely meant to be revered in their capitals, give every appearance of taking refuge from their subjects who would much prefer to have them within reach; where day in day out, ambition, avarice, revenge, and pride drive a herd of hapless wretches who, riding on wings of boredom, pay homage to each passing fashion; where the élite of the French aristocracy, who could render useful service by staying at home on their estates, are instead only too keen to loiter in the humiliating antechambers of the great, pay base court to door-keepers, and on bended knee beg a dinner (never as good as the one they could get at home) as a favour from one or other of those persons whom Fortune raises brief-ly from the mists of obscurity only to send them back whence they came a moment later.*

His business done, Monsieur de Raneville got into one of those court carriages known as a *pot-de-chambre*, where he found himself quite by chance thrown into the company of a Monsieur Dutour, a very talkative, very fat, and very dull-witted, supercilious man who, like Monsieur de Raneville, was also something in tax, though he was based at his birth-place, Orléans, which, as we have said, was also Monsieur de Raneville's home town. They began to talk and soon Raneville, as laconic as ever and giving nothing away about himself, was acquainted with the Christian name, surname, origins, and

business of his travelling companion long before he had
even opened his mouth. Having conveyed these details,
Monsieur Dutour then enlarged upon society matters.

'So you have been to Orléans, sir,' said Dutour. 'I
believe you said you had.'

'I lived there for some months a long time ago.'

'And did you, pray, ever meet a Madame de Raneville,
one of the most consummate harlots ever to live in
Orléans?'

'Madame de Raneville? A rather pretty woman?'

'The very same.'

'Yes, I did run across her in society.'

'Well, I can tell you in confidence that I had her. It
lasted three days. The usual thing. If ever husband was
a cuckold, it was surely poor old Raneville.'

'Do you know him?'

'Only in this connection. They say he is a thoroughly
bad lot who is ruining himself in Paris with whores and
other rakes like himself.'

'I can't tell you anything about him. I never met him.
But I do feel sympathy for cuckolded husbands. I don't
suppose you are one by any chance, sir?'

'Which of the two do you mean, husband or cuckold?'

'Why, both. These days the two are so closely linked
that it really is very difficult to see daylight between
them.'

'I am a married man, sir, and was unfortunate enough
to hit on a wife who never learned to put up with me.
Mark you, I never myself much cared for her character
either and we agreed to an amicable separation. She
wanted to go to Paris and retire from the world with a
relative of hers who is a nun at the Convent of Sainte-
Aure.* She has gone to live there. She writes to me now
and again, but I don't see anything of her.'

'Is she very devout?'

'No. Perhaps I'd rather she were.'

'Ah, I see. So, although your current business obliges
you to remain in Paris for some time, you have not been
sufficiently curious about her to enquire how she is?'

'No. To tell the truth, I don't care for convents. I'm a man who likes a spree and a good time. I was meant for the pleasures of life and I am very much in demand. I have no intention of rushing off to some convent parlour and run the risk of having to put up with my lady's vapours for the next six months.'

'But a woman . . .'

'. . . is someone who has a claim on our attentions for only as long as she serves her purpose. But you must be firm and send her packing the minute you have good cause for parting with her.'

'What you say is rather callous.'

'Not at all. It's philosophical, it's the modern way, it's the language of reason. You have to go along with it, otherwise people will think you're a fool.'

'But that assumes that your wife is in some way guilty. What do you mean exactly? A defect of nature, some failure to please, something to be desired in her behaviour?'

'A little of all that, sir, elements of all those things. But pray let us drop the subject and return to dear Madame de Raneville. By God, I cannot believe that you were in Orléans and never had some sport with the trollop. Everybody had her.'

'Not everybody, for as you see I never did. I do not care for married women.'

'I have no wish to pry, but pray tell me, sir, with whom do you spend your time?'

'Business acquaintances in the main, but there is also a rather pretty creature with whom I have supper now and then.'

'You are not married, sir?'

'I am.'

'And your wife?'

'Is in the country. I leave her there just as you allow yours to stay at Sainte-Aure.'

'Married, sir! You are married! And would you be a member of the Antler Club by any chance? I'd be obliged to know.'

'Did I not say that husband and cuckold are synonyms? The moral depravity of modern manners, the taste for luxury,* so many stumbling-blocks to make a woman trip and fall.'

'That, sir, is true, very true indeed.'

'You speak like a man well versed in these matters.'

'Not I, sir. But I take it then that it is a very pretty woman who consoles you for the absence of a neglected wife?'

'You are quite right. A very pretty woman. I should like you to meet her.'

'Sir, you do me too much honour.'

'Oh, come now, let us not stand on ceremony. But here we are. I shall not insist this evening because you have business to attend to. But tomorrow without fail I shall expect you for supper at this address. Let me write it down for you.'

Raneville was careful to supply a false identity to which he immediately alerted his servants so that anyone who called asking for him under the name he had given would be able to locate him without difficulty.

The next day, Monsieur Dutour duly appeared at the appointed time and, arrangements having been made for him to find Raneville at home, in spite of the assumed name, he was admitted at once. When the initial civilities were over, Dutour appeared uneasy at not yet catching a glimpse of the divine creature he had reckoned on meeting.

'Such impatience!' said Raneville, 'But I see what you are after. You were promised a pretty woman and are anxious to make a start on her. You are used to deceiving the husbands of Orléans, and I sense you have a mind to hand out much the same treatment to the lovers of Paris. I wager you would be highly delighted if you could put me on the same footing as the unfortunate Raneville you told me about so entertainingly yesterday!'

To this, Dutour replied like an irresistible womanizer and accomplished fop, which is to say foolishly, and the conversation brightened for a moment. Then, taking his friend by the hand, Raneville said:

'Come, you heart-breaker, prepare to enter the temple where the divine creature awaits you.'

And so saying, he ushered Dutour into a sensuously decorated boudoir where Raneville's mistress, primed for the jest and fully in the picture, was reclining minimally but fetchingly clad on a plush-covered ottoman. She wore a veil. There was nothing to hide the grace and lushness of her body: only her face remained concealed.

'Zounds! what a beautiful creature!' exclaimed Dutour. 'But why deny me the pleasure of admiring her face? We have not strayed into the harem of the Great Turk by any chance, have we?'

'No. But keep your voice down. There's her modesty to consider.'

'Modesty?'

'Absolutely. You don't think that all I have in mind is to let you see my mistress's figure and the way she dresses? My triumph would not be complete if I did not demonstrate how fortunate I must be to have full rights over such grace and beauty, and for this I shall need to remove her veils. But she is an unusually modest young woman and what I propose would be highly embarrassing to her. She has agreed to it but on the express condition that her face remains hidden. You know what modesty and niceness of manners mean to women, Monsieur Dutour. A man of taste and fashion like yourself would never allow himself to be put off by such things.'

'No, really, are you going to show me . . . ?'

'Everything. I told you. There is not a man alive who has less jealousy in him than me. I always think one-sided happiness is a poor thing. For me, I can only take delight in love that is requited.'

And to convince him of the truth of this notion, Raneville began by removing a film of gauze, thereby revealing the most beautiful bosom imaginable. Dutour licked his lips.

'Well?' said Raneville. 'What do you think?'

'Why, these are the orbs of Venus herself!'

'Believe me, breasts so snowy and so firm were made to inflame a man's passion. But touch them, feel for yourself, my dear fellow. Sometimes our eyes deceive us. In matters of pleasure, my view is that we must allow all the senses to be brought into play.'

Dutour held out a trembling hand and rapturously squeezed the most beautiful bosom in the world, quite unable to understand how his friend could be so unbelievably accommodating.

'Let us fix our sights lower,' said Raneville, lifting the filmy chiffon petticoat above her waist, 'and let there be no limit to the foray. Well, what do you say to such thighs? Tell me, did ever temple of love stand on such fair columns?'

And good Monsieur Dutour ran probing hands over the features which Raneville proceeded to enumerate.

'I can read your thoughts, you rogue,' continued the complaisant friend. 'This comely temple decked with fine-spun moss by the Graces themselves . . . you burn to open these portals, do you not? And yearn to plant a kiss there, I wager?'

The dazzled, stammering Dutour's only answer was in the violence of his sensations which were stimulated by all he saw. He was encouraged to go further. His libertine fingers caressed the portico of the temple which was unlocked by sensuality in response to his desires. Then the divine kiss which he was allowed was duly planted and savoured for a full hour.

'Friend,' said he, 'I can bear no more. Either turn me out or allow me to go further.'

'What do you mean, further? Where the devil do you want to go, pray?'

'You do not take my meaning. Alas, I am mad with love and can contain myself no longer!'

'But what if the woman turns out to be ugly?'

'No woman who possesses such divine attributes could possibly be ugly.'

'But if she were?'

'Let her be whatever she likes! My dear sir, I tell you

I can control myself no longer!'

'Then, my fiery friend, so be it. Since you must be gratified, go to it. But at least say you are grateful for my complaisance.'

'I do. Wholeheartedly.'

Gently, with one hand, Dutour began pushing his friend away, intimating that he should be left alone with the woman.

'Leave you? I couldn't possibly do that,' said Raneville. 'Surely you aren't so particular that you would find satisfaction in my presence impossible? Between grown men, scruples like these are hardly the thing. Besides, those are my conditions: either it is done with me here or it is not done at all.'

'I wouldn't care if I did it in front of the Devil himself,' said Dutour, unable to contain himself any longer and making a rush for the sanctuary where his incense was to be burned. 'If you insist, I agree!'

'But,' said Raneville phlegmatically, 'are you sure you have not been misled by appearances? Are the sweet pleasures promised by so many charms real or illusory? Still, I never saw a more seductive sight in my life.'

'But this damned veil, sir, this perfidious muslin, am I not to be allowed to remove it?'

'Why of course, but at the last moment, at that truly delicious instant when, with all our senses beguiled by the rapture of the gods, a woman makes us as blest as they, and indeed often more so. The surprise will heighten the bliss: to the charm of possessing Venus herself you will add the inexpressible delight of gazing upon the face of Flora,* and with every sensation combining to swell your joy, you will plunge all the more ecstatically into that ocean of delight in which a man finds such sweet consolation for his existence. But you'll have to say when.'

'Oh, you may count on it,' said Dutour. 'I shall work myself up to that instant.'

'So I see. You have hot blood, sir.'

'None hotter! Ah! dear friend! the celestial moment

approaches! Strip away, tear back the veil that I may look upon heaven itself!'

'And so you shall,' said Raneville, whipping away the muslin, 'but have a care lest there be but a step between this paradise and hell itself!'

'Good God,' exclaimed Dutour, recognizing his wife. 'Upon my soul! *You*, Madame? Sir, what bizarre joke is this? You deserve to be . . . This harridan . . .'

'Hold hard a moment, O man of hot blood. It is you who thoroughly deserve everything you've got. Mark me, my dear fellow, and learn: a man needs to be a little more circumspect with people he doesn't know, and a great deal more so than you were with me yesterday. The unfortunate Raneville whom you treated so abominably in Orléans—I am that man, sir. You observe that I hereby return the compliment in Paris. You will further note that you have succeeded far better than you ever imagined. You thought that you were making a cuckold out of me whereas you have just cuckolded yourself!'

Dutour swallowed his medicine. He held out his hand to his friend and agreed that he had got everything that was coming to him.

'But as to this perfidious creature . . .'

'But has she not simply followed your example? What barbaric law is it that binds her sex with inhuman chains while granting us men total freedom? Is such a law equitable? And by what natural right do you lock up your wife at Saint-Aure while you cuckold husbands in Paris and Orléans? My friend, it is simply not just.* This charming woman whose worth you never appreciated came in search of other conquests. She was right to do so. She found me. I have made her happy: you may do as much for Madame de Raneville, you have my permission to try. Let all four of us live happily, and let not those whom Fate has brought low also turn out to be the victims of men.'

Dutour saw that his friend was in the right but by an impenetrable twist of fate he now fell madly in love again with his wife. Though Raneville was an extremely caus-

tic man, his heart was too noble to deny
ing that she be returned to him. The yo
consented and the whole episode, which is p
unique, furnishes a most singular example of the w
ings of destiny and the waywardness of love.

The Husband Who Said Mass:
A Provençal Tale

BETWEEN the town of Menerbe in the county of Avignon and Apt in Provence,* there stands a small, isolated Carmelite monastery, called Saint-Hilaire, perched on the flank of a hill where even grazing goats venture with difficulty. This modest place acts more or less as a dumping-ground for all the Carmelite communities in the area, for to it each consigns those Brothers who have brought dishonour to their calling. It may easily be deduced that the company in such a house is far from wholesome. Drunkards, womanizers, sodomites, and gamblers, such broadly speaking are the noble elements of which it is composed: so many recluses foregathered in scandalous retreat to offer up to God as best they can hearts which the rest of the world does not want. One or two châteaux close by and the town of Menerbe, no more than a league from Saint-Hilaire, form the entire social purview of these goodly monks who, their cassocks and calling notwithstanding, do not find all doors open to them in the surrounding district.

For some considerable time now, Father Gabriel, one of the saints of this holy place, had coveted a certain woman of Menerbe whose husband—one of life's natural cuckolds—was called Monsieur Rodin. Madame Rodin was a black-haired little thing of 28, with a pert eye, a round bottom, and everything required of a dish to set before a monk. As for Monsieur Rodin, he was a decent sort who went calmly about his business. He had sold cloth for a living and served as Provost† and was therefore what is called an honest burgher. Not altogether certain of the virtue of his better half, he was enough of a philosopher to realize that the best way of keeping the horns that sprout on a husband's forehead

---

† A municipal appointment equivalent to the office of local magistrate. [*Author's note*]

to reasonable proportions is to appear unaware that any have sprouted at all. He had studied for the ministry, spoke Latin as well as Cicero, and regularly played draughts with Father Gabriel who, sly and attentive wooer that he was, knew that it is always important to decoy the husband if you want to hook the wife. Among the sons of Elijah,* Father Gabriel was a stallion. The mere sight of him was enough to give anyone every confidence that the business of propagating the whole human race could safely be left to him, for if ever there was a begetter of children, it was he. With a solid pair of shoulders, a back a yard wide, swarthy, tanned features and the brow of Jove, he stood six feet tall and was, people said, as well endowed as the province's finest mules (always a distinctive feature of Carmelite friars). What woman would not be irresistibly attracted to such a lusty brute? And he did indeed most marvellously appeal to Madame Rodin who was anything but accustomed to encountering appurtenances quite so sublime in the lord and master her parents had picked out as a husband for her. Outwardly, as we have said, Monsieur Rodin appeared to notice nothing. But this does not mean he was not jealous. He never said anything but he was always there, and he was often there at times when he might have been wished elsewhere. But the apple was ripe for plucking. The naïve Madame Rodin had brazenly told her lover that all she was waiting for was an opportunity to respond to desires which seemed to her much too ardent to be resisted any longer, while on his side Father Gabriel had given Madame Rodin to understand that he was quite ready to accommodate her. In a brief instant snatched when Rodin had been obliged to go out, Gabriel had even shown his delicious mistress credentials calculated to make up the mind of any woman who might still be inclined to hesitate. All that was needed now was an opportunity.

One day Rodin called on his friend from Saint-Hilaire to invite him to lunch, with a notion of suggesting they might go hunting together. The two of them having emptied a few bottles of Lanerte wine,* it struck Gabriel that circumstances had conspired to favour his desires.

'By God, Provost!' said the friar to his friend, 'I am very glad you're here. You couldn't have come at a better moment for my purposes. There's something I must attend to, most urgent, and you could be a great help to me.'

'What is it, Father?'

'Do you know a man in town called Renoult?'

'Renoult the hat-maker?'

'That's him.'

'What about him?'

'Well, the rogue owes me a hundred écus and I have just heard that his business is about to go to the wall: even as I speak he might be clean away and across the county boundary. I must get away and see him, but I can't.'

'What's stopping you?'

'My mass, for God's sake, I have to say mass. If I had my hundred écus in my pocket, mass could go to blazes!'

'Isn't there any way you could be excused?'

'Excused! Out of the question! There are three of us here and if we don't spout out three masses between us every day, the Superior who never manages to say any at all would report us to Rome. But there is a way you could help. Do you want to know what it is so you can think about it? It's entirely up to you, of course.'

'I'd be glad to help. What do you have in mind?'

'There's just myself here and the sexton. The first two masses have been said and all the friars have gone out and about. No one would know. The congregation won't be very big, just a handful of peasants and that nice woman, very devout, who lives in the château of —— just half a league from here, an angelic creature who believes that by strict observance she can make up for all the wild oats her husband keeps sowing. I believe you once told me you studied for the priesthood?'

'That's right.'

'So you must have learned how to say mass?'

'I can say mass like an archbishop!'

'Then, my dear old friend,' Gabriel went on, throwing his arms around Rodin's neck, 'for God's sake, slip my habit on, wait until it strikes eleven—it is ten now—and when it does would you say my mass for me? Please? The Brother who is the sexton is a good sort. He won't give us away. If anyone says they did not think it was me, we'll say it was a new Brother just arrived, and the rest needn't be told anything. I'll get to Renoult's house, the rogue, as quick as I can, kill him or have my money, and I'll be back here inside two hours. Wait for me. Put the sole on the grill and the eggs in the pan and draw the wine. When I return we shall sit down and eat, and then we'll go and hunt. O yes, we'll go hunting and I have a feeling that this time we might just bag something. I'm told that a pair of antlers was spotted near here only just the other day. By God! I'd love us to pot it, even if it meant saddling ourselves with twenty lawsuits from the lord of the manor!'*

'The plan is excellent,' said Rodin, 'and I'd do absolutely anything I could to help out. But wouldn't it be sinful?'

'Sin doesn't come into it. Perhaps it might if mass were said and said badly. But if someone who is not qualified celebrates it, then whatever is said would be the same as if nothing was said at all. Take it from me: I am a trained casuist and in this matter there is nothing which might be described as a venial sin.'

'Would I have to say the words?'

'And why ever not? The words mean something only when they are said by us: the power is in us, not in them. Look here, I'd only have to say those words over your wife's belly for the tabernacle of your conjugal devotions to be immediately transformed into the body of Christ. No, only we have the power of transubstantiation. You could say the words twenty thousand times and you would never persuade the Holy Spirit to descend on anybody. And even with us it doesn't always work. It's entirely a matter of faith. With an ounce of faith a man can move mountains, you know, Jesus Christ Himself said so. But a man who has no faith cannot move anything. Take me, for instance. Sometimes when I'm giving mass, my mind is more on the girls and the women in the congregation than on that damned bit of wafer I wave about in my hand. How do you think I could manage to get anything to descend then? I'd be better off believing in the Koran than filling my head with that sort of thing. Which means that your mass will be to all intents and purposes just as valid as the ones I give. So don't give it another thought. Go to it! Brace yourself!'

'By God!' said Rodin. 'But haven't I an appetite on me! And lunch isn't for another two hours yet!'

'But what's to prevent you having a bite to eat? Here, we've plenty.'

'But what about the mass I'm supposed to say?'

'God in heaven! What difference does it make? Do you think God is more defiled if He fetches up in a full stomach than in an empty belly, or if there's food under Him or on top of Him? I'm damned if I can see it makes the slightest difference! Listen, if I had to go to Rome and make a clean breast of things every time I broke my fast before saying mass, I'd spend all my time on the road. Anyway, you aren't a priest and the rules don't apply to you. All you'll be doing is making it look like mass, not actually saying it. So you can do whatever you want before or after. You could even pleasure your wife if she was there. Just do what I do, that's all. You won't be celebrating mass or consummating the sacrifice.'

'In that case,' said Rodin, 'I'll do it. Don't give it another thought.'

'Good,' said Gabriel, making off and leaving his friend well recommended to the sacristan. 'You can depend on me. I'll be back inside two hours and then I'm your man.'

Overjoyed, the friar hurried on his way.

With an expeditiousness which is only too easily imagined, he rushed round to the house of the Provost's wife. Surprised to see him there when she believed he

was with her husband, she asked what the reason was
for this unexpected visit.

'Let's be quick, my sweet,' said the breathless friar.
'Hurry! We have only a few moments to ourselves. First
a glass of wine and then to work!'

'But my husband?'

'He's saying mass.'

'Saying what?'

'Yes, by God, saying mass, my pretty,' replied the
Carmelite as he tumbled Madame Rodin on to her bed.
'It's true, light of my soul. I've turned your husband into
a priest and while the booby is celebrating a mystery
divine, let's be quick and consummate a passion profane.'

The friar was strong and there were few arguments
that could be put up against him once he had come to
grips with a woman. Anyway, the case he made out being
so conclusive, he quite won over Madame Rodin. Since
he did not find the business of convincing a pert little
thing of 28 summers and a combustible Provençal disposition in any way irksome, he put his case more than
once.

'Oooh, you angel man,' said she at last, now perfectly
convinced. 'But look at the time! We must part. If our
revels are supposed to last as long as it takes to say mass,
then he must have got to the *ite missa est* long ago.'

'Not at all, my sweet,' said the Carmelite, who still
had one argument left to put to Madame Rodin. 'Come,
dear heart, there's plenty of time. Just once more, my
dear, my sweet, once more. Beginners like him don't
rush it as we do. Believe me, just one more time. I'll
wager that husband of yours still hasn't got to the part
where God the Wafer has to be held aloft.'

But part they had to, though they did not separate
without promising to see each other again and agreeing
several new strategies for doing so. Then Gabriel went
off to rejoin Rodin who had said mass as well as any
archbishop.

'The only part I got slightly wrong,' he said, 'was the

quod aures. I started eating instead of drinking. But the sexton put me right. Now what about your hundred écus, Father?'

'In the bag, my son. The rogue tried to put up a fight. But I got hold of a pitchfork and, by God, I gave it to him. On the head and all over.'

The meal came to an end and the two friends went hunting. When he got home, Rodin told his wife all about the good turn he had done Gabriel.

'I said mass,' the great booby announced gleefully. 'Said it like a proper priest, by God, while our friend went off and took Renoult's measure with a pitchfork. He browbeat him, light of my life, what do you say to that! Raised great bumps on his head! Ah! Dear heart, it's so funny! Anyone who ends up with bumps on his head makes me laugh! Now what about you, my dear, what were you doing while I was saying mass?'

'O my sweet!' said the Provost's wife. 'Heaven must surely have inspired us both today! Don't you see, we were both filled with the celestial spirit and never knew it! While you were saying mass, I was reciting the beautiful prayer which the Virgin offered up to the angel Gabriel when he appeared unto her and announced that she would be with child by the Holy Ghost. O my dear! we shall surely both remain on the road to salvation as long as each of us, in our separate ways, goes on performing such good works.'

The Lady of the Manor of Longeville, or a Woman's Revenge

IN the days when the aristocracy ruled their lands like despots—those glorious days when France contained within her boundaries countless sovereign lords and not thirty thousand cowed slaves bending the knee to a single man*—the Lord of Longeville, master of a fief near Fimes in Champagne, resided on his not inconsiderable estates. With him lived his wife who was small, dark of hair and pert of face, vivacious, not very pretty but brazen, and passionately fond of her pleasures. The Lady of the Manor was perhaps 25 or 26 and her Lord and Master 30 at most. They had been married for ten years and being both of an age to relish whatever might relieve the tedium of wedded bliss, they each set about satisfying their needs as well as could be managed out of what the locality could furnish. The town, or rather the hamlet of Longeville had little to offer. However, a pretty little farmer's wife, pleasing to the eye and with the bloom of her 18 years still on her, had succeeded in catching his Lordship's fancy and for two years past she had fitted his bill most satisfactorily. Louison, as his darling turtle-dove was called, came each evening to her master's bed by a secret staircase built into one of the towers which housed his Lordship's apartments, and decamped each morning before Madame, as was her custom, arrived to breakfast with her husband.

Madame de Longeville was fully aware of her husband's unseemly little *amour* but being herself nothing loath to enjoy similar sport, made no comment. There is nothing sweeter-tempered than faithless wives: having such good reason to hide their own dealings, they do not look into other people's lives as keenly as do the prudes. A local miller named Colas, a young dog of 18 or 20, as pure as his own flour, as muscular as his mule, and as pretty as the roses which grew in his little garden, came each night just as Louison did and let himself into room adjoining Madame's apartments and thence, when all was quiet in the château, into her bed. There was no more tranquil sight to behold than these twin ménages. If the Devil had not taken a hand in the business, I am convinced that they would have been trumpeted loud throughout the province of Champagne as examples to be followed.

Do not smile, reader, no, you should not scoff at the word *example*. When there is a want of virtue, vice suitably garbed and discreetly hidden may properly serve as a model: is it not a thing as worthy as it is deft to sin without scandalizing one's fellows? And when the offence is not made public, where can be the harm in it? Come, decide for yourselves: are not such trifling irregularities preferable to the spectacles furnished by the manners of the present time? Would you not prefer the Lord of Longeville duly and tranquilly settled in the arms of his pretty farmer's wife, and his respectable Lady installed by the side of a handsome miller whose good fortune is known to no one, to some Paris Duchess or other who publicly changes gallants once a month or takes her pleasure with the servants while her lord and master works his way through 200,000 écus a year with one of those despicable creatures who are gilded by wealth, base by birth, and cankered by the pox? I say again: had it not been for the discord distilled by life's poisons over these four favoured children of Love, nothing could have been sweeter and more exemplary than their charming little arrangements.

But the Lord of Longeville, cruelly believing like many unjust husbands that while he had a right to be happy his wife did not, and imagining, like the partridge, that he was invisible because he kept his head buried, discovered his wife's little intrigue and was not amused, as though his own behaviour did not fully justify the conduct which he now took it into his head to censure.

From discovery to revenge is but a small step for a jealous mind. Monsieur de Longeville decided to say nothing but to rid himself of the knave who had caused horns to sprout on his forehead: 'It is one thing for a man of my rank to be deceived by a gentleman,' said he to himself, 'but quite another to be cuckolded by a miller! Monsieur Colas, you will please be good enough to do your grinding in someone else's mill, for from this day forth it shall never more be said that my wife's took in your seed.' Now seeing that the hatred of the little sovereign despots of those times was ever cruel to a degree, and since they regularly abused the power of life and death which feudal law granted them over their vassals, Monsieur de Longeville determined upon no less a course than to have poor Colas thrown into the waters of the moat which surrounded his château.

'Clodomir,' said he one day to his head cook, 'I want you and the rest of the kitchen staff to rid me of a vassal who is fouling Madame's bed.'

'At once, your Lordship,' replied Clodomir. 'We'll slit his throat if you like and serve him up trussed like a sucking pig.'

'No, nothing like that,' said Monsieur de Longeville. 'It will suffice to put him in a sack with some stones and drop the sack and him with it into the moat.'

'It shall be done.'

'Yes, but first we'll have to catch him and we haven't got him yet.'

'We will, your Lordship. He'll have to be pretty smart to get away from us. We'll have him. I guarantee it.'

'He will be here tonight at nine,' said the injured husband. 'He'll come through the garden and proceed directly to the rooms on the ground floor. He'll hide in the little room just off the chapel and stay there until Madame thinks I've gone to sleep. Then she will come, let him out, and take him off to her apartment. You must let him go through all the preliminaries—we will merely keep watch—but the moment he thinks he is safely hidden, we'll seize him and give him a long drink that will put out his fire.'

This scheme was excellently contrived and poor Colas would certainly have been food for the fishes if everyone had kept their mouths shut. But his Lordship had told his plans to too many people and he was betrayed. A kitchen lad who was very fond of his mistress and perhaps hoped one day to share her favours with the miller, surrendering more to the feelings which his mistress stirred in him than to the jealousy which should by rights have made him rejoice at his rival's imminent downfall, hurried away to tell her of the plot that was hatching and was rewarded by a kiss and by two shiny gold écus which he valued less than the kiss.

'His Lordship,' said Madame de Longeville when she was alone with the maid who assisted her in her intrigues, 'is most assuredly a very unjust man. Why, he does whatever he likes and I never say a word; yet he takes exception to my making up for the quantity of abstinence he requires me to observe. I won't have it! I simply won't put up with it! Listen, Jeannette, are you prepared to help me carry out a plan I have thought of which will not only save Colas but also put his Lordship in his place?'

'O yes, Madame. I'll do anything: Madame has only to say the word. Poor Colas is such a nice boy. I never saw a boy with so strong a back on him nor with such colour in his cheek. O yes, Madame, of course I'll help. What must I do?'

'I want you to go this very minute,' the Lady said, 'and warn Colas that he is not to come to the château unless I first send to him. You will also ask him to lend me the complete suit of clothes he usually wears when he . . . visits. When you have them, I want you to go and find Louison, my false husband's love-pet, and tell her that his Lordship sent you. Say she is to wear the clothes you have in your apron pocket. She mustn't come her usual way but through the garden, across the courtyard, and into the ground-floor rooms. Once she's in the house, she must go to the little room next to the chapel† and

† The physical disposition of the Château de Longeville is unchanged to this day. [*Author's note*]

hide there until his Lordship comes to fetch her. She will probably question you about this new arrangement, and you will say the reason is that Madame is jealous, that she knows everything, and that she has ordered the route she normally follows to be watched. If she is frightened, reassure her, give her some present or other and above all tell her that she must not fail to come because tonight his Lordship has matters of the greatest consequence to impart about what happened after Madame's jealous outburst.'

Jeannette left, discharged both errands to the letter, and at nine that evening the unfortunate Louison, wearing Colas's clothes, was hiding in the little room where, according to the plan, Madame's lover was to be apprehended.

'Forward!' said Monsieur de Longeville to his men who, like him, had been keeping a sharp look out. 'Go to it! You all saw him as plain as I did, did you not?'

'O yes, your Lordship, and by God he's a fine-looking lad.'

'Now open the door quickly, throw these clouts over his head to stop him from crying out, then stuff him into the sack and drown him without further ado.'

All this was done to perfection. The mouth of the unfortunate captive was so tightly gagged that she found it impossible to identify herself. She was put into the sack, at the bottom of which large stones had been carefully placed. Then from the window of the same room where her capture had taken place, she was thrown into the middle of the moat. Once their work was done, all the men withdrew and Monsieur de Longeville returned to his apartment, being most eager to welcome the wench who he knew would not be long in coming and who he never imagined for a moment to be lying in so chill a bed. Half the night went by and no one came. As there was a large, bright moon, the anxious lover thought he would venture as far as her house and see for himself what motive there could be for her not appearing. He went out and in his absence Madame de Longeville, who was aware of his every move, got into her husband's bed. On reaching Louison's house, Monsieur de Longeville learned that she had left as usual and that she must certainly be at the château. No one said anything about her disguise because Louison had taken no one into her confidence and had slipped away unobserved. His Lordship returned home and the candle he had left in his room having gone out, went over to his bedside to fetch the tinder-box to relight it. As he did so, he heard breathing, assumed that his dearest Louison had come while he had been out looking for her and that, growing impatient on not finding him in his apartment, she had gone to bed. He did not hesitate. In a trice he was between the sheets caressing his wife with the words of love and the expressions of tenderness he normally used with his darling Louison.

'Why did you make me wait, my pretty? Where were you, dearest Louison?'

'So, you hypocrite!' exclaimed Madame de Longeville at this juncture, exposing the flame of a dark-lantern which she had kept hidden, 'I can no longer entertain any doubts about your behaviour. Behold your wife and not the whore to whom you give what rightfully belongs to me!'

'Madame,' said the husband without losing his calm, 'I believe I may be allowed to be master of my own actions since you yourself play me false in so essential a matter?'

'Play you false, sir? And in what manner of wise, pray ?'

'Am I not aware of your intrigue with Colas, one of the sorriest peasants to disgrace my estate?'

'I, sir?' his Lady replied haughtily, 'I? You think I would stoop so low? You are imagining things. There has never been a word of truth in what you say and I challenge you to produce your evidence.'

'In truth, Madame, the evidence would indeed be difficult to furnish at this moment seeing that I have ordered the knave who dishonoured me to be thrown into the moat. You shall never see him again.'

'Sir,' said his Lady, rising to an even higher pitch of effrontery, 'if you have indeed ordered the unfortunate man to be thrown into the moat on the strength of your suspicions, then you are certainly guilty of a great injustice. But if, as you say, he was punished simply because he came to the château, then I am greatly afraid that you have made a grave mistake, for he never set foot here in his life.'

'Truly, Madame, you make me fear for my wits!'

'Let us look into the matter, sir. Let us cast light on it. Nothing could be simpler. Give the order yourself and send Jeannette here to fetch this peasant fellow of whom you are so mistakenly and ridiculously jealous, and we shall see who is right.'

His Lordship agreed, Jeannette set off and brought back Colas who had been told how to behave. When he saw him, Monsieur de Longeville rubbed his eyes and immediately summoned all the servants out of bed, commanding them to waste not a moment in finding out who it was, then, he had ordered to be thrown into the moat. They rushed off but all they brought back was a body, the corpse of the unhappy Louison, which they set down for her lover to see.

'O just Heaven!' cried his Lordship, 'an unknown hand has been at work in this business. And yet that hand was guided by Providence and I shall not complain of the blows it has struck. Whether it was you or another, Madame, who was the cause of this unfortunate occurrence, I shall not enquire. You are now free of a woman who made your mind uneasy. Do as much to rid me of the man who troubles mine and see to it that Colas goes away and does not come back. Will you agree to this, Madame?'

'I shall do more, sir. I join with you in ordering him to go. Let peace be restored between us. Let love and mutual respect come into their own once more and let nothing dislodge them ever again from their rightful place.'

Colas left the district and was never seen again, Louison was given a decent burial, and never since that time was there a more devoted couple in the whole of the province of Champagne than the Lord and Lady of Longeville.

in Paris in her modest circles and carrying with her
besides a fair ... uncle Mathieu
and her cousins, Mathieu's daughters, Rosette was as well

The Confidence Men

THROUGHOUT history, there has always been a class of
men in Paris who go abroad into every part of society,
their sole business consisting of living off other people.
The degree of art and cunning which these malefactors
bring to the execution of their multifarious designs is
without parallel. Their invention and wit in devising
stratagems of one sort or another to lure their victims
into their snares know no bounds. While the main body
of the force operates within the city walls, detachments
work the flanks, scattering throughout the countryside
and travelling mainly by public carriage. Having solidly
established these grim facts, let us now turn to the young
and inexperienced woman for whom we shall presently
shed tears when we observe her fall into such evil clutches. Rosette de Flarville, the daughter of an honest
Rouen merchant, had so plagued her father that she had
finally obtained leave to spend the time of Carnival* in
Paris with a Monsieur Mathieu, her uncle, a wealthy
money-lender, who lived in the rue Quincampoix.* Rosette, though somewhat naïve still, was turned 18 and
had a charming face, fair hair, pretty blue eyes, dazzling-
ly white skin, and a bosom which, beneath a light muslin
handkerchief, gave notice to connoisseurs in these matters that what she kept hidden was at least the equal of
what was visible. The leave-taking had been tearful. For
the first time, her doting father was to be separated from
his daughter. She was good, she was capable of looking
out for herself, she was going to stay with a kindly
relative, she would be back for Easter, all good grounds
of course for consolation. But Rosette was pretty, Rosette was very trusting and she was going to town, a
highly dangerous place for any of the fair sex who travel
up from the country and step down from the coach,
imbued with innocence and a goodly share of virtue.
Nevertheless, the lovely creature set off, furnished with
every necessity which would enable her to cut a figure

in Paris in her modest circles and carrying with her besides a fair store of gems and gifts for Uncle Mathieu and her cousins, Mathieu's daughters. Rosette was well recommended to the coachman, her father embraced her, the driver cracked his whip, and tears were shed on both sides. But the love felt by children is set at a much less tender pitch than the love of a father: Nature allows a man's daughters to discover, in pleasures which turn their heads, diversions which, without their intending it, distance them from their parents and readily chill their hearts against those feelings of tenderness which are palpably more one-sided, more ardent, and much more sincere in the hearts of mothers and fathers. Parents are keenly aware of the fatal insensitivity of their offspring which, by making them indifferent to the former pleasures of their early years, explains why they come to regard their elders as no more, so to speak, than sacred vessels which transmit life.

Rosette was no exception to the general rule. Her tears soon dried and having no thought save than for her pleasure in seeing Paris, she was not long in getting to know the other passengers who were going there and who seemed to know the city better than she did. Her first question was an enquiry as to the whereabouts of the rue Quincampoix.

'That's my part of town, Mademoiselle,' said a tall, well-built fellow who, partly on account of a uniform of sorts which he wore and partly because of the loudness of his voice, was dominating the much-jolted company's conversation.

'Really? You live in the rue Quincampoix?'

'Been there twenty years and more.'

'Well, in that case,' said Rosette, 'you must be acquainted with my Uncle Mathieu.'

'Monsieur Mathieu is your uncle, Mademoiselle?'

'O yes, sir. I am his niece. I'm going to see him. I shall be spending the winter with him and my two cousins, Adelaide and Sophie. I expect you know them too.'

'Of course I know them. How could I not know my

closest neighbour Monsieur Mathieu and his daughters, since, I might add, I have been in love with one of them for these five years past.'

'You are in love with one of my cousins! I wager it's Sophie.'

'Not at all. It's Adelaide. Such a wonderful face.'

'That is just what they all say in Rouen. I cannot say myself for I never saw them yet. I'm going to town for the very first time in my life.'

'So, you have never met your cousins, Mademoiselle. Nor your uncle either, I suppose?'

'Good heavens no. Monsieur Mathieu left Rouen the year I was born and has never been back.'

'He really is a most proper gentleman and he will be delighted to welcome you into his home.'

'Is it a grand house?'

'Yes, but he lets part of it. All he keeps for himself is the apartment on the first floor.'

'And all the ground floor too.'

'But of course. And I believe he also keeps the use of one room at the top of the house.'

'He is a very wealthy man, but I shan't let him down. Look, I've got a hundred shiny double louis. My father gave them to me so that I can appear dressed in the latest fashion and not make my cousins feel ashamed of me. I also have some lovely presents for them, like these earrings. They are worth over a hundred louis. They are for Adelaide—the one you love. And this necklace which cost at least as much is for Sophie. But that's not all. Look, this gold casket with my mother's picture in it was valued just yesterday at over fifty louis: it's for Uncle Mathieu, a present from my father. I'm pretty sure that all told, with my clothes, the money, and the jewels, I have probably got more than 500 louis with me.'

'You didn't need all this to be heartily welcomed by your uncle, Mademoiselle,' said the predator, eyeing the girl and her money. 'I'm sure he would be just as pleased to see you if you were to arrive without any of these baubles.'

'That is of no account. My father is a man who likes to do things properly and he does not want us to be looked down on just because we live in the country.'

'To speak plainly, Mademoiselle, there is so much pleasure to be got from your company that I could wish you would stay in Paris permanently and that Monsieur Mathieu would be agreeable to your marrying his son.'

'But he doesn't have a son.'

'I meant his nephew, a well set-up young man . . .'

'Not Charles?'

'That's him, Charles, my best friend, by God!'

'Really? So you knew Charles too, sir?'

'Knew him! Why I can say better than that—I still know him. The only reason I'm going to Paris is to see him.'

'You are mistaken, sir. He is dead. Ever since I was a little girl, he and I were intended to marry. I never met him but I was told that he was terribly nice. Then he took it into his head to be a soldier. He went off to the war and was killed.'

'Capital, capital, Mademoiselle! I see that my dearest wish will come true. Take it from me, they have a surprise in store for you! Charles is not dead. Everyone thought that he was, but he came back six months ago. He wrote to me to say that he was getting married. And from this other quarter, you are now sent to Paris! There can be no doubt about it: it is a surprise! Four days from now, you will be Charles's wife, and the things you are taking with you are really wedding presents!'

'Indeed, sir, what you surmise seems all too likely. If I put together what you have just said and a number of my father's comments which now come back to me, I can see that your predictions are all too likely. And so I shall be married in Paris! I shall be a Parisian lady! How wonderful, sir! But if all this is true, then at the very least you must marry Adelaide. I shall not rest until I have made my cousin agree to it and we can go out together as a foursome!'

Such, as they drove along, was the conversation which

took place between sweet, unsuspecting Rosette and the wicked man who, as he probed her to see how the land lay, was bent on carrying off maximum booty at the expense of this inexperienced party who in all innocence had delivered herself into his hands. What a splendid catch for the dissolute gang: 500 louis plus a pretty girl! Now tell me if you can which of our senses would not be tickled by such a prospect? When they neared Pontoise,* the villain said:

'Mademoiselle, I have an idea. I shall get out here and hire horses which will post me to your uncle's before you arrive and allow me to announce your coming. I am certain they will all come to meet you, so at least you will not feel alone when you get to the city.'

The plan was agreed, the rake jumped on to a horse and galloped off to alert the actors in the charade he had devised. They were all apprised and given instruction, and two cabs carried a counterfeit family to Saint-Denis. They got out at the inn there, the confidence man took charge of the introductions, and Rosette found waiting for her Uncle Mathieu, Charles, who was tall and lately out of the army, and her two charming cousins. They embraced, Rosette handed over her letters, and the good Monsieur Mathieu wept tears of joy on learning that his brother was in good health. In Paris, people do not wait for presents to be given out and Rosette, only too anxious to make a show of her father's generosity, eagerly handed them over. There were more embraces and renewed protestations of gratitude. Then they all repaired to the sharpers' hide-out which they gave their pretty dupe to understand was the rue Quincampoix. They arrived at a genteel-seeming house, Mademoiselle de Flarville was settled in, her box was carried up to her room, and then all thoughts turned to table-matters. At dinner, good care was taken to ensure that she drank enough to fog her wits. She was used to taking nothing but cider, but being persuaded of what she was told, namely, that champagne is the juice of Paris apples, the compliant Rosette did as she was bid and finally became utterly befuddled. Once she was no longer in a state to defend herself, she was stripped of all she possessed and the whole gang, not happy until she had left on her person only the charms which Nature had showered on her, and loath to leave her even with these intact, spent the rest of the night taking full and glad advantage of her. Finally, satisfied that they had got out of the poor girl everything that could be got, and content that they had deprived her of her reason, her honour, and her money, they threw a wretched coat over her and, shortly before dawn, took her and abandoned her on the top steps of the church of Saint-Roch.* Their unfortunate victim, opening her eyes just as the sun began to shine and confused by the appalling state to which she was reduced, felt herself all over, racked her brains, and wondered whether she was alive or dead. The lewd riff-raff of the streets crowded round her and made lengthy sport of her. In the end, she was, at her request, taken to the watch. There she told her sad story and begged that her father be written to and that meantime a place of refuge be found for her. The officer of the watch detected such innocence and honesty in the wretched girl's answers that he took her into his own house. The good burgher travelled up from Normandy and after many tears had been shed on both sides, took his darling daughter home. It is said that for the rest of her life she never wanted to see the civilized capital of France again.

Gentle Reader, adieu! Health and Happiness be with you! Thus in times of yore said our forefathers as they ended the tale they had to tell. Why should I not imitate their courtesy and candour? And so I say to you as they once did: Gentle Reader, adieu! Wealth and Pleasure be yours! If my scribblings have brought you a measure of both, set me to advantage on your bookshelf. If I have bored you, accept my apologies and consign me to the flames.

EXPLANATORY NOTES

THE MISFORTUNES OF VIRTUE

I   *the angel Jesrad in Voltaire's* Zadig: the eponymous hero of *Zadig* (1747), like all the heroes of Voltaire's tales, is preoccupied by the problem of evil. The angel Jesrad, expressing the philosophical optimism of Leibniz (this is the best of all worlds possible) and Pope ('Whatever is, is Right'), informs him that man has only a partial sight of God's mysterious ways; that His vast designs are not to be questioned; and that ignorant mortals must have faith that God is as good as He is powerful. Zadig's protests are overruled and he submits—unlike Voltaire who, increasingly aware of the horrors of life, never accepted that wars, natural disasters and man's inhumanity can be explained away in such cosy terms. By evoking Voltaire at the outset of his own tale, Sade clearly signals his own rejection of the optimistic solution to the problem of evil. See note to p. 127.

3   *Cythera*: one of the seven Ionian islands which, in Greek mythology, was sacred to Aphrodite, goddess of love and beauty. In the imagery of 18th-century French gallantry Cythera stood for sexual licence. By Sade's day, the word had lost most of its idealistic connotations—as expressed, for instance, in the paintings of Watteau—and was used ironically to characterize the sordid morality of contemporary manners.

4   *tax-farmer*: the tax-farmer (or *fermier-général*) was a private citizen who bought from the King a licence to raise taxes in a given area to an agreed amount. If, as invariably happened, he raised more money that he had contracted for, he kept the difference. Tax-farmers were rich and heartily detested.

7   *risk to health*: that is, free of the danger of venereal disease. As Sade indicates, avoiding action (ranging from the use of condoms fashioned from the stomachs of sheep to sodomy and worse) was taken by those wishing to escape infection.

9   *500 a month*: Juliette's success may be measured by the fact that a gentleman would normally expect to pay one

louis for a girl in a brothel and from 25 to 100 louis for
a night with a high-class courtesan. Her monthly rental
is similarly stratospheric. In the 1760s (when Sade paid
Mademoiselle Colet 25 louis a month), most kept
women happily settled for anything between 8 to 30 louis
and the most sought after never charged more than 100.
Juliette's rates reflect less the economic realities of 18th
century prostitution than the gigantism which led Sade
to exaggerate the size of the physical attributes of his
priapic heroes and the quantities of food and drink which
they consume.

9   *to abortion*: by both civil and ecclesiastical law, abortion
was a capital offence.

10 *the injustice of men*: this ironical rejection of the view that
virtue is its own reward was not specifically Sadean but,
in various forms, a commonplace of a certain strain of
his century's philosophic thinking. Thus Rousseau argued in *The Social Contract* (1762) that priests and pol-
iticians had used the promise of an afterlife to keep the
poor (who are always with us) in subjection. Closer still,
Diderot's materialism led him to the view that there is
no more merit in acting well than in behaving badly,
since good and evil are effects of physical disposition or
education over which we have no control.

11 *magistrates' courts*: the first of many slighting references
to the courts, magistrates, and lawyers which Sade, who
had no cause to love the system which kept him locked
up, makes in these stories and tales.

12 *the larger part of my misfortunes*: at this point, the first of
a series of marginal notes in Sade's manuscript not re-
produced here or in the standard French text, Justine's
modesty in her dealings with Dubourg is defined as the
first of her virtues which will be punished. See introduction, p. xxix.

17 *in the rue Quincampoix*: this street, which runs from the
rue des Lombards to the rue aux Ours, still exists. It was
an important financial centre. John Law set up his Ban-
que générale there in 1718 and since the 14th century it
had been the home of the Guild of Drapers, one of the
richest of the Paris corporations.

17   *denier*: for this and other currency values, see Note on
      Money.

20   *that I should ever escape it*: the opposition of Destiny to
      human desires was not only a staple feature of tragedy
      and prose fiction but also the inescapable terminus of
      materialist thought: the hero of Diderot's *Jacques the
      Fatalist* (written 1773–4 but not published until 1796) is
      quite convinced that everything which happens was pre-
      ordained because the chain of cause and effect ensures
      that what is could not be otherwise. For the materialists,
      'Fate' and 'Destiny' were alternative names for philoso-
      phical necessity. All created life is subject to natural laws
      and all phenomena can be explained by them: Justine's
      misfortunes are therefore inevitable, given her tem-
      peramental meekness and her constitutional inability to
      jettison the idea that virtue is rewarded and vice inevit-
      ably punished. Sade frequently uses this view of Fate to
      undermine the role of Providence, generally regarded as
      its Christian equivalent. The 'Dialogue between a Priest
      and a Dying Man' also makes much of this brand of
      philosophical determinism.

21   *to my bedside*: at this point Sade notes that Justine's refu-
      sal to steal from Du Harpin is the second of her virtues
      which will be punished.

      Palace prison: that is, the prison of the Palais de Justice,
      better known as the Conciergerie, on the Île de la Cité.
      Begun in the 11th century, it was the residence of the
      Kings of France until Charles VII (1403–61) made it over
      to the Paris Parlement. It had long been a fashionable
      meeting-place and there were numerous shops in the
      area under the galleries surrounding the Sainte-Cha-
      pelle: for this reason it was also known as the Palais
      Marchand.

22   *refusal to take part in a crime*: the theft of which she was
      found guilty was punishable by death.

      will catch fire: the prison of the Palais de Justice was
      destroyed by fire in 1618 and again in 1776, when the
      conflagration began in the part of the building which
      housed the prison. Though there is no internal evidence
      to suggest when the action of *The Misfortunes of Virtue* is
      set, it is possible that Sade here avenges himself on the

Paris Parlement by having its lawcourts burned to the ground by a bawd.

22 *the forest of Bondy*: an extensive wooded area, near Saint-Denis to the north-east of Paris which was a notorious haunt of footpads, highwaymen, and robbers.

25 *while the class*: Sade's use of the word *classe* (rather than the more usual *condition*) injects a modern, pre-Marxist note into his analysis which, however, notwithstanding his known Revolutionary sympathies, is framed in terms more of metaphysics than of politics.

a state of equality: here Sade makes Providence synonymous with Nature which on page 24 also made us equal at birth.

27 *sacrifice her to our pleasures*: Sade makes Justine's refusal to join the robber gang in the forest of Bondy the third of her virtues to be punished.

30 *rarely a compassionate man*: an instance of Sade's psychological acuteness. The question of whether the libertine depersonalizes his victims because he was born with an affective aphasia or because he is desensitized by repeated acts of cruelty has yet to be decided.

31 *Themis*: daughter of Heaven and Earth, Themis bore to Zeus both the Fates and the Horæ (Equity, Justice, and Peace). She was held to enshrine order and especially Justice and in art is represented holding a sword in one hand and a pair of scales in the other.

37 *an integral part of her essence*: according to standard materialistic theory, movement was one of the basic characteristics of matter (some also believed matter to be sentient). The point was important. For if matter moved and was everlasting, then talk of Creation is redundant for there can be no Creator of what was never created but has always existed through the action of the universal laws of physics.

41 *any vivifying ingredient*: there were many speculations about the mechanics of reproduction, ranging from spontaneous generation to the theory of the matrix: life is already implicit in an egg or a womb down to the finest details. Sade was not alone in denying the female a vivifying role. Restif de la Bretonne (1734–1806) argued

that the female is responsible for providing 'corporeity', but insisted that only the male 'gave life'.

41 *old enough to appreciate it*: Sade's fiction provides many case-histories consistent with psychopathological principles which have become known only since Freud. But remarks such as this indicate clearly that his insights were experimental and that he had no concept of the unconscious.

42 *which gives him pain*: an echo of the current utilitarian pleasure/pain principle which explained human psychology by the alacrity with which we seek pleasure and flee pain.

46 *a lettre de cachet*: under the essentially paternalistic legal system of the *ancien régime*, a direct application could be made to the King to remove an erring relative from circulation when the interests of families were threatened by his or her reckless or even criminal behaviour. After receiving advice, the King signed a *lettre de cachet* ordering detention or house-arrest of the offender. The system was open to abuse and came to symbolize the injustice of the law. Sade himself was held 'during the King's pleasure' at Vincennes and the Bastille on the strength of the *lettre de cachet* against him granted to his mother-in-law.

47 *physiognomy*: the old claim that character may be judged by facial characteristics had recently been revived and refined by Johann Caspar Lavater (1741–1801).

49 *to punish murthers*: the line ('Le parjure est vertu quand on punit le crime'), which cannot be traced in the works of any of 'our tragic poets', is possibly taken from Sade's only tragedy, *Jeanne Laisné* (1783), which was never performed. The text has not survived.

51 *my countenance was suffused*: Bressac's reaction here perfectly illustrates the central characteristic of the sadist: pleasure is derived from the infliction of pain.

here and now: by Sade's reckoning, Justine's refusal to poison Madame de Bressac is the fourth of her virtues which will be punished.

54 *Claye*: that is, Claye-Souilly, near Meaux (Seine-et-Marne).

61 *to admit everything*: Sade makes her refusal to take part in murder in Rodin's house the fifth of her virtues to be punished.

61–2 *thieves are branded*: branding was a staple part of the punishment for a variety of civil, canon, and criminal acts. Though its use was declining, prostitutes and thieves in particular continued to be marked. French convicts carried the letters TF (for 'travaux forcés') until 1832, when the practice was discontinued.

62 *Lieusaint*: on the road to Melun. Justine will continue to head in a south-easterly direction to Sens and thence, following the Yonne, to Auxerre in Burgundy, 170 kilometres from Paris.

63 *the Dauphiné region*: Sade, a native of Aix-en-Provence, was familiar with the area. Justine's belief that she will be happy there reflects the current image of the Alps made famous by Rousseau.

64 *Recollet Friars*: the Franciscan order was founded by St Francis of Assisi in 1208. The Recollet branch, one of the stricter variants, was introduced into Spain in the 16th century by John of Guadalupe and many of the new Brethren were among the first Spanish missionaries to the New World. The order was approved by Pope Clement VII in 1532. The Latin *recollectus* means 'gathered together'.

66 *her miraculous statue resided*: for Sade, Justine's sixth virtue to be punished is her piety: 'She makes her way there to take the sacraments and is raped for her pains.'

70 *Lucretia*: not Lucretia Borgia but the wife of Tarquinius Collatinus who was brutally raped by Sextus Tarquinius. Summoning her husband and his friends, she called on them to drive out the hated race of Tarquins from Rome and, unable to survive her shame, committed suicide. She came to symbolize the proud and virtuous woman who prefers death to dishonour. The subject was used by Shakespeare in *The Rape of Lucrece*.

71 *Joigny*: on the Yonne, 27 kilometres north-west of Auxerre.

76 *pain is conducive to pleasure*: of course, sadism predates Sade. The link between pleasure and the giving of pain

had been long if discreetly acknowledged. Nor was sadism peculiar to Sade: the police inspector Marais, in a report dated 10 May 1765, expressed surprise at how many brooms were in regular use in the brothels of Paris where flagellation was an established practice. But no one before Sade, or since, has expressed the phenomenon quite so clearly or obsessively.

77   *those around them suffer*: this thought echoes the fashionable cynicism of the 1780s, best exemplified in Laclos's *Dangerous Liaisons* (1782) or the maxims of Chamfort, which itself reflected the example set by La Rochefoucauld (1613–80). Cf. 'We are all quite strong enough to bear the sufferings of others.' (*Maxims* (1665), 19.)

80   *every infringement is punished*: some critics see in such moments a prefiguration of Kafka. The labyrinthine settings of many of Sade's torture scenes, which may partly be accounted for by his own years of imprisonment and partly by the current vogue of the Gothic novel, help considerably to create an atmosphere of claustrophobia.

      nine in the morning: this detailed account of the timetable of Sainte-Marie-des-Bois does not merely reflect the obsessions of a long-serving prisoner: it echoes the 18th. century taste for detailed plans, schemes, and projects. The Utopia of Tamoé, which Sade had already described in *Aline and Valcour*, is reported in similar terms.

81   *could such bizarre whims ever be catalogued?*: but this is precisely what Sade had already done in *The 120 Days of Sodom*, a catalogue of 600 'passions' which, after the initial shock, is as interesting to read as a telephone directory and considerably less instructive.

90   *no trace of his intemperance*: though there was a small decline in artificially terminated pregnancies during the 18th century, the techniques of abortion had become more sophisticated. Of course, none was as effective as Antonin's and his *tisane* is to be understood rather as the symbol of the magically invulnerable power of the friars who not only hold the women in their power but also defy the law of men and of God with impunity.

95   *Vermenton*: 24 kilometres south-east of Auxerre on the Avallon road.

101 *the Order of St Francis*: the Recollets were Franciscans: see note to p. 64.

104 *to give to the woman*: Sade makes charity her seventh virtue to be punished.

105 *Vienne*: that is, Vienne-sur-Saône, 30 kilometres south of Lyons.

107 *Virieu*: that is, Virieu-le-Grand, due west of Lyons, 40 kilometres from Aix-les-Bains.

108 *my present environs*: Justine has been led not so much into a Gothic landscape as into another labyrinth, which is the physical and psychological substructure of all Sade's fiction. See note to p. 80.

109 *to work for coiners*: counterfeiting the coin of the realm was a capital offence. Dalville is therefore no petty robber but a man who plays for the highest stakes. The crimes of Sade's ogres almost invariably carry a metaphysical overtone. Few are simply mean-minded like Du Harpin and most are in open revolt against the laws of man or God or both. That they are rewarded for their defiance only makes Sade's case against virtue the more shocking.

a storage cistern: Sade notes here that saving Dalville's life is the eighth of Justine's virtues which will be punished.

110 *for giving yourself pleasure?*: Dalville here expresses a vital implication of materialist doctrine. If man is indeed a machine, human actions are perforce mechanical. Though society and morality may make distinctions between actions, the concepts of good and evil are artificial constructs. Nature promotes the pure search for pleasure while remaining indifferent to the forms that pleasure takes. Predetermined mechanical responses, temperament, and education therefore leave us no choice but to behave according to our lights. Now where there is no free will, there can be no morality. Justine is no more to be congratulated for her compassion than Dalville is to be censured for his sadism. Both act naturally, according to preprogrammed promptings over which they have no control. While Diderot never finally saw a way round this difficulty which he believed was a recipe for anarchy, Sade found it liberating: it meant that he could not be blamed for what he was.

110 *the weakest or the poorest*: Rousseau argued that in the natural state, before the creation of human societies, men, though physically and intellectually different, were born free. But with the introduction of property, natural inequalities were built into a socio-economic system which gave the strong (who became rich) power to enslave the weak (who became the poor). But while Rousseau viewed the institutionalization of natural inequalities as the source of the corruption of society, Sade welcomed it. The division of men into masters and slaves was a logical consequence of the transformist (that is, pre-Darwinist) doctrine which explained the survival of species in terms of adaptation to environment. Besides, there was as little point in regretting what Nature had decreed as there would be in regretting that water is wet.

117 *to have money without working for it*: Dalville's materialistic argument is an acid counter to the sentimental philanthropy of the times. He redefines modern moralistic society, with its lamentable concern for the poor, as a conspiracy of the weak to overthrow Nature. While Rousseau believed that a social contract could preserve the rights of all, Sade's preferred mode of social organization was anarchy which alone ensured that the fittest survived and prospered. Sade, who was to support the social and political upheaval brought about by the Revolution, never showed much sympathy for the underprivileged who, whether deserving or undeserving of their miseries, were Nature's failures.

118 *Andronici . . . and Wenceslas*: Andronicus was the name borne by four unsavoury Byzantine emperors who flourished between the 12th and 14th centuries: Andronicus I (1110–85), for instance, rose to power by strangling his predecessor, ruled by terror, and was finally put to death by the enraged mob after suffering horrible mutilation and torture. The other tyrants mentioned here are the Roman Emperors Nero (AD 37–68), Tiberius (42–37 BC), and Wenceslas IV (1361–1419), Emperor of Germany and King of Bohemia, who thoroughly enjoyed earning his reputation for debauchery and cruelty: thousands of Jews were massacred on his orders in 1390 and he once had his chef cooked alive for failing to supply his table.

119 *Monsieur Servant [sic]*: Michel-Antoine Servan (1737–1807) was appointed Advocate-General to the Grenoble Parlement at the age of 27. He resigned his post in 1772 in protest against a verdict of the court which was in his view unjust. Servan was well known for his defence of truth and his common charity. Sade may have consulted him as early as 1774, and Servan is the only lawyer the Marquis ever spoke of with any enthusiasm.

125 *a matter of opinion and geography*: Diderot had similarly argued, in his *Supplement to the Voyage of Bougainville* (composed 1771; published 1796) that most of what is considered moral and legal is no more than the product of history, religion, and custom. However, unlike Sade, who draws the conclusion that morality is no more than a convenient form of social control, Diderot argues that certain acts—like murder—are proscribed in all societies and that such sticking-points suggest that there exists an as yet unwritten but universal natural moral code.

126 *with my conscience*: in the Christian tradition, conscience meant the awareness of original sin. Philosophers agreed that conscience was a reminder to man of his duty to be just, truthful, and charitable, but disagreed as to whether it was innate or a learned response. Rousseau held conscience to be a spark of the Divinity placed in all of us whereas for Kant it meant practical reason. While for some, then, conscience was the spiritual principle in human character, evolutionist systems regarded it as a collective code of conduct which favoured actions and attitudes which have contributed to the well-being of societies. The logic of Sade's materialist philosophy led him to the latter view. But if God is an illusion and society a conspiracy of the weak, man is bound by no moral authority and is free to shape his own conscience. For Sade's view of remorse, see note to p. 159.

127 *the Wheel*: a barbaric method of judicial murder. The criminal was spreadeagled on a horizontally slung cart-wheel and his limbs were broken by successive blows with an iron bar until death ensued. When mercy was recommended, the victim was strangled before the sentence was carried out or, to expedite matters, the executioner was allowed to deliver heavy blows (the *coups de grâce*) to the chest or stomach. The introduction of the

guillotine (first used on 25 Apr. 1792) was widely regarded as a humanitarian measure worthy of the new
regime.

127   *to prevent it*: according to the paradox of Epicurus (341–
270 BC), the existence of evil casts doubt on the received
idea of the nature and power of God. If God could, He
would surely wish to expel evil. But evil exists. It follows
therefore that either He is not good or He is not omni-
potent, for He cannot be both. Sade's century was preoccupied with the problem of evil and various
philosophical solutions, in addition to ecclesiastical ex-
hortation to accept the mysterious ways of God, were
proposed. Notably the 'Optimists', like Leibnitz and
Alexander Pope, believed it reasonable to assume that
the created universe, for all its faults, could not have
been bettered and was in its 'optimum' state. 'Evil' is
therefore a name we give to forces which we understand
imperfectly. Madame Dubois's answer is much simpler.
By denying God, she demythologizes the problem and
reduces the whole question to a matter of practical action.

128   *Piedmont*: the area comprising Savoy (transferred to
France in 1860) and north-west Italy which were then
part of the Kingdom of Sardinia. Sade had himself fled
to Piedmont to avoid the attentions of the French authorities in the 1770s.

131   *more like to be suspected than she*: as Sade notes, Justine's
attempt to prevent a robbery is the ninth of her virtues
to be punished.

133   *Châlon-sur-Saône*: in the Saône-et-Loire, 125 kilometres
north of Lyons.

135   *Villefranche*: that is, Villefranche-sur-Saône, 31 kilometres north of Lyons on the Mâcon road.

137   *no harm would have come to her*: Justine's tenth virtue to
be punished, according to Sade, is that 'she saves a child
from death by fire and in so doing brings criminal proceedings on herself.'

rules of procedure being strictly observed: Sade's ironical
voice may be heard behind Justine's naïve observation.

140   *this town of bankrupts*: Sade's generalized contempt for

legal procedures is here compounded by his detestation of Lyons where he had been imprisoned between May and November 1768 as part of his sentence for his treatment of Rose Keller.

147 *Carmelite Convent*: there were three Carmelite Convents in Paris: one in the Faubourg Saint-Jacques, another in the rue de Grenelle, and the best known, the Couvent des Carmélites de la rue du Chapon (now the rue Beaubourg). All were soon to be closed by the Revolution.

DIALOGUE BETWEEN A PRIEST AND A DYING MAN

151 *a Socinian*: Socinianism was the doctrine of two Italian heresiarchs, Lælus Socinus (1525–62) and his nephew Faustus (1539–1604), which, with some differences, resembles that of modern Unitarianism. It argued that the only foundation on which Protestantism should be based was human reason, and Faustus combated the principal dogmas of the Church: the divinity of Christ, original sin, propitiatory sacrifice, and everything which could not be justified in rational terms. The Socinians were admired by Enlightenment *philosophes* who saw in them early exponents of deism, or natural religion.

152 *grant you a Creator*: philosophers had long argued that the universe is composed of two substances: matter and spirit. Eighteenth-century materialists like La Mettrie and D'Holbach allowed only the existence of matter which, far from being inert, was made of molecules which were sentient and capable of movement. When molecules were arranged in sophisticated ways (as in animals, which possess a central nervous system, as opposed to rocks or plants, which do not), these two qualities were deemed sufficient to account for all living phenomena: the vitalists went so far as to believe that even the planets were living organisms. Sade's argument assumes that matter is active not inert, eternal not created, a view adopted by the extreme materialists.

provided by my senses alone: sensualist epistemology, which the French 18th century derived principally from John Locke, started from the denial of innate ideas. The soul at birth is a 'clean slate' upon which the hand of experience writes. All knowledge is derived from our senses, for only by seeing, touching, etc. do we acquire knowledge of the external world. Like others before him, Sade uses sensualism to oppose the Christian doctrine of the soul as an immortal spark of God within us. His intention here is to maintain man as an existential phenomenon subject only to physical laws.

155   *a voice of thunder!*: this line, a French classical alexandrine and italicized in Sade's manuscript, seems intended as a quotation, though no source has been found for it.

to be sceptical: ever since the controversial exegetical work undertaken by the Hebrew scholar Richard Simon (1638–1712), anticlerical writers had attempted to undermine the authority of the Bible by arguing that it was written by fallible men and not by the hand of God. Closer to Sade's time, Diderot had pointed out that the trial and death of Christ were unrecorded outside the (therefore) suspect writings of the disciples and of Jewish historians such as Josephus.

156   *Apollonius of Tyana*: Apollonius of Tyana (4 BC–97 AD) was a celebrated disciple of Pythagoras. He travelled widely and preached moral reform and the adoption of neo-Pythagorean ideas. He was one of the most virtuous and learned men of his day, and was popularly regarded as a worker of miracles and a divine being. In England, Charles Blount (1654–93) compared him with Jesus as did, nearer Sade's day, Jean Meslier, Voltaire, and Diderot.

157   *your blasphemies*: in a similar vein, the Diderot of the *Conversation between a Philosopher and the Maréchale de **** (1777) had suggested that if God indeed exists, then the doubter who is in good faith is more likely to be welcomed by God than the man who believes blindly.

talked nonsense: free-thinkers had traditionally viewed Jesus, Muhammad, and Moses as 'impostors' who had abused human credulity in order to gain temporal power over men in the manner described on page 154. In *The Philosopher in the Bedroom* (1795), Sade added to the list of 'great knaves and despots' Lycurgus of Sparta and Numa Pompilius, second King of Rome. The *philosophes* suspected power-seeking priesthoods but admired lawgivers who devised sound moral and social systems. Voltaire viewed Christ as the man with the perfect ethic and both he and Diderot—as does Sade here—praised the social and moral values of Confucius the Wise.

158 *does not deserve to live*: accusations that Jesus was a seditious, destabilizing influence were not unusual in anticlerical circles. It is interesting to note that in 1782 Sade, like many of his contemporaries in the run-up to the French Revolution, was concerned to defend political stability: by 1785 at the latest, he had come to the view that Nature prefers despotism, even anarchy, to anything resembling a rationally ordered society. His defence of patriotism, intended to combat the fashionable 'cosmopolitan' ideal of his day, was also to change. As a supporter of the Revolution, his concept of 'Frenchness' was to be quite different from the orthodox loyalty to King and country he recommends here.

if not eternal life?: for materialist thinkers, matter is eternal, not created; finite, but fixed in quantity. In the cycle of life and death, matter takes different forms but it cannot either increase or decrease. Death expunges the individual, of whom nothing remains (save a memory in the minds of his fellows). The molecules of which he was made become available to the constant cycle of rebirth which therefore excludes all possibility of an immortal soul.

159 *with its sting*: Sade accepts the fatalistic implications of his materialist philosophy because it frees man of the burden of moral responsibility. Diderot's discussion of the implications of scientific determinism in *Jacques the Fatalist* is more subtle. 'Everything which happens to us here below for good or ill was written in the great scroll in the sky', says Jacques who, however, is still able to function as a man with valid moral choices.

to avoid criminal acts: if this statement comes oddly from a convicted felon, it should be remembered that Sade never accepted that he was in any way guilty in the Rose Keller and Marseilles affairs. His position here, in 1782, is close to that of the moderate materialists who argued that Nature inevitably punishes (with remorse, for instance) what society overlooks. By 1787 his ideas had hardened: none of the ogres of *The Misfortunes of Virtue* are troubled either by Nature or the law. For since there is no God and punishments exist in this world (there being no other), and since all desires are natural and open to whoever is strong enough to impose them on others, then the man who is sharper than his fellows or uses his socio-economic power to defeat human justice is free to do whatever he will. Sade's torturers succeed because they are strong and they despise remorse as Sade himself does here. The relish with which he allows them to succeed suggests that he did not blame them but society for failing to contain their activities. Morality thus becomes not the responsibility of the individual but the duty of society: it must be imposed from without for it cannot come spontaneously from within. But since society cannot be perfected (it will *always* be corrupt), the solution lies in the anarchy recommended in a notorious section of *The Philosopher in the Bedroom* (1795): in conditions of permanent revolution, the weak would go deservedly to the wall and the strong would rightly prosper.

159 *you yourself would be*: variants of Christ's 'Do unto others' were common in the writings of a range of late 18th. century ethical writings.

160 *wars and scourges on earth*: Sade fully shared his century's fervent anticlericalism, of which the most effective representative was Voltaire. The same objections to established religion appear in his philosophical poem *The Truth* (1787?) and are expressed with increasing violence in the major novels.

THE PIMP WELL SERVED

164 *the Regency*: Louis XIV (1638–1715) outlived his immediate heirs and on his death, Philippe d'Orléans (1674–1723) was appointed Regent during the minority of Louis XV (1710–74). A man of dissolute habits, he gave the tone to a period of French history which is noted for its general immorality and sexual licence.

[We shall summarize]: a suggested reading. The manuscript is defective at this point.

rue des Déjeûneurs [sic]: this street, just east of the Bourse, was in existence in 1633. It was then part of a road circling the Paris of Louis XIII and from 1640 onwards was a favourite place for bowls and other games. It was in fact first known as the 'rue des Jeux-neufs' which gradually became the present rue des Jeûneurs.

166 *Duke de Vendôme*: Philippe, Duke de Vendôme (1655–1727), held the rank of Grand Prieur and was a noted soldier and rake.

THE WINDBAGS OF PROVENCE

168 *an Ambassador from Persia*: Mehemet Riza Bey, though holding the rank of Kalender, or tax-collector, was nevertheless fully accredited by the King of Persia. He landed at Marseilles on 23 Oct. 1714 and on 7 Feb. 1715 arrived in Paris where he was received by Louis XIV. Watteau made ten drawings of members of his retinue. He was exotic, highly irascible, and notoriously mean, and doubts were cast on his credentials. In his *Persian Letters* (1721) (chap. 91) Montesquieu mentions this 'personage got up to look like a Persian ambassador'. Saint-Simon believed that he was a fake and that his appearance at court had been engineered to flatter the elderly King. He was, however, exactly what he claimed to be.

Parlement at Aix: the Parlements were sovereign courts of law, though they aspired to a political role. Their publicly expressed views were often liberal, but in practice they resisted constitutional and financial reform and jealously guarded their corporate rights. Sade's hatred of them, however, was less ideological than personal. He believed that, after the Marseilles affair, the attitude of the courts had been influenced by the political rivalry which set the Parlements, which were predominantly staffed by middle-class professionals, against the hereditary aristocracy, of which he was a member. The Parlement at Aix-en-Provence, created in 1415 with Hugues de Sade at its head, had sentenced Sade to death by decapitation in 1772.

François I: François I (1494–1547), protector of the arts and a key figure in the development of the modern French nation, is here remembered for his persecution of the Protestants of southern France.

170 *Mérindol and Cabrières*: Mérindol and Cabrières-d'Aigues, small communities in the Vaucluse near Sade's château

at La Coste, were the scene of the brutal massacre of Protestant Vaudois, suspected of heresy, by the Catholic forces of François I in 1545 under Meynier d'Oppède, First President of the Parlement of Aix. Sade rarely mentions religious tyranny without quoting these examples.

AN INEXPLICABLE AFFAIR

175 *Grande Chartreuse*: the celebrated monastery founded by St Bruno in 1084 in the Alps near Grenoble.

THE PRUDE

179 *infamous rulings*: during his trials, Sade always made it clear that he regarded prostitution as an uncomplicated exchange of services and money. The authorities, however, took a different view and attempted to contain the rapid expansion of the capital's flesh-market by unofficial police controls. The 'two or three . . . officials' Sade denigrates here were the two most recent Lieutenant-Generals of Police: Antoine de Sartine (1729–1801) (who was born in Barcelona but became French in 1752, and is the 'dishonest Spaniard' of a few lines earlier), and Charles-Pierre Lenoir (1732–1807). Sade also probably includes the police inspector Louis Marais (d. 1780), the scourge of whores and their keepers, who kept substantial records of the current state of prostitution based on a vast network of spies and informers. From about the middle of the century, brothel madams were required to make written returns containing details of the activities of their customers. In this way, the police hoped to trace criminals and other undesirables, though, as Sade rightly points out, their major success was in apprehending a surprising number of clerics *in flagrante delicto*. Many objected to the 'inquisitorial' methods used by the forty-two police inspectors charged with surveillance of the vice-trade, but Sade is less than fair to Sartine and Lenoir who were no more corrupt than the average functionaries of the *ancien régime* and who were faced with an impossible task. But both had a hand in keeping him in prison and for this Sade could not forgive them.

180 *The celebrated S. J.*: Sade was well known in the brothels of Paris in the 1760s until he was banned from frequent-

ing them. 'S. J.' may shelter a bawd named Jourdan who figures in Marais's police reports.

ÉMILIE DE TOURVILLE

184   *a provincial Lieutenant-Governor*: Sade himself had held a similar office. He succeeded his father as Lieutenant-Governor of the provinces of Bresse, Bugey, Valromey, and Gex in 1764.

190   *rue des Arcis*: this street, which dates from the 12th century, became part of the rue Saint-Martin in the third *arrondissement* in 1851.

196   *passed through our hands as you could*: in the absence of official statistics—the first census in France dates from 1801—contemporary observers put the numbers of Parisiennes involved in prostitution as high as 1 in 7. This figure, however, was inflated by honest but poor women forced to supplement their income by casual soliciting and, as Madame Berceil points out, by those who, for a variety of reasons, deliberately exploited their attractiveness to men.

199   *between Coucy and Noyon*: Coucy-le-Château, on the edge of the forest of Saint-Gobain, is 23 kilometres north-west of Soissons and 29 from Noyon, which lies on the road between Compiègne and Saint-Quentin.

206   *[Author's note]*: an instance of the chauvinism of Sade who was always eager to defend his native Provence.

207   *excellence of character*: that is, Sade so hated lawyers and magistrates that he found it difficult to understand how any honest man would willingly want to become either. The President de Tourville is clearly an exception, like Servan: see note to p. 119.

209   *their contemptible persons*: Sade's outburst against the legal system is directed mainly against the *lettre de cachet* (see note to p. 46) and is part of the routine philosophic case against injustice and the corruption of law. But it is given point by his hatred of his mother-in-law, Madame de Montreuil who, like Émilie's brothers, set up as the avenger of the family honour and turned into the tormentor of her unhappy victim, as the opening paragraph of this tale puts it. To this extent, *Émilie de Tourville* is a symbolic version of Sade's own experience; it also fea-

tures a paternalistic figure who is much more kindly than his own father, who, like Luxeuil, was also a Lieutenant-Governor.

AUGUSTINE DE VILLEBLANCHE

210 *immortal Sappho*: Sappho, famed for her poetry and amorous liaisons, was born on the island of Lesbos about 600 BC. Her affection for three women friends was generally supposed to be lesbian in nature and she was given the name Tribas, though she killed herself for love of a youth named Phaon who spurned her. Sapphic love, known frequently as 'tribadism', had recently gained ground in the fashionable world, mainly through the well-publicized scandals provoked by actresses like Mademoiselle Raucourt. An echo is found in Laclos's *Dangerous Liaisons* (1782), where Madame de Merteuil hints that she is not insensitive to the charms of Cécile de Volanges (letters 38 and 63).

a Cujas or a Bartole or a Louis IX: of celebrated jurists like the Italian Bartole (1313–57) and the Frenchman Jacques Cujas (1522–90), Sade remarks in *Aline and Valcour*: 'Imbecile lawyers! Or rather a race of hellish maniacs who spent their sad, unhappy lives demonstrating to other pedants like themselves just how many different ways there are of doing away with one's fellow men . . .' Louis IX (1215–70), known as St Louis, took a harsh line with blasphemy and heresy, a broad category which included sexual practices which were deemed unnatural. Until the 18th century, the connection between heresy and homosexuality remained strong, and sodomy was a capital offence, as Sade knew to his cost. Sentence of death on sodomites was carried out publicly on at least three occasions: as late as 1783, a former priest named Pascal was broken alive on the wheel for repeatedly stabbing a youth who had refused his advances. Lesbians never risked such harsh treatment and when they fell foul of the law were jailed (for 'outrage to public decency') on the same basis as their heterosexual sisters. Even so, there is no denying that Augustine is a thoroughly modern young woman.

212 *the Three Graces . . . Eros*: the Three Graces, Aglaia, Thalia, and Euphrosyne, were daughters of Zeus and

personified grace, gentleness, and beauty. They were usually represented holding each other by the hand or locked in a triple embrace in contrast with the more virile face of sexuality represented by Eros, the God of Love.

temples of Venus: an 18th-century euphemism for brothel. Paphos, on Cyprus, was famed for its temple of Venus. According to contemporary practice, the use of classical references made writing about unseemly matters decorous.

214 *to that Psyche*: Antinous, a youth of Bithynia of whom the Emperor Hadrian (76–138) was extremely fond. Adonis was beloved of Aphrodite, not Psyche, though Psyche was so beautiful that many mortals (including Sade evidently) regularly mistook her for Aphrodite.

at Carnival time: a festival which originally began on the day after the feast of the Epiphany and continued until midnight on Shrove Tuesday. It was kept principally in Catholic countries. In 18th-century France, it was generally restricted to the final week before the beginning of Lent.

THE LAW OF TALION

223 *title*: the system of talion is found in early Hebrew, Greek, and Roman law, and still operates in primitive communities. It requires a punishment to be inflicted on the wrong-doer in proportion to the evil suffered by the injured party: in effect, 'an eye for an eye and a tooth for a tooth.'

one of the great writers of our century: an ironical reference to the Comte de Tressan (1705–83), a leading figure in the recently revived interest in medieval literature. In the preface to *The Crimes of Love* (1800), Sade contemptuously dismissed all medieval romances ('long, boring, superstition-ridden sagas [written] with such barbarity and coarseness'), though he admired the 'pretty tales' of the troubadours, especially of Provence (see note to p. 206) In his view, Dante, Boccaccio, and even Petrarch owed more to the troubadour tradition than was commonly granted.

has given to Literature: Saint-Quentin, in north-east France, was famous for the siege of 1557 but not for producing writers. Sade's irony may be motivated by some obscure memory of his military service in the area.

223   *to be got out of them?*: as the old system of patronage declined, the artist was increasingly forced to seek alternative funding from the sale of his work. From 1759, Diderot, the founder of French art-criticism, covered the biennial exhibitions held at the Louvre, and newspapers followed the progress of the art market. Technical developments had brought down the price of engravings and, as Sade notes, publishers eagerly exploited the public appetite for the visual.

225   *Lucretia*: see note to p. 70.

THE SELF-MADE CUCKOLD

227   *Capuchin monks*: a Franciscan order (so called because of their distinctive *capuche* or pointed hood), dating from 1528, who were dedicated to a life of rigour and mortification.

229   *a moment later*: the system of privilege and favour which had dominated the French court since the time of Louis XIV was, to Sade the patrician, the symbol of the emasculation of the hereditary nobility. Among his reasons for welcoming the Revolution was a certain satisfaction at seeing the end of the decadent court of Versailles.

230   *the Convent of Sainte-Aure*: one of a number of establishments set up at the end of the 17th century for the reclamation of 'repentant courtesans' and fallen women. From 1690 until 1792 when it closed, it was located in what is now the rue Tournefort in the Latin Quarter. Part of the community was used to educate girls: Jeanne Bécu, the future Madame du Barry, was a 'pensionnaire' in the 1750s. Sade's wife had rooms at Saint-Aure for a period in the 1780s.

232   *the taste for luxury*: the problem of luxury divided intellectual opinion in a century torn between the traditional Christian and aristocratic mistrust of money, and the capitalist spirit of the new bourgeois order. On the one hand, luxury was deemed to corrupt; on the other, it was defended for its ability to make wealth circulate between rich and poor. Sade, like his ogres, was more interested in having wealth than in earning it honestly, and, though

impoverished, continued to take a moral, anti-bourgeois line with vulgar lucre.

235 *Flora*: mother of Spring, and goddess of flowers and gardens. Another instance of the classical allusions to which Sade's age was addicted.

236 *not just*: an echo of the pro-feminist tone of Sade's times. Louis Thomas's *Essay on Women* (1772) had noted pointedly that women were no better than slaves in a male society, and Laclos's essays on female education in the 1780s argued for the rights of natural woman in terms not dissimilar to those used by Rousseau to defend the freedoms of natural man: indeed, *Dangerous Liaisons* may be read as a defence of women who, by education and marriage, were singularly ill-prepared to deal with the likes of Valmont. Sade's view of the question is more complex than Raneville's progressive stance suggests. Although in his life he normally adopted a consumer view of women, he admired and respected Marie-Constance who shared the last twenty-five years of his life. And while liberal views do not have a place in the spectacularly illiberal Sadean universe which interprets life as a war between the weak and the strong, we have seen him allow Madame Dubois and the Juliette of *The Prosperities of Vice* to thrive. His fictional villains may be more numerous (and more villainous) than his villainesses. Yet he was clearly prepared to allow women to succeed in their endeavours on the same terms as men.

THE HUSBAND WHO SAID MASS

238 *in Provence*: Ménerbes (*sic*), on the north face of the Luberon mountains, overlooks the road which links Avignon and Apt, 50 kilometres due east. Sade's château at La Coste, now a ruin, is a mere 6 kilometres from Ménerbes.

239 *the sons of Elijah*: though an iconographical tradition shows Elijah surrounded by fifty young men, they were not his sons but the progeny of the faithful prophets. The reference here is to another tradition which ascribes the founding of the Carmelite Order (established in 1154) to Elijah the Prophet.

240 *Lanerte wine*: Sade, very much on his home ground, gives the two men a local wine to drink.

241 *lord of the manor*: until 1789, when noble privileges were abolished, infringement of the feudal but still widespread game laws was treated severely: in some cases, the penalty was death.

THE LADY OF THE MANOR OF LONGUEVILLE

245 *bending the knee to a single man*: Sade's pre-Revolutionary political views reflect a mixture of patrician conservatism and the progressive values of the Enlightenment. Like many of the old nobility, he resented the erosion of aristocratic power and privilege which had been the centralizing monarchy's policy since the time of Richelieu: see note to p. 229. Yet at the same time, he was opposed to the excesses of the old feudal tyranny: see p. 247.

THE CONFIDENCE MEN

253 *the time of Carnival*: see note to p. 214.

the rue Quincampoix: see note to p. 17.

257 *Pontoise*: 35 kilometres from Paris on the Rouen road, the last posting-stage before Paris, though coaches also halted at Saint-Denis before travelling the last 10 kilometres into the centre of the city.

258 *the church of Saint-Roch*: in the rue Saint-Honoré. Sade had been married there in May 1763.

THE WORLD'S CLASSICS

A Select List

TOBIAS SMOLLETT: The Expedition of Humphry Clinker
Edited by Lewis M. Knapp
Revised by Paul-Gabriel Boucé

ROBERT LOUIS STEVENSON:
Treasure Island
Edited by Emma Letley

ANTHONY TROLLOPE: The American Senator
Edited by John Halperin

GIORGIO VASARI: The Lives of the Artists
Translated and Edited by Julia Conaway Bondanella and Peter Bondanella

VIRGINIA WOOLF: Orlando
Edited by Rachel Bowlby

ÉMILE ZOLA: Nana
Translated and Edited by Douglas Parmée

A complete list of Oxford Paperbacks, including The World's Classics, OPUS, Past Masters, Oxford Authors, Oxford Shakespeare, and Oxford Paperback Reference, is available in the UK from the Arts and Reference Publicity Department (BH), Oxford University Press, Walton Street, Oxford OX2 6DP.

In the USA, complete lists are available from the Paperbacks Marketing Manager, Oxford University Press, 200 Madison Avenue, New York, NY 10016.

Oxford Paperbacks are available from all good bookshops. In case of difficulty, customers in the UK can order direct from Oxford University Press Bookshop, Freepost, 116 High Street, Oxford, OX1 4BR, enclosing full payment. Please add 10 per cent of published price for postage and packing.